THE
GOBLET

THE DARK WORLD BOOK V

S.C. PARRIS

PERMUTED
PRESS

A PERMUTED PRESS BOOK

ISBN: 978-1-68261-552-2
ISBN (eBook): 978-1-68261-553-9

PERMUTED
PRESS

Permuted Press, LLC
New York • Nashville
permutedpress.com

Published in the United States of America

To everyone, it had to be done.

I'm (not *that*) sorry.

Table of Contents

Chapter One: Red Skies 1
Chapter Two: Visions 21
Chapter Three: The Etrian Hills 32
Chapter Four: Christian's Fear.. 50
Chapter Five: Dracula's Granddaughter 60
Chapter Six: A Usurper's Plan...................................... 76
Chapter Seven: Surrounded 94
Chapter Eight: Hands of the Order 104
Chapter Nine: Churning Blood 113
Chapter Ten: Deadly Training...................................... 127
Chapter Eleven: An Exchange 135
Chapter Twelve: Bagabills 143
Chapter Thirteen: The Base of the Mountain 154
Chapter Fourteen: The Room 176
Chapter Fifteen: The Choice.. 192
Chapter Sixteen: The Uninvited Guest............................. 205
Chapter Seventeen: Betrayals 218
Chapter Eighteen: Storming the Gates 226
Chapter Nineteen: The Winter Ball 237
Chapter Twenty: The Brothers Delacroix 246
Chapter Twenty-One: The Goblet of Existence 252
Chapter Twenty-Two: Phoenix Fyre.. 257
Chapter Twenty-Three: Golden Blood 261

About the Author.. 271

Chapter One

RED SKIES

"He's gone?" Aleister whispered, clutching his heart with a scarred hand.

Philistia felt he would keel over at any moment, such was the pain that graced his once-handsome face, but he remained standing, if only by another hand clutching tight the arm of an armchair most nearby.

They stood in the abandoned cottage the Enchanter had vacated two days before, and though it was full to the brim with Vampires, two strange Elite Creatures, and herself, one of the three Creatures here capable of magic, she found she felt safe. Safer than she had been out there, at any rate.

Before Nathanial could have dragged Xavier onto the ice, Xavier went mad, or at least, that's what it seemed to her. Even the Phoenix appeared bewildered, and stopped hurling its balls of fyre at them:

She had watched from the ice as Xavier's eyes became completely black, no white to be found in them at all. Before where he moved with fear, with weakness, he suddenly seemed to exude remarkable skill.

He had pressed a hand against Nathanial's chest, catching him off guard, and with a word, a whisper, rendered the Vampire immobile at his feet. He then turned to her, ignoring the Phoenix entirely and with a snarl, he raised a pale hand with the palm facing her, and said, *"It is time to come home."*

And from his hand several bolts of black smoke appeared, their sharp points piercing the air before she could think to prepare the proper counter or whisper her astonishment. It was then that she stared helplessly at the black-eyed Vampire and saw him for what he really was.

An Elite.

But when?

And as the sharp daggers of black entered her midsection, she let out a bloodied gasp, and clutched the wound, her blood pouring past a gloveless hand.

He'd blinked the moment his spell struck, appearing astonished, and he'd looked to the skies as though called there. And she stared as well.

There were hundreds of them.

Winged, darkly-colored monsters hovering abhorrently in the blackened sky, and despite the pain, she felt shame canvass her. *Had Equis been right?*

The leader of these…things landed lightly upon the grass several feet from Xavier, and Philistia prepared her spell to see she, Xavier, and Nathanial to safety, for Nathanial was still alive: she could smell his cold blood in the air though he had not been cut.

But she could barely ready herself before the leader of the winged ones held out a long-nailed claw, the skin stretched and webbed, the veins beneath straining against its translucent thinness.

She dared not breathe, for Equis couldn't have been completely right, he could not have been correct in giving up on the Vampires, for Xavier Delacroix needed to be given his chance. He needed the chance to prove he could right the wrongs of his breed—

But, much to her dismay, he took Eleanor's clawed hand, hesitantly at first, he clasped it within his own, and in a burst of wind, a wind she had not felt in centuries, they were all gone.

Xavier included.

And she relayed this to a most grief-stricken Aleister Delacroix for the third time. He had not wanted to believe it to be true. But it was.

Xavier had joined her and was perhaps, one of her Creatures right now.

But no Creature in the small home wanted to believe it, it seemed. They all shook their heads fretfully, or, in the case of the two hopeless-looking Elite Creatures, stared silently into space, fear full on their faces.

"We can track him down, bring him back," Dragor Descant said from the couch where he, Lillith Crane, and Yaddley Caddenhall were squished together.

Philistia glanced out the window nearest her again, the sky red, but not from the coming dawn, no, something stirred: she could feel it in the air.

Turning back to the room at large, she sighed. "I don't believe he will come. When he turned on me and Nathanial," she eyed the still unconscious Vampire propped carefully against a stone wall to the back of the room, "his eyes…He looked, moved…with the presence of a bloody King, Mister Descant."

"That's because he is!" Dragor shouted, his brown and gray hair shaking against his neck as he sat forward on the couch, his sword on the floor nearby. "He is the King—our King, not hers! If we don't get him back do you know what will happen?!"

Aleister looked up from his grief with anger in his eyes. "What will happen, Descant? Hm?! He will turn on us all? Kill us all? Is that what you mean to imply? That my bloody son would sooner see us all dead at his hand than do his bloody duty?"

"He's done *nothing* thus far!" Dragor shouted back. "And he has turned on you, Aleister, have you so easily forgotten?! Your son has no duty! His duty has always been to Eleanor bloody Black! And we've been damned fools stringing him along this World with that knowledge in the back of our heads!"

Aleister seemed to recoil into a state of further shock: his mouth shut abruptly and he moved from an armchair Minerva Caddenhall sat in, opened the door. Before anyone could say a word, he exited through it with a slam.

"He'll burn," Aurora cried, letting out a sound much like a mother most cross with their child. No one said a word as she swept from the stairs where she'd sat, passed Minerva, and exited through the door as well.

Once it closed, Christopher Black, who had busied himself with the small pile of books upon the floor near the unlit fireplace, looked up, much to Philistia's surprise: she had thought he would never emerge.

"Send me," he said, staring at Philistia now.

She met the stare with confusion, rubbing her bandaged wound beneath her bloodied robes. Concern filled her mind: No magic had been able to heal it fully. "What, forgive me, do you think you'll be able to do, Mister Black?"

"I'm her bloody brother," he said, running a hand over a book he had seemed to favor: he had not released it for some hours now, its weathered purple cover aged greatly, but still the words *The Ancient Elders & Their Secrets* could be seen upon it. "If anyone can—should—be able to…speak sense to her, wouldn't it be blood?"

Peroneous Doe, who was shrouded in darkness at the top of the stairs and had not spoken a word since they arrived in Cedar Village said, "You're gifted with certain knowledge Dracula wished you to hold, Vampire, but do not believe this to give you a marker of power. You saw the state of the World out there. You have been kept from it for years. Not in the thick of things. And you saw the way Xavier behaved. Turning a sword on Aleister, running to Eleanor, kissing her—bloody hell he wouldn't listen to us," and he waved a hand to Aciel, "when we tried to keep him from climbing up Merriwall Mountain. He is not to be toyed with, not at all." And Philistia noticed his gaze darkened considerably.

"What more do you hold from us, Peroneous?" she asked, bringing all eyes to him.

He squirmed slightly atop the old step before rising to his feet, bowing slightly as he descended them, and when his bloodied boots touched the old floor, he said, "After I…subdued the Enchanter… you were all…badly injured. I…began to see what I could do for all of you, when Xavier…he shook atop the rocks. He was…turning… becoming what Darien was…what you say Eleanor now is, Madame Mastcourt."

"What?" the Order of the Dragon whispered together. Even Amentias and Aciel looked up from their stupors in surprise. Philista thought of getting Aleister and Aurora when the Enchanter went on.

"I gave him my blood…and there is…protection in place to keep Vampires from taking too much Enchanter blood, but he bypassed them all and…he continued to drink. He was healed from his… impending transformation, but he apologized once he tore from me, and kicked me in the head, knocked me out cold."

Philistia stepped away from the window. "And he began to climb the mountain," she finished for him.

"Yes," he said, though his gaze was still shrouded in deep thought. "But I see now that he was driven only for a desire to know what Eleanor Black held from him, he desired to be closer to her. By climbing the mountain, he desired to see what power, what greater power could exist in this World that had her of all Creatures *scared*," Peroneous said quietly.

Dragor snarled. "You're saying that he wanted to see the Enchanters' power for himself to see what power would be higher than Eleanor's? Why would he—?"

"Because, if what I sensed from him is right," Philistia whispered, understanding Peroneous's reasoning now, "he was always bidden to go to Eleanor. If not consciously, then subconsciously—something in him is drawn to her. Be it their blood—"

"It's his love for her. It's driven him mad, it has," Aleister said from the now open door. He stepped inside, the sun's light not pressing upon his back, Philistia noticed, as he moved into the shade of the cottage.

Behind him stepped Aurora and a most-stricken, teary-eyed Elf who hobbled with a white cane into the cottage, his thin lips trembling greatly, his robes bloodied and covered in what looked to be gray sand.

Dragor grabbed his sword and stood from the couch, Aciel and Amentias tensing as well. "What the bloody hell—Arminius? Where have you been?" he yelled.

Arminius said nothing, nothing at all, and as Philistia closed the door behind them, he sank to his knees, the cane clinking loudly to the floor at her feet.

"What's wrong with him?" someone asked.

"Give him air!" Aleister roared, spreading arms so everyone was pushed as far away from the Elf as possible.

Philistia watched from beside Aciel and Amentias as the Elf coughed, his long black hair covering his face. She noticed how greatly his long-fingered hands trembled and clawed at the wood as though angry.

And then from behind the curtain of black, he spoke, though it was so low Philistia hardly thought he spoke at all:

"Nicholai is dead. The Phoenixes...k-killed him."

"But why?" Lillith asked.

The Elf looked up at last, staring around at them, though his hands never left the wood. His eyes were red with tears, their black color striking in the dim of the cottage as the sun rose, pouring light past certain Creatures that were not Vampires: all colder Creatures had stepped back deeper into the reaches of shade if they did not sit.

"He was the first." He coughed and blood left his lips. "The first Dracula let see the Phoenixes. He took him to the Nest—their home. He...I...I made it happen. I made him relive a memory with my persistence to *know*." And he raised a hand from the floor, pointing it toward Aleister. The Vampire obliged at once, helping him to his feet, and Philistia reached for his cane, handing it to him once he was fully upright.

Taking it with a badly shaking hand, he clutched the golden handle tight and stared around at them all. Aleister still held him upright with a firm grip on his arm, and it was a long while before the Elf said, "Dracula had many...many *Vampures* in place should any fail. And Nicholai was his first serious choice, as I understand it, to see his will done. But Nicholai...when he was sent to watch over the woman, the Alexandria Stone, he...he did magic on her. To keep her from Dracula's clutches. Even he knew, then, that Dracula could not...did not have the best interests of all involved at heart.

"He was truly a monster," he coughed, "truly. I saw him reprimand Nicholai for losing the woman. He became...this creature, this winged...bat-like—"

"You saw him change form?" Peroneous Doe said from near the stairs.

Philistia eyed him. He looked quite ready to move forward and strike the Elf where he stood.

"Aye," Arminius breathed. "He changed. The power with which he moved...he spoke not with his mouth, he spoke to Nicholai through the mind. Called all his plans disappointments—all of us, disappointments."

"Then he would not be pleased to know about Xavier," Christopher said.

"But getting back to his transformation," Peroneous said coldly, stepping forward. "The Vampire could transform? I made it so he could never take that bloody form again. You're telling me you *saw* him do it? Nicholai saw him do it?"

"I did," Arminius whispered.

Peroneous looked as though he wished to cry but instead he said, "Then I failed. That potion was meant to bind him, if not kill him, make it so he never graced his original form. But how...how could he return to it?" He stared at Arminius expectantly.

But the Elf's eyes had closed sometime while the dark Enchanter had spoken; he now slumped in Aleister's hand. As Minerva Caddenhall vacated her armchair and Philistia helped Aleister place the Elf within it, Dragor said, "This is just ridiculous. If Dracula could switch forms whenever he pleased why couldn't Darien do the same?"

No one said a word and Philistia raised an eyebrow. "Who is this Darien?"

Lillith, who had perched on the edge of her cushion at the mention of Darien's name, said, "Darien Nicodemeus. He's...changed into... something else...an original Vampire."

"But how?" Philistia asked.

Lillith's blue eyes seemed to shine in the dim. "I gave him my blood...drawn to do it, I suppose."

She narrowed her eyes upon the Vampire, realizing she had never seen one so young before. Not born as such, no, for she knew Vampires were born human until they reached their Vampire Age. So she must have been turned. But turned so young? *How terrible.*

She began to think on the young woman's many afflictions, the growth of the mind while the body failed to follow. But perhaps the young woman had not reached her Age, not yet. But still, she recalled the vague stories she'd heard of Dracula's secret Vampire, a young girl with light hair, fair skin, blue eyes. How he trained her to perfection, but for what, no one readily knew.

How interesting.

As Christopher Black stared at the back of Lillith's head, Philistia cleared her throat, and said, "What on Earth would possess you to give Darien your blood? I thought this was a forbidden practice among your kind."

"It is," Dragor said coldly, though his gaze was on the floor. "Most forbidden. Now we know why." He looked up at Philistia at last and she saw his eyes were black. "The blood of a Vampire makes us those Creatures. The blood of a human," and he eyed Peroneous Doe who looked as though he would be sick, "keeps us as we are now."

"Something I did not think would happen," Peroneous said coldly, arms folded across his chest. "I did not mean—"

"We know you did not mean for any of this. Merely doing what you were bidden, as were we all," Aleister said with a touch of annoyance. "What matters is that we know a bit more of Dracula's... nature. And it stands to reason that if Dracula could...change form, then Eleanor Black could do the very same. We find her, we attack her when she is most vulnerable, and we get my son back."

No one said a word to the stone-faced Vampire, his words passing through the air with a touch of finality. But then, quite suddenly, Philistia found the thought: "How do you propose we do that, Aleister?" For she'd heard of Division Six's troubling tactics to take down Lycans, rogue Enchanters. Indeed, she had heard they had gotten into a scuffle with a few rogue Enchanters some years ago, given their scars. But now the Vampire worked not for the safety of the World, but for his son. She had a feeling he would move heaven and earth for Xavier; she just hoped he did not put the others or herself in harm's way: More unnecessary bloodshed would solve nothing.

He turned his green gaze to her and much to her further surprise, he smiled coldly. *More of a grimace, really*, she thought. "We use your...considerable skill, Madame, all of your considerable skill. We stand together as the Order of the Dragon. All of us. We may not want to be here," he said shrewdly, for Peroneous had opened his mouth to speak, "but we are. And it is high time we stand as one to do as Dracula desired and see Xavier Delacroix to the bloody Goblet."

She saw it mirrored in all their faces: the words they had shared before Aleister had come bounding through the door. *He did not want to believe that Eleanor Black had had her fangs in his son; he had dismissed it outright, but the fact remained,* Philistia thought, recalling the sight of Xavier at her side in the dark, *that Xavier did not do Dracula's work. Not anymore.*

She moved back to the window as the others began to whisper amongst themselves and stared once more at the sky. Something was wrong: The Mountains of Cedar should have been littered with Dragons, teeming with them, but they were empty. Not a red and yellow scaled Creature remained atop their snow-covered peaks. A fresh fear washed over her with the strange sight.

"Oh dear," she breathed, not tearing her eyes from the horizon.

"What? What is it?" someone behind her asked.

She inhaled sharply as she turned from the window to eye a most curious Dragor. He had stood from his seat and held his sword aloft. "The Dr-Dragons," she managed to whisper. "They're gone."

* * *

The skies never lightened into dewy morning, though the Creature thought, vaguely, that they should. *Perhaps,* he thought, *it was the nature of our energy now. There is far too much on the Earth, far too conflicting.*

For he had felt a multitude of clashing energies the moment he landed here, on the mountain. He had felt like the World was no longer his. *But of course it wouldn't be. Too much had changed.*

He stared at the charred body of Equis Equinox, remembering him when he was a boy, a brother. Not the maddened, power-crazy man he had become.

"Shame, really," Caligo Manus said, returning his bloodied sword to its sheath at his side. "If he wasn't so scared of your power, he could have been essential to helping the Abominations."

"He was scared of the magical arts returning to the Elves," Syran said, "more so than he was any power I possess."

"But it is a fearsome power all the same," Caligo said, his black eyes not shining in the sun's glare.

Syran surveyed the dark-skinned man for moments more, seeing his rage, his madness, how well contained he kept it. He thought briefly that that madness would have to be unleashed upon the World. *What were they calling it now? The Dark World? Dark, indeed.*

"Come, my son," he said, spreading his wings wide, their flames licking the air, never burning him, "we've much to reclaim."

Caligo tensed at his side, his black wings not opening, and for the first time Syran felt fear in the beautiful Creature.

"What is it?" Syran asked, not closing his wings.

Caligo's black eyes did not glisten in the light of the sun or the fire of Syran's wings, but Syran could see something within them all the same. Something he had never seen before. *Was this fear?* He folded his wings at once, overcome with a strange sensation: Caligo was never scared. *This did not bode well.*

"What do you sense?" he asked the dark Creature, placing a steadying hand on his broad shoulder.

Caligo flinched under the touch, not used to it at all, but said all the same, "There is something here…something that holds traces of our blood…your blood. Did you ever give the Abominations your blood?"

He shrank away, the thought ridiculous. "Never," he said, aghast. "How could you say—?"

"It is on the Earth!" Caligo yelled, and Syran raised an eyebrow. The dark Creature recoiled, and said quietly, but still viciously, "There are traces of your blood on the Earth, father! Can you truly not *feel* it?"

He narrowed his eyes upon his son, unsure what had happened to cause such an outburst, one as ridiculous as this lie. For it had to have been a lie. There was no possible way his blood could have reached the Earth in centuries…

The gasp left his lips as he felt it in truth: faint, but there, lying amidst the turmoil of the World, no, the Dark World. It was his blood, his energy, his power. Concentrated, collected. Imbued with other blood, lesser blood…Abomination blood.

"H-How could this have happened?" he breathed as the flames licked the air high above their heads.

"The Abomination…the Primus was a crafty Creature. I told you I did not trust him! Did not believe him!"

"I saw in him a Creature worthy of redemption!"

Caligo's eyes widened and beneath the blackness Syran saw rage. "They were never meant to exist, Syran! Never! I know you wanted to correct what you've done—giving Primus—*Dracon* the chance to do it for his kind, but a monster will only ever *be* a monster!"

He stared. "And I should have cast you out, should I?"

Caligo retreated, his rage waning with the words softly spoken. "You know you should have," he said after a time of equal staring.

He sighed, his heart, as large as it was, growing perhaps, even larger. *I care. I care so damned much.* "I do not regret what I have done. For you, or the others. I gave Dracula the chance I gave you. He stumbles, yes, but as I remember it, so did you."

Caligo said nothing and Syran let a smile turn up his lips. "Now come. Let us fly this new *Dark* World and uncover what new presence that crafty Abomination has wrought upon our World. I am eager to meet it. Thank the thing that allows us passage after all these silent years."

Caligo said nothing but nodded, spreading his dark flames wide.

And without another word both Phoenixes lifted into the air, spreading their colored flames against the morning sky. Syran eyed the mountains in the distance, feeling the strongest desire to head there.

With a nod of his head he was off, feeling the searing, yet still somehow cold heat of Caligo at his heels, their collective fyre sending trails of golden light to bathe the jagged rocks below.

* * *

Damion Nicodemeus listened to the voices swirling through his mind from the blood. Gritting his teeth, he willed them away, eyeing the idyllic town several yards from his high perch.

Something is wrong, he thought for the tenth time since he'd landed atop the Mountains of Cedar two days before. He had flown across the village once he had his bearings on just where he was upon leaving Eleanor's tunnels, but upon reaching the mountains, he suddenly felt strangely compelled to remain where he was.

The goblet wrapped carefully at his side grew hot, the snow it rested on beginning to melt as though the sun itself beamed directly upon it and it alone. Staring at it, he thought of releasing it from its burned, bloodied home but thought better of it once it started to shake madly against the quickly melting snow.

"Give the Goblet to the Dragon! Give the Goblet to the Dragon! Protect the Dragon! Spare all! Protect the Dragon!"

He exhaled a cold breath, closing his eyes, willing, once again, the voices from his mind, for that was all they said once he'd sat upon the mountain's peak, unsure where else to move.

"Cedar Village," he said once the voices died and the Goblet no longer glowed with heat. He remembered this as the place he had first sent Lucien, the place where, it had been told, Xavier did battle with her Creatures, had acted strangely.

He recalled the green-eyed Vampire's calm, almost resigned expression as they'd shared words in Cinderhall Manor those weeks before. *How he had tried to figure out what I did*, Damion thought, a small smile lifting his lips, *sorry Xavier. I, myself had no true idea what I was searching for.*

He eyed the Goblet again as a strong wind blew past. *If this is Dracula's true power and the sword is not...then Xavier must be close.*

And sure enough the once quiet village began to stir: doors opened against the chilly morning air and Enchanters and beautiful Fae, blonde and dark haired, light skin and dark emerged from their homes, all eyeing the air as though expectant.

But there was one cottage just behind the bubbling stream that held Damion's attention. Its doors did not open with everyone else's, and the more Damion stared, the more he felt the answer he sought was within its stone walls.

Focusing his new power as best he could (for everything was much more vivid now), he centered on the cottage, hoping, indeed, to pick up wisps of Xavier Delacroix's scent or anyone else's known to travel with the Vampire. Once he'd gotten the Goblet to the Vampire, he hoped to face Eleanor again. Whatever she'd gained from adding his own blood to that toxic mixture scared him. But he was changed himself. And he had no doubts that he would not be able to face her now.

Yes, he saw it all. The coward he had been. Running from her, her cold stare for all these years, when the World…the workings within it were so much bigger than his hurt feelings.

Thinking of Xavier again, he straightened where he sat, wondering what the Vampire did now, just where he was. Surely he was still moving just as the others did to retrieve the Goblet, to stop Eleanor.

But then, in a flash of pain, he recalled the way Xavier's eyes had fogged over, the similar smoky blackness within them then, just before he had taken Dragor's sword and slashed he, Damion, across his throat with the blade.

Doubt marred the memory with swiftness. *Smoky blackness—not the smoky blackness that covered Eleanor's Creatures, surely?*

"Damion Nicodemeus, you have been chosen…where Xavier Delacroix has failed. You hold the Goblet of Existence in your grip, my Lord, that makes you the Dragon. The chosen."

Lucien's words filled his mind just as the wind grew stronger, spreading his hair over his shoulders and face. He could barely think on their importance before the terribly large white Dragon soared directly overhead, large wings flapping powerfully as it swerved through the air, and then, gracefully, quietly, it landed upon the empty plains at the mountain's base.

Its claws were gold as they tucked into the earth, and staring seriously now, Damion could see the tips of the Dragon's wings were gold as well, as was the end of its long, sharp tail that swished patiently in Damion's direction.

It faced Cedar Village and as it tucked its wings against his back, a tall Creature rose from atop it, his long white robes sweeping across the Dragon's back. Moving swiftly, the tall man landed in complete silence atop the grass at the Dragon's side.

A long golden staff littered with glowing words emerged from the man's long-fingered hand, and his hair, terribly long and blonde fell freely down his shoulders and back. And as this man stared in the direction of Cedar Village, the door that had not opened with the others finally did.

Damion stood at once, narrowing his eyes against the distance and the strange light of the morning. He nodded in amusement for there was Dragor Descant, Lillith Crane, the Caddenhalls, and every other Creature that had remained in Cinderhall Manor those weeks before.

Knowing that these special Creatures were his reasoning for remaining here, he knelt and grasped the Goblet in its bundle but immediately dropped it: It burned madly through the cloak. He watched in astonishment as the cloak itself began to burn in high, leaping flames.

"Bloody hell," he whispered just as the strange newcomer began to speak:

"Patrons of Cedar Village, you hold amongst you a person of great import! I know this modest place has seen recent misfortune, but it can be avoided again if those that bear the medallions step forward now and claim your places. Quickly," he added, his voice a rush of power and age, "there's not much time at all before many things go wrong."

Damion watched as a dark-skinned Enchanter he had never seen before stepped toward the rushing stream, and as she moved, a scarred Vampire that looked quite like Xavier followed. After him was the young Lillith Crane, a dour-looking Vampire that did not seem to wish to leave her side, the Caddenhall twins, and Dragor Descant. Narrowing his eyes upon the large Vampire he was surprised to see the unconscious frame of a red-haired Vampire draped over Dragor's shoulder. And then two familiar-looking Creatures emerged from the house, one of them carrying an unconscious Elf: the familiar white (though heavily stained) robes draped about the body told him that much.

In the man's hand was a white cane, and as he stepped onto the path with the others, he closed the door behind him with it.

They spoke amongst themselves, that much he could tell, for their mouths moved as they eyed the tall man, though none stepped farther than the rushing stream: it seemed uncertainty held them in place.

"Come forward!" the old, tall man said as the Dragon released short puffs of black smoke from its large nostril slits.

The dark Enchanter made a move forward, but the scarred Vampire held out a hand. *How curious*, Damion thought, *that none of them burned*. And then he trained his gaze on the lighter female Enchanter whose hands were held at mid-level, the fingers definitely wiggling, keeping some sort of spell afloat.

"Not until you explain what it is you mean!" the scarred Vampire roared, causing all other voices to dim: All Enchanters and Fae now watched him from the roads or around the corners of their cottages, eyes wide. "You say we hold a person of great import?! The only person I know of great import to an Ancient Creature such as yourself is Xavier!"

Hushed whispers filled the air, and even from where Damion stood atop the mountain, it reached him as a restless wind. Terror suddenly claimed him though he knew not why. Moving quickly, he kneeled, keeping his gaze on the village. He reached for the Goblet, its gold cool to the touch, his cloak gone. It was now ash atop the black rock.

Securing it under an arm, he no longer felt as though he needed to be threatened by it: he understood it would not harm him now. He felt it something that would aid him from whatever came next, a bloody white Dragon proof of that enough.

He had never known a breed of white Dragon with golden claws, and he knew them all, the Wedderwiles to the west, the Feilong to the east, the Artic Rinebacks to the north, all of them any magnificent sort of color, scales glittering in the suns or gleaming in the night. But *never* white and never with *golden* claws.

Who was this Ancient Creature?

As a hush fell over the village, all clearly awaiting the Creature's response, a voice, cool and soft entered his mind: *"Return the Goblet to the King."*

He did not turn his gaze from the scene below but clutched the gold to his chest all the same, and watched as the Dragon's gold tail swished lazily against the mountain's body, the rock beginning to crack as the gold spikes dragged through.

The mountain trembled with the sudden loss of structure and Damion let out a cry, teetering on the balls of his feet to keep his balance. Below the Dragon let out an aggrieved growl. The rocks from its careless swing had hit its tail and scaled back roughly, some landing atop the snow-covered grass at its golden talons with little abandon.

His cry had reached the curious old Creature and immediately Damion felt the piercing stare of the Creature's gaze. Straightening, for the mountain ceased its shaking, he maneuvered the Goblet underneath an arm, fear beating hard in his chest.

The tall man seemed to want Xavier Delacroix and the others, even threatened their existence if these things were not given to him. *Surely*, Damion thought suddenly, watching the man's blue eyes reach the Goblet and then widen in horror, *he was not working for Xavier's best interest.*

A shuddering breath left the man's thin lips and then the glowing staff was lifted into the air pointing straight at him, and Damion leaned into the many demanding voices that teemed through his mind, though it was the commanding boom of Dracula's voice that rose above all:

"Save the World, Damion Nicodemeus. I trust you."

And before the brilliant flash of golden light could reach him atop the mountain's peak, he turned his gaze to the left and saw the brighter trails of gold that were heading toward them. A greater fear claimed him at the sight and turning back to the old man, the spell cast his way, he felt the Goblet burn white hot beneath his arm. He removed it then, holding it high in his grip. Not knowing what more to do, but feeling all eyes from the village and below upon him, he focused on the heat from the Goblet. The red light that had begun to pour from it covered him and he allowed himself to be carried to hopeful safety.

* * *

Evert the Ancient Elder roared in anger. Staring at the spot the dark Vampire had stood, the glowing Goblet in his bloody hand, he sent yet another spell to smite the mountain where the Vampire had just been.

"Ease, Evert," the Dragon said quietly, and he turned to eye her. She was staring at him with disapproval, her red eyes bright in the darkened morning.

He sighed beneath her gaze, pressing the staff to the grass once more. He turned to her fully letting a feigned smile lift his lips. "Very well. For you, Vetus, I shall. But that Vampire was why we were called here—he holds the Goblet!"

"And the chosen ones shall retrieve it," Vetus said calmly, her red gaze moving toward the village.

And sure enough, Evert following the gaze, the Order of the Dragon were marching through the stream, moving as one to reach them. Some of their gazes were centered on the mountains above their heads and he wondered if they had seen the dark Vampire as well.

It was not long before Aleister had reached several yards away from the Dragon, and the others stopped some ways behind him, their stares now wary, uncertain, some trained upon him, most on Vetus.

Smiling as best he could, Evert stepped forward, the glowing words embedded in the golden staff's dimming slightly as he moved. "Thank you," he said, "for crossing the barrier. For allowing the Order of the Dragon to—"

"That Creature atop the mountain," a scared-looking Dragor interrupted, sword held unsheathed at his side, "that was a Vampire. Why'd you attack him?"

Frowning, he glanced at Vetus for the briefest of moments, her answer clear in her cold gaze: *Ease.*

Clearing his throat, he turned back to the large Vampire that had walked close enough now for Evert to smell the cold and death that filled him, that filled all the nightwalkers.

"I did what I deemed necessary for the protection of the Order of the Dragon," Evert said before Dragor could demand an answer again. "And like you Dragor, I am a Defender of the Order. Higher in rank than you, assuredly, but my job is to *defend* the King and that is what I intend to do."

The staff had warmed in his hand as he'd spoken, the glowing words sending a few of the members of the Order to hide their eyes behind their arms. It was with a breath that the words dimmed once more. But at his side he felt the ground tremble, and without turning to look, he knew Vetus was shifting her footing, impatient, demanding, and he silently agreed.

Throwing forth a hand that sent Dragor stumbling back in alarm, Evert let an old breath leave his ancient lungs and said, "Take your place Defender of the throne, Dragor Descant, at my feet."

Moving as though bidden, Dragor stepped forward, falling to his knees just before Evert's white robes. He placed the sword atop the grass just in front of himself, and as he knelt his head, Evert saw the medallion beneath the Vampire's bloodied, ripped shirt was beginning to glow.

Evert waved another long-fingered hand. "Magic Holder for the throne, Peroneous Antiquitus Doe, take your place." And all watched as Peroneous moved just as Dragor did, brushing past Lillith Crane and Yaddley Caddenhall to kneel at Evert's feet beside Dragor, head bowed, medallion's red light blaring despite being beneath his robes.

One by one Evert called the remaining members of the Order:

"Magic Holder for the throne, Aurora Borealis..."

"Etrian Elf, Arminius, Wisdom of the throne..." And here he watched in bemusement as the unconscious Elf was laid carefully next to Aurora, medallion blaring bright.

Evert stared at the Elf for a moment, wondering why he was gone to the world before he refocused, eyeing the Vampire that stood behind a young Vampire with blond hair. "Step forward Christopher Black, Defender of the throne."

Once the Christopher was in line with the others, he stared at the defiant-looking Vampire who had watched the others kneel against their will with darkened green eyes.

"Aleister—"

"I moved because of what he made me do to my boys," Aleister Delacroix said before Evert could get very far. "I did what Dracula wanted because—because I was bloody compelled to listen. And now Xavier is...he's a bloody mess, isn't he? And you want me to—to kneel *again* when my boy is out there getting worse by the second? What do you propose we do if I kneel here, Ancient? What can you tell me will make me *want* to kneel?"

"Aleister," a dark-skinned woman in deep black robes said from behind him.

"No," he spat, though his gaze, bathed as it was in red, did not falter, "I need to know. Back there I was prepared to do what I could—what we could on our own. What will this...added power do? Will it guarantee I get my son back to his right mind? Or will it only further push him away?"

Evert's lips pursed and this time he did not stop himself from looking to Vetus for assistance. The Dragon, far well versed in how best to handle unhelpful Dark Creatures than he, seemed to smile.

"What do you mean push him away, Creature?" Vetus asked, much to Evert's surprise. Why, her question was calmly asked, rather than rushed and demanding as he was used to. *What did she know that I do not?*

Aleister blinked his surprise at being spoken to directly by the white Dragon, but quickly relented, and said, "Before, while we journeyed across this World to get *The Immortal's Guide* for Xavier, and then to retrieve Dracula's sword for Christian, and then again to see what the Enchanters knew about the entirety of the situation—at every turn Xavier made questionable choices, choices I should think no one bearing the title 'Dracula,' would ever make if they were in their right mind. He was lost, lost to her even longer than he held the title King of All Creatures. He's lost even now. And I'm hard-pressed to think it's because of Dracula's…light that he runs to her. Something in it turns him away, and something in her…dread pulls him in." He looked as though he struggled with any number of grand emotion, then, but he said, "If we locate him…and we find it is his choice… free of any coercion on her end *or* ours to remain at her side, *if* that is where he is now, what are you prepared to do, Dragon, Evert?"

Evert opened his mouth to speak, but Vetus said with a grand swish of her tail, "If the Vampire is lost to her, or if he is not, but does not wish to take his place as rightful King and do what must be done for this World, then he will die. It is the only way," she added as Aleister opened his mouth to speak.

"And who will take his place?" the dark-skinned woman asked from Aleister's side now. "There must always be a King. Who shall it be?"

A steady stream of black smoke issued from Vetus's nostrils and all Enchanters coughed as it reached them. When it passed, the white Dragon was standing taller, her full height towering over the Creatures by several feet. "Kneel Aleister Delacroix, Protector of the King. You will protect the King while there is still a King to protect. *We cannot fail.* Xavier Delacroix was the last chosen by the predecessor. And I daresay we want to have our brave faces on before they reach us."

As Aleister moved much against his will, kneeling at the unconscious Elf's side, the red light blared from his chest. And Evert turned his gaze to where he felt the rush of peculiar, familiar energy.

Damn, I thought we had more time.

The remaining Members of the Order, alive with red light, went up in a collective burst of green flame, and though they did not burn, screams of fright and gasps of shock left the remaining Creatures in the field.

But Evert merely stamped the staff against the grass and the Order of the Dragon were gone, taken where he knew they would be safe from the wrath of a bloody Phoenix. *The* bloody Phoenix.

For he was heading this way Evert saw through the red morning, and his questions, Evert was sure, would be numerous.

Chapter Two

VISIONS

Xavier Delacroix wrapped himself around her lithe body, taking in for the millionth time her scent of perpetual lilac and blood, death and life, decay and rebirth. She held traces of all these things on her skin and now that he was close enough to notice it, he realized she held something else. It was something he had not been able to pinpoint the past day or so, but now it was becoming clear: besides the blood of an Elite, besides the dread that was now not dread at all to him, but merely the essence of her; something to be cherished, sought after, there was the clarity of her now. It no longer inspired fear, a need to run, but now excitement, eagerness, a need to get closer, indeed.

"Lost in thought again, my sweet?" Eleanor Black said, maneuvering a leg around his hip. The sensual embrace only boiled his blood further, the surge of lust thickening his groin. She moaned in delight at the feel of it and he smiled against her neck.

"Lost in you, Eleanor," he whispered, cursing himself for suppressing his desires for her for far too long, for ignoring the sweetness of her hair wrapped in his fingers, the power that radiated off her body in droves, the words whispered with promises of secrets to be divulged in his ear…Secrets, he had felt he would be able to retain, now, Dracula and his myriad, pointless plans be damned.

She laughed in his ear, and he pulled away, curious to see what caused such an outburst. Covering a hand with her mouth, she settled, removing it not long after to say, "Before you *drown* in me anymore, my love, let us talk business at last, hm? Grateful though I am you came to me at last, we haven't had time to talk at all."

Grunting, he leaned to her side on an elbow, never taking his gaze from her flushed, human face. Though it made her features markedly plainer than normal, he found her still enthralling no matter what her face, though there was one he could do without seeing again…

Returning to the present, he blinked. "You want me to officially become your King, become an Elite Creature," he said, able to see this desire in her ever-changing eyes from the moment she shed her 'new' form to one more approachable.

Shifting atop the black sheets, she sat up, propped against the many pillows at her back, her naked form revealed to him in full though he still held a cold hand on her hip, refusing to release it lest this was a dream. Sweeping her black hair over a shoulder, she smiled down at him. "You already are in all but blood and title. They listen to your word, will do as you ask, nay, command, but I cannot be a Queen to a King that is not fully an Elite." And her eyes darkened to gray, sadness within them at the thought, perhaps, that he would deny her again…

He stared up at her, all that had transpired within the past few months churning within his mind. He thought of Dracula, the mad way the Vampire had looked within Carvaca's castle those months ago, he thought of the sword that now remained on the stone floor of Eleanor's room, cold to the touch, no longer glowing with a red heat, and he stared back into her eyes: the flicker of power, of righteousness he had felt whilst in his dream world where he and she ruled completely returned in a strong wave.

He sat up, pulling her into his arms. And as her head rested on his chest, he placed a strong hand in her hair and said, "When I told you I wanted to be King, that I wanted to rule the Dark World, I meant it. It never seemed fair to me that Joseph Gail got to choose whether he ruled the Vampires or the humans of his province, whilst I was kept," he pulled away from her slightly, cupping her cheeks in his hands, catching tendrils of her hair beneath them, "forever at Dracula's side, in the dark, unknowing. I played my part of the sycophantic schoolboy well when it came to him. But you, Eleanor," and he stared her deep in her eyes, willing her to see the truth of what he had come to know, "you, with your knowledge, your courage to know—to reveal what was kept from us, you have only opened my eyes wider. I see what I have always known Dracula to be—a coward, a true liar.

"He never wanted me to rule as he did—he only desired I continue his quest to become…become lesser? How can we become lesser? How can I or my brother return to humanity after all it has rent upon our heads? Even my father forewent the chains of humanity to become a Vampire." He thought of his dream whilst under once more, remembering the sight of Christian and Alexandria Stone, Darien Nicodemeus holding Alexandria tight in a dark hand. "No," he finished after a time, "we cannot return to humanity, but we must surpass it—make the entire World surpass it."

Her smile was wide, wider than he'd ever seen it before; tears fled her soft brown eyes but they were cold as they touched his skin. He knew they should be warm. *I should be able to feel it all*, he thought coldly.

He was pulled from his thoughts when her lips once again pressed against his. Her tongue slithered its way past his lips and he could think of nothing more.

* * *

The tunnels were strangely quiet, though it was not the silence that bothered him; it was *her*. She had turned them all with some manner of horrible magic, no doubt, turned them all into these… monsters, and what was worse, he thought as he threw up what little he had eaten the night before, he would never, truly, see Mara again. This realization, so complete and resounding horrified him more than what he had become two nights ago.

He had not been able to stop thinking about her, dreaming about her, and to know that there was no way, truly, to bring her back, no woman with red light and kind eyes coming to wave a hand and give her back or, better yet, kill him, and send him to her, was absolutely revolting.

Desiring a reprieve from such stressing thoughts, Thomas Montague dropped the bucket at his feet and turned to eye his modest room. Slathered in slightly more black, rich fabrics than the others' rooms, he had known it was a statement of his standing at Eleanor's side, but now that she had Xavier…and had not been seen since he was acquired, he truly wondered what his purpose was—had ever been—at her side. He felt quite pushed aside and what on Earth did she do with the bloody Vampire for days on end?

But he grimaced, knowing full well what they did. It was what he would do if he had his lost love at his side, after all.

Moving for his bed, shaking off such dizzying thoughts, he sat atop it, resigned to his fate without his wife at his side. How strange; he had felt hope the two months since she'd been killed, but now it was gone: He could feel nothing but a resounding numbness, a grand loneliness where her love had been.

The tears began to fall, no longer burdened by any good feeling; no lie to keep them in place. What, truly, had his life become? Burdened by Eleanor's voice, her power, lost, indeed, where he had once had purpose at his father's side, his focus on destroying Xavier Delacroix—

And now that very Vampire was only feet away and Thomas felt oddly compelled to leave them alone, though he knew, in a better mind, he would have moved to kill the Vampire without a second thought.

"*Damn,*" he said, a snarl leaving his lips with the word, anger hot in his heart, his blood. The rage of the Lycan settled beneath his skin, his blood boiling with its heat, but instead of urging him to transform, he felt the rage change. Something else was there now, and as he glared at his hands clenched into fists, he saw the strange black wisps leave his skin. Confusion quickly replaced the anger: he opened his hands, surprised when the black wisps pulsed strongly as he flexed his fingers.

What the Devil?

And in a flash, images of blood, gray and black winged monsters, and the misty black sky appeared before his eyes and he inhaled deeply, the smoky dread filling his lungs. "*Lycan of Old,*" a new voice said from somewhere close by, "*why do you feel sad?*"

Blinking in the penetrating dark, he looked around, no longer in his room, it seemed, but transported to a new place: Encroaching, gnarled branches pressed toward him, a penetrating blackness surrounding all here, wherever here was. He could see nothing but his shaking hands before himself as he moved the black, twisting branches away, doing his best to peer past them—still unable to see a thing.

What now? he thought bracingly, just as the voice returned:

"Lycan of Old." It was much closer now, and through the black he thought the voice terribly familiar. *"You do not need to mourn what you have lost."*

He stepped forward, brushing past the branches, which, he realized, protruded from nowhere. Before he could think how utterly strange it was that the branches held no trunks, no roots tying them to anything solid, the cabin appeared. How familiar it looked save the long, twisting vines enshrouding its old face. The old, wooden door was bare, save its peeling, cracked body, and in the light of what seemed to be a dim moon, though he could not see it in the murky blackness above him, he stepped past the dark branches, free from their cutting fingers, and into the clearing.

"Who a-are you?" he called, his voice cracking, sounding low and weak against the silky echo of the voice that had led him here.

"Come, Lycan of Old," the voice called, decidedly feminine now, even more familiar the longer he stared at the cabin. He recognized it now as the place Eleanor had sent he and another Elite, the place she had sent he and Javier Theron flying through the dark.

He stepped forward, unaware he had ceased walking upon reaching the clearing, and though there was no light to pass across the cabin, he could see it clearly:

The door was black the more it was he stared, and he could see its old knob turning in the low light. Tensing, he thought briefly of slinking back into the sharp shade of the branches when the figure emerged from behind the door.

Illuminated in the vague light, Mara Montague stood resolute against the darkness beyond the door, her frame appearing to glow with her own brilliant light. It cast a brighter glow over the clearing, and seeing her in full now, he staggered forward, though his knees felt like stones beneath him.

"M-Mara," he breathed, doing his best to reach her, but failing miserably: The more steps he took the farther away she and the cabin appeared.

"*Lycan of Old,*" she said, her lips—the lips he remembered so sweetly—parting, and even through the distance he could feel her breath, cool and soft against his face. He blinked as the wind passed, sinking to his knees with its touch.

She was here.

"Mara—please," he gasped, his heart suddenly piercing with great pain the more he watched her. She wore a simple black dress tied with a single black rope at the waist, her hair, still slightly frizzy and brown hung as it once did at her back and she made no attempts to tie it into an unfathomable creation atop her head. She wore it as she did—as she once did—as if she were preparing to sleep in their bed, and with the sudden thought, an aching gasp left his throat and his gaze clouded with tears. "Mara—how—?"

"*Lycan of Old,*" she said, her voice cold, cutting across his whispers with ease, "*you need not mourn what you have lost. For I am here. Still here. Always, I have been and always will I remain.*"

He blinked several tears away and once they were gone, before new ones could fall, he moved his lips and tried to form proper words: "What do you mean, my love? Where—what is this? A-Are you even real?" For he had a sinking feeling she would disperse, leave him to his terrible pain, his grief all over again. It was a pain he was not keen on experiencing again, now that he had reprieve from it in the sight of her, whether this be a dream or otherwise. He rose to his feet slowly, finding it strange how his knees still felt like stone but he could stand. *This must all be in my mind*, he thought, wiping away a tear.

Mara took a step from the door and he flinched, his gaze moving to her feet with her movement. He was surprised to find her feet bare. *She always wore shoes*, he thought, remembering when she would go as far to chastise him when he would return from a hunt sans shoes, never mind the blood that would blanket his skin.

She stepped clear of the door, her gray eyes reflecting something like contempt, but he could not be sure: his tears marred his sight as well as sense.

She moved as though a ghost, her feet not making a sound on the ground strewn with twigs and dried leaves as it was, and then she was before him, a hand outstretched as though to grasp his face.

Her fingers never did grace his skin: she held the tips mere inches from his lips, her stare keeping his breath still, his mind horribly blank.

"Thomas," she breathed and he blinked at last, fresh tears threatening to fall. How he had wished for her to speak his name for many a night and now she was.

Mara.

"*The ring,*" she whispered, a breath just as soothing as it had been whilst she stood before the door. It was gone, he realized, with a quick glance behind her. The cabin, the vines, the clearing, indeed. All of it, gone.

"*Creature,*" she said, bringing his gaze back to her, "*the ring.*"

"Ring? What ring?" he breathed, doing his best to focus on her: suddenly all seemed to darken as though this were a dream and he was to wake up, regrettably, at any moment.

"*The ring of the constable,*" she whispered.

And all at once he remembered the fawning Vampire as they'd stood in the darkened alleyway of London, how easily Eleanor had ripped him apart...

"What—what of the ring?" he asked, voice low.

"*Take the magic that holds it fast...*" she was saying as darkness encroached her in full.

"And?" he breathed, daring to rise to his feet, keep her in his sights, yet he made it no farther than a knee off the ground before he was pushed back down by an invisible hand. And still the vision of Mara Montague spoke on:

"*...place the ring within the Goblet of Existence, and you will know freedom from suffering, Creature.*"

He blinked hard. All was black now, her grey eyes, her light now gone. Then, with a cold breath, he was back atop his bed, clutching his heart tight. The darkness that had pulled him in that vision now cleared, and quickly.

"Wh-What on—?" he breathed, staring around the room where all seemed quite normal, all seemed untouched...and yet, he could not deny there was a difference in the air.

Yes, something was off…and it was not the essence of Eleanor and Xavier's energy spiraling throughout the tunnels, no, it seemed to come from within him, himself.

The ring.

He stepped across the cold, dirt floor, toward his dresser where he kept what little clothes he owned. Pulling the topmost one open, he quickly removed what little rags remained there, eyeing the single golden ring at the bottom.

"A Vampire's ring," he breathed, lifting it up, holding it between his pointer finger and thumb. "Do you really hold such magic little band?" Mara's words whispered in his mind, resolute against Eleanor's wispy dread, something that struck him as strange. *How was it possible Mara's words could do that?* The glint of gold pulled his attention back to what he held. "Magic…the Goblet of Existence. True freedom?" He thought of his wife again, smiling as the sight of her passed across his vision. A dream it may have been, but it was the most real he had ever known since her death.

If she spoke this, he decided then, staring at the slight glow that emanated from the ring, *then it must be true. Mara,* he thought, feeling his heart, battered and weak as it was, begin to warm with hope, *would never lie. Not to me.*

* * *

The stone burned in his pocket but he ignored it, thinking again if he had been foolhardy in revealing the stone to Christian Delacroix, but no, the Vampire would not gain curiosity in it, this he was sure.

He had seen Christian's look of hurt before he'd left them at the gates to the Vampire City; he had seen the seed of doubt that had been planted: Whatever had flourished between the Vampire and Alexandria Stone would wither. And they would not move to complete their goal.

Yes, he thought triumphantly, staring at the bloodied grass before Cinderhall Manor, *I will remain Dracula's creation forever.*

A searing pulse of heat from the stone drew him from his reverie, and he sniffed the air, dismayed; it suddenly smelled of Eleanor's dread.

"Master Vonderheide," a strong voice said from behind him.

He turned just as the stone grew cold.

Standing in the puddle of dried blood where a Vampire's head rested beside the base of a tree were several of his Elite Creatures, their hoods down against their backs, their eyes alive with relief, yes, but something else lingered there as well.

The one that had spoken stepped forward out of the black blood, his eyes dark in the morning's light. His hands were clasped behind his back, his cloak just as tattered as the others that stood at attention behind him. "Master Vonderheide, you must return to the tunnels," he said, black beard splattered with what looked to be dried blood, not yet black. "Eleanor desires it."

"Does she?" he whispered, doing his best not to roll his eyes. He had no intention of returning to her damned caves ever again.

"Yes," the Elite Creature said, stepping out of the puddle, toward him, and closer now, Victor recognized the greedy glint in the Creature's eyes. *Gregory.* "You must return. She's changed us all."

He blinked in the light. "Changed? What do you mean?"

The others stepped forward as well, stopping just beside the Creature, and Victor suddenly felt he should prepare for an attack. "She's...made us better," Gregory said, "made us...more."

A flare of fear rose in his cold heart and the stone began to warm as if in response. "What more has she done?" he asked, unsure if he desired to hear the answer.

A look of uncertainty passed across a few of their faces, and Gregory said, "We are not...entirely sure. But she has made us stronger...our rage drives us, we hold the ability to fly, and we hold the majestic shape similar to the Phoenixes. If I had a chance to name it, I would call us gods, Victor. And she needs you home to bear witness to her new creation."

Majestic shape similar to the...? "What on Earth are you talking about?"

Gregory moved, stepping swiftly up to him in four steps, and Victor felt the stone flare with a greater heat as if to protect him. "We are tied to her, Victor," he whispered, and for a brief moment Victor almost thought he saw the Vampire's black eyes darken with insurmountable fear. "If you won't come back for her, come back for us. *We are scared.*"

He could not speak against that voice, against the fiery heat that now soared up his thigh, moving to his gut. He merely opened and closed his mouth, not sure what he was hearing.

"Victor," and Gregory placed a strong hand upon Victor's arm, squeezing it tight. Victor could feel the sticky darkness that oozed off the Elite Creature in droves now. *Changed, indeed.* "*Please.* If you will not do it for us, do it for your creator's legacy. If you come back… if you…end her before she can turn you, turn Xavier, then you can lead us…end this torment."

He stepped away, the Elite's long fingernails ripping lines in his sleeve as he moved. He blinked, unsure if he were truly seeing the way the Creatures' eyes were turning entirely black, unsure if that were truly the searing heat of the stone sending sudden waves of a warming heat over his entire body.

Blinking through the heat, he focused on Gregory as best he could. "What do you mean turn Xavier? He is with her?"

"Yes, Master Vonderheide. And we fear it is a matter of time before he succumbs as we all have."

Victor stared, unsure what to believe. "If Xavier is with her," he began thoughtfully after a time, "then would he not be most eager to bend her ear? To know her secrets? Become one of hers immediately?"

Gregory shifted his footing atop the dried blood. "He has not, not yet, but there is no telling when he will. For he *will*, Lord Vonderheide, and he *cannot*. Not by any means."

The stone flared with greater heat then, and Victor stifled a scream of pain as the Elite Creatures tensed or released their weapons from their cloaks. They had seen his grimace and perhaps, figured he were to attack. Placing a hand over his pocket, willing the stone to cool, he straightened as best he could, trying to ignore the heat as it rose from his thigh, spreading up his side, flushing his face with its strange fire. He felt he should be sweating or some form of profusion, but all that happened was that he blinked as the heat passed across his eyes, gasping in alarm immediately.

The Creatures before him were covered in a sickly black energy. It radiated off them as though unstable, flaring from their heads, not with a steady ebb and flow, but with a wild, uneven pulse that repeated the more he stared.

And blinking in the strange sight, he noticed Gregory's eyes, how they shined with a lighter illumination than the rest of him. If Victor were not incredibly confused, he would have thought it the faintest bit of light of the Creature's soul doing its best to shine through.

He blinked several more times in the light of the sun seeing the strange blackness radiating from the Elites, and then it was gone. Once it was, he rubbed his eyes, now free from the strange heat. It had, while he had been staring, retreated into the stone.

"Master Vonderheide," Gregory said, expectantly.

Victor stared back upon him, unsure what he had just witnessed, but quite sure it was, once again, the power he had been afforded by the Phoenixes. With this empowering thought in mind, the meeting with Eleanor, with a newly-turned Xavier did not seem quite as scary. *For if I can see what...remains of their souls*, he thought, taking a step toward Gregory, *I can discern the truth of all of this at last.*

Reaching out a steady hand for the Creature to take, he waited, the strange smell of old blood, death, and lilac filling his nose.

And then, with a slow, wide smile, Gregory extended a rough hand and shook.

Chapter Three

THE ETRIAN HILLS

The Elves spoke loudly amongst themselves, their many voices filling the large hall. The sound echoed deeply in the Elf's ears, sending his brain to further pound against his skull.

He lightly stroked the faded gold embedded into the arm of his chair, his long finger smoothing over a groove burned into the arm over a long period of time.

The thin crown atop his head had slumped forward some time before, and he had not bothered to place it upright. It was a position that had long left him, after all. It was all for show, indeed.

"My King! Alinneis! We've just received word!" the red-haired Elf shouted, stepping briskly through the harried crowd of other orange-eyed men and women. In his raised right hand, the scroll waved wildly above the heads of the others as the Elf passed them, his long, stained robes sweeping rhythmically around his feet as he moved.

When he was just before him at last, Alinneis lifted a finger in the air, sending the crowd to fall into silence, all eyes upon the messenger.

"It would seem," Alinneis called to the crowd, "we've stirrings in our…derelict side of the World. Let us be kind enough to see what our dear Specter has prepared for us this time, hmm?"

Though the sarcasm was thick on his tongue, the orange eyes of the other Elves were glued on his. They were wide, some with exasperation, others anticipation, all a trickle of fear.

The Specter kneeled, his orange eyes glistening in the light of the white large ball that hovered overhead the King's faded gold throne. "My King," the Specter breathed, the hiss long in the air while he spoke, "we've just received word from Latharius." And he extended the scroll in a long-fingered hand.

Arminius waved a hand, and one of his guard, a long-nosed Elf with long black hair stepped forward, grabbed the scroll and undid its seal, unrolling it with haste.

He cleared his throat, gathering the attention of the very few Elves who had not been paying attention toward the back of the hall, and read:

"The Enchanters have regained control of magic."

Alinneis sat up higher in his chair, headache gone. He nodded to the Elf to continue.

The Elf squared his shoulders and said, *"Equis has placed a call for a Summit, your Graciousness. And we Etrian Elves have been invited.*

"I write to you in place of my presence because I have found the roads to be treacherous, the Dark World burdened with a crushing energy—it constricts.

"I will return to the Fields when I learn more about this energy, your Graciousness.

"As it is, Swile has not returned, I have watched him closely as well, but he lost me somewhere around the Bagabill Mountains. His disobedience will not go unanswered.

"Latharius—your loyal servant."

All eyes returned to Alinneis as the scroll was hesitantly closed.

And the slow smile lifted his face.

"…My King," the Specter began slowly, rising to his feet.

The guard lowered the scroll to his side and stepped backwards down the stairs, leaving the throne.

"No, no," he said quietly, staring at the dark stone of the dais his throne rested upon, "there will be no anger this day." He looked up to stare at the waiting faces before him, seeing the fear and confusion within himself mirrored in their gazes. "We must do all things as we have always done—with decorum. Latharius is right in moving as he has, but he knows it is best—always best—to return here to report back to me. We are not...desired Creatures in this World.

"But we have done things the way the other Creatures would have them done. We have sent and sent our letters, our requests for our freedom, and we have been denied. Now magic has returned to the Enchanters when its rightful place is at the hands of Elven kind?"

"I wonder, as do any of you, what Latharius has done to warrant this motion by one of my greatest spies, but rest assured this matter will be handled accordingly.

"You are all to return to your chambers, I must speak with the Etrian Wing."

A low murmur of voices filled the hall as the many Elves filed out through the large stone doorway opposite Alinneis's throne.

When the last long-eared Elf passed through the doorway and the large gold doors closed, the remaining Elves moved around the throne to stand just before it.

"Our King," they said in unison, their orange eyes gleaming in the light of the ball.

Alinneis watched them in silence for a moment, taking in their apprehensive faces. "Things have gotten out of hand," he said calmly.

"As we are aware, your Graciousness," one nearest the end of the line wheezed, the strangled hiss leaving his old lips in something of a whistle. "We have already begun deciding how best to proceed."

He stared. "You have, have you? And what, dear Trolig, is the best way to proceed?"

Trolig said nothing more, his orange gaze finding the floor.

Alinneis moved his gaze to the others, waiting for a response. When one did not reach him, he sighed. "No? Nothing? Were those words merely said to ease my great, old mind?"

"Of course not," another Elf hissed, "what Trolig means to say, your Graciousness, is that we have begun to discuss the matter."

"And?"

"And," Trolig said, recovering, "it has been decided that Swile is no longer one of us."

He fought the urge to roll his eyes. "As I have already decided," he said cruelly, sitting up higher in his chair, "we must move on this matter seriously my dear Wing. As we know, Swile has told this new King how we entered the *Vampures'* city. I can only guess that Damion Nicodemeus has finally revealed how that horrid attack came to pass. Twisted Swile's arm as it were..."

The Elves eyed each other in alarm, one of them sputtering out, "That *Vampure* would never reveal the truth—that would throw him under the horse as well, surely!"

He closed his eyes at their simplicity. "Damion Nicodemeus was made a Member of their *Vampure* Order after the attack for *successfully*," the word drowning in sarcasm, "fending off our own. He betrayed us then, I daresay I would not put it past a *Vampure* to repeat the same offense twice."

No one said a word which was just as well for Alinneis: he had taken to thinking deeply on the events of that strange time. A *Vampure* in the Etrian Fields...No one would have believed it unless it was seen...and seen the dark *Vampure* had been.

"I want you," he said, opening his eyes to glare upon them, "to track Damion Nicodemeus down...and bring him to me."

He was well prepared for the sputtering tongues, the aghast exclamations of disbelief, but he raised a hand to silence them and with the other adjusted the crown atop his head.

"Bring him to me, Etrian Wing," he repeated coldly.

They stared at him for moments more, and then Trolig bowed, the others following suit soon after. "As you wish, Alinneis," he whispered with a hiss, "as you wish."

* * *

Damion rested beneath the large tree, his brain pounding against his skull as fear washed over him. He knew not what more to do having fled the Mountains of Cedar and now clutched the Goblet tight in his hands.

He felt greatly exposed, quite wishing his brother were there only in the Vampire form, he, Damion had come to know. Not the form of the monstrous, winged beast that flew about the World now.

Yes, if Darien were here he would speak sense, Damion thought, hearing the birds chirp high above his head. *Darien would know what to do. He'd always had a better head on his shoulders than I.*

The memory returned as though it waited to be called up, and with nothing else to do, he allowed it to take him to sleep.

He walked alongside him through the dark, the rain falling heavily upon their cloaks but they did not stop until they reached it.

The large white house stood resiliently amidst the thundering rain and it was here that he removed his hood, letting his face succumb to the rain he could not feel. "Manners Darien," he reminded the Vampire who walked behind him.

Darien nodded silently.

Together they set off for the black gate. It was not locked at all; it slid open rather freely with the small push of his hand.

He flew up the old wooden steps and lifted a hand to knock at the door when it flung open; a hollowed, tiny woman stood there, a grave look upon her small face. "Harm him anyway you see fit," she said.

With a low snarl, he smacked her aside with a careless movement of the hand and she flew to his right, hitting the wall, which was only just repaired from the many other times he'd smacked her to the very same spot.

"Darien," he called for his brother, never turning as they moved further into the house, climbing the stairs, for he knew where the newborn would be, and he marched to the room at the end of the hall. The door flew open although he hadn't touched it and his gaze fell upon the tall blonde Vampire who stood near the crib, his eyes wide with surprise.

But the Vampire had only lifted a hand when Damion moved quickly, appearing just before him, pushing him against a wall where he did not resurface.

"Did you have to hurt him?" the voice of Darien sounded from the doorway.

"He was going to try and stop me," he said harshly, waving a hand to the crib. "Do it now!"

Darien swept for the crib without another word and he stared down at the baby, doing nothing.

"Do it now!" he snarled harshly. "You must do it before he awakens! Have you not forgotten the way she was murdered, Darien?! Do it! Brand this child so we may take our leave—and quickly!"

But Darien would not lift his dark hand, instead he said, much to Damion's displeasure, "It has happened many years ago. May we not lay rest to this madness?"

"Madness?!" he cried. "Our mother was massacred by this family—!"

"No, she was not!" he yelled incredulously, and Damion fell silent, eyes narrowing in disbelief. "This family did not do it and you know it! It was Renere Caddenhall. And where is he brother? Dead! Have you not gotten enough of your damned revenge?"

He knew his impatience to increase with the Vampire's rude words, and Darien snarled warningly, his hood hiding his black eyes. "I dare you."

"Father would be disappointed with you, Darien...he always spoke of it. You were more human than Vampire, more human than Creature, pathetic in every right, in every way," he spat, his words aiming to hurt.

Darien's eyes shone angrily yet he remained where he stood. "We must leave," was all he said after a few terse moments.

"Leave?" Damion laughed. "We cannot leave! We must secure the child! Were you not complaining about Minerva and Yaddley Caddenhall being to your dislike? This is your chance to secure another Caddenhall! You must do it!"

"I did not say Minerva and Yaddley were to my dislike—they must be set free! Damion you are a fool for contacting that Enchanter. Do you have any idea what you have wrought, dragging me along with it?!"

Damion stepped toward his young brother, disgust lining his eyes. "They will never be set free, Darien. Nepenthe—our mother!—was destroyed by Renere, and I shall not rest until I feel satisfied that the Caddenhall family tree has suffered enough."

And much to his bewilderment, Darien smiled: a thunderous noise from below filled the house. Damion rounded on his brother, waving the door closed with a hand. "Who did you call here?"

"The Chairs," he said tersely.

"The bloody Chairs?!"

"I hear them—they're up here," a voice from outside the door sounded.

And before Damion could do a thing to stop it, the door swung open and in stepped Westley Rivers, accompanied by a younger Armand Dragon; Craven Winger held the pale, sallow woman who'd been flung against the wall. She appeared to be dead, but Damion could smell her blood clearly...

"Damion!" Westley said, stepping forward, eyeing the sleeping baby within its crib. "Armand, secure the child."

Armand rushed over to the baby and lifted him gently from the bed, glaring at Damion, before falling back in line with Craven against the wall.

Westley turned his glare upon Damion. "Invader, your reign upon this family ends here," and he eyed Darien as well before saying, "both of you will be escorted to the Vampire City under my close watch. I want no funny business do you hear me?"

Damion scowled while Westley wrapped a strong hand around his arm, dragging he and his brother out of the room. When he passed Craven, he jerked his head toward the unconscious Vampire whose back remained against the wall. "Take care of him and the others, I must take these two to the City. Caught 'em at last! Armand, bring the boy. We shall return shortly, Craven..."

Damion and Darien were pushed through the narrow doorway and down the stairs, out of the house into the pounding rain, which had not slowed at all since their arrival.

With a firm hand around his arm, Damion's grimace could not be concealed. Betrayed! He'd called the bloody Chairs! Had us captured! Why, if he weren't my only sibling, I would have killed him long ago...And then he caught the slew of blonde hair peeking through Armand's cloak, new anger spreading through him—

And then it happened.

His eyes narrowed, the boy flying from underneath Armand's cloak, Armand staring after it in alarm. The child hovered in the air and with Westley's attention momentarily distracted, Damion threw a punch to his jaw.

The Vampire flew back and landed on the muddy ground, his cloak soaked in it, his gray hair clinging to his shocked face.

Damion leapt for the Caddenhall child who still hovered bizarrely in the air, drenched in the hard rain, but as he did so, he was knocked aside by something strong, something heavy and dark.

He flipped through the air and slid in the mud on his knees, a growl of anger and frustration leaving him. Darien had grabbed the child and was attempting to shield him from the oncoming rain, by placing him in his cloak but he was upon him once again.

"You will regret defying me brother!"

Darien bared his fangs and jumped back, much to his dismay, far away from his thrown fist, the small baby nestled safely in his arms. The child that should already be under their consummate command...

"Darien!" he screamed in rage.

"Damion!" the deep voice roared from behind him, causing him to turn. Westley was on his feet and although covered in mud and drenched in water, there was no denying his anger: his eyes gleamed red through the rain. He started for Damion but had barely made a step before Damion felt a rather hard blow to his face, knocking him back through the night.

As he flew, he could just see the livid eyes of the blonde Vampire he had pushed aside. Evan Caddenhall, he thought vaguely, before the Vampire was atop him, pressing him down into the mud with strong, pale hands.

He stared up into the Vampire's red eyes, the large droplets of water from his hair, falling against his face, and he knew, then, that there was nothing for it. While the Vampire had him, touched him, he knew he would have to do it. Change the tides of battle to his favor...

It was with a strained tongue that he managed to whisper, "Serve...me...Caddenhall..."

And Evan's grip loosened, he stood at last, allowing him to rise to his own feet, a hand rubbing bracingly at his neck. He stared at the

Vampire who merely stood in the rain, not saying another word, and there on his arm appeared the jagged cross.

"Get the boy," Damion commanded, Evan nodding, moving for Darien and the boy he held close.

Darien, much to Damion's surprise, did not move from the Vampire, but merely allowed him to grab his son; he did not even stop him as Evan turned from him and moved back to Damion, the blankest of looks upon his face.

Westley and Craven were moving for them, Damion knew, but with the utterance of a new voice, the one of a terrified Sessa Caddenhall from the doorway of her home, Damion grabbed the child and said the three words he'd whispered only moments before.

He stared down at the child, eyeing its pale skin, its tufts of blonde hair; it stared up at him with large brown eyes, the mark appearing on its small arm the more it was Damion stared, and he did not realize that Sessa was still screaming as she ran down the steps of the old house and moved toward him, her voice forever echoing on in his ears the more it was she reached him:

"LUCIEN!"

Damion Nicodemeus opened his eyes.

He blinked away the memory with haste. It would not do to focus on things that no longer mattered, for Lucien was gone, as was Darien. There would be nothing to gain from lingering on painful pasts. No, he had done that for far too long as it was...

He stood, stepping in a direction that seemed best, and though it was feeble, he found his thoughts moving to Lucien, and where in the World the Vampire could have been. The Caddenhall Curse was no more, this he instinctively knew, if he didn't have a Caddenhall near to test the theory: it was in the way he found it difficult to focus on anything that was not Xavier nor Dracula, that was not, and this he found curious, the Phoenixes. He recalled the way the sight of the winged Creatures heading toward him atop the Mountains of Cedar had filled him with a new fear.

Bloody Phoenixes filling the sky, white Dragons allowing Ancient Creatures to ride their backs...goddamn Xavier Delacroix—gone.

What the hell am I supposed to do now?

And just as the thought left him, he heard the faint voice through the trees and stopped dead. As the voice drew closer, he pressed up against a tree, doing his best to determine from whence it came, holding the Goblet close to his chest, ignoring the heat of it against what remained of his shirt.

"What else am I supposed to do Latharius?" The voice was closer now, but still some ways off, and the more Damion listened, the more he could make out the distinct lingering hiss beneath the angry words. "Go back with you to Alinneis? I cannot. Not after what I've done. He'll kill me for my treachery."

A new voice, one Damion assumed to be this Latharius, said, "And what do you think I am here for, Swile?"

Swile? Damion peered around his tree at the name, doing his best to see just where the Creatures were. And there, standing some ways off ahead of him through the high, thick trees were two Elves. The one with silver hair and a short black cloak over a black button-up shirt and black worn pants held, in a steady, gloved hand, a glowing blue dagger pressed against Swile's throat.

And the black-haired Elf with orange eyes Damion knew as Swile attempted to step away from the dagger, but Latharius stepped with him, the dagger resolute.

"I know you were just here to track me down, Latharius, not kill me. As that is Alinneis's decision to make as the Etrian King, not yours," Swile said, the dagger against a vein sliding slightly against his skin as he talked.

"Who said he hasn't already made the decision, Swile?" the silver-haired Elf said.

"What do you mean?"

"I sent letter when you left the *Vampure* City and did not immediately return to the Etrian Fields," he said coldly. "Alinneis has sent the signal to end you."

"Signal?" he breathed, and it seemed he was unsure just what this signal was.

"Yes," hissed the assassin, and Damion understood just what this Elf was.

He remembered them when at Alinneis's door, the first Etrian Elves he met: *Elipsum Etrianos Cara*: The Death of the Earth.

They'd pulled two daggers from their cloaks, though the blades had not glowed as this Elf's did. They were quite dull in that respect, in fact, but sharp: Damion remembered their cuts as they sliced his throat in various places before he could very well speak.

Fear pulled at his every sense but he stayed, watching what happened next, for he remembered these particular Elves as inherently ruthless in their quests: To fulfill Alinneis's word no matter what it was. And if this particular Elf had already received their sacred symbol then Swile was as good as dead, Damion knew.

Shuddering slightly at the memory, he blinked in the sparse light of the sun and watched as Swile closed his eyes, for Latharius had moved his wrist, slicing the orange-eyed Elf's throat far too easily.

The Goblet against his chest pulsed with a steady warmth and he tore his gaze from the sputtering, bleeding Swile to stare down at it.

The blood was black.

Blinking upon it rapidly, for it could not be true it had changed so easily, Damion was torn from his confusion when a brilliant burst of blue light shined through the trees.

Looking up, he almost dropped the Goblet, for there were several Elves, all clad in black cloaks, their silver hair all bound high upon their heads, their ears sharp and revealed.

The one known as Latharius kneeled to these Elves, the blood of Swile still on his blade. It remained in his hand, gleaming in the sparse sunlight, and Damion narrowed his gaze on Swile who remained slumped against the tree, eyes dull in his death.

Gratitude swarmed the fear, for with Swile dead, the Elves couldn't have ever told anyone that it was he who led them into the Vampire City, indeed—

"The deed is done, my brothers," Latharius said.

One Elf said, "Alinneis will soon receive word of Swile's deeds and that you move to subdue him, brother."

Latharius did not look up from the ground. "But I have done my task. Surely he seeks my return to the Fields."

"No," one of them said, this voice low. "We will not return to Alinneis. Not yet."

At this, Latharius looked up. Damion could see the confusion in the Elf's shoulders as they sagged. "Why not?"

"Because," another said, this one opening his cloak to reveal numerous daggers, "we are not alone. And as you know Latharius, no Creature that is not an Elf can gain passage into the Etrian Fields. Not after the *Vampure*," and the word rang with disgust, "Damion Nicodemeus."

* * *

Aleister cursed as they marched blindly in a direction he was not sure was anything more than a waste of their time.

Xavier. I need to get to my son. Not be pulled here...wherever here is.

He stared around at the rolling plains, seemingly endless, though he knew they had to end. From his journeys across the World, he knew he had to be somewhere near the Elven and Enchanter town of Pinnett, but there was something in the air that made him doubt that guess.

It was as though he could not make out their place in the World, and how strange that was.

"Where the bloody hell did that damned Ancient Creature drop us?" Dragor asked angrily, hand on the worn leather of his sword.

"The middle of nowhere, it appears," Aurora said in exasperation, clutching at her medallion.

Aleister lifted a scarred hand to clutch at his own, for it had begun to warm, and from the painful expression on Aurora's face, he was sure hers did the same.

Stifling the anger at being made to move for the Ancient Elder once more, no doubt somewhere that took him farther from his son, he focused on the others.

They were all staring around at the wild plains in bewilderment, some had their hands on their weapons, others grasped at the medallions beneath their shirts, but Arminius, Aleister saw, lay over the shoulder of a grim Peroneous, still unconscious.

Wondering why indeed the Phoenixes would bother killing Nicholai Noble, a rush of fear swept over him. The Phoenixes had him killed because, as Arminius said, Nicholai was the first to have seen them. The first Dracula let see them. And he had failed. *So then,* and he tightened his grip on the burning medallion with the thought, *would they not move to see Xavier killed?*

Not desiring to entertain the thought further, he stifled the snarl that arose, feeling powerless despite the blare of red light from their medallions, the words of Evert repeating in his mind, *"There's not much time at all before many things go wrong."* It mattered not what the damned Ancient Creature said, if Xavier was struck down by a bloody Phoenix. But if the Vampire had moved to join Eleanor, he thought then, what would a Phoenix matter? Surely, as an Elite Creature, Xavier would be able to fell a Phoenix.

Snarling in frustration at his, Aleister's, lack of actual power against the state of the ever-changing World, he cursed himself for not moving sooner. For not moving as soon as possible to aid Xavier in his tasks, for letting Eleanor Black's dread keep he and the others at bay, amplifying his fears. The fear that he was not as strong as he'd thought. That he would only see Xavier die. That the Dark World would fall to Eleanor before he and Xavier could stop it—

Various shouts filled the air ahead of where they remained and all Creatures ceased their mindless walking immediately.

Pulled from his thoughts, Aleister stepped ahead, unsheathing his sword, mind heavy on Eleanor's Creatures and if they had somehow located them...

He climbed the hill, the medallion glowing fiercely at his chest and stared down. Through the many exceedingly tall trees, he could see the colorful cloaks of various slender men as they darted in and out of view, their long platinum blonde, silver, or black hair swaying with prominence as they moved. Their long-fingered hands were weaving expertly through the air as far as Aleister could see. Streams of light left their fingertips here and there directed, it seemed, at a badly bruised figure further into the woods.

Doing his best to sense just who it could be, he was distracted for the slightest of moments when Aurora placed a hand on his shoulder. He eyed her, her dark brown eyes alive with concern. It was a look he was sad to see grace her face more often than not. "The Etrian Elves," he said to her and she stared down the hill as well, narrowing her eyes.

"And they have their magic back," she said after a time of observing the flashes of colorful light.

"Of course they do," Peroneous said, joining them, the black hair of Arminius swaying across his back. "But who are they attacking?"

"Who wouldn't they attack?" Dragor said, standing beside Aleister now. "They have any number of enemies in the Dark World, don't they?"

"Still," Aurora said, her medallion's glow giving her face an ominous hue, "so many against one Creature. It isn't exactly fair. The Elves' magic is much more…grounded than ours. They have an advantage in the woods as they are."

Aleister blinked in the collective red light. "Advantage?"

She did not eye him as she said, "The Elves—all kinds—are the Creatures we Enchanters get our magic from. Their magic comes from the earth; the trees, the grass, the dirt, the sky. They use the elements, the spirit of the earth if one will, to their better gain. It was said before Vampires their beauty was never surpassed. It is supposedly a brilliance they have lost with the appearance you Vampires currently hold."

At this Aleister saw Peroneous shift his footing atop the grass.

"Regardless," Aurora repeated, bringing his gaze back to her, "if the Etrian Elves are free of the original Dracula's hold then we have more to fear than the Phoenixes and Eleanor Black."

Aleister's brow furrowed. "Why is that?" He could not believe the Elves were any true threat, so long had they been encumbered. Curious to their current state, he listened to her intently as the shouts below continued:

"*Nam Cora*," she said as though that explained everything, "it is what the Etrian Elves use to connect to their magic. Unlike we Enchanters that were taught to pull magic from our minds, ourselves, the Elves believe the purest magic is what we have around us. All of their spells end with the affirmation 'Nam Cora.' As I understand it, it roughly translates to, 'to name the core,' that is, the core of the earth. They pull the earth's energy, the very essence of it, into their spells, into themselves. They believe it…impure to merely shout a spell and have it come from the self."

"So why did the Elves teach the Enchanters to do the very thing they feel is impure?" Aleister asked, confused.

Peroneous cleared his throat. "Because I gave Dracula the potion of immortality. I made that potion with material from the earth, the elements, and blood. An abomination as far as potions had gone before then. I was desperate, clinging to whatever dark arcane arts I could manage. Indeed, I had many knocking on my door, begging me to join my brothers at Shadowhall but I turned them down. I could not face what I had done—I did not see pleasure in the darker arts. Since then, the Enchanters and Equis, were taught to pull magic from within themselves, and it was no loss to Equis, he thought it a better use of the art. And then Dracula was given control of the art and," he waved a free hand to the trees below where more spells darted through the air, hitting the bark of trees with sickening sounds, "now that he is gone, here we are. Chaos."

Aleister stared at the dark Enchanter as though he had never seen him before. "Exactly how old are you Peroneous? You seem to have been present for everything."

Peroneous merely grinned, but his gaze darkened as he stared down at the trees again. Sliding Arminius off his shoulder, he raised his hands as though prepared to cast a spell. "Elves," he said.

As Aleister followed his gaze, he saw few Elves clad in dark cloaks were running up the hill, their dark eyes upon them. They moved at an ungainly speed, and before one was just in arms reach, dagger drawn and prepared to strike, Aurora waved her hands through the air and said fiercely, *"Symbolia Rocare!"*

The Elf stilled as though bound by invisible threads, the dagger dropped brusquely to the ground, and his black eyes closed though by the rapid movement beneath his lids it seemed it was not his preferred state.

Before Aleister could do a thing, another Elf appeared just before Peroneous and held two glowing daggers in his pale hands, but before he could use them Peroneous waved a hand and the Elf tripped over his own feet, the daggers, lodged in the grass as he landed brusquely. He did not rise.

Dragor ran forward for another approaching Elf and before the Elf could release his daggers from beneath his cloak, the large Vampire raised his sword and reached the Elf in a giant leap, slamming the blade into the Elf's heart. Aleister watched as the Vampire and Elf went down together, Dragor hopping up with a flourish, pulling the sword out of the Elf's chest.

"Aleister," Aurora said, bringing his attention back to her, to the Elf she still held encumbered before him.

Regaining himself, he lifted his own sword in hand and sent it through the Elf's chest with ease. Piercing past rib and heart, the Elf slackened, and Aleister pulled the long blade out, giving it one nice shake to remove the blood. As Aurora released the spell, sending the Elf to crumple to the grass, Peroneous stooped to grasp Arminius once more when the Elf's medallion, that had not glowed as theirs did, began to glow profusely, bringing all eyes to it.

"What's going on?" Christopher Black asked as he stepped forward at last, the only one that had not moved to fell the Elves. He held in a hand Arminius's white cane, his white bow and numerous arrows still placed along his back.

Aleister let out a 'tsk' of disdain. *The Vampire had not even moved to help.*

"Hell if I know," Peroneous answered as all Creatures moved to surround the Elf who was back atop the grass, for it seemed Peroneous was wary to touch him.

The light from the medallion was immense: it easily overshadowed their own glowing medallions, the heat palpable as well; Aleister could feel it from where he stood some ways off from the unconscious Elf.

"Creatures!" a new voice called from down the hill.

All turned, and Aleister narrowed his eyes in confusion, for there was a rejuvenated Damion Nicodemeus near the line of trees that marked where the woods began, in his hand, though Aleister could not believe it, a golden goblet seemingly full to the brim with a black substance.

The dark Vampire was moving toward them, brown eyes alive in the morning sun, and Aleister felt all Creatures behind him tense with anticipation though he raised a scarred hand, keeping them from moving at all.

"No," he said, eyes still on the golden goblet, that, the closer the dark Vampire got, the more Aleister could see was remarkably plain: nothing was upon its body, no marks or glowing words of power, indeed. "Let the Vampire come."

And once Damion was close enough to speak, Aleister asked, "What were you doing atop the Mountains of Cedar before, Vampire?"

Damion's eyes were wide with fear, with bemusement, indeed, before he finally said, *"The Death of the Earth*—how—how did you kill them?"

At this Aleister chanced a glance to Aurora who returned the stare equally: one of utter confusion. "What are you talking about? Those Elves? Easy, a bit of magic and swords always does the trick, doesn't it?"

"B-But that should be impossible," Damion said, and he reached out a hand to grasp Aleister's shoulder. Aleister flinched under the touch: The Vampire's hand was incredibly hot. "No one can harm *the Death of the Earth* let alone kill them! What special magic do you Creatures hold to be able—?"

Four Elves clad in dark robes appeared just behind Damion in the next moment, and before he could continue his words, one held out a glowing hand, and placed it atop his shoulder. The dark Vampire's eyes went wide in bewilderment but before he could say another word or turn his head, indeed, a giant shadow swept over all.

Turning his gaze from Damion to the sky, Aleister exhaled a needless breath as the large…Creature swerved with jagged grace overhead.

"What the bloody hell?!" an Elf shouted in absolute fear.

But Aleister knew what—who it was, as did the others behind him, and they moved as one, away from the stricken Elves, the immobile Damion. And the large Creature landed roughly atop the grass beside Damion pushing the Elves out of the way, its bat-like wings spreading wide, sending a burst of air pressing against their clothes and hair. And as Damion stared in what seemed to be relief upon his brother, Darien extended a large claw toward Damion, grasping the arm that held the goblet.

Much to Aleister's surprise Damion did not drop it even as Darien beat his massive wings, and with a horrible screeching scream ascended into the air, carrying his brother and the goblet with him over the trees.

Everyone watched them go in absolute silence, and it was not until they could no longer be seen that one of the Elves said, tears in his eyes, "You Cr-Creatures trespass on the Etrian Hills! And you a-allowed the most-wanted *Vampure* by Alinneis to escape! You must answer for your insolence!" And he placed a hand in the folds of his robes and pulled out a long staff that could not have fit on his person at all.

As everyone tensed, an Elf next to his comrade whispered words Aleister could not catch and the angry Elf lowered the staff by an inch. His watery eyes, no longer dripping with tears, were wide with incomprehension as he listened to whatever it was his comrade told him, and then he blinked, several more tears falling freely.

Lowering the staff completely now, he stared upon them with much more focus than before, eyeing each Creature, their red medallions for far too long a time, and then he turned, giving them his back.

"Come Creatures," he said, his voice no longer shaken, indeed it seemed quite controlled, "Alinneis awaits you."

Aleister stared at the Elf's back, watching his silver hair sway as he stepped from them further down the hill, the others joining suit, and then Aurora said, "Alinneis knows we're here?"

"Nothing would surprise me anymore," he responded, squaring his shoulders. With the appearance of the strange Elves, Damion Nicodemeus, and Darien he was rudely reminded that Evert the Ancient Elder had brought them here for some reason, and Damion held a goblet in hand. *It could not be the Goblet of Existence, could it? That would have been far too easy, far too easy, indeed. But what did it matter if Xavier was not here to drink from it?*

What the bloody hell is going on? he asked the air as he, bidding the others looks of resignation, followed the Elves' backs, beginning his descent down the hill.

Chapter Four

CHRISTIAN'S FEAR

"**W**e have moved as best we could down here!" Evert yelled to the glowing, beautiful Creature before him whose anger was unmatched.

Indeed, Evert felt Syran was distracted by something else, something he, himself could not readily place.

"And what do you have to show for it, Evert?" Syran asked, blue eyes almost seeming black against the brilliance of his wings. "Tremor withers away for what? For you to finally move when I show? Where did you place those Creatures before I arrived?"

"To safety," he said shortly, not desiring to explain. It would make nothing better. The Creatures needed their weapons, needed to completely become the Order of the Dragon they had not been since given the medallions.

Syran said nothing for a while, his gaze thoughtful as he turned from Evert at last. He stared at the remaining Creatures that had not moved when he and Caligo had landed.

Evert watched him pace before the line of scared Creatures before pointing a hand to the dark Enchanter, turning the palm toward the sky as though he were to beckon her forward. He never did. He merely watched her for what Evert considered quite a long time, and then said, "Philistia Mastcourt. Speak. You were Equis's right hand for so many years. How did this happen?"

"How did wh-what happen...?" she breathed, red lips trembling despite the coldness in her dark gaze. Behind her Lillith Crane, the Caddenhall twins, and two strange Elite Creatures lingered, fearful. Nathanial Vivery still lay atop the ground at Minerva's feet, still unconscious, almost forgotten. Almost.

"Do not profess ignorance now!" Syran yelled, and for a moment the sky appeared to darken. The sun returned from behind invisible clouds before long, however, and Syran went on softer this time: "Please. Help me understand what has befallen my World. Equis hoped to regain control of the magical arts before I arrived, yes?"

She looked as if she wished to scream or cry, her gaze darting every which way, seeking solace it would seem in Evert's gaze. He would not grant it.

"He did, your—my—my King," she stammered, hesitation sending her breath to hitch with the words.

Evert stared as the Phoenix stepped from her, seemingly aware of the bewilderment his presence caused. He turned to the Dragon, a hand over his heart as he said, "My dear, sweet friend. I beg your forgiveness for the death of your family. We mourned the loss of your Herald as we did a loss of our own."

Vetus lowered her head to the grass, her red eyes closed, and Evert knew she was thanking Syran as only a Dragon could: A Dragon's silence and closed eye before the appearance of Vampires and Lycans meant peace. Either the Dragon acknowledged the Creature attempting to make peace with them or they wished nothing to do with the Creature. That Vetus faced Syran while closing her eyes and not turning away told Evert all he needed to know: The Dragons had not forgotten the times from before where they worked together with the Phoenixes.

It was not until Vampires and Lycans became many across the World that they took to defending other things, be it towns, cities, hills, or indeed, though quite rare, humans or Vampires, themselves.

Smiling at her acceptance, Syran turned once more to Evert who met the gaze austerely. "We must move for the one this Dracula has chosen in his stead. Where is he, Evert?"

"I do not know," he said, "I was hoping I could rouse the others before you arrived."

"Why did you not rouse them before?"

He felt the ridicule burn him with Syran's stare. "I was weakened," he said, not desiring to explain he had hoped the Creatures assigned to their tasks would move with as little assistance as possible. A false hope if ever there was one.

Ignoring the feeling that Syran knew this, he turned his attention to the darker Phoenix who stood a ways off behind Syran. The endlessly black eyes pierced through everything as though little of it mattered.

Caligo Manus. A shiver of fear ran down Evert's spine at the sight of the dark-skinned Phoenix, the Creature who, it was said, was more death and darkness than anything else, more blood and cold breath, true decay, unlike the Vampires. He was quite simply death itself for his sadistic skill with sword, dagger, staff, hands, fingers, and nails. Anything he could get his hands or mouth on, indeed.

Evert was unsure why Caligo was down here with Syran, but then it did not make sense for the King of the Phoenixes to be without his most volatile son. Caligo needed looking after, but then, so did many others up above, Evert felt.

Caligo's completely black eyes moved to him in the next moment and Evert inhaled. He turned away, doing his best to ignore the deathly glare he now felt burning his face. He stared once again on Syran, the Phoenix's simple brilliance illuminating everything it cast its glow on; Lillith Crane and Philista Mastcourt looked most beautiful in Syran's glow, though their eyes belied the fear they felt at being in the presence of the Head Phoenix.

"We must move for Xavier Delacroix," Syran said, and his blue eyes were locked on Evert this time.

Vetus exhaled a plume of black smoke. "That is what we are attempting to do, Syran, but the others—the Order of the Dragon— must be recovered, told what is best at last. They have been elusive, for the better part of few months as I understand it."

Syran looked thoughtful, an expression that looked somehow misplaced upon his face, and then he said, "Very well. You will lead me to them, Vetus, Evert. Now. The sooner you do, the sooner I can uncover what has allowed me to walk atop the Earth once more."

Before Evert could ask what it was he meant, Syran had spread his wings and had ascended into the air, leaving trails of golden dust to fly to the grass. Philista stepped forward the moment Syran had done so, given lease to move now that he was no longer directly before her, and she waved a hand, a trail of blue light leaving her bare fingernails.

At once Evert felt the thought enter his mind:

You can't bring them to Xavier. If she is with him—if he is an Elite Creature, Syran will destroy him.

He opened his mouth to respond when Syran cleared his throat sending their gazes upward. The Phoenix was staring down at them impatiently, arms folded across his chest. "What keeps you Evert?" he asked.

"I…nothing, my friend." Giving Philistia his back, he stepped for Vetus, climbing atop her scales, settling himself between her wing blades. Without gazing upon the dark Enchanter, he whispered to Vetus to rise, and as she moved, removing her gold talons from the earth, beginning to ascend into the air, Caligo did the same, his black wings of fire flapping steadily as he moved.

Unnerved at how closely the dark Creature seemed to watch him, Evert turned his gaze to Syran who had watched him rise with narrowed eyes, and nodded. "I placed the Order at the Elves of Etria," he told him, ignoring the wild beating of his large heart.

"Then that is where we go," Syran said. And without further ado, he turned in an elegant whirl and began to fly toward the trees to the right of the Mountains of Cedar.

As Caligo Manus passed, gaining speed to match Syran, Evert chanced a final glance to Philistia below, knowing what he would see. And indeed, her gaze was terribly fear-filled, her brown eyes wide in her loss, for the World, her World was ending, had ended, and once Syran knew that his chosen Vampire had become an even worse Creature, the World would suffer for it, remaining Vampires and Lycans be damned.

He bid her a silent promise to figure something out before they reached the Order, and commanded Vetus to follow in the trail of golden dust that filled the sky.

* * *

Westley watched the shadow fidget behind the curtain, thoughts on the purpose of Victor Vonderheide's visit two days before fresh in his mind. The former General looked defeated even as he whispered his words to Christian. And whatever he'd said had seemed to drive a miniscule wedge between the infamous Vampire and the enigmatic Alexandria Stone. They could not look the other in the eye, nor could they speak more than three sentences at a time to each other, stilted sentences though they were.

How strange.

Westley hoped this would not interfere in Christian's continued duty to protect Dracula's granddaughter, though the more Westley spoke to her, the more he wasn't so sure Alexandria needed the protection at all. She was strong-willed, her blood strong as well, her gaze unyielding, not demure and downcast like the various Vampire women not of royal title, but there was still something in the slight frown of her lips that denoted a perpetual sadness.

He had figured it to be her sadness at being turned at first, but remembered his own transformation and recalled it a devastating one: It took him many years to come to terms with what he was, but that could not be it for her. Her sadness seemed more personal, something deeply buried, untouchable, indeed.

The pale hand appeared at the dark curtain's edge and he blinked as Christian pushed it back, revealing a positively gaudy dark blue velvet suit jacket layered atop a beige vest and tan ruffled blouse. "Does this one work for appearances sake?" Christian asked, smirking slightly as he spread his arms wide, turning from side to side, sure to show the absurdly long coattails that trailed alongside his long legs that were covered in dark blue velvet as well.

Westley sighed, taking a seat at the dark round table toward the back of the room. They frequented Xavier's old office, the black dresser against the wall was disheveled from its usual state of perfect use: the clothes once folded and placed perfectly within the designated drawers were now across the floor. Some clothes Christian was prepared to wear were draped unceremoniously over the drawers' edges, and the makeshift curtain was strung up, cutting the room in half, effectively cutting off the vastness that was once Xavier's office.

"It works if you were prepared to join the Gibbering Elves in their tower, Christian," Westley said in exasperation, "but not for the bloody Winter Ball."

Christian's smirk would not leave his lips as he stepped with flourish behind the curtain once more. As he began removing his clothes, he said, "Why go ahead with the ball at all, Westley? Once London was destroyed I figured anything to do with the Vampire City would be pointless."

He drummed his dark fingers against the table's wood. "It was in plans for up to a year before Dracula's death, before London's destruction. And London has been rebuilt, Christian, as you very well know. Xavier did an excellent job in restoring connections to other Vampire Towns and Cities, but now that he has vacated his seat, as has Nathanial, I take place as Temporary King. And I desire for the Winter Ball to resume as normal. A bit of normalcy, I feel, will go a long way to restoring what morals, what decency we Vampires have lost with all the betrayals, all the madness about."

Christian reappeared with simple black pants, unbuttoned though they were, and his chest bare. His black hair lay unbound against his back, some swaying over his shoulders as he stepped past the curtain, ignoring the mess behind him. He stopped just before the round table, and in the slight darkness of the large room, he crossed his arms over his chest. "Upgrading your protective measures has everything to do with that I imagine."

"Aye," he said, staring up at the Vampire, marveling at how much he looked like Xavier from this angle. Indeed, if his eyes were green one would not have been able to tell the difference. "Protective measures…you surprise me, Christian. To take the step you have to throw yourself willingly into Dracula's plans—I must imagine the doubt that plagues you is immense."

An eyebrow rose in the slight darkness, and a pale finger was placed upon a chair's back through the Vampire never did sit. "A decision borne of foolishness, though I do not doubt it. I can no longer, not when it has placed me in such close proximity to a most incredible Creature."

"You speak of Alexandria Stone."

"I speak of the Vampire she has become. The human she was, though I never really got to know *her*, was far too scared to move, the rage burning beneath her tears never given lease to rise. She faced the knowledge of her impending death with absolute fear, resisting it to the very end. But the Creature that arose from that death, Mister Rivers, is…I have no words."

At this Westley sat higher in his chair, staring in renewed wonder upon the Vampire, dismissing any notion that he resembled his brother. Christian was his own Creature, his words about Alexandria were telling of this enough. Xavier would never expound upon another Creature, let alone a woman, even Eleanor with such admiration, at least not openly, nor to he, Westley, indeed. "You feel for Miss Stone, don't you?" he asked at last, the question he had desired to ask since he'd laid eyes upon them given lease with Christian's words.

He did not balk or feign toughness as Westley expected him to. Instead, Christian pulled the chair back with the very same finger that had remained upon it, and sat heavily, his black stare on the smooth wooden surface, though if it were to avoid Westley's gaze or if he were in thought, Westley could not know. It was a long time before Christian said, "I feel…I've a desire to see her happy more than anything…and it is strong, stronger than I've ever known myself capable of feeling for another person, beyond my brother. And I've had my share of dalliances, Westley, this is…it is something else."

He narrowed his eyes, knowing the Vampire couldn't be talking about love. That would be unheard of. "Does she share in your sentiments, Delacroix?" he asked instead, knowing it a touchy subject for the Vampire most incapable of heavy emotions—as much as a Vampire could feel, anyway.

At this he looked immensely confused. "Share?" He laughed. "I dare say she hardly knows how I feel. I barely know it myself. I've tried to chalk it up to our connection. Me being the one to turn her. I've never experienced such a connection before—I've never turned another before, so I wouldn't know, would I? Do you know of the one who turned you, Mister Rivers? Were your feelings for them similar?"

"The one who turned me is dead now, but their influence lives on. I hear it in everything I do, the blood I consume, the battles I have fought—it never wanes even if their presence has. But what you have explained sounds mightily like something else, Mister Delacroix. Emotions I don't think I've ever seen in a Vampire. Not even Xavier with his beloved Eleanor," he said seriously, seeing Christian in a new light, indeed. "What you feel toward Alexandria will only strengthen your ability as the one who turned her. I will not belittle her brilliance by calling her your charge as it seems she holds the reigns over your heart and not the other way around as it usually is, but you can use the transformation that took place to understand her better, to let her spread her wings as a Vampire, but be there if—when things begin to overwhelm her as they are wont to do for those new to this life. But you can't be there for her if you're avoiding her." And he gestured to the curtain behind Christian. "You've been trying on outfits for the Ball for hours now, and the Ball isn't for three days. You've a nice enough sense for clothes, Christian. My only guess as to why you'd spend your day with me in your brother's old office and not where you truly want to be is because you're avoiding it. And you can't avoid things for long. They have a way of building up in nasty ways."

Christian took in his words with darkened eyes, an understanding within them. But he did not move. "It is what Victor said. That Alexandria holds great power but we don't know the full truth of it. In truth, we don't know much of anything about her."

Westley smiled slightly at the sentence that was not uttered, though he heard it clearly: Christian did not know anything about her, in truth. No one did. And it appeared the couple had been chased and under the threat of constant permanent death to ever have a sit down and get it all out. "All the better to speak to her now, Christian. You have an advantage most never will. She is tied to you. Talk to her. Openly. Learn what she likes, what she dislikes, who she was before she was turned, what her hopes, her fears, her dreams were, and in that you will know what is the truth: If there is more to her power or not. We cannot take Victor Vonderheide on his word anymore, I'm afraid. And I am very interested in discovering the truth of her power as well."

Christian said nothing, he merely stared some place past Westley, above his head, and Westley turned to see what held his attention, not surprised at all when he saw the painting of Xavier's stallion, Knight.

Knowing nothing more would be gained by trying to get the Vampire to do what it was he feared most, Westley excused himself, adjusted his empty sleeve behind the remaining stump once more, and exited the room, leaving Christian to what it was Westley knew would overwhelm him for as long as Alexandria still lived.

The most damning of emotions, however guarded from a Vampire's cold heart.

Love.

* * *

"You still have your arrows with you, Miss Crane?" Philistia asked her.

The young Vampire turned her gaze from the sky, blue eyes wide with fear. "O-Of course," she said, blinking what Philistia felt should have been tears.

"Very good," Philistia said, adjusting her disheveled robes. The fabric felt strange beneath her bare fingers. *Gloves no longer matter*, she thought wistfully, returning her gaze to those that stood around her.

The unconscious Nathanial Vivery still remained on the grass, Yaddley and Minerva Caddenhall stood behind her, some ways off, looking wary, and the most curious Creatures Philistia knew as an Aciel and Amentias stood beside them, looking equally worried. *A band of ragtag Creatures if ever I saw them*, she thought with a small smile, shaky though it was.

Stepping from beside Lillith, she motioned to the larger Caddenhall twin whose blue eyes narrowed upon her with question. "Get Mister Vivery, if you please, Yaddley. We will regroup back at that Enchanter's home, and gather our...nerve," she told him, hoping they did not detect the fear in her voice. It was known that Vampires could know fear intimately, smell it, feel it, somehow, in their very blood. It was a thought that chilled her to the bone.

"Where are we headed after?" Lillith asked, blue eyes narrowed inquisitively.

Philistia smiled at her, admiring her in a new light despite the cloud above her head, placed with her, Philistia's protection. *So very smart, this Creature*, she thought. "Lane," she said. "I have a friend there most eager to help us in our cause."

"And what cause is this?" Aciel asked as a harsh wind blew past.

"The cause, my dear Creature, of helping Xavier Delacroix regain his mind. There are Enchanters in Lane still eager to help."

"Do you think it can be done?" Minerva Caddenhall asked from beside her brother, who now stood with a limp Nathanial hanging over a broad shoulder. "I mean with what we've just seen..." But her gaze moved to the sky, and whatever words she was to say left her mind.

Philistia nodded, doing her best to suppress her own doubt. "We have no choice," she said after a time, voice shaking despite herself, remembering the piercing gaze of the Phoenix. "We must or else we'll all suffer under Syran's wrath, indeed."

Chapter Five

DRACULA'S GRANDDAUGHTER

He had only caught glimpses of her between the restless crowds, not having been there when she and Christian Delacroix had first appeared, no, he had missed that piece of scintillating news. It had not taken long for Civil Certance to realize the woman had been turned by Christian, and by the time he had pieced this together, half of the Vampire City had realized it as well.

Richard Yore, who had been present when Westley Rivers strode into the Clearance Committee Building, Elisa and her soldiers in tow, relayed the news to Civil that Christian Delacroix had finally arrived in the Vampire City. And with a woman no less.

Civil had merely brushed it news of no consequence, until he saw her.

He had been striding the halls of Dracula's mansion, stacks of pressed parchment in hand, when out she strode from an open door, hands clasped with the Queen of Chrisanti, Odette Chrisanti. The red-haired, vibrant Vampire looked positively radiant as always, but the mysterious woman at her side was what held Civil's attention.

Her face was rather plain for his standards, a heart-shaped face, curt lips that were wide with her laughter at a joke shared between the two women, and her eyes, briefly passing across his own, were rather dull, the oddest mixture of brown and green, the colors not mixed together, but distinctly separate.

As her long brown hair bounced blissfully down her back, he only thought it odd that it was not up in a sophisticated hold atop her head as were the other women here for the Ball.

What held his gaze all the more as they walked further away from him, parchment all but forgotten in his hands, was the smell of her blood.

Brilliant. Strong. Familiar. Eerily so.

But it could not be.

Now Civil Certance stood in what used to be Dracula's office, though he knew it was off-limits to those not of royal blood, but that was why he stood there at all. Dracula's blood. It trailed through the air since the woman's appearance, but he had not placed where it had come from, though he had entertained, briefly, that it could come from her. But what nonsense that would be.

Pressing a pale hand against the vacant desk, he sniffed deeply, faint traces of Dracula's blood still lingered in the air, here. *But he could not still live, could he? And wouldn't I know about it if that were so?*

The door opened and in she stepped, a slight gasp escaping her lips as she looked up from the floor. "I—er—I'm sorry, I didn't realize anyone else was here."

"Nonsense," he whispered at once, unsure why the words left him as swiftly as they did, "it is not my office…far be it from me to keep you from any corner of this great mansion."

And she seemed unsure of his words: her furrowed brow, and hesitant tongue, resting between her lips relayed that much. He found he could not blame her, he, himself, was unsure of just why he'd said what he did. Known for being most curt to other Vampires, other Dark Creatures, he found it utterly puzzling that he simply give her the room—a place most off-limits as it was, until she stepped deeper into it.

The door closed behind her and with its closure, he smelled it. Wafts of Dracula's scent, his blood filled the room, thickening in its strength, its power. He stepped from her in one swift movement, and she merely smiled warmly upon him.

"I…require time to myself, if you do not mind…"

"Civil Certance," he obliged at once, waving a hand gently through the air in way of proper introduction. "And y-yes, yes I shall…please, let me…" And without another word, he stepped forward, nodding slightly as he passed, unable to eye her straight on any longer. But as he brushed against the folds of her many white skirts, he felt the strangest sensation wash over him.

It was as though all that had just transpired, all thoughts of her strangeness, the curious sensations of bemusement that plagued him when he eyed her, simply vanished. Left, he was, as he opened the door and escaped into a less-Dracula-filled hallway, with musings of a faint need to kneel.

As various Vampires passed in the large hallway, all talking excitedly to themselves, he was most surprised to realize, with a blink, that one of these very Vampires heading toward him was none other than Christian Delacroix.

Straightening at once, for he had remained slumped against the door as he rethought this curious need to kneel, he blinked blearily as the pale-skinned, black-haired Vampire neared.

Civil blinked rapidly, Christian coming into better view, and he almost let out a cry of alarm. Except for the ever-steady black of his eyes, Christian Delacroix resembled his brother outright. Right down to the haughty way his eyes would glaze over all, making one feel mightily inferior.

After a moment of staring, Christian's lips turned upwards at a corner, his gaze appearing to soften. "Hello, Vampire," he said, his voice not as resounding as Xavier's to be sure, but still commanding.

"Hello, Lord Delacroix," he whispered back, unsure if he should call him that at all. It became more apparent the longer he stared at the Vampire, that Christian was not the bloodthirsty Vampire he had heard him to be. Indeed, Xavier's brother seemed to be quite capable, assured…almost born of Dracula's training room as Xavier had been…

"Pardon me, but there is someone I must speak to beyond the door you guard," Christian said, his black gaze roving to the wooden door Civil felt behind him.

"Someone you must…" he began, when reason and thought reached him, "ah—yes, of course. Forgive me…" He stepped briskly from the door, unsure of why he moved so willingly at all, and turned to watch Christian open it and disappear behind its polished wood.

It was only when the door closed, the brief whiff of strong blood reaching his nose, that his eyes widened, but as it passed, the notion was gone.

Blinking blearily in the torchlight of the hallway, he straightened, trying to remember just why he was before Dracula's office at all.

* * *

Alexandria did not turn to eye him, though she smelled his blood clearly, felt his confusion, his worry, and knew their days selectively avoiding each other were at an end.

Though she was not expecting the softness of his voice as it pressed against her back.

"I trust you have found your way in this gargantuan city better than I?"

She rubbed her gloved hands together, feeling restricted suddenly against the golden choker at her throat, the dress about her body, the tightness of the golden corset beneath her breasts…*Bloody hell, these clothes are driving me mad—*

"*Repel it…*"

At once the feeling of heaviness retreated and she found herself able to relax ever the slightest though his gaze still burned into her back. It was a gaze she could feel, even as he remained near the door, never stepping forward. *But goodness, that gaze…*

"Why have you sought me out, Mister Delacroix?" she asked the green curtain toward the back of the room. "You've made it perfectly clear you did not desire my company after Victor's words above ground."

"Can you fault me, Miss Stone?" And she could not help but wince at his pronunciation of 'Miss.' "Victor reminded me…that despite all that's transpired between us…I know nothing about you in truth."

"*Do not taint it…*"

She opened her mouth to respond, but found the words would not rise in her throat. She shifted her footing in her high white heels instead. "And what," she asked after a time, "would possess you to want to know about my past now?"

She could practically hear him wringing his hands before himself, but did not turn to look and see if this was the case. "I…had a heartfelt discussion with Mister Rivers…"

At this she turned, amusement on her lips as she regarded him in full. He wore a positively stuffy, black suit jacket buttoned at his front, and beneath it, poking out of the suit jacket's opening was a ruffled collar, the white shirt it was attached to peeking through the ends of the jacket's sleeves. At his hips was a black and gold sheath in which the Ares was housed, and on his legs were the darkened breeches Alexandria had quickly learned were designed for Vampire royalty. She'd seen quite a few men of Vampire title wearing very similar breeches in her time throughout the city. His hair was tied up in a long hold behind his head, and she found it made him look all the more misplaced. Why, he looked as though he desired to tear off the clothes he found himself in.

His hands were covered in black leather gloves, and true to her thoughts, he wrung them together as though a child caught in a lie.

After a time of staring, she collected herself, and said, "And Mister Rivers talked you into coming to see me to figure me out, is that it?"

He had stared upon her as though he had just seen her for the first time when she first turned to him, and now his gaze darkened with the familiar look of need she had seen in few other Vampires…

"I have come," he said with an unsteady voice, "to know you, yes. But that is not all." He took another step, yet no farther than the desk. "I have come to strengthen our connection, our bond."

"Bond? I daresay I am *bound* to you—but there is no bond, here, *Mister* Delacroix."

"I have angered you with my avoidance, I know it. But damnit, Miss Stone, as powerful as you are, as…much influence as you have over me, we owe it to ourselves—to Dracula—to work together. To understand each other—this connection—as best we can."

She laughed, though she had not meant it to leave her lips as harshly as it did. "You know all you need to know of me, Mister Delacroix. That I have been preened and kept by this Dracula my entire life, forbidden the notion of a happy, normal…anything…only to become his—his weapon upon the event of my natural death…" She regretted the words as soon as they left her lips: the stare of confusion he placed her with next made her curse aloud. The questions would be endless, now.

And so they were.

"What do you mean kept? Forbidden the notion of a happy—what? Alexandria what did he do to you? As a child?" He stepped the remaining space between them in what should be a breath, a tentative hand on her cheek, and despite the burning anger at his questions, she found she could not—did not—wish to remove it. "Please, Alexandria," the pleading, fearful voice echoed on somewhere above her. "What has he done?"

The anger burned in her with fresh resolve, though she knew not the reason for it, and then the memories returned, swirling visions of color, sound, and Christian disappeared, as did the office they had been in.

She stood in her living room, and it was just as she remembered it. Modest brown furniture stood around the modest wooden room, hardly-used, endlessly clean. And yes, the more she looked around, the more she saw her dolls atop the circular dark red rug beneath her feet, the dark of the room reaching her as strange, though she knew, deep within, that it was night, here.

"Listen to me, mother," a voice whispered harshly from beyond an archway leading to a darkened kitchen, "we cannot protect her for much longer. I fear he's reached out to her as it is."

Another voice spoke next, this one sending a thrill of fear through her, though she knew this was the past—her past.

"I know that Patricia! Which is why I moved away. Better to protect the child from his plans. After you wouldn't bend to his hand, he took precautions, I'm afraid."

Curious, Alexandria stepped deeper into the room where the voices were loudest, and peered around a corner.

There, leaning against a high counter was her mother, Patricia Hatfield, still in her day dress, brown hair hidden beneath a sleeping cap. She eyed the woman opposite her, who sat at a long, brown wooden table, her eyes no longer the soothing brown Alexandria remembered but a piercing, worried, red. The red Alexandria recognized as Christian's.

As a Vampire's.

But how could it be? Grandmama had died when I was just eight. How in the world could she have been a Vampire?

"You've protected nothing," Patricia said, soft green eyes alive with indignation, "you've done sod all to protect me from his…his plans. But you've given him free reign of her with your move!"

"You fault me," the older-looking Vampire said from her seat, "for returning to Egypt to escape his hand—what he's made me—and in-turn help keep Dracula off your rear end? Pah, you're ungrateful, after all." There was a finality to the way she said this that made Alexandria's blood run colder than normal.

She could tell from the smell of the blood in the air that the woman was old. Turned years before. But she still looked quite youthful, save the burgeoning wrinkles appearing at her brow. Her black hair was not covered like her daughter's, but instead flowed freely down her back, giving her a more youthful appearance. She wore a black day dress that only strengthened the paleness of her skin, and around a finger was a gold ring, a red gem glowing atop it.

Alexandria could not tear her gaze from it, even as Patricia spoke: "Ungrateful? Mother, you made it so I would never become like you—like Father. Can you really call me ungrateful? I only want the best for Alexandria—it's not my fault the man who seduced you turned out to be nothing short of a monster."

"He does what is best for the Vampires he created," she said quietly, the anger suddenly gone. In its place was a sort of kind recollection. *Perhaps on all of Dracula's deeds*, Alexandria thought, wondering next just how much her Grandmother had known.

She would know nothing else, for just then the door to the back of the kitchen flew open and there he appeared looking downright devilish, handsome, save for the twinkle of knowing anger in his eyes. He looked young, younger than Alexandria had ever seen him in any memory or dream, his brown eyes piercing, hair not white but a soft brown, yet still it trailed down his back. And as the women stared upon him in alarm, he smiled, though it was quite cold, murderous, even. "My dearest Patricia," he said coldly, gazing almost lovingly at the woman still held up by the gleaming counters, "how you try to keep me from my granddaughter."

"Dracula," Evelyn breathed, not rising from her seat, though she'd turned her head to eye him all the same. "What kept you?"

His cruel gaze shifted to her, something like softness blanketing it. Alexandria found it an odd expression that did not suit his face. "Ah, my sweet Evelyn Stone," he whispered, his voice a far cry from the harshness that had filled it just seconds before, "you are always a ray of light in the darkness that fills my life."

She left her chair now, running long-nailed hands over her black skirts, shaking back her black hair. "Charming as ever," but the words left her with venom. "I thought I'd bought myself some time."

"Egypt was…as encumbering as I remember, my dear, and the spell that brilliant Aurora Borealis placed on you to further hinder my progression," a low whistle left his lips, "was a masterpiece. To make me smell your blood in all its…beautiful glory in every passing human left me chasing my tail for months. But a kind Dragon set me straight. The Atem are a marvelous breed. Discerning, you know. They have a natural gift for seeing through the spells placed on one—for seeing the magic within the blood. But do not think me," and he placed a hand over his heart, "unable to smell the blood of the woman I turned, the woman I made, the woman I defied the limitations of my kind with!"

"Mother," Patricia breathed, fearful, "what's he talking about?"

Dracula's eyes narrowed in the dark, suddenly mischievous. "She hasn't told you?"

And in the silence that greeted him, he had his answer.

A laugh left him, void of life, mangled, almost a strange sound, between a snarl and a roar. Patricia noticeably coiled further into herself, shrinking against the sound as though it would strike her with its unnaturalness. "I cannot bear children, not naturally. There is magic in place to ensure those with Vampire blood are turned before they would reach their Age. But you, Patricia, your mother had you spelled—"

"What?" Patricia breathed, and she released her vice-like grip from the counter, stepping toward the table. "Mother—you've had me spelled?"

"Quiet Patricia," Evelyn whispered harshly. Then to Dracula, "You don't know what you speak!"

All manner of amusement fled his being and in the rain his eyes were now red. He suddenly looked quite old, no, that wasn't it, Alexandria decided, he looked monstrous. Veins protruded from his skin beneath his eyes, dark and unseemly. They stretched against his skin, which suddenly seemed quite translucent, his blood just barely seen beneath it, quite dark, and his hair lifted from his back, the rain all but gone now.

A fierce wind had blown up with his sudden manic appearance and a surge of rain water and cold wind blew into the room blowing up the clothes and hair of the woman vigorously, but Alexandria noticed Dracula would not step past the wooden doorway though it seemed that's what he wished he do.

He was snarling viciously, bent double, his head up, red gaze held on Evelyn as though he wished nothing more than to kill her. "You play games with my bloodline, Evelyn!" he yelled, his voice terribly deep, resounding on in Alexandria's ears long after he'd spoken. "You know what the child means for Vampire kind! What she means for the Lycans! With her blood we can end all of this! Keep my daughter away from me, if you will, but know this: I will have Alexandria Stone. I don't care if I face my death trying. She will keep the Lycans at bay, she will control their blood—our blood—she will keep us from our cravings while I work to keep my successors in place!"

Evelyn took a step forward amidst the roar of the wind that had only strengthened with Dracula's words. Patricia let out a cry of panic, perhaps at the thought her mother would venture toward the Vampire, but she stopped just before the door, just out of his snarling reach. "The brothers—the boys, really, what you did to their mother is despicable. All to keep them under your watch. And what if they don't succeed when you are no longer here to grace us with your presence, *my love*?" The last words canvassed in sarcasm.

Dracula snarled and lunged for her, yet his hands slammed against an invisible wall within the doorway and he was pushed back onto the wet ground with a squelching sound. Alexandria could not see from where she stood what had happened to him, but when he emerged, she knew he had fallen: his hair, face, and clothes were slick with mud.

"Everything I do is for the sake of this world, Evelyn," he said, his voice no longer loud and menacing, but low, and it seemed the fight had been taken out of him with her words or his fall. Alexandria could not be sure. "Everything. The Nicodemeus brothers are resourceful—their proclivity to keep the Caddenhall line under their hand is quite impressive. Very useful. It may come in handy one day. All of you may be of use to me. One day. One day soon."

"Yes," Evelyn hissed, stepping from the door, much to the relief of her daughter: Patricia sagged noticeably against the counters, tears streaking her cheeks, "because we are your endless pawns, Dracula. Your endless pieces to this maddening puzzle you insist you must fix. You have created—nay—*helped* your Creatures endure—thrive in this World, in a most respectful manner. We blend in seamlessly with the humans—the Enchanters are in-line with your desires, enchanting the necklaces so that the few of us not lucky enough to be graced with your blood may walk in the sun, enjoy the human pleasures this world has to offer. You need fix nothing you mad man. You're chasing after a fantasy—a mad affliction that's tearing your mind in two."

He merely stared at her, fascinated, and then he said, his voice impossibly low, "You don't know what you speak, you simple woman. You are but new to the ways of a Vampire. All you know of is the lust—the blood—the power we supposedly possess. These are but lies! These are the true fantasies—the true affliction is not the damned blood, nor is it the power to trick and tease the humans to our wills! You know nothing of why it is preferred we are this way, you know nothing of what I really am."

"Then tell me, Dracula," she said.

A great look of sorrow appeared on his mud-splattered face and his eyes resumed their natural brown glow. "Alexandria," he said, much to everyone's surprise. They looked at him, Patricia from her seat on the floor, with confusion. "I will be returning for her. If you try to stop me, if either of you try to stop me, I will kill you both." And before a word could leave their lips, he was gone, leaving them to stare upon the open doorway, the heavy rain returning as though it had never ceased. The dark hills were in the distance, and before the door was closed, Alexandria remembered when she would play on those hills, visit with her few neighbors, laugh in the sun...

"Mother!" Patricia wailed, rising to her feet, running to the woman who embraced her greatly.

And Alexandria, watching as the human sobbed frantically onto the Vampire's chest, closed her eyes in resignation.

* * *

"Alexandria? *Alexandria?*"

She blinked in the torchlight at last, and he released her, quite pleased she showed signs of life once more. She had begun to glow her red color vividly some moments ago, and she stared past him, not responsive to any of his attempts to rouse her.

That was when he noticed the vast portrait of Xavier against the wall to the back of the room, and he wondered whose office this was. It was with a quick look around, his hands still held on her arms, that he noted the books on their shelves above the unlit fireplace, the grand windows to his left that displayed the city in all its vast splendor, and at last he turned his head to eye the dark desk near the door, and a strange feeling that he should not be here overcame him.

Now he stepped from her as she ran a hand across her forehead, her unfocused eyes getting steadier the more the seconds passed.

"Christian," she breathed after a time, "I saw my grandmother—she was a Vampire."

He blinked. "What?"

He listened in silence as she recounted her vision, eyes widening at the mention of Dracula and her mother who was, astonishingly, still human.

"Aurora Borealis worked with your grandmother to protect you?" he asked once she was done, the most stunning revelation keeping his thoughts tied. "Why would she then work with the others to help Xavier?"

Her gaze darkened with deeper thought. "I don't know, but my grandmother mentioned the Nicodemeus brothers—said Dracula had something done to their mother. Dracula all but confirmed it was to keep his plans in motion. Keep Damion and Darien under his control. I think he was to choose one of them to take his place before you and Xavier came along."

"We were given to Dracula by my father, Alexandria," he said, remembering when the curse placed upon him had been lifted in Cinderhall Manor. "He was the one that turned us. Xavier, however, was the one that met with Dracula."

"You did not?" The question was innocent, gone any malice, at least none he could detect.

He relaxed in her curious gaze, glad, at least for the moment that he was not under the ire of her cold heart. "No," he said, "I was away—feeding." He did not meet her stare, sure it was disapproving.

"You feed more than I have ever known your brother to."

"I find the taste of blood alluring…and it seems my brother did not need as much of it as I once he returned from meeting Dracula."

"He was given Dracula's blood, I'm sure of it."

"He never mentioned—"

"Since you've had my blood," she cut across, driven by encouraging thought, "have you felt the need to have it daily like before?"

"No."

She nodded, her waves of brown bouncing as she did. "That's it then. My blood…Dracula's blood enables the Vampires strength they wouldn't have before; indeed you could walk in the sun after you turned me."

"I have thought on this significance," he admitted, unsure where she was going with this.

She moved from him, striding past, heading toward the desk. He turned once she reached it, staring down at it as though some great answer would reach her from its black wood. "Dracula's fear is what drove him, Christian," she said at last, "he was terrified of…returning to his true form. Our true form. I could feel his fear as he spoke to my grandmother. Whatever fear I felt from becoming a Vampire is nothing to what he felt. Daily."

He stared. "What are you getting at?"

"He did far more than any one Vampire alive can know, I suspect," she said, and he was unable to see anything other than how brilliant the extravagant white gown she'd been given to wear complimented her eyes which were still focused on the desk. "Damion and Darien failed him, that Vampire, Nicholai Noble, failed him. Eleanor Black and Victor Vonderheide failed him. He only wished to become human, and even my mother—my grandmother kept him from that end."

Christian thought of the heaviness upon his brother's shoulders, the sorrow in the Vampire's green eyes, and he nodded. "Dracula has a knack for placing insurmountable burdens upon those he chooses to bear them," he agreed, "but are you saying you agree with him? After all he's done…made my brother undergo? Made us…made us…" He gestured toward her then back to himself, lost for the proper words. *What were we, anyway?*

"My grandmother was never a forthcoming woman…well, Vampire, as I remember her. My mother was barely there as well. We were shunned at Court because those of royal blood…Vampire blood now I realize, were intimidated by my grandmother's never-changing beauty. My mother's plainness in comparison confused them. I see now that they did not know who my grandmother's master was… and I…by the time I reached sixteen, I was expected to already have a husband, or at least, be promised to be wed to another. Yet every meeting with what my grandmother called a 'suitable prospect'— those of title—I soon found them to disappear, or no longer be able to meet me for morning walks through town."

The silence lingered on with a hint of despair, and Christian pieced together what she could not say. "Dracula had them killed or turned into Vampires," he finished.

She nodded, greeting his gaze at last. "You can imagine growing up thinking myself most unsuitable, most unsightly, if all these prospects continued to disappear." She smiled wistfully. "At what seemed like my mother's disapproval to my lack of child-bearing, I'd lock myself in my room for days, writing my letters to Count Dracul. Now I realize she was torn between what she knew Dracula had been doing—perfecting me, my blood—I believe she knew…knew she could do nothing to stop it. It is alarming to know how little of my life was truly mine."

He stepped to her, finding it impossible to merely stand there any longer and listen to her lamentation. He could not understand her acquiescence to the monster that was Dracula's goals. After all, those plans had taken Xavier from him, it had driven he, Christian from his home, across the Dark World, and into her arms.

It had changed him, those goals, the blood that coursed through him, the sword at his waist, all of it had changed him into something he barely recognized, but he could not return to what he was before. He was not sure if he hated Dracula for that, all he knew was that it was Dracula's fault any of this was happening at all.

She looked up at him in alarm at his movement, her lips slightly parted, bracing herself for his next move, but he merely stared down at her, unsure what more he should—could do.

Oh yes, he wanted to kiss her, deeply, madly, he wanted to grab her and taste her lips, her skin once more, but he did not know if she would welcome it, he did not know if she, in her sorrowful state, would welcome any part of him, especially after what he'd done to her.

"Christian," and the word left her in a whisper, "what are you—?"

The door to the office opened without a sound, and they both turned in alarm to eye the dark-skinned Vampire whose wide gaze befell them, immediately replaced with incredulity.

Christian stepped from her at once, appearing before the long table against the windows, blood burning in his shame.

He heard the Vampire step into the room, the door closing softly behind him. "Pardon the intrusion my Lord, Miss Stone, but your blood is quite the allurement," and Christian could hear the urgency in his voice.

He blinked, realizing that her blood filled the entire mansion, had done so since she'd glowed with her red light. He turned slightly, just his head, watching them over his shoulder.

Westly had stepped before the desk and was staring at Alexandria, his gaze red. She looked quite flustered, perhaps even embarrassed, her eyes wide. Apparently, she had not known her blood left her in droves as well.

"I—pardon me," she stammered, and Christian thought she was doing her best to avoid his gaze. In an instant, the smell of her blood was gone from the air, and Westley released a sigh of relief.

"Our guests were in a dither below, wondering just where the blood so similar in smell to Dracula's was stemming. I'm glad I got the thought to head here…" he said, his dark gaze shifting to Christian's.

He did not meet it, but turned his gaze to the table's smooth surface instead, practically feeling the Vampire's amusement reach him with the stare.

Good on you, Christian, the voice said suddenly, and he closed his eyes in exasperation.

Leave, damn you, he retorted.

And with a chuckle, another apology for the intrusion to Alexandria, Westley stepped from the room, and Christian did not dare turn until the door had closed.

Alexandria was staring at the door's dark wood, her own gaze red in color. "Well, Christian," she said after a most suffocating time of silence, "seeing as how neither of us has a companion to this Winter Ball I hear so much about," she eyed him, "would you accompany this entirely ill-equipped, newly-turned Vampire to it?"

He did not believe what he was hearing. "I…you're asking me to the Ball?"

She turned to him in full, her gloved hands coming together before herself in sublime elegance, and he suddenly felt the inexplicable need to kneel. "I am. What better Vampire to accompany me than the one who turned me, than the one who holds my grandfather's sword, than the one who was chosen by Dracula," and at this the need to kneel overwhelmed him; he was suddenly on his knees, a hand bracing the table at the abruptness with which he found himself there, "to aid me?"

His voice would not leave his throat, his mind suddenly blank. And in a sudden flash of inspiration, he thought, *Alexandria, what are you doing?*

Protecting my grandfather's legacy, she returned, but there was not coldness there, indeed, he stared up at her, and of all things a smile graced her beautiful face. *And I need your complete focus on the task at hand if I am to do this.*

Focus on the task? Alexandria, release me from this bind!

I do not bind you, Christian. You are free to move as you will.

He lifted a hand from the floor, pushing himself up with the other on the table, relieved to know he could do so. Once fully on his feet, he stared at her, unsure what he should say or do next, indeed. "I felt the strongest need to kneel...it was as though I could do nothing else in your presence. You seem vastly different..."

"Perhaps I am merely understanding how my grandfather felt," she said, her red gaze lingering on him, and he could not help but feel as though he were being sized up, his worth determined with her next word.

"Perhaps," he whispered, remembering Westley's words to him just hours before:

"...*you will know what is the truth: If there is more to her power or not.*"

He suddenly felt far more over his head than he had before, and found he had the answer he had come to seek:

He knew nothing more of her power, save her brilliance against the blood of those around her, but he had learned that she was far more capable, much more than he to face any of this. She had accepted her life, indeed, and with this thought Xavier's words to him returned in a humiliating wave, "*I think it would be best if you...were not alone with the woman...*"

He watched a smile lift her red lips, felt his blood boil with desire, and knew Xavier had been absolutely, right.

Chapter Six

A Usurper's Plan

Victor felt the stone burn in his pocket but did his best to ignore it. The darkness of the air here, despite the late morning, made him feel sick, and what he'd been told just moments before had done nothing to ease his spirits.

The cave's entrance was bare, a familiar smell reaching him where he stood, a smell he could hardly believe, but could not deny.

Xavier Delacroix.

"Master Vonderheide...at your word," Gregory said from his back.

He turned against the twisted air, seeing the number of hooded figures, Gregory's hair the only one revealed against the sparse sunlight. Staring at the heavily bearded Elite, Victor managed, "And if she sees through the ruse?"

"She won't," he said with confidence, confidence Victor could not help but admire. "She's too wrapped up in the Vampire. Once the others see you, they will know you've decided to move at last. To aid us. Save us from her wretchedness."

Such belief in me, he thought with slight shame. Doubt that he could not live up to their belief in him, to their desire to see him lead, usurp Eleanor right under her nose resurfaced in a harsh wave of greater sickness, but he swallowed it down. *It would not do to lose my cool now,* he thought, remembering how he had faced Christian before the gates to the Vampire City. *I have already set my plans in motion. Having these Creatures at my beck and call will only serve to aid me in ensuring I am forever Dracula's Creature.*

The stone warmed in his pocket as if in response to his thoughts, and with a sigh, he swallowed the last remaining traces of fear. *This was coming the entire time,* he told himself, feeling the strong hand on his shoulder. *I was never going to join her. Never going to become one of those...things. Dracula...may have left me, but I needn't leave him. Yes—yes, I will remain a Vampire, and lead these Creatures as only a pure Vampire can.*

And besides, he thought further, reaching into a pocket of his cloak, closing a hand around the warm stone, *I have power neither Creatures have.*

Assured with this knowledge, he stepped forward, allowing Gregory's hand to slide off his shoulder, satisfied when he heard the many footsteps follow behind him as he descended the few steps before the mouth of the cave.

The tunnel stretched onward as it did, but where it met wall and branched off in separate directions, there were two darkly cloaked figures that stood at attention as he and his Creatures drew near.

"Lord Victor!" one said in surprise as he passed the many torches along the walls. This Creature moved to meet him, reducing their hood to reveal a long mane of wild black, curly hair. Her dark skin glistened in the orange light, and as she neared, her red irises appeared to glow amidst the natural dark that was always here, no matter what light was shed. "We've waited for your reappearance with bated breath—she hasn't said a word to us since *he* arrived—locked themselves up in her chambers—"

"Madison," he said, recognizing this Creature as one most skilled with the Lycan form despite being a Vampire first, "as overjoyed as I am to know you've missed me, that is no way to speak about the Queen. Never mind if she has been occupied...I am sure it has all been for good reason…" He winked upon her and her gaze drifted from confusion to comprehension at once.

She could be listening, he thought toward her.

Of course.

"Now, Madison, Gregory, Percival, take me to my chambers. I am most weary from my travels," he said, the stone burning in his pocket now.

The Elite Creatures moved ahead of him as the others dispersed, half going right, the others left, all lit up with a brilliant black energy that he could see plainly, here. *Changed to something else, indeed.* With the three ahead of him, they turned as one, rounding a corner to the left, moving swiftly.

They walked in silence for quite some time, the excitement, however, burning in their blood: he could smell it. Thick, unyielding, greatly changed, indeed, that blood. It was somehow foreign to his nose, despite their ability to turn from Vampire to human to Lycan and back. Very changed.

As they walked, the dread within the tunnels was thick, so much so he could hardly see, the stone doing its best to keep the dread away. It flared greatly, its heat engulfing him in full, protecting him, indeed.

He felt its influence as they rounded another corner and entered deeper into the tunnels, the clattering of low voices filling the air the more they moved. The dread seemed thickest here, yet it was not until they entered through the large doorway, that he felt it in overwhelming droves. Wave after wave of sickening dread attempted to line his blood, but the stone burned with a stronger heat keeping it at bay before his skin, and in the light of the numerous torches around the vast circular hall, the many tattered cloaks were illuminated with the strange black smoke. It filled the dread-thick air, and taking an unnecessary breath, he stepped forward with the others, the group of Creatures already assembled turning to eye them as they moved.

He recognized a few of the faces beneath their hoods, their eyes shining white just as Gregory's had done, and he stepped further than the others, feeling the liquid ripple at his feet. He looked down, brow furrowing upon the blood. Why he had not smelled it at all. Indeed, it covered every inch of the dark floor.

"What happened?" he asked the Creature that had left his back and now stood at his side.

"This is where she turned us," Percival said, hood still atop his head.

"Indeed," was all Victor said. He felt quite misplaced before them, though he was no stranger to leading a group of Creatures into battle, but the battlefield's face was quite different from any he'd fought on before. He was not well-versed in secrecy and subterfuge. *No*, he thought with a frown, *that had been Dragor's job.*

The Creatures stared at him expectantly, and he knew he should offer a word of thanks, but the words would not find his lips. What did one say to a group of Creatures prepared to risk their lives and follow behind him to a place he could not yet know?

But the words needn't leave him, for, from another tunnel came hurried footsteps, and all heads turned. He released the stone that had gone cold some time before. His hand instead wrapped around the handle of his sword.

He thought of Xavier and Eleanor, though found he could not smell the newcomer's blood, indeed, he could smell nothing but sickening dread.

It was not long before the footsteps reached the tunnel's opening, not long at all before the figures appeared in a white light that followed them as they emerged into the circular hall, a strained silence filling Victor's ears.

And then Eleanor said, "Brilliant, Victor, you've arrived!"

And as the light left her back and drifted up to the ceiling, shedding light atop all Creatures' heads, Victor laid eyes on the Vampire at her side.

His hair was undone, trailing down his back as it always was. He wore the same dirtied, bloodied buttoned-up shirt and breeches Victor had seen in him but days before when he'd flown to Eleanor over the jagged rocks.

It had been just before he, Victor, had been prepared to join her.

How silly that was to him now.

Xavier's green eyes were studying the circular hall as though fascinated by its dark stone walls, but Victor thought he could hardly call them completely green any longer. They were so dark they were almost black, and of all things a slight smile curled the corners of the Vampire's lips.

Smiling, are you? Victor thought, remembering the last time he'd seen that faint smile ever present on the Vampire's countenance. Back when Xavier had trained alongside Eleanor and the other Members of the Vampire Order, back when Dracula had taken pride in the Vampires he had chosen...back when Dracula had prepared these Creatures to take his place...

With the dark thought all wonder fled his mind, and he turned his attention to the woman clad in her usual ruffled blouse and black breeches. She stared around at the Creatures present with much more interest than before, bemusement lining her Vampiric features. Her skin had paled as she'd approached in the light, Victor had noticed, and he thought it had something to do with the lake of blood they stood in.

"What's this?" Eleanor whispered, her gaze meeting his with pleasant curiosity. Though he knew the pleasantry hid a greater darkness just beneath her beautiful surface. "A meeting Victor? Or perhaps a gathering to celebrate your return?" She eyed someone behind him. "Thank you for fetching him, Gregory."

"Pleased, your Grace," the gruff voice whispered.

Xavier had now turned his attention to the proceedings, having taken his full of the architecture. He stepped up to Eleanor, and Victor watched in abhorrence as he placed a hand around her waist. "Hello Victor," he said, his voice still as Victor remembered it—deep, commanding, and tinged with haughtiness, "lovely to see you again."

Was he under a spell? It seemed quite funny, indeed, that the Vampire so bidden to seeing Victor's return to Dracula's hand would approach him as though nothing had happened. As if they both had not defied Dracula's very word, left the Great Vampire completely in the face of his crushing absence. Indeed, Victor perused the Vampire's waist for any sign of the Ascalon. It was not there.

He felt quite uncomfortable now, remembering suddenly Xavier's brilliance with speed in battle, how he had felled many a Lycan with his bare hands should his sword be kept from him. The feeling of incapability returned just as Xavier swung out his free hand, and Victor, of all things, flinched.

Xavier's brow furrowed, as did Eleanor's, and recognizing his mistake, Victor corrected himself, shaking the Vampire's hand curtly. *Still a Vampire*, he deduced at once, smelling the blood beneath his skin as their hands tightened around one another's. "Likewise," he whispered, unsure what to feel now face-to-face with the Vampire he had loathed without reserve since Dracula's death.

They released hands and Eleanor's smile widened. "Now that we're all back together again, let's say we make it official, hm?"

Incessant witch, Victor thought coldly; panic flaring in his cold heart. But Percival stepped in-between he and Eleanor, bringing all gazes there. "Er, pardon me, your Grace, my Lord, but Master Vonderheide was prepared to be informed of all that's happened since he's been absent. We've barely begun to brief him on your goals, as plentiful as they are."

"Indeed?" Eleanor asked, eyeing Victor over Percival's shoulder. "Is this true? They did not tell you of my plans? Then what convinced you to return?"

Heat that was not from the stone burned his ears, and he blinked in the ball of light, thinking quickly. "Worried were you, that I would not return?" he asked after a time, figuring a question would serve better than an answer he did not have.

"Oh never," she said with a laugh, yet he no longer desired to smile as it danced through his ears, "where would you go? Especially when Darien Nicodemeus blankets the skies in his...new form? Though it pales in comparison to ours, now, doesn't it my Elite Creatures?" She looked around the room for approval and was pleased when it was met with meager sounds of assent.

"Though I have yet to witness this new form, your Grace," Victor found himself saying, "I am sure it is as captivating as any that lives on the earth."

"Truly," she agreed. "Now, let us walk, my dear Vampires, and talk more of your coming transition."

Percival did not leave Victor's front as she and Xavier began to turn away from them, and this caught Eleanor's eye. She placed a hand on Xavier's shoulder, bidding him to still, and shook herself out of his grip, turning.

"Creature," she said to the still-hooded Elite, "why do you keep Victor from moving forward?"

Fear swarmed the hall at once, and what steady dread and blood that had filled his nose since he'd arrived had thickened greatly.

Gregory and Madison stepped to his sides, and he knew it was their fear he smelled: it trailed on their blood as they moved.

"He is feeling a bit out of sorts," Madison offered, gripping Percival's arm, attempting to pull him from Victor's front but not at all succeeding.

Anger rose in Percival's blood and the stone roared to life with it. And here Victor heard the Creature's thoughts as though they were directed to him alone:

"*You cannot become one of us. You must remain pure! Stall! Stall!*"

Moving swiftly, he removed himself from behind Percival, planting himself beside the Creature. Placing a strong hand atop the Creature's shoulder, he squeezed, bidding his silence. "Your Creatures are merely excited at the prospect, I imagine, of who shall take Joseph Gail's place as your right-hand," Victor said to a most curious Eleanor. "And I believe as it was I who obeyed your commands faithfully these past weeks, they wish for myself to take his place."

"But Victor," she whispered, her words quite low amidst the murmurs, "you, yourself went against my word, taking matters into your own hands—"

"I brought you Alexandria Stone and Christian Delacroix!"

"Well, yes," she agreed, reluctantly, "yet you also released the barrier allowing Damion Nicodemeus unfettered entrance!"

He blinked. "Damion?"

Xavier turned in full as well, dark gaze narrowed.

She scoffed, looking around the room with distaste. "It is a matter I would have liked to explain in the seclusion of my throne room, but very well," she exhaled deeply before continuing, "Damion Nicodemeus's…changed blood is the reason I was able to change forms."

"What?" he asked, feeling the stone burn once more, though he did not dare reach for it.

"Her blood is forever changed," a haunting, shrill voice said from somewhere behind Xavier, "because of the dark one."

Xavier and Eleanor stepped aside, allowing the newcomer to enter the circular hall in full, and Victor narrowed his eyes. "Friandria Vivery." Yes, he remembered the woman when he'd returned to the caves with Eleanor some days before, how she'd slunk about and lingered near Eleanor as though tethered, as though a ghost.

She crept past Xavier, Elite Creature robes and cloak tattered and covered in dust, much too large for her small frame. Her red hair trailed behind her head, a fiery crown against the orange torchlight, her gray eyes dull as she surveyed the room at large. "Hello Mister Vonderheide," she breathed, her voice lifeless, a whisper of wind passing her pale lips.

"Hello Friandria," he said uncertainly, the stone flaring to life at the smell of her blood, which was no longer laced in death, but something else, indeed.

"Damion Nicodemeus holds the Goblet of Existence," she continued, "trapped in the bowels of her home, he was granted the... knowledge to drink from its rim."

He stared from Eleanor to Xavier and then back to Friandria. The latter of whom was staring dimly past him, at a location he did not care to place: what she'd said rattled him greatly.

"He...holds the Goblet?" he asked, and he could not tear his gaze from Eleanor, now. "How could he hold the Goblet? And how did he drink from it but we all remain...as we are?"

"Indeed!" Eleanor said, stepping up to Friandria, placing a bracing hand on her shoulder. "How, indeed! Thank you, Friandria, for your wonderful...illumination, but I'll take the rest from here—it would not do to place too much on Victor, now."

He blinked at her words. "Let her speak if that's her desire," he said, eager to hear more, "there isn't a need for secrecy, surely." And he could not help but let his gaze travel to Xavier. The Vampire looked quite interested in the proceedings as well.

Eleanor chuckled softly, clasping her hands together. "But there is a nature to the history of things that must be carefully understood," she said, "and to spout it off at anyone's behest is quite simply," she eyed Friandria coldly, "rude."

Friandria's eyes fluttered briefly, but she said, "Mister Vonderheide, Damion Nicodemeus holds the Goblet because Javier Theron worked beneath Eleanor's very nose and granted him the blood necessary to gain passage to Dracu—"

Blood left Friandria's lips, her gray eyes went black, and before Victor could react, Friandria fell to the ground beside Eleanor who did not look down. "Enough from her," she said coldly. "I do not care to be reminded of my one mishap. Those that betray me," and her ever-changing eyes met Victor's coldly, "do not deserve life."

Coldness blanketed the room, a deep coldness, and no one said a word, but the stone, which had been burning steadily in Victor's pocket since Friandria appeared, flared with heat and suddenly the room was not so quiet:

Have we been discovered?

Nonsense.

We'd all be dead if that were the case!

Dead and ash, truly!

Will all of you just calm down! I'm sure Victor is thinking of something, aren't you Victor?

Damn. Aloud, he said, "Javier Theron? Betraying you? Helping Damion Nicodemeus? How on Earth did that happen?" And he remembered the smell of Dracula on the young Creature, how he had thought it his memory. He cursed himself now, staring at her, how she had been duped. How they all had been deceived. *Dracula, again, right under my nose and I dared not believe it.* Shame washed over him, dousing the stone's heat, allowing it to cool, the thoughts to dim. With it, clarity was allowed to return, the dread he had felt since he'd laid eyes upon Xavier, Eleanor, to disperse.

"I ask myself this same question every day," Eleanor said, "but, again, if you would accompany myself and Xavier into more secluded parts of my home, we may better—"

"My goodness," a new voice said from behind Xavier, and the Vampire turned. Eleanor, however, did not. "What is the meaning of this…varied party? Discussing our new faces? Ah, Victor! I thought I smelled the blood of a *normal* Vampire. What brings you back to the tunnels?"

Thomas Montague stood beside Xavier, formidable in height, a smile on his haggard, sunken face, but there was a gleam in his brown eyes that showed greater life, indeed. "Victor, welcome home," he said, the gruffness to his voice telling of its lack of use, Victor thought, or from screaming his pain: the whites of his eyes were quite red, most likely from tears.

"Thomas," he said with a nod.

Xavier, however, stepped away from the former Lycan, surveying him with a greater breadth of coldness. Victor wondered why, when Eleanor finally turned to Thomas, the smell of her displeasure clear in the damp air. "What brings you out of your room, Mister Montague?"

"I thought it prudent to eye the new smells in our ever-growing home," he said, still smiling beneath his unkempt scruff.

"I was just going to take Xavier and Victor to my throne room," she said, "enlighten them on the next steps to further my plans."

"Ah, but we all know your plans are set—have been even without their imminent transformations," Thomas countered coyly. "What is it you truly desire to do with them, Eleanor?"

Victor narrowed his eyes upon the smiling Elite. *What did he know?*

"It's quite simple, really," she said, and she turned back to Victor, a smile on her own face, "I will explain to them the truth of what we are, and they will finally join us in the sun."

* * *

They ventured through the enshrouded wood, the sun barely reaching them here, but they did not slow. The Elves on either side of them forbade it: every time someone would ask them where or what they moved for, the Elves, daggers brandished at their heads, would let out a collective hiss of warning.

Dragor Descant kept his hand on his sword. He walked beside Peroneous and Aurora, who whispered their spell to keep the sun from sending any of the colder Creatures to burst into flame, not bothering to pay heed to their frantic thoughts, for his were just as dark.

He focused on the memory of Darien, now greatly changed, and remembered the night he had moved, at Dracula's command, to kill the pure Vampire, Nepenthe Nicodemeus. A formidable opponent, if ever he faced one. There was gratitude in his cold heart for the previous battle with Renere Caddenhall. *If they had not fought,* he thought with a small smile, then, *I would not have been able to end her with an Enchanted dagger to her cold heart.*

Of course, it was not that easy. Nothing ever was easy. It had been quite the chore to wipe the memory of the great old Vampire, Renere, for he had seen me deal the killing blow, his confusion quite apparent. Thank the birds Dracula granted me that difficult spell.

It was harder, still, to kill Cewenthe, he thought suddenly, as the trees began to thin and the ground began to slope downward, the Elves hissing orders to them all. Arminius's arms and hair swayed wildly at Peroneus's back as they ventured down the deeply sloping dirt, that was now not dirt at all, but hard stone steps, Dragor realized.

Looking up, he eyed the wide, old wooden doors set into the base of a large, grassy hill, and as they stopped just before the closed doors, the Elves that had chased Damion left their places around the Order of the Dragon, and moved to stand before the doors. They were at attention, and, curiously enough, glowing, as though something from within them emanated greater beauty.

One of the Elves moved for the doors, and the others stepped aside, allowing this Elf to push them open. At once, the acrid smell of stale death pressed against Dragor's nose, and he immediately chose not to breathe any more of it in. Darkness greeted them where the sunlight could not touch the seemingly endless stone tunnel, as tall as it was wide. And as the Elves turned as one, their dark cloaks sweeping the leaf-strewn, dirt-splattered stone floor, Aleister, who had taken up the rear of their party was pushed unceremoniously forward, and he stumbled onto the stone of the tunnel, a new smell reaching him as he straightened, walking of his own volition now.

There were no torches, nor balls of light to illuminate their walk, so when the doors closed loudly behind them, they found their silent journey a harrowing one. Nothing but the silver of the Elves' hair shone any light through the thick dark, and Dragor thought again on the glow that left their frames. *Had to be magic, couldn't be anything else. And with magic restored...Syran preserve us.*

For he knew the turn of magic to the rightful Creatures would spell death for those not truly of this World, he knew it well. Dracula, after all, had been annoyingly endless in reminding him of his role in the Enchanting Arts. *A role that was but a sham*, he thought with a smaller smile.

The walk was mindless, endless, indeed, and in the silver light of the long-eared Creatures before him, he found his hand restless. It tightened around the handle of his sword and in his unease, he felt the coldness with which the leather straps greeted him. *No longer bidden magic*, he thought with greater fear. *What more can I do against these magical Creatures if not with my Spell of Greater Strength?*

He remembered the way the blue light used to light up his sword, how quickly the magic was taken from him as Dracula's death took hold on the World, its influence catching on all things the Great Vampire had touched...

Something of a shiver crept up his spine, the thought just out of reach, but he would not face it now, not when he had to be on guard, he the Defender of the throne, whatever that had meant.

The whispers of the Enchanters had ceased when they'd entered the dark of the tunnel, and Dragor wished for it to return, for something more than the near-silent footsteps of those beside him as they walked along. The fear that they had left, would leave, would face their deaths just as Nicholai had done would not cease its hold on his mind. *What a bang up job of Creatures we are!*

Gone, lost, chained to a dead Vampire, forced to move this way and that, and for what we don't know! And our supposed leader is off with Eleanor Goddamn Black, probably one of her Creatures, and what were we meant to do for any of it?! What, indeed, can we roughshod Creatures do?

Anger boiled his blood, for he had played his part dutifully, gone along with it all as he was meant to—as he was *forced* to—and here he found what he'd been told completely at odds with what was meant to *be*. Thrust with these Creatures, tied to this Order, forbidden any other choice but to obey or face permanent death.

Dragor remembered the face of Arminius as the door had been thrown wide and the Elf had relayed the demise of Nicholai Noble, and he suddenly wished it was he that had met his end at a Phoenix, for the mindlessness of the World now, of the Creatures mad for power, the Elites growing stronger by the second was far too much to bear.

And without magic, without that little hope at his side, he found he could not endure to fight, not any longer. *Not*, he thought in despair, *when it meant nothing but death for us all.*

Indeed, these dark thoughts placated him for the rest of the blind walk, but it was not until the Elves lifted glowing daggers into the air, illuminating further the path ahead, that Dragor felt, for the first time in the past hour, the least bit of hope.

The end was in sight. Its face was a set of better-kept golden doors which reminded Dragor very much of the Vampire City's layout with its unkempt gate and white doors the deeper one ventured through the tunnel.

Relief washed through him for the briefest of moments before more fear replaced it. *It would not do to get excited*, he reminded himself; *we could be walking to our deaths*. For who had ever heard of the Etrian Elves awaiting visitors? Let alone the Order of the Dragon?

The Elves closest to the doors sheathed their daggers in hidden pockets of their robes and reached out long-fingered hands for the equally golden handles. They moved as one, an Elf on each side, and they pulled them open, revealing a grandiose entrance hall, covered in all manner of blackened shrubbery, dark vines that draped across the walls and floor, and the distinct smell of all old, forgotten things.

The walls were as golden as the doors, and stretched high above their heads, higher than the hill the caves were set in. And they walked through, Dragor doing his best to ignore the glowing orange glares of the Elves who had stepped aside to allow them entrance as they moved.

"Dracula gave them this place?" Peroneous asked in awe, causing Dragor to look around.

Indeed, they had stepped onto gold floors, though covered in dirt and various wildlife as it was, it still held a certain gleam as though it had been polished dutifully throughout the years.

And it had been three, last Dragor remembered.

There was a statue of a stoic-looking Elf with a bejeweled crown atop his head in the center of the room, though this was solid white stone, not gold as was everything else. Various armchairs surrounded it as though those who sat in it would look upon nothing but the statue's delicate detail. The Elf was crafted finely, the folds of its robes numerous as it flared out around its boots, which were obviously armor of some kind, and in the Elf's long-fingered hand was a sword raised high as though the Elf were prepared to do battle.

Dragor's eyes perused the sword for some time, for he felt he had seen it before, when the small book, barely noticeable in the Elf's other hand caught his gaze. He could hardly begin to formulate theories as to why the Etrian King would hold a book and a sword in the statue of his likeness, when someone spoke.

"Well," Aleister asked the large room, and looking around, Dragor could see two more large doors situated on the other side of the statue, leading, he guessed, to more nature-filled opulence, "this is quite an entrance hall. Not bad for a group of Creatures most bidden to live out their remaining years in solitude." There was a tinge of unease to his words, but Dragor knew better than to remark on it.

Christopher Black, however, did not.

"The Elves are luckier than most."

Aleister eyed him. "The Etrian Elves were scourges on our heads. Always demanding more. Though if," and he glanced at Aurora, "it is true that they were the true holders of magic and Dracula took the art from them...they cannot be faulted for their indignation."

"Indeed," a new voice said, cool as it echoed against the walls, "we cannot."

All heads turned as the Elves finally closed the doors behind them, brushing the Order further into the large hall, closer to the statue and the new figure that had appeared before the doors beyond the sculpture, a splitting image of the hard stone, indeed, save for the sword and book his counterpart held.

The Etrian King sauntered forward with all the grace and pomposity one could expect from an Etrian Elf, his long black hair flying out behind him as though a second cloak, the one he wore a deep red, offset by the paleness of his skin. As he opened his arms wide as if in greeting, his gold-embroidered vest, shirt, and breeches could be seen, though they were all white, and despite the dirt on everything around him, his clothes were quite clean.

Too clean.

The Etrian King's smile was wide as he took long strides around the armchairs to reach them, and once close enough, he said, "But indignation, my dear *Vampure*, is better saved for other Creatures, is it not?"

Aleister unsheathed his sword and the Elves at their backs let out further hisses of warning. "Speak plain, Alinneis," the scarred Vampire said, "how did you know to gather us? Why do you wait for us? What part do you play in all of this?"

"The part I have always played, naturally," he said, appraising Aleister with distaste. "To be sent here was a small price to pay to one day regain what was naturally ours."

"Your control of magic," Aurora finished.

Alinneis nodded. "My Elves did not understand, nor would they ever, I'm afraid, but sacrifices had to be made. Sacrifices, Creatures, are always being made, and further still must more be made." And before Dragor could pinpoint the discomfort he felt with the Elf's words, his cold stare, Alinneis waved two long hands through the air and Dragor felt the cold of a blade in his back.

Letting out a cry of pain, he whirled, brandishing his sword, just as Aleister did the same, Christopher flourishing his bow, a hand on an arrow. Peroneous and Aurora readied their hands for a spell, yet they were lowered slightly from their normal spell-ready positions; they bled profusely from their backs where the blades had struck.

"What the Devil is the meaning of this Elf?!" Aleister roared, though his gaze would not leave the Elves that now formed a line before the doors they just came through.

The voice of Alinneis came in cool and cold as the Elves stepped forward as one, "Tear them apart."

Dragor silenced the frustration that he had been terribly right as he swung his sword.

A bolt of red fire flew past his head, but still he moved, hearing the sharp slices of air as Christopher released his arrows.

The Elf jumped out of the way, just missing the tip of his blade, and Dragor felt the wetness of his blood drench his back, heard it splatter against the floor. *I'm not healing*, he thought just as Aurora and Peroneous let loose lightning from their fingertips, aimed straight for two Elves most near the doors.

The Elves avoided the attack with ease, the bolts hitting the white wood leaving black marks that faded far too quickly. Thinking this curious, Dragor took his gaze from the Elves where the others did battle, and eyed Alinneis behind him.

The Elf was smiling, a bright gleam in his eyes as he watched all that transpired.

"Aleister!" Dragor called to the scarred Vampire.

Aleister did not tear his gaze from the Elf that held two daggers to his sword. "What, Dragor?!"

"Cease your fighting!" For he could see now the hint of something more in Alinneis's eyes. And turning his gaze to the sword the statue held, he narrowed his eyes in disbelief.

The Ares.

"Why aren't you fighting, Dragor?!" Peroneous yelled, the still-unconscious Arminius at his feet. The dark Enchanter was sending blue and green blasts from his palms, attempting to strike an Elf that moved as swiftly as the light left Peroneous's hands.

Dragor turned his gaze back to the Elf he had been fighting. The Elf merely stood, dagger in hand, panting heavily, but he did not move. Something of a smile lit up his face, and Dragor smiled back despite himself.

Dracula. Of course.

He could feel the familiar tug and pull of the Vampire's hand, no matter if he were dead. *I should have known.* Turning to Alinneis in full, he sheathed his sword with a snarl. "What," he began, with more conviction than Aleister this time, "is the meaning of this Elf?"

The tall Elf appraised him for moments more, before letting his wide smile fade. "Dragor Descant," he said as the sound of arrow, sword, and light smashing together continued on through the hall, "you are quite the clever *Vampure*. Though, you always have been."

Dragor remembered it now, how he had seen Dracula speaking with Alinneis but five years before, though they had taken a visit to the Elven Council to meet with the Heads of the many Elven Wings. It had been a long and arduous journey to get to that desolate place, the grass of Europe a kind of middle-ground to the Elves' natural places of heat, though they always made sure there were plenty of water nearby. Despite the encumbering appearance of the Vampires and

Lycans, the Elves—all kinds—had kept their peaceful relations with the Merpeople of the World.

He remembered the way Alinneis had fought with Dracula on some matter—but he, Dragor, had been too distracted by a nearby Fae and her exquisite beauty to truly pay attention. How he wished he had.

"Forsaken your title as 1st Captain to your Armies, have you?" Alinneis continued, much to Dragor's surprise.

He rethought sheathing his sword as the words pierced his ears. "I take it you played a part in all that transpired during that, now I see, false attack on the Vampire City?"

"It is the very reason Dracula desired me pay for my crimes," he said, a lingering hiss trailing behind his words, "the very reason he locked me and my kind away. To better keep what must be kept. I imagine the guise of forced solitude would help him further his plans. Perhaps it worked too well—you Creatures don't seem to know why you are here."

At this Aleister pushed the Elf that had had him pinned down to the floor with his daggers off him, and jumped to his feet, sword shaking with anger in his grip. His green eyes were alive with malice as he stepped up to Alinneis, a snarl escaping his lips. "Did I hear you correctly? That Dracula *planned* this from the very start?"

Dragor motioned to the sword and book in Alinneis's statue. "*The Immortal's Guide* and the Ares," he said, and Aleister let out a sound of incomprehension as he eyed them, "Dracula's tools. Why else would Evert send us here? We are the Order of the Dragon, are we not?"

By now the others had ceased their fighting, and upon realizing the Elves would not attack, they moved to surround Alinneis as well. "What's all this?" Peroneous asked.

Aleister would not tear his gaze from the Elf. "We move at Dracula's behest…again," he said coldly, sheathing his sword. "Now, tell us the truth. What's the meaning of this attack? Why send us here if to try and kill us?"

"Kill you?" Alinneis asked. "No, I merely moved to demonstrate how useless your weapons are. How baseless. Ill-fitting. How lacking in…proper magic they truly are."

"What the Devil are you on about, Elf?" Dragor asked, grown quite tired of Alinneis's voice: it was quite cool, yes, but closer now it held the distinct air of ridicule.

Alinneis clapped his long-fingered hands together, and the Elves near the doors appeared behind their king on a knee, their silver heads bowed. "Simply, Creatures," Alinneis said, his face serious, and for the first time Dragor realized there was no torch or light to illuminate the room. All should have been in darkness, indeed. But the subtle glow from the gold upon the walls and floor served as their light.

"You couldn't lay a hand on my Elves, could you? Couldn't get a scratch off them, yes?" Alinneis's voice continued on, droll, much to Dragor's displeasure. As all Creatures looked around at each other and the blood that littered the floor from their wounds alone, dark realization dawned on their faces.

Dragor, however, snarled. "*What* is the meaning of this?" he asked again, not at all liking the Creature's implications that they were weak, that they could not stand a chance against the magic of the World, that the Elf was right...

"Simply, *Vampure*, that your weapons, your standing as this Order of the *Dracon* lack. And *have* lacked since your rather crude formation. Foreseeing this, or perhaps, dreading it, Dracula enlisted myself to aid you in your pursuits. Indeed, how can the one meant to take *Dracon's* place do anything more than wound their enemies if all their protection held were plain staves, bows, and horribly dull swords?" Alinneis said.

Before anyone could respond, he turned in a whirl of red cloak and black hair, his Elves rising to their boots as well, and stepped around the statue, moving for the doors to the opposite side of the room.

"Follow, Dark Creatures," the voice trailed in the large hall. And the Elves stared at them, expectant.

Without another word, Dragor trudged forward, knowing the others took up their places behind him, and as they reached the white doors that remained open, revealing a grander hall, many more doors placed on the walls throughout, Dragor realized with a start that the wound to his back had closed.

Chapter Seven

SURROUNDED

"**B**ut what *is* he, Remington?"

"I can't say. His blood doesn't reach the nose, does it?"

"How curious."

"The *whole World's* curious these days."

James Addison thanked Alexandria Stone in silence. He knew he would go mad if he had been forced to smell the Vampires' blood the entire time they were here. Forced to fight off waves of them once they were able to smell his own…

He walked through the mansion, eager to seek solitude, for the numerous Vampires desiring to know where he'd come from, how he'd known Lord Christian and Miss Stone would not cease since they'd arrive to a large din of gossip.

It had amused him at first to hear how many of the women and men immediately scorned Alexandria upon seeing them side by side, for they had known Christian was a bachelor, had, apparently, desired to bend his ear, be known as the one who tamed the untamable.

And as for Alexandria, the number of Vampires interested in her at all were numerous, far more than Christian's admirers. As it was, no one could smell her blood, for it was what she desired, perhaps weary of their reaction, and James laughed quietly to himself as he remembered the number of Vampires that had tried, and failed, in the two days, to request her company and gain her attention in any capacity.

He felt their stares as he walked mindlessly through the halls, his lack of available blood making him, not the spectacle Alexandria was, but something of an enigma, and though it had been brief earlier, his blood had been available, and those that were near glared at him with red eyes, unable to believe they smelled the blood of a Lycan in their city.

He had been able to escape thanks to the quick thinking of Westley Rivers, who merely explained away the Lycan scent by assuring it was he that carried it, that he had just felled quite a number of the horrid beasts.

This had eased them, though there were very few Vampires desiring to know more of him after that.

This suited James perfectly.

He had spent the time exploring where he could, he had seen the offices of Lillith, Victor, Xavier, Eleanor, and Damion, though they were all quite empty, and some left in states of use as, he had been told, "They'd left in a hurry, then."

He looked up from dark thought as the darkness from the hallways grew. Yes, seldom torches rested on the high walls here, and yet he still walked further, the doors becoming fewer and far between. It was not until he reached the very end of the hall, the darkness all but crushing here, almost so thick he could not see—and yet, he could—that he saw the door. Simple in its wood, he took a breath and turned on its handle, eager to see what lay beyond it.

A small desk sat a few feet before the door, bright torches high above the square room, large as it was tall. Indeed, it seemed to stretch on forever above him, and as he stepped in, closing the door behind him, the smell of Vampire—terribly strong, impossible to ignore—filled his nose.

It was instantaneous. The smell of old blood, strong blood filled all he dared breathe and at once he doubled over, clutching his sides, for he burned with the rage that sat in his blood, quiet until it needed to be unleashed.

"*Not now*," he gritted through sharpening teeth. "*Vampires—everywhere.*" And the fear that he would be smelled, that he would be found and instantly attacked did nothing to quell his growing fury.

Must destroy.

"No."

Walking sticks of decay.

"No!"

Obey Lore. Kill. Kill the woman.

"NO!"

A loud howl ripped through his throat, burning like fire as it passed, and at once the pain grew, almost unbearable in its tenacity, and he instantly found his thoughts and senses turned to the one that had bitten him under the moon's glow.

Lore.

He was not here. He had left me. Where had he gone?

Find him. Find him. Help him. Save him. You are his blood—

"I am not his blood—he merely used me then left me when things seemed lost," he reasoned with the blood-filled air. Looking around the stone room with a Lycan's clarity, he could see the splatters of blood that lined the walls and floor, the many bloodied, old weapons that lingered here and there along the floor, and he blinked in the light of the many torches.

A training room?

Lore is not here.

The door opened with a slam then, and James stared as the Vampires, eyes red with their confusion, anger, and bloodlust, glared at him.

He stepped back on large, hairy hind legs, just now noticing the new clothes he had been given upon being taken to his room now lay in scraps upon the bloodied stone floor. His heart beat loudly in his chest, large as both were now, and he took a slow breath as the dark Vampire stepped into the room, his only arm brandishing a glowing blue sword. "James," Westley Rivers said slowly, somehow commanding calm to the Vampires at his back despite never once laying eyes upon them, "ease. Calm. Please."

Calm was the last thing he could manage now, not when the old blood of the room still filled his nostrils, sensitive to the exactness of the Vampire that had held it. *Old blood, indeed.* "Mister Rivers," he growled, lifting a large paw off the ground, shifting his footing on his haunches, "her blood does not work, not like it should. I am tied to her, but it is not enough." He could feel it now. The waning influence of Alexandria Stone's blood, how it did not compel like it did when out in the World. Here it was lesser, and why was she not keeping the blood of Dracula from reaching his nose, now?

The Vampire soldiers at Westley's back looked wary, and James could smell the cold weaponry they held in their hands. Silver. Indeed. Lore had told him they would use the weapons as it was one of the only things that could stall a Lycan.

Why do I think of Lore now? He abandoned me—

Westley took a step into the room. "James, return to your human form," he said, his red gaze focused. It gave James the thought that the Vampire had had his fair share of fights with Lycans, how calm it was he looked, quite unlike Christian Delacroix some days before. "For the sake of all Vampires here, I implore you." And then to the others at his back who had not stepped into the room, "Get Lord Delacroix and Alexandria Stone. Bring them here, immediately."

They were gone in a burst of wind that hit James's nose roughly, a distasteful growl leaving his long throat with the smell of their blood. "You knew I was a Lycan when you first saw me, didn't you, Vampire?" he asked instead of doing what he truly wished.

"Aye," he said, closing the door behind him, sealing in the smell of his blood much to James's growing displeasure, "I knew you were the Lycan cub Dracula had saved to help further his plans."

"What plans?" he growled, the need to rip and pull clawing at his mind, but he held it at bay, the Vampire's words keeping him still.

Westley lowered his sword though he did not sheathe it. "Vampire and Lycan distort the blood of all natural Creatures. It is not we that give the title of 'Dark,' other Creatures bestowed it upon us. When Dracula heard of the woman married to the Lycan Lord Reginald Addison, he moved quickly to ensure the child born of a beast's blood could be kept."

Wariness crept over him. "Kept?"

"Dracula," Westley began, and there was an exasperated way he said the name that made James even more curious, "was…scared. By that time, he'd fought numerous Lycans, many that did not survive the need for destruction that overwhelmed their large, hairy frames. It is a curious thing, the blood of we forsaken Creatures. Before potions were made to ensure our longevity, our blood seemed to work to kill us—we were prisoners of our decaying, monstrous bodies, quite inhuman, mad with little rhyme nor reason.

"Dracula gained this reason. And after he'd secured the form you know we Vampires to hold best, he began to think of ways best to overcome his enemies. How better, indeed, then to gather one for his own?"

"But that does not explain why he kept me in Xavier and Christian's home—as their servant of all things—"

"What better way to ensure your protection from other Vampires?" Westley said simply, and before James could respond, he went on. "They could never be touched once Xavier was placed as Dracula's favorite, James. And once he was, Dracula deemed it important, I imagine, to keep you safe, and curious to see if a Lycan and Vampire could live in the same home, unknowing of the other's nature. As we know, they could. You would have turned eventually, once your hot blood boiled by some insurmountable rage, I imagine. How fortunate it is, then that Lore took the opportunity to further along the process, himself, and when Xavier was along for his journey, no less."

"Dracula kept me there?" he growled, voice low.

Westley nodded, the sword never lowering in hand.

"He took me from my father…my mother…kept me and my aunt to work beneath strangers—Vampires?! When I, the blood of a Lycan, bended backwards to fulfill Xavier's ever whim?!"

The rage was breathing through greatly now, and all manner of Alexandria's blood vanished from his heart, his mind. And the voice continued on, and somewhere, somewhere not quite lost, the thundering heart of Lore resounded in his head, a ferocious beating that sounded more akin to the heavy padding of paws as they tore up ground…

"I'm coming."

And there it was, as clear as day, Lore's voice piercing through all. And suddenly the Vampire before him seemed quite small—

The door opened with a slam and behind Westley stood the Vampire soldiers from before, their eyes still wide, still fear-filled, but Christian and Alexandria had joined them and were now stepping quickly past to enter the room. But before they could get to Westley's back, James let out a roar, fear replacing the rage.

The woman. He focused on her as Christian threw out an arm to keep her at bay, her red eyes wide with what looked like fear, but James could not be sure. And what did it matter if she felt fear, for wasn't *his* anger, *his* fear at being turned, *his* rage at being lied to for his *entire* life what truly mattered?

He recalled the vision of Alexandria in the woods, what she'd said of her grandfather, how he needed James to help keep the blood. *Kept.* A growl of disgust left him as the memory morphed into Xavier staring upon him with blank, monstrous coldness in the hallway of Delacroix Manor one dark, cold night.

Even then, James thought with disdain, *there was contempt.* Yes, he could recall with a startling clarity the green gaze of the Vampire as he'd looked down upon him. He, James, had been a boy, then. Young, and scared. Something in that cold green gaze always warranted grand fear, he'd known it even then, but he could never place it. Now, however, staring upon the older Vampire with Lycan eyes, he could see it: The contempt, the desire for the blood he could not have, the absolute loathing. *He hated me because I was human,* James thought with renewed wonder. Did he hate all the humans, or was that merely what being a Vampire reduced the rest of the world to? A grand sense of loathing, looking down upon others from a supernatural pedestal few could climb if not given to death?

Christian's snarl brought him back around to the present; the Vampire quite similar in face to Xavier was staring upon him in wary distaste. *Vampires. All of them. Why should I have to hide behind their backs? Why can I not be what I was meant to? A bloody Lycan, indeed!*

The rage boiled in his gut, the smell of Vampire blood very near complete revulsion now, and how maddening it was that he stand there and take it when he could very well rid them all of it if he so wished!

"James," Alexandria said, her voice tremulous, yet laced with the same contempt he knew all Vampires to hold. Her gaze was not red, however, and he stared at her more than he glared upon the others. "Change your form, please."

"Why?" he repeated aloud. "Why should I? You bloody Vampires—I have served you for my entire life! Why must I forgo my power in order to placate your delicate senses when you would not show me the same courtesy?!"

All was silent in the tall room, his words seeming to linger painfully in their ears for moments longer, and James found reason, a sliver of it, but it was enough, to heed the woman's words. He was indeed surrounded by Vampires—in their very home—it would not do to run roughshod through their halls, their streets, and get himself destroyed. Especially not with Lore on his way.

Yes, the Lycan King was coming; he could feel it in his blood. And how it seemed to be blood that Alexandria Stone could no longer touch.

As he sighed deeply, allowing his beastly form to disappear, he heard the relieved sighs of the Vampires as they stepped forward, a strong dark hand wrapping around his arm, pulling him from his knees. He looked up into the Vampire's now black eyes, the fangs still bared within his mouth. The shiver the sight should have sent through his spine was subdued: the thunder of Lore's paws matched the beat of his heart and calmed him somewhat.

"James Addison, you're to be kept in the Chambers of Waiting 'till we can figure out what to do with you," Westley said, and while his hand still gripped James's arm, he looked toward Alexandria who had stepped forward a minute before. "Miss Stone, are you comfortable with your power?"

"I believe I am gaining a better understanding of it as the minutes pass, Mister Rivers," she said, her brown-green gaze much more assured than James had ever remembered seeing it.

"Good," the dark Vampire said, swinging James around to eye the Vampires in full. He was very naked, but modesty was better left for humans, he thought, the smell of the Vampire's blood an annoyance, but he would not allow himself to turn, not when Lore was close.

"Men, take him to the Chambers. I must speak to Lord Delacroix and Miss Stone about the severity of the power they wield."

James growled slightly as Westley pushed him toward a waiting soldier, all manner of hospitality gone.

It is just as well, James thought as he and the soldiers left the bloodied room, not chancing a glance back to the wary Vampires, *this makes it easier to kill him—kill them all once Lore arrives. How quickly their natures change when faced with the blood of their enemy.* He smiled as the door was closed loudly at his back.

* * *

"Getting right to it," Westley said once the echo of the door was all that could be heard. Relief passed through him as the smell of beast left with it. "Miss Stone, you must gain a better understanding of your power. I was aware, as much as I could be, of the Lycan plan Dracula had concocted. But if you cannot keep his blood subdued...this spells disaster for Dracula's intentions: to keep the blood of Lycans from our noses, to keep our blood from theirs, so the King of All Creatures can reach the Goblet, drink from it, and we can end all of this."

"I am aware," the woman said, and Westley fought the desire to kneel with her voice, regal if ever he had heard a voice of royalty, "I don't know what happened..." But the slight shrug of the shoulder closest to Christian gave way her truth.

So the Delacroix boy is a distraction, hm?

He thought back to their closeness once he stepped into Dracula's office, the heady gaze of desire that filled Christian's eyes, indeed her unadulterated lack of control over the scent of her blood, all of it filling the air. *Love, indeed.*

"Just as well," Westley said, returning his attention to the tense Vampires before him; the sight of Lycan never did rest well with a Vampire even after the Lycan was felled or managed (although rarely in his case) to run off, "let's get to the bottom of it." He bent and picked up the sword he had dropped when James had returned to his human face.

Christian and Alexandria's gazes were on it wearily.

He smiled. "What, you did not think you were merely here for safety, did you?"

"Well, no," Christian began, stepping forward as well, "we thought you would have more information on what's going on—on Alexandria's power."

"Information—no," he said, his sword's blade beginning to warm. *Oh, the small privileges we damned Creatures are afforded.* "Training, yes."

"Training?" they said together, bewilderment lining their pale faces.

"Yes," Westley said, the sword in his only hand beginning to glow with its blue light. A Member of the Order, he was, though he was never officially given a medallion. The emblem of a sword in flame his marker of his place in all of this. In Dracula's hand. As he lifted the sword into the air, he wondered if Philistia had gathered Evian, if they, at least, had moved to defend their part in the larger plan.

The blue light left the sword and zoomed straight for Alexandria, who immediately glowed with her red hue, a burst of cold air blowing past them all as the blue light touched it.

When the wind died, Westley stared in pleasure upon she and Christian.

The black-haired Vampire held the sword across his face, the gem in the guard just before his eyes, and Alexandria Stone's eyes were glowing their familiar red.

Good job, Dracula, Westley thought, as he pressed the tip of the blade into the stone at his feet. The blue light wormed its way against the floor, moving and stretching until it pressed against all walls, and Alexandria's red light lessened slightly in its glow.

As the Vampires look around the room in confusion, Westley pointed his sword to them. "Let us begin, Vampires. Christian, defend her, Alexandria—attack me. I will not go easy."

They shared skeptical glances, but Westley was upon her in the next second, the sword's sharpened point just before her eyes. Christian moved with great speed, clashing the Ares against the sword, fury in his eyes, perhaps at the fact that he had let Westley get so close.

As Westley reappeared behind the desk, Christian did not move from his place in front of her, but was much more tense, indeed.

Westley could see the anger that she could have been harmed clear in Christian's red eyes. "Good, Delacroix. You must learn to get used to having a charge—what it means. She is tied to you, she is an extension of you, another body that houses your blood, if you will. You must never let harm come to her, you must never let her be touched."

"Trust me," Christian Delacroix said, renewed purpose filling his blood; Westley could smell it, "I won't."

"Good," he said again, lifting the sword and slashing the old desk in half. As it crumpled at his feet, he looked up at the waiting Vampires again. "Now, come. Make Xavier proud."

And with that Christian was flying toward him, hair lifted from his back, the sword erect, headed straight for Westley's heart, Alexandria not far behind.

* * *

The afternoon sun lined the horizon, but through the trees he thought it flames. It was not until he reached the clearing that he saw the red half-circle in all its glorious splendor, and he immediately spit out the blood.

It splattered against the already bloodied grass, weighing down the green blades, and he continued his run down the path, feeling the blood that was not his, the power of the boy—no, *man*—grow stronger with every large step he took.

Somewhere overhead, a large shadow passed, and he looked up at it, a most curious sight filling his eyes, but he never did slow. It was only when it was gone that he thought how strange it was that he'd see a true Vampire fill the skies again.

Thought Dracula'd gotten that under control.

Wondering what more the dead Vampire was losing control of, he ran faster, knowing he could not let James escape him again, not when the World, already teeming with power and strangeness, was descending into greater madness. A madness he hoped he could overcome.

Chapter Eight

HANDS OF THE ORDER

They had followed the tall, slender back deeper into the once-lavish cave that looked more to Christopher like an underground palace. What little he had heard about the Elves from Dracula seemed more and more like some far-off tale, made to subdue him into staying complacent, sure the Etrian Elves were merely part of this plot to kill him had ever they lain eyes on him. Now, looking around, he knew it had been a lie.

Every corner they turned, every untarnished golden door that was opened, more Elves peered at them, at him, with unadulterated interest, some with scorn, yes, for they were foreign Creatures trespassing on a place of exile, perhaps what the Elves had grown to think of as home, but nothing in their gazes, to Christopher Black at least, warranted any unease. They were merely as curious to the new faces as the Order of the Dragon were to being there.

And just why they had been placed here, and the slight on the weapons they held by Alinneis had not left Christopher's mind since he'd seen the sanctimonious Etrian King. The unease he had felt when stabbed in the back by the Elven soldiers never did entirely leave, even when their wounds closed, the blood ceased from spilling down their backs. It was all still too strange.

He had attempted, as they walked, to speak to Dragor about it all, for it was the strong Vampire that had seen through the Elves' ruse and attempted to speak to Alinneis about his true plans, but Dragor did not wish to speak: his dark eyes were held on Alinneis's back, a large hand on the handle of his sword.

It was not until they reached a door to the back of a most ostentatious throne room, that Alinneis turned to them, his soldiers falling back to stand behind them once more. "Now," he said, placing his fingertips against one another, "Order of the *Dracon*, enter this door, traverse the steps, and see what true power is. I, myself, am eager to see it taken from beneath my feet. Maddening, it is."

Without another word Dragor stepped forward first, pushing down on the golden handle, a brilliant light blinding them the moment he pulled on it. As they raised their arms against it, Dragor managed to yell, "This isn't some trap, is it, Elf?"

"Trap?" Alinneis answered, and Christopher turned his gaze to the Elf against the light. He too stood back with his arm raised against his eyes, his high brow furrowed in bewilderment, perhaps at the question asked. "Don't be bloody ridiculous, *Vampure*! This is the power I've hoarded for your beloved Dracula for years! Now go to it and see it removed from my place of rest! It is most encumbering to reside here whilst the power of the bloody Phoenixes rumbles beneath ones feet!"

At the mention of 'Phoenixes,' Dragor had already stepped through the door, Aurora and Aleister giving each other skeptical glances before disappearing in the white light as well. Peroneous, carrying a still-unconscious Arminius, swore loudly while stepping through, and Christopher, resigned to the worst (for he had been taken from Lillith and what use was it fighting the damned medallion at his chest), followed suit.

His foot hit air and he let out a cry of alarm as he quickly recovered, finding the step below him. He proceeded like this slowly, using the stone walls on either side of him as his railings, and he only knew he would reach ground soon when the exclaims and curses of the others in front of him finally did cease.

Once he stepped onto ground, passing his boot across the floor in front of him to be quite sure, he blinked, annoyed with the continued blare of white light. It had not ceased the least as they'd descended.

"What now?" he heard Peroneus ask the room warily.

"You wait," the deep voice of Alinneis sounded from behind him. He jumped despite himself, feeling the Elf brush past him to move elsewhere, but nothing else: it seemed the soldiers had been ordered to stay above.

They waited for what seemed an eternity, the white light never dimming, never ceasing in its crazed glow, and then, quite suddenly, the wood from the bow in his hand burned hot, a heat he could earnestly feel, not unlike the medallion.

Letting out a curse and a cry, he dropped it at once, the arrows at his back beginning to burn through their casing as well. Quickly, he tore it from his back letting it fall to the floor, confusion filling his mind as the arrows clattered against the stone, able to be seen against the white. And indeed, with the others' cries he looked up, surprised to see the weapons the others wore all glowed and emanated their heat being dropped to the floor in surprise or anger, and once this was done the white light lessened considerably.

They stood in a modest stone room that resembled his tower the more he stared at it, but save a rather uncomfortable bed made with far too few feathers and hay, there were six wooden chests, lined before them on the floor, their latches closed. They were all old, their wood peeling, but they had been painted different colors, and it was a black chest to the far end of the row that held Christopher's rapt attention. It was larger than the others, and it was this one Alinneis stood beside as he surveyed them with cold eyes.

"These are your true weapons, Knights of the *Dracon*," he said, his tongue clicking against his mouth as he spoke. "All different but all serve a purpose in your service to the King of All Creatures."

No one said a word, and it was not until Peroneous dropped a suddenly frantic Arminius that anyone said anything at all, and it was Arminius to do so:

"Where the Devil are we?!"

He'd struggled out of Peroneous's grip and landed brusquely atop the floor, looking around in absolute bemusement. It was not until he eyed Alinneis that he jumped to his feet, but not before snatching his cane out of Peroneous's dark hand, and letting out a stream of curses in Alinneis's direction.

"You! How dare you show your face to me! Not after what you've done to Dracula—!"

Peroneous placed a hand on the Elf's shoulder, bringing the black gaze around to him. "Relax, Arminius. Alinneis is working with Dracula," he said, though his voice was still shaky.

"Working with—? How did we get here? What happened in Cedar Village?" Arminius asked and all stared at him with pity, sure the conversation to explain all that had transpired would be a long one.

But it surely cannot be one to have now, Christopher thought, and sure enough Alinneis waved a long arm over the chests and the black latches undid themselves, but the contents of each chest remained unseen from where they stood near the stairs. And it seemed no one desired to get too close for no one moved.

"Come Creatures, and see the true gifts of the Phoenixes," Alinneis said, and slowly, carefully, Aleister stepped forward, a resigned expression on his face and Christopher was sure he thought only of Xavier as he moved. Next was Dragor, then Aurora, then Peroneous, then Aleister, and at last he followed suit, peering over the dark Enchanter's shoulder to see what lay within the chests.

In the black one was a large crossbow, fashioned out of some sort of metal he did not recognize, though it was painted black, and parts along it shone with gold, but there was a darkness around it: it was as though it did not wish to be seen.

At once his medallion began to glow as did the others' as they looked into the other chests, each drawn, Christopher thought vaguely, to the weapons that called to them most. He did not look up to see, but brushed past them as he moved to the chest the crossbow was housed in. He reached for it without waiting for Alinneis to tell him to, and the moment his fingers graced its cold metal, his hands were shrouded in a black mist.

He shrank away in surprise, drawing the curious gazes of the others, but Alinneis merely chuckled, bringing all gazes to him. "You must be Christopher, the *Vampure* kept from all, Dracula's secret. How curious we find ourselves, Creature. You kept from the World now given freedom with Dracula's death, and I find myself and my Elves in the opposite situation."

"But you are surely free now," Aurora said, reaching a hand into her chest for her weapon, "now that Dracula is dead, I mean."

"Oh magic-wielder," Alinneis sighed, watching as Aurora surveyed her rod, no taller than her forearm, littered with glowing symbols upon its surface, symbols that glowed orange the moment her hand clasped around it, "just because the *Vampure* is dead does not mean I am free from his wrath. Though I suspect you all know what it is I speak of."

"Far too well," Peroneous said lowly, holding a tall golden staff that could not have possibly fit into the golden chest he'd pulled it from. He was surveying it intently with black eyes, the words all across its body glowing just as Aurora's did, though its words were black instead of orange.

Dragor was swinging a glowing sword made from what seemed black steel, a vicious gleam in his eyes as he did so. "I fear we will never be free from his hand," he said, never once taking his gaze off the sword.

Christopher lifted the crossbow from its place now, feeling how light it was in his arms; indeed, it should have been much heavier, much too heavy to wield. He was wondering where the arrows were to ready the thing when one appeared in the flight groove, made of the same black mist that covered his arms now, and as he thought of how strange it was that it would appear, a brilliant burst of light shone from down the row of chests.

He eyed it, just as the others did, narrowing his eyes on Aleister Delacroix, who looked quite unrecognizable now, a steady light settled around him. In his hand was the silver handle of a beautifully-crafted sword, and it too glowed just as Dragor's did though its blade was not black.

But the sword he held was not why they continued to stare, for the Vampire's scars were completely gone, and with the appearance of his clear skin, Christopher marveled at how much like Xavier Delacroix the Vampire looked. The slightly furrowed nature of his brow, the brilliance of his green eyes, even the slight disheveled elegance of his eyebrows slightly thicker than most was the same.

It made Christopher uneasy, but he was reminded that this Vampire was not Xavier when he spoke:

"What is everyone staring at?"

"Not a thing," Aurora said happily, tears leaving her eyes. She sidestepped Dragor and Peroneous with ease, throwing her arms around the Aleister's neck, standing on tiptoe, the rod all but forgotten in her grip, and she kissed him deeply, a surprised grunt leaving his throat, but he returned the gesture of affection equally, wrapping his strong hands around her waist.

All averted their gazes as the couple kissed, and Christopher was grateful when Arminius hissed into the only other chest not touched, "What am I meant to do with a bloody cloak?"

Turning his thoughts reluctantly from how Lillith's lips would feel upon his, Christopher blinked at the haggard-looking Elf. "What's that?" he asked.

"A cloak, a cloak," he repeated with all the anger of a rather old man not given his supper in a timely fashion, and he reached a slender hand into the chest and pulled out a dark purple cloak, indeed, golden words littered all across it as well, "what am I meant to do with a cloak? Being of a magical nature, wouldn't it make sense for me to wield a rod or staff like the others?" And it was to Alinneis he addressed his question.

"That cloak is not for you," the Etrian King said with all the enthusiasm of a Vampire quite satiated in a room full of humans, "it is for Nathanial Igorian Vivery. You already hold your weapon, brother."

He hissed loudly. "I am *not* your brother. And last I was aware the *Vampure* was not an official member of Order of the Dragon—he doesn't bear a medallion."

"Doesn't he?" Alinneis answered, bored-like. "Ah, I had thought he would. All the same, that cloak was meant for him. It'll allow him to use his magic unencumbered. Useful for a magic-learned Dark Creature, I imagine."

Arminius dropped the cloak, anger thick on his voice, "And about me? I'm just to hobble along behind the rest of the Order, barely able to keep up with their newfound weaponry?"

"Don't be daft, Arminius," Alinneis said as Aurora and Aleister finally dislodged, wiping their lips, "you've been holding your weapon the entire time." As all Creatures eyed him in confusion, the Elf went on. "Your cane. Look, it's already started to wake up."

And indeed the Elf's white cane was beginning to glow with similar words as Peroneous's staff, the words gold as well. And the more the Elf gripped the cane, the brighter the glow became until it was all anyone could see, and then at last it was gone and Arminius pressed his injured foot down with its full weight as though testing something he daren't put much faith in.

He smiled once his boot touched the floor, and he looked around at them, throwing the cane up in the air, catching it in the middle. "Healed," he whispered, tears leaving his eyes. "I'm bloody well healed!"

Whispers of congratulations left the other Creatures, but the joy was short-lived for Alinneis shouted, "You must leave! At once!"

"Why?" Aleister asked, sheathing his sword.

"Don't put your weapons away! Out! Have them out!" The tall Elf swept from beside the chests and moved to the stairs though he did not climb them. He pressed his ear to the wall beside them, terror flooding his long face. "By Tremor—the birds—the Phoenixes! They are on their way," he whispered, the words barely leaving his trembling lips.

Arminius was the first one to his side, the fear full in his black eyes. And Christopher remembered how scared, how angry he was when he'd appeared in the cottage yesterday. Because of the Phoenixes. "They are coming here?!"

"Yes," Alinneis hissed, "and all of you must leave! I've done my part, I daresay I don't deserve to die this day after all my time hidden from the sun!"

"But why would you die? Why would the Phoenixes harm any of us? Didn't they kill Nicholai because he broke their promise to them?" Aurora Borealis asked, securing the purple cloak within her brown satchel.

Alinneis eyed her as if she had several heads. "Don't be daft, woman! Syran is not known for his kindness—especially not toward Darker Creatures, not after it is your energy that has kept him from the Earth. No, I fear he seeks you all out—seeks out the *Dracon*— and if you all are not to his liking, I am sure he will end you all where you stand."

No one said a word as his frantic voice filled their ears.

Would they really kill us after all we've done? After all Dracula has done? Christopher wondered, securing the crossbow at his hip with the leather strap from the arrows' casing.

"So these weapons are just for show, then?" Dragor asked, anger filling his voice.

"No! But you were meant to secure them much sooner—meant to learn how to wield them—for these are the weapons of the Phoenixes themselves!" He pointed to the dark blade Dragor held. "Sword forged by Caligo Manus, Syran's right hand," he said his voice trembling. He pointed to the crossbow. "Made from the woven air of Bel, the Bird of Air and Syran's left!" He pointed a shaking finger to the sword at Aleister's waist, the rod in Aurora's hand, and the staff in Peroneous's. "Forged from Agliarept, fashioned from Adar, and created by Barbas! Now go—go—out—*out*! I have done my part, indeed! Stain my sight no more!"

And in a whirl of confusion and terror, Alinneis waved his long-fingered hands and Christopher felt himself be swept along darkness, an aching feeling to see Lillith Crane's darkened blue gaze strengthening to a roar as he went.

*   *   *

They'd moved for the better part of the day, and despite the speed of the Creatures' wings and the Dragon's, they'd reached the Hills of Etria by nightfall.

All the while, the clawing anxiety that had plagued Ewer with the sight of Syran and Caligo had not waned, indeed, it had grown. He had no better idea how he was to placate their senses, for he knew not what he would tell them, and even the slight admonishments from Vetus for a better part of the trip could not ease his frazzled mind.

Doomed, we are doomed. The Creatures surely have not been given their weapons yet—weapons they should have already had!

As he wondered exactly why he was comfortable to rest when Dracula's plans had been put into motion, a brilliant burst of light filled the dark air from the trees several miles ahead, and squinting in the dark, Evert's blue eyes saw it came from the grassy plains, the hills.

Relief dressed his large heart.

They had their weapons at last, he thought while beneath him Vetus let out a snort of black smoke in equal pleasure, yet the realization that this news would not make Syran any more satisfied sank upon him with equal fervor, and he frowned.

Eyeing the two Creatures that flew ahead of him, their wings of fire, orange and black, he focused on their skill, their standing, a shiver running through him with the thought.

If they are not pleased with the state of the World—what they have come to find—the World will surely burn.

He thought of Philistia Mastcourt, a rush of hope running through him, as the Phoenixes and Vetus began to descend.

Chapter Nine

CHURNING BLOOD

Damion allowed himself to take morbid pleasure in the sight below. The old Vampire city of Rore was still its glass enclosure, and he smiled at its never-changing nature. Though he had not walked its glass-like roads in quite some time, it reminded him of when he was a younger Vampire, when he had not been swept up in Dracula's madness. But as they passed over it, his brother's large talons digging deeper into his shoulders, though he was numb to the pain now, he turned his attention to the jagged, snow-covered mountains in the distance, his thoughts immediately turning to Dammath and if she were okay.

For he could see the spirals of fire that lit up the darkened sky, and knew they could only come from one thing. Dragons.

And not just any.

The Bagabills.

He had stayed in his home whilst the Bagabills destroyed all of London along with the Giants, his magic keeping his castle well-protected, but if Darien were taking him to their place of rest, he was not so sure he'd survive the encounter.

After all, it was known far and wide that he had taken the egg of a Reganor Dragon whilst its mother was away, daring he had been back then, all the more surprised when he had been inducted into the Vampire Order and Dracula had let him keep it, let him watch it, let it grow alongside him. And while most Dragons were weary of Vampires, despised them, even, he knew it was because Dammath had only known him that the Dragon was so complacent to his needs. And as such, she protected his home from Creatures, and himself if ever need be. Yes, she was the perfect line of defense, that Dragon, but cradling the Goblet filled to the brim with the black liquid, he was quite terrified that she would not come to his rescue this time, and indeed, perhaps never again.

* * *

Christian Delacroix bared his fangs, blood pouring past them, the anger in his eyes thick and unforgiving, but Xavier would not falter; he withdrew the sword at his waist, and how light it felt in his grip, though he knew it was not the Ascalon, long ago had he rid himself of that dull blade...

He swung, the black mist surrounding the sword lingering on the air as he spun, bringing the steel down again and again with all his might, his target always gone before the blade could strike.

The sound of the sword slicing air seemed an echo after a time of mindless spinning and slashing in the dark, and then the hand was on his chest and he opened his eyes, alarmed at the touch.

She stared down at him, concern etched into her now-brown eyes. "You were writhing in your sleep," she whispered.

He sat up at once, recognizing his surroundings with every passing blink. The dark stone of the walls gleamed in the vague lone candlelight, casting her face in greater shadow for the candle was placed on the bedside table at her back. She drew the sheets up over her chest, but even through the dark he could see the worry gleam strongly in her eyes. *Worry that I would change my mind.*

"Bad dream," he sighed, bringing her close, tendering a kiss to her forehead as they slid back into the sheets, and he could feel the smile upon her lips as she nuzzled his chest in relief.

"Another about Christian?"

The hand that had been absently stroking her hair ceased with the question, but resumed it after a time, and he knew he could never—truly—keep anything from her. How even the night at the cabin she had known it had been Christian that wished to feed..."It is like my years-long dream, yet only flashes now. He hates me in them—indeed, it feels as though he is my greatest enemy and there can be no reprieve from that. And it is always because I have done something to the woman...that Alexandria Stone."

Eleanor lifted herself up and stared at him, resting her head on her shoulder, elbow pressed into the bed. "You harm this woman in these dreams?" she asked.

He had told her of the dream he had suffered whilst knocked unconscious upon journeying for *The Immortal's Guide* many weeks ago, and she had enjoyed it greatly, indeed she seemed to know what had transpired before he'd told her. He knew she knew of the answer to her question, just wished to hear it again. Wished to hear it said that he had killed Alexandria Stone—the woman that threatened everything Eleanor was trying—nay—was succeeding in accomplishing.

He smiled with the thought as he said, "I end her life with relish." And he rose up once more to meet her lips. Kissing her softly, he pulled away but not far, nuzzling his nose against hers as he finished with, "And it is always Christian that takes her blood—it is he that gains something from her blood. He always comes back stronger... more able...far too much like..."

He lingered on the word, not desiring to say it lest he make it true or she laugh at him. Indeed, it did seem a foolish thought, that Christian, hard-headed as he was ever become like he, Xavier. After all, the Vampire survived no training, was more of a nuisance than anything to look after for all the years, and had the most astounding knack of getting the most damndest of things—emotions—tied up in places and people they didn't belong. It was how they'd been turned into Vampires at all, and, he thought with further disdain, it was why the boy had feelings for the untouchable woman. Feelings that were all the more dangerous if she ever returned them.

But wasn't she dying? And he surely wouldn't bite her, would he? Couldn't could he? That most sacred act left to the Vampire most capable of it—but Dracula was dead, so what did that mean for Alexandria?

Eleanor shifted slightly and he blinked upon her, a waiting smile upon her lips in the dark.

"Far too much like you, my love?" she whispered after a time of staring.

"Yes," he breathed, chuckling slightly at her ability to pull the truth from him, "far too much like me."

"How sure are you that this will happen?" she asked, and it was as though she addressed one of her soldiers; he could see the militant gears turning in her mind.

"What are you thinking, Eleanor?" he asked, narrowing his eyes, the smell of her blood sending him to nibble at her lip despite the change in her tone.

The smile never wavered beneath his love bite, but she pulled away, her skin now pale in the dark, her eyes red, and he remembered her whilst she walked through the Vampire City years before, clad in a dark red dress, hair up as was custom for those of title. She had held no true title, but being one of Dracula's chosen Vampires offered one all the prestige one would need to go anywhere—do just about anything—and they had. "Just that we may be able to use this—if it is true. If the woman is now a Vampire and Christian has turned her... bears the blood of Dracula in any form...he may well be next in line for the throne."

"Throne? His title means nothing, now. I have forgone the title of King of All Creatures. Surely it is void now?"

"It is not a mere title given in just word, Xavier, but passed down through magic—through blood—to ensure it is binding. Indeed, I believe a bit of the potion that gave Dracula his human form is in this transference of power. If Christian has taken the woman's blood never mind if she is alive or permanently dead, he is next in line to become King. But so are any number of pureblood Vampires still alive today."

He sat up in full with her words, not daring to believe she said them. "Is it not enough that I have made my decision? I have renounced Dracula and have chosen you—why—how should my brother be next in line to be King?"

"You needn't worry," she said, though he didn't see how that was so, "if this is indeed the case, we have Vampires here who can confirm or deny our fears, don't we? And we can move to end Christian if he does hold the power Dracula once did…but of course if you object in anyway—"

"No," he said before he could stop himself, "I don't object. Wouldn't it be saving him, if we were to end his life? He need not suffer with Dracula's voice urging him on an insane quest for objects or a cup that will turn all Vampires and Lycans human." The words traced the air with a touch of finality, a finality that scared him, but he was sure he had said them. And in the flickering dark, Eleanor's eyes had turned a misty, penetrating black that made him feel all the more unsure…but then it was gone as she ran a hand through his hair, her touch unyielding, and he remembered what he sought in her arms, and how much she held in them:

Freedom, truth, the chance to be a true King, in charge of his own destiny, not bidden to the voice of a dead Vampire, but alive with an Elite Creature by his side—a reign that proved fruitful by the respect and reverence her Creatures held in their gazes when they eyed her.

The words he had uttered so fiercely just moments ago seemed quite far away, indeed, but as she kissed him, her black mist wrapping around him as it often did when lost in their lovemaking, all grief and lingering regret faded away and the thought of killing Christian Delacroix was somehow, absolutely right.

* * *

"We cannot just stay here!" Gregor whispered harshly, but Victor waved him down.

"And what do you think she will do when she and Xavier rise from their slumber and see the majority of her Creatures gone?" he countered coldly, the stone burning in his hand; he tightened a fist around it as he had done for the past two hours.

They had met in the large hall from before, Victor able to convince Eleanor to hold off on the transformation, all the better for he to rest, and gather what little things he would, say goodbye to just being a Vampire and all that. He had found it a terribly weak excuse but she had agreed at last and gone off with Xavier in arm, surely to celebrate their many successes the only way they knew how.

Now he stared at the vast number of her Creatures that had heard he had returned and sought him out to see what they would do now, for they were all convinced if he turned into an Elite they stood no chance of getting out from under her rule. A rule that seemed to be destroying them more than anything.

They were terrified, indeed, her voice seemed to fill their minds more and more as the days went on, and their new forms made them stronger, yes, but at the cost of an increased blood lust while in Vampire form, or increased rage—to the point of mindlessness—while in Lycan, and their human forms now felt rather dull: They could no longer enjoy food or use any of their bodily functions, indeed, it was as one Elite had said, "We feel dead as humans—ghosts in flesh form."

And when he had asked if Eleanor Black had brought up any of this to them or mentioned feeling any differently or some such, another had said they hadn't been able to talk to her since the transformation, for she had been wrapped up, as he had known, in Xavier Delacroix and had not been seen since he, Victor, had returned to the tunnels.

"They will see that they have no kingdom!" Gregor went on. "They will see that we will not be used as pawns in her twisted games to be better than Dracula—a Vampire that's all but *dead and gone!* Why mangle what has been for the past few centuries?! I, for one, was quite happy as a Vampire and now I'm this—this—monster! She suckered me, as she did us all, she lied to us even, withholding this last bit of information lest we run before she could divulge it, locking us in here while blood poured from her throat making us worse. We are stronger, yes, but at what cost? Victor, I beg of you, let us leave here at once and formulate better plans!"

He had flinched at the words "Dracula" and "dead," but Gregor had not seemed to notice. Indeed tears left the gruff Creature's eyes in droves, and many in the crowd shed tears as well. Regret, terror, and grief marred all the faces that could be seen in the light of the torches, and he all at once found himself the leader of yet another group of Creatures that he felt quite incapable of leading.

How often I find myself in this role, he thought in exasperation, but aloud, as the stone burned miserably hot in his hand, he said, "I beg of you all to relax. I assure you I will not be turning into her Creature—"

"But what *will* you do?" another asked, and he found it fascinating he hesitated.

But indeed, the words would not rise to his lips, the thought would not find lease. *What will I do? Besides run from Creatures greater than I?*

The stone flared white hot for a second and he released it with a cry, feeling all eyes upon it as it rolled across the black dirt, never ceasing in its brilliant shine, and all Creatures let out murmurs of question, gasps of alarm, and a voice, one he had heard somewhere quite some time ago, filled his mind, "*Protect the Dragon.*"

"The Dragon?" someone asked, and Victor blinked in the light of the torches, realizing with a start that he had not been the only one to hear the words.

"Who's the Dragon?" another asked. "And why does it need protecting?"

"Victor?" someone asked, someone close by, but he was no longer there in the room with terribly curious Elite Creatures, no, he stood within a grand hall, the light of the stone revealing this place the more he stared.

He stepped forward on the pristine, white floor, wondering dimly if he had died permanently, gone someplace reserved for those better than he, when an impossibly tall man appeared out of nowhere, his auburn hair wavy as it fell against broad shoulders and down his back.

He had strong eyes, piercing in their gaze, and Victor was glad it was not to him the man looked. No, his blueish-black stare was placed on a letter he held in a large hand, and with a lunge of fear, Victor saw the other was held on an equally large sword at his waist, partly hidden in the many folds of his thick, long dark blue robes.

"Departed, eh?" the man whispered, a chuckle leaving him, but even with the heaviness of his voice, the sky (for Victor could see the clouds here against the endless ceiling, wherever here was) darkened from a glittering blue to a tumultuous storm with swirling clouds and jagged bolts of thunder. He crumpled the paper in his hand, bringing Victor's gaze back to him. "I better prepare the others."

And he was gone.

Victor blinked hurriedly, staring in alarm at the wide-eyed, hooded faces of the Elite Creatures, the stone no longer glowing with a white light: it was now quite dull and black against the dirt. Without thinking, he moved for it, scooping it up lest anyone else get the thought to. Placing it back into the pocket of his cloak, he straightened as best he could, staring at the Creatures, trying his best to keep a sense of calm, yet how brazen the tall man had appeared, how untouchable, and how much lesser, he Victor, felt now, against those man's eyes.

And with another cry of alarm, it came to him. *A bloody Phoenix!* And somewhere, he knew, Dracula had known that man, had seen him, and suddenly the grief that marred his heart was lesser, somehow, and the gazes of those in the large hall were brighter, or perhaps, he were seeing it all as brighter with the power he held, now.

"Creatures," he said, and all tears ceased with his words, "I hold in my possession something of great power—something greater still, than the power you all possess now, I believe, and it is this power we will use to end Eleanor Black's reign—perhaps even before Xavier becomes her Creature for good."

"But how?" Madison asked, stepping out of the crowd, her large brown eyes wet with her regret.

He stepped to her, feeling a new heat fill him, and how curious it was that it did not come from the stone, but from within him, indeed. Yet it was not until he placed a hand on her shoulder, attempting to comfort that he felt it came from the ring in his other pocket, a soothing, calming heat. At once his hand flew from her shoulder as though pushed, and it stared upon her anew, able to see the darkened energy that floated around her, around them all.

"*Protect the Dragon,*" he whispered, feeling as though he were meant to be elsewhere, protecting someone else, something else, indeed. Not here, in her halls, with her Creatures—

Gregor stepped forward as well, black eyes curious in the torchlight. "My Lord?" And Victor blinked once more, staring at the gruff Elite seriously. "You were saying you held something in your possession? Something that will help end her reign?" Gregor asked.

"I—er—yes, well," and how the words would not form correctly in his mind, how nothing made sense, nothing at all. He was supposed to stop her—and yet, he felt as though he were supposed to defend someone that was not riddled with stretching dread...

"My Lord?"

And how thickening it was now, this sense of needing to be elsewhere, doing more for the stone in his pocket, for the blood of what was not on Earth...

"Victor?"

"What do you possess?"

"Is it that stone?"

"Yes, is it that stone?"

But the words would not lift to his lips, nothing would rise but the stark realization that he needed to be with the sword—the Ares—with the King—the Dragon, for was that not right? Was that not just?

And somewhere far from where he stood, surrounded by Elite Creatures, the crowd parted and before he knew it, he stared, though somewhat blearily on a terribly curious Thomas Montague. The man looked unhinged, as though something within him threatened to eek forth, and he blinked in the light of the torches, but his brown gaze never did clear. "What was that?" he asked, voice hoarse, and all at once Victor knew the man had been crying. Again.

"What was what?" he asked, the ring still burning in his pocket.

"That voice—that light," Thomas went on, and he would not be deterred, "I felt it—heard it. Mara...what *was* that light?"

"Thomas I don't know what you're talking about—"

"DO NOT LIE TO ME! THAT LIGHT! THE VOICES! WHAT WAS IT?! I KNOW IT CAME FROM HERE—CAME FROM YOU!"

"Keep your voice down Lord Montague!" Percival began, shrugging his way past the crowd to reach the former Lycan, but he could barely move two steps before Thomas turned on him, long hair lifted from his back, a horrific snarl leaving his throat.

"Stay where you are!" he yelled. "All of you—stay where you stand! Do not interfere!" He turned back to Victor, and Victor was taken aback by the tears in the Elite Creature's eyes. "Mara—she told me there was power in the rings afforded you Vampires when Dracula was alive, but that—that was something I have never felt before. What was it? What power do you hold?!"

"I hold no power!" he roared, despite the fear in his heart; it beat a terse rhythm against his chest, and he prayed no Creature took notice. "Clearly you are addled, Thomas Montague to suggest such—"

The golden ring glowing a strong red was held up before his eyes, silencing him immediately. "This ring holds power. Whatever it is you hold, holds even more. This ring reacts to it. Have out with it, Victor. I will not be kept from my wife, again," Thomas said coldly.

He blinked in the torchlight, feeling the eyes of all upon him, watching, judging, indeed, doubting his position of leader…"I've no honest clue what you're on about, Montague, but I will not partake in it. Now if you will excuse us…" and he waved a hand to his left, gesturing in the general direction of the many tunnels, though all entrances surrounded them.

But Thomas would not move. He held ground, glaring daggers upon Victor, and Victor almost thought him to attack when the foreboding dread returned in a sickening, sudden wave.

Damn.

"What is the meaning of this gathering?" Eleanor Black's sultry voice called through the air.

Victor shook his head to rid his ears of its lingering echo, watching in disdain as the crowd reluctantly parted to allow her entrance. His brow furrowed upon her: she was alone.

"I was prepared to ask Lord Vonderheide the very same, my Queen," Thomas said smartly, smiling as Eleanor reached his side, ever-changing eyes moving to all Creatures in the room with bewilderment before turning with resolution upon Victor.

It was a gaze he found entirely uncomfortable. He felt incredibly surveyed, and beneath that gaze the ring had died with its heat and Thomas had returned his own ring to a pocket of his breeches. *What secret is that?* Victor thought when Eleanor said, "Well, Victor? Out with it. What do you have *my* Creatures here for? And in this hallowed place, no less?"

Hallowed. Ha. Aloud, he said, "We met to merely discuss Xavier, Eleanor. His place at your side…how eager we all are for him to take his rightful place, to turn."

Her gaze became red and in the light of the torches he thought he saw a flicker of the winged monster she had become, no, always was, but she opened her mouth and said, "How glad I am to hear this. And indeed, it seems fortune smiles upon me…Xavier and I were just speaking of matters that would interest you deeply, Victor. Come, walk with me." And she held out a slender hand.

He felt Gregor's fear-filled gaze heavy upon him but didn't dare turn to greet it. *It's all going to hell!* With all eyes upon him, including a still-fuming Thomas, Victor reached out and took her hand, remembering for a brief moment when he had first touched it like this, when she had been just a Vampire, welcomed into the Vampire City by himself and Dracula. *Dracula.*

With the thought of the Vampire, he almost pried his hand from hers, but her grip was strong despite the frailness of her fingers, and she led him, as the others watched, solemnly, past them all, back the way she and Thomas had come.

He looked back only when they left the torch-lit hall, the back of Thomas Montague quickly swallowed by the crowd as they gathered together once more, sure to regroup, to rethink, to do their best to escape her hand.

But he found himself gripping it still as she led him down the darkened corridors, not a word leaving her lips, and he almost found it eerie that she would not speak, would not look to him at all, but pull him along into darker parts of the tunnels he had never been before.

Yes, the ground they traversed now was riddled with mud, the stone walls wet with perspiration, and he imagined it was hot here, but if it was he could not feel it. The only heat he could feel blared from a stone and a ring and both were decidedly cold and dull within the pockets of his cloak.

He thought hopelessly how, if possible, he was to escape her grip, leave the caves and search for what still burned in his scared, beating heart, the image of the tall man flashing in his mind. *A bloody Phoenix.* The fear reclaimed him anew, and he snarled involuntarily as Eleanor took the Vampire form: her hand was suddenly cold. Yet it was not until they reached a painfully narrow, lower tunnel that she whirled to him at all, waving a hand as she did so.

He felt the wall at his back and felt immensely closed off, and with the red-eyed Vampire glaring him straight in his eyes now in the close space, quite vulnerable. It was all he could do to keep from shaking. His hands now free, for she had released his as she turned to him, he placed them in the pockets of his cloak, willing either object to flare to life, to protect him from her dread, from what she would do next. For he had some idea.

There was a battered old door just behind her, here. Its wood was peeling, damaged from the water that dripped incessantly against the ground, why the door looked as though it was barely holding up on its hinges, and as he swallowed, he was aware a great menacing wave of dread came from the cracks in the door, the slits the ill-shape afforded it, and a greater fear claimed him, still.

"*Victor*," she breathed, and her voice was heady, calling, and try as he might resist it, he found it impossible all the same. Soon, he was speaking:

"Yes, my Queen?"

"*Alexandria Stone. Is she a Vampire?*"

"Yes, my Queen."

"*Who turned her?*"

"Christian Delacroix, surprisingly."

"*And is he different? Is he like Xavier in any way?*"

"He can walk in the sun sans ring—holds the authoritative tone that made his darling brother famous, of course."

Somewhere in the saner parts of his grief-stricken mind, Victor Vonderheide watched her lips move, he heard himself speaking, but he could not stop what he said. And then she was snarling, and somewhere in his mind, dimmed to be sure, he thought she would bite him…turn him into one of her Creatures, for isn't that how it was done? But she reached out for an arm, swung him forward, and barreled him against the old door which gave way as soon as he pressed against its deteriorating wood. And as it fell, splintering against the cold, black floor, he blinked in the brazen wind that filled the endless space where a room should have been.

Slowly, he rose to his feet, hands pressed against the outside of his pockets, ensuring he had not lost either trinket in his fall. He breathed a sigh of relief, but it quickly turned to terror as she stepped in, the wood from the door rising from the floor to reform itself in the doorway behind her, and with a start, he realized where exactly he was and why exactly it terrified him so.

She was changing now, no longer pale of skin, but gray, long, leathery wings extending from her back, her face elongated, her chin sharp and pointed, ears stretching up and outward like an Elf's, and her teeth were all fangs, sharp within her large mouth.

She stepped toward him on large, webbed claws, and he pressed back, agreeing with Gregor's words. *Monstrous, indeed.*

And in the face of what she was, what she desired to make him, all he could manage to whisper was, "No," the fear of becoming, truly, what they all were, what they sought so desperately to escape was insurmountable now, and with some wild last hope as it reached out a terribly large clawed hand toward him, he thought only of Dracula.

He pressed against something soft just then, and turning quickly, he eyed the Vampire whose long white hair was billowing about his head, but his brown eyes were soft as they gazed straight ahead. And he smiled, much to Victor's bemusement. "Dracula?" he dared whisper, only tearing his gaze from the very solid Vampire before him to eye the coming Creature.

She had stopped with Dracula's appearance, an angry screech leaving her lips, but she did not step forward.

Dracula would not take his eyes from her, and Victor's brow furrowed with question despite the racing of his heart, from fear, joy, whatever. *Even now, at my darkest hour, he would still ignore me!* And with the thought, Dracula's brown eyes found his own and the gasp left Victor's lips.

"What do you wish to do, Victor?" he asked and Victor felt his knees shake with the voice.

He blinked in the wind, doing his best to focus on what the Vampire was saying. "What do you mean?"

"What do you wish to do?" Dracula repeated. "I cannot hold her off for very long. You have entered a page of *The Immortal's Guide*, do you wish to use it to aid the World or will you become her Creature? Either way, your journey through this room must end with a choice made, and blood taken."

"Blood taken?" he repeated, unsure. He looked from Dracula, to Eleanor and back. "I have to drink blood? Her blood?" He grimaced with the thought.

"Hurry, Victor," Dracula said, and the edges of the Great Vampire were beginning to fade as though he were disappearing slowly, becoming one with the wind. "Search for what is lost, but make your choice all the same. Become like her, or stay mine."

"But I'm dying!" he shouted before he could stop himself. "I shed tears—my heart beats! I don't stand a chance as a Vampire—I won't be one for much longer!"

He was fading faster, his outline gone, now. Only the trails of his cloak were solid, but his brown eyes were still penetrating as he stared at Victor in what seemed amusement. "You need not die if you would protect the King—get the Goblet to him, allow him to drink," he said, and he seemed so confident, Victor blinked and he faded more—*at this rate he will be gone for good*. And then...

He cast a glance to the still-waiting Eleanor-Creature, brow furrowed in disgust. *Not if I can help it*, he thought, knowing some things were a fate worse than death. To what was left of his Creator, he said, "But Xavier is here—with her!"

He spoke to air. Dracula was gone, and in his absence, Eleanor, tall and monstrous, charged.

Chapter Ten

DEADLY TRAINING

He wiped the blood from his lips as Alexandria's red light warmed around him and the sword, and then he was moving on air again, the Ares wet with blood, his own and Westley's. He reached the dark Vampire before long, prepared to bring the sword down, but he felt the change in the air before he saw it.

Westley was gone from before him, and with the slight tug of the red light at his boots, he knew the Vampire was behind him, near Alexandria. He whirled in mid-air, the cry strangled in his throat, for Westley had the sword's point at her neck, and Christian realized the reason the dark Vampire had gotten so close was because she had been too busy protecting he, Christian, as Westley attacked.

We've been too careless, he thought harshly, moving on the air to reach Westley before he could do anything more, *she's been focusing on me, always on me, when it is she that needs the most protection. They will always go after her. Always!*

The dark Vampire turned as Christian moved, his red eyes sparking with pride.

"Finally, Delacroix," he said, dropping the sword, "you understand."

Christian stopped, still hovering above ground, but he kept the sword pointed at Westley's broad back. "I don't understand why you did not just tell me this, Mister Rivers," he said, Alexandria's shoulders sagging slightly now free from Westley's sword.

"But I did," he said, of all things a smile lifting his lips, "I told you that you are tied to her, Christian, and as such you must protect her, but she must protect you. You place too much on defending her before anything can befall her but she has been harmed before and she will be harmed further still. You cannot stop all these occurrences, but you can better prepare for them. You are not just Vampire and charge, but something more, and seeing you both in action, I see it is something that can no longer be denied."

The words washed over him, their implication quite lost to his frazzled mind: he still thought on her, indeed he still watched her over Westley's head, her strong gaze meeting his with that familiar steel, that unwavering focus. *Even facing death she was stoic*, he thought.

"Well what is it, Westley?" he asked after a time of waiting, bringing his gaze reluctantly from her (for he thought he saw a message in her eyes, words she wished to spill on sparse air, but he dismissed it at once for what could she want to say?), the sword not leaving his hand.

Westley's mouth twitched, but he stepped away from Alexandria, turning fully. A stronger wind pressed against the stone walls as the dark Vampire left the ground, moving, Christian realized with a start, to hover just as he did: Christian now stared the dark Vampire in his black eyes. "The path you were destined to take," Westley said, and his voice was grave with an importance all but he seemed to know.

"What path, Vampire?" he said with a snarl, but a steady fear rose with the impatience that was beginning to grow; he dreaded what he would hear for a reason he could not name, Alexandria's gaze all but gone from his mind.

"You, Christian Delacroix, were chosen to wield that sword—"

"I know that!" he said before he could stop himself, the fear insurmountable now. Something was coming he did not desire to hear. "Dracula—"

"Desired you take Xavier's place if ever he failed to lead, and he has."

He merely stared as the words pounded against his ears. And what he had known, perhaps had always known had trailed on the air in this bloodied dungeon and what did it mean? What did *that* mean? That Xavier had failed? As far as he was aware, his brother had moved with the others for the Goblet. So what was this? He had *failed*?

"*What?*" The whisper was soft, but it was not his own. He glanced behind Westley to eye Alexandria through his bewilderment once more, and her red light was still blaring, but softer than before. "Christian to lead *what?*"

Westley turned to her, giving a shocked Christian full view of his black shoulder-length hair. "To lead the entire Dark World…as King, of course."

King.

The word was foreign to his ears, at least in the blood-stained room with a dark-skinned Vampire highly-skilled in battle, and a Vampire with terrifying power that stunned him into feelings most deep when he least expected it. It was…odd.

Strange.

But there was that feeling of somehow having always known it would come to this—but that was not true, no, no, he had never known his brother would fail. The Vampire that had looked upon him far too many a time with hatred, the Vampire that had said time and time again he should stay away from Alexandria Stone, that she was not to be courted, that he, Christian, would not be the one to bite her, to turn to her…

The sword pulsed in his hand as if in response.

No I cannot hate my brother, I could never—

He is lost.

He blinked in her red light. *Dracula?*

The sword pulsed once more. *Lost.*

Alexandria, he thought frantically, *Alexandria can you hear this?*

But only silence returned to him. Silence and greater fear.

He opened his mouth, his tongue feeling like lead between his lips. "But…isn't Xavier—what's happened to Xavier?"

The red gaze was back upon him. "I do not feel he is best for what must happen, Christian."

There was the dread again. "What must happen?" he asked, his voice a whisper.

"Simply," he said, sheathing the sword at last, dripping with blood as it was, "you must drink from the Goblet. End all of this madness." He pointed a finger toward the door. "Stop that beast within our walls from continuing to turn. Allow we wretched Creatures to live as humans."

"But my brother—" *Is lost.*

"Is not here, nor has he been! We are running out of time—no, we have no time! The Phoenixes are here on the Earth and there is no King on the throne. There is no Dragon on the seat! It must be you!"

And before he could say a word, Westley was surrounded in a plume of massive, green flame and Christian felt the Ares grow hot in his hand. He moved away from the fire that engulfed Westley, now, expecting a cry of pain to fill the room, but Westley did not burn yet he seemed tormented all the same: his mouth opened in agony, but his eyes closed, and it was a long while before he said anything at all, and when he did it was: *"I will prepare for your arrival, my Lord! I will prepare! The others are already in motion!"* And the moment his lips closed, the flames dispersed, and Christian blinked in astonishment upon the dark-skinned Vampire whose eyes were open, the irises a bold golden color in the torchlight and Alexandria's luminous red light.

"We have less time than I thought," Westley said, golden eyes appearing to glow.

Christian blinked in wonder upon him, not understanding any of it. Not *wanting* to understand. Though he knew he did. Knew it perfectly well although he did not *wish* to. "What must happen?" he asked again, for it was the only thing he could manage to do as the sword in his hand continued to grow hot.

Westley landed at his feet, and Christian followed suit, staring as the Vampire now glared past Alexandria, toward the door.

"Westley?" he asked, the sword beginning to pulse beneath its heat.

"The Ball is in two days' time, you two," Westley said after a painfully long time, Alexandria all but forgotten to him, it seemed. "You must be ready to face the Phoenixes, to hold the mantle of King before then." And then he was walking to the door, all manner of rips Christian had managed to cause in his clothes forgotten completely: He no longer limped, but moved with purpose.

"Westley," Christian said, unsure just what more he could ask him. He knew it all, knew it well, though he wished it were not true. Not true at all. Xavier could not be lost, he could not be King, and he, Christian, could not face these Phoenixes, whatever they were. He was just…he was quite…he felt rather small, then, incapable of holding the sword despite the blood that flowed through his veins. How the blood had invigorated him, yes, allowed him to walk in the sun sans ring, but it was not enough. No, he was certain one needed more than special blood to be King of All Dark Creatures, and he was just Xavier's brother, the roughshod, foulmouthed, bloodthirsty Vampire all knew and all rightfully despised. He was no King.

The door had opened and closed with a resounding echo Christian found harrowing. His mouth closed abruptly, and he stared at the old wood, blinking in the light of the torches, brow furrowed with a question he could not speak just yet.

It was not until he felt the hand on his shoulder that he turned to eye her, her brown-green gaze strong. "Christian," she whispered, but she said nothing more, and he could see the confusion burning in her own gaze.

"K-King," he breathed at last, finding lease to speak with her touch, her stare, "did he mean what he said? That I…? But Xavier— what's happened to my brother? Why can he not lead?"

"Westley knows better than I, Christian," she said, and whatever happiness he felt at hearing her say his first name with such softness was dimmed in the madness that filled his mind, now.

"But does he? Can you not feel my brother? Sense the truth of the situation?" he asked desperately, remembering when she was able to tell that Xavier had not been harmed when Victor had pulled them into a trap.

Her furrowed brow would not straighten and a flair of fear filled him more. "I cannot sense him, I can sense no one," she said after a time, "but perhaps Westley is not certain himself, after all he did say he did not feel it would be best to have Xavier lead. Whatever he knows that we do not, it is clear he is tied to these Phoenixes—that fire, what he said…"

"Yes, it is unnerving," he agreed, remembering the golden glare Westley had bade him. "If what he said is true, we don't have any time at all. The Phoenixes are on the Earth…wouldn't they come after Xavier if that were true? Is that why you cannot sense him? Why he feels Xavier cannot be saved?"

Her silence told him all he knew but did not wish to admit. That she had very little idea what was true as he did. And then he countered the confusion with another question, "Did you hear Dracula's words?"

"Dracula's what?"

"His words? He spoke to me while Westley did. Told me that Xavier is lost—"

"Then that settles it, doesn't it?"

"Settles what?"

"Xavier. That Xavier is lost…perhaps to Eleanor Black? That he cannot lead the Dark World?"

"But that's—Xavier wouldn't…" Yet the words failed him as they journeyed through his mind. The Vampire had not been right since Dracula's death, this Christian had been able to see clearly though he did not wish to admit it. Of course, things were made infinitely worse with Eleanor Black's crushing dread everywhere they dared turn.

A look of sympathy crossed her face. "If—and it's quite a large if, Christian—Xavier is lost to her, we can get him back," she said softly.

He stared at her, watching the way her lips moved as she spoke, the way her brow furrowed slightly with her words, watched her red eyes search his face for any sign of ease. Somehow, he smiled, though it was small, able to see, for the first time since Westley opened his mouth, that things would be sorted. He would not be King and Xavier would not be lost to anyone or anything. Yes, they would see to it…

"It is a wonder how quickly you are able to ease me of my doubts, Miss Stone."

"Alexandria," she reminded him, slipping an arm around his own, beginning to steer him toward the closed door. "Now, we need to freshen up, don't we, my Lord? I've a date with a prince of some foreign Vampire country today."

"A date?" he asked, not even capable of feeling jealousy: by the slight curl of her lips, he could tell she was doing his best to keep his mind off all that just transpired. "How'd you manage that? We've only been here two days."

As she pushed open the door, ignoring the tattered folds of her skirts, she said, "Unlike some people I am quite able to make friends wherever I go."

"Is that so?"

Her gaze darkened noticeably in the dimmer torchlight in the vacant hallway, the scent of all their blood lost with the door's closing, and he knew she remembered some unbidden time from her past.

"It is what one learns when they are a pariah to the court, Lord Delacroix," she said, and she flashed him a dazzling smile, continuing to pull him along the hallway toward the more active parts of the mansion. "Though I suspect you are no stranger to loneliness."

"Quite right," he said, a slight snarl escaping his throat as he thought on the memory, quite enjoying the feel of her pulling him along with surprising strength, "I was banned from court after my third year of attendance. We'd been freshly turned, Xavier and I, and though I hadn't known it at the time, our queen was a Vampire. She didn't like the young maidens of title showing up dead year after year. None left for her, after all."

"That was you?" she asked, brown-green eyes wide now, and the chatter from the rest of the manor became louder the more they walked. "I remember the scandal at all the women being found drained of their blood. I'd attended sparsely after that. I was in such a state; I was delirious when they found me. Couldn't get two words out of me, and I was sent back to the country to live with grandmother for a bit."

He stopped dead causing her to jerk slightly as she stopped as well. Her stare was quite curious, but he merely let out a harsh laugh. "That was *you*? I caught sight of you as they hauled you off in that carriage with the roses painted on the side. Bloody hell, small world, isn't it, Miss Stone?"

"The smallest, Lord Delacroix," she said, replacing her arm through his, though she did not lead as they continued their walk: he was quite comfortable to match her stride, feeling immensely at ease, now. He did not even notice the sword burning with a vast heat in its home at his side.

Chapter Eleven

AN EXCHANGE

Victor dodged her large claw, the dread around him suffocating despite his attempts to not breathe it in: it entered his nose and clogged his veins with far too great an ease.

He rolled along the dirt, feeling the air change: she was pressing forward again, yet another claw outstretched to swipe at his head—

The stone burned madly in his pocket, and he felt the heat rise, covering him entirely, and as he knelt on the dirt, he looked up at her silver talons—they crashed against an invisible wall, and he felt the heat flare the greatest at his nose where her claw struck.

He blinked as she flew back, a horrible screech leaving her throat with her pain, and her wings folded brusquely beneath her as she slid against the dirt.

He rose to stand, feeling the heat rise to his head within him, warming his blood, filling his mind with its fire. He thought of Dracula again, and stared around, expecting the Vampire to appear once more but Eleanor rose to her large clawed feet and let out a roar. She lifted from the ground, stumbling slightly as her long limbs fought to hold up her large yet slender frame and her wings flapped hard at her back as she roared again, pushing off the dirt, headed straight for him.

Fear. He expected fear. That was why he did not fight it when it danced in his blood, sending its coldness to flush to a freeze. The warmth he could feel, aside from the rapid pounding of his heart, was what came from the stone and ring.

She barreled into him with blinding speed; he was thrown off his feet, the blaring heat from the stone and the ring covering his front where she had struck his shoulder and blew her away once more. He braced himself against the dirt, stumbling slightly as he gained his footing, once again watching her struggle to large silver-clawed feet looking all the more weakened.

He knew it would not end, her constant barrages. He had no idea how long it had been since they had entered the room, nor did he care, he merely wished, desperately, for it to be over—

"*Protect yourself,*" the whisper sounded from the air around him.

He gasped as the stone flared far too strongly, burning a red hole through his cloak. He could barely eye it before Eleanor was upon him, pressing him to the ground, her entirely black eyes wide as her many fangs gleamed against the dark. Her breath was hot against his face, and for a brief moment, he was alarmed that he could feel the heat at all...

He wrapped his hands around her large throat, doing his best to push her long mouth away from his face, thick beads of saliva dripping onto his cheek as he turned his face against the dirt. "Is this... my...choice, Eleanor?" he managed to whisper between involuntarily snarls, still feeling the heat from her breath and the heat from the stone that had rolled away along the dirt.

Why can I feel her breath? he managed to wonder beneath her loud growls, and just as this thought reached him, he felt his strength go, his hands around her throat loosen their grip, though he strained, pressing harder, doing all he could to keep her sharp teeth from reaching his skin—

His strength left him entirely in the next moment, and she pressed down, her large claws on his shoulders breaking the bone, and with his cry of anguish she pressed down harder: He felt his spine blindingly snap clear in half down his back before all went blissfully black.

* * *

Eleanor stared down at the creature below her with little comprehension. His mouth lay slack, his tongue hanging limply out the side of his mouth, his violet eyes dull in the darkness that surrounded them. Slowly, she slid off his broken body and stood, bruises beginning to form along his face, which was no longer pale, some human part of her noticed, but held slight rosiness, though that was quickly fading as death, permanent death, filled him.

Rage, the nameless rage filled her, but in this form it was all she could feel regardless. She knew, vaguely, what waited for her when she released it, for the grief was beginning to fill her large, black heart, but as best she could stomp it down, it grew.

With a sound half-sob half-sigh, she regretfully released the form that so filled her mind with the darkest thoughts, and stared, with Vampire eyes (for she couldn't bear to be in the room in any other form, indeed) upon the utterly dead Vampire—no, *human*—that lay on the ground before her bare feet.

Victor, she thought, the tears that wished to fall staunchly pressed back by the coldness of her blood, *you damned fool*.

She would not have attacked him had he willingly given himself over, but no, he was never going to join her, she knew it. No more than three seconds into the room and he'd called for Dracula. Readily. Eagerly.

Weakling.

Eleanor Black crossed her bare arms beneath her breasts, staring at the unnatural way his chest and torso pressed upwards in the middle signifying the breaking of his spine she had known she caused. Her fingers twitched against her skin but she dared not stare down at them in horror or disbelief. She knew what she had done, would own up to it readily, never mind if the bloody Vampire had trained her, had watched over her, had cared for her like a daughter...

Never mind if he had been the most beloved Vampire in the Vampire City those many years before.

Never mind if he had been the strongest, most resilient Vampire she had ever known.

Until Xavier showed up at Dracula's door.

Yes, Victor had been formidable, a pillar of strength for the remaining Vampires in the World, back when it needed him.

But when it didn't…

She closed her eyes, remembering how scared he had been when she'd come for him in the Vampire City that night, how vulnerable…

He had become a shell of himself, a lesser Vampire with Dracula's death. She had hoped she could convince him to be more, to join her, but with his constant refusal, she knew it would never come to pass. He was far too tied to Dracula to let anyone else take the Vampire's place.

And how he had suffered for it.

"By Tremor, may you rest well, my old friend," she whispered, the words barely leaving her lips in the cold wind that filled the endless place, had filled it since her transformation to Vampire.

With a needless sigh, she knelt at his boots, caked with dirt as they were, no longer able to smell his blood, how rich and powerful it had been, and touched them. The dirt clung to her fingers as she trailed the ends of it, and she thought of the Goblet and where it was now, what would have happened if Victor had been brave enough to take her blood while she remained in her Elite form. Would he immediately look as she did, or would he struggle with the transformation to Lycan?

A wistful smile falling upon her lips, she stood, pressing the dirt into the pads of her fingers.

Her grief fled her presently as she turned her thoughts to the Vampire that waited for her in her bedroom, how she had waited for him to finally be there, be here, in this place she had called home for quite some time. And now he was.

And though Victor would not join their family, it was just as well, she thought, she already had Thomas Montague to deal with, and that was enough in itself: the bloody Creature was becoming a nuisance. She felt it only a matter of time before she give the order to end the Creature's life, and she found it suitable that Xavier be the one to do it.

Letting her hair fly out behind her, she stepped for the door that had reappeared some time she did not know, and the unnatural blackness of the room fled as she walked to reveal a rundown cabin, the wooden boards that made up its floor and shoddy walls peeling. Placing a hand on the handle of door, she pulled it open, thinking only of falling into the arms of the Vampire she loved, eager to tell him what information Victor had imparted before his death, that Christian had indeed turned Alexandria Stone, that he, indeed had to be felled. That he, Xavier, would need to end his life.

But Xavier would need to become an Elite before he would have the strength needed to end the life of one with that woman's blood.

She shivered as she closed the door behind her, remembering how Aciel and Amentias had gone crazy when they held the Ares, driven to madness by Alexandria's blood, Dracula's blood.

It was all she could do to retain a solemn face as she stepped along the muddied ground, the mud squishing between her toes as she stepped for her room and the Vampire that awaited her.

* * *

They'd landed where the light was strongest, Vetus resting roughly atop the grass. Evert slid from her back, doing his best to slow his beating heart.

He had seen them, standing in a line before the trees, their new weapons held uncertainly in their hands as they had neared, and now up close he could see the Creatures were trembling with equal fear.

Syran and Caligo had landed some time before and illuminated the dark with their burning wings, their heads turned toward the line of Creatures. Evert figured they were appraising the Knights of the Order, and it was a long while before Syran said, "Creatures of this... World...as I understand it you have been slow to move for your better gain these long years. What I wish to know," he paused, "is why? Why have you stilled in moving as you should, knowing it would spell your end?"

All the Creatures had stilled in their shifting with his words, bidden, it seemed, to listen. *Of course they would*, Evert thought with a small grin, remembering the Creature's rousing speeches, *once Syran spoke, it was all that mattered.*

Syran spread his arms wide, waiting. "Well Dark Creatures? What say you?"

No one stepped forward for quite some time, but it was Aleister to move at last, his glowing sword held tight in a hand. "We were...

held back...by my son...Xavier, Xavier Delacroix," he said, voice shaking, and Evert noticed the many scars that had littered his face had disappeared completely. *How much like his son he looked.*

"Held back?" Syran whispered, and Evert thought it a strange sound, Syran whispering. It was rarely done. "How can the...Vampire, as you Creatures call them, hold you all back from doing your duties? From seeing him to the Goblet?" His tone darkening the more he questioned them.

Aleister's shoulders sagged under the weight of the questions, the accusations thrown their way, and Evert knew their incompetence thus far was weighing heavy on the Vampire's dead heart. *He's not happy*, Evert thought, *he'll kill them.*

He had just stepped a foot forward when Dragor stepped beside Aleister, his sword's blade black, glowing with a powerful light as well, illuminating the small space between the Phoenixes and the Order. "Xavier Delacroix has been corrupted, Phoenix," Dragor said coldly, and Caligo roared much like a Dragon would when prepared to strike: The sound pressed against Evert's eardrums with ferocity, making his ears ring. Dragor flinched, recognizing his error. "Er... your...Holiness?" he added softly, uncertainly, the words etched into the black blade glowing their golden hues.

Syran's arms folded across his naked chest. "How has the chosen King for you Creatures been corrupted?"

Evert could feel the burgeoning anger in the Head Phoenix settle beneath the Creature's skin, licking through his pores just as his winged flames did. The flames Evert and his brothers had forfeited many ages before.

"Eleanor Black," Christopher said, at his hip a large black and gold crossbow. He did not step out of line with the others but remained near the woman Enchanter, his black eyes held on the dark-skinned Phoenix with grand unease.

"Who?" Syran asked.

"My sister," Christopher said, turning his gaze to the light-skinned Phoenix now. He blinked, adjusting to Syran's brilliance for a moment, before he went on. "She's become something more than Vampire or Lycan...your Holiness."

"And who let this happen?" Syran asked, and Evert could hear the confusion on his voice.

Peroneous Doe stepped out of the line next, bringing all gazes to him. He shrank slightly under the attention, but said, "Dracula. She… uncovered his secrets. Journeyed through *The Immortal's Guide*, became…a hybrid Dark Creature."

Caligo let out an animalistic sound, but Evert could not place its meaning. "It seems the *Dracon* is not the only resourceful Creature on the Earth," he said, his voice deep, mangled as though he spoke through a heavily scarred throat.

Syran ignored this. Instead, he kept his stare on the line of Creatures. "The…thickness of the air, is that her doing?"

They nodded as one, Arminius the Elf the only one not saying a word or showing he cared to join the discussion: he remained staring at the grass beneath his feet.

"And where," Syran went on, shifting a bare foot atop the bloodied grass, "is this Eleanor Black?"

"We do not know," Peroneous said.

"But Xavier has her, yes?"

"We believe so."

He scoffed, then. "Do those medallions do nothing but sit against your chests looking pretty, Creatures?" And at their confused gazes, he undid an arm from its fold and pressed a hand toward them, palm flat against the air.

At once a golden light swirled through the darkness and struck all of their medallions, Evert's included, with its light, brightening them so that the field and trees around them were lit up in a brilliant golden glow.

"That is much better," Syran said after a time of blinding gold filled Evert's vision; he could see nothing beyond it, indeed. "Now, put the beacons to good use and lead me to this Eleanor Black, allow me to see the woman that has outsmarted the Dark Creature I once believed to hold the greatest brilliance of his kind."

And without another word the line of Creatures moved forward, marching past a curious Syran, and even through the still blaring light of their medallions, Evert could see the amusement on his handsome face. *Why, he thought this all a joke*, Evert realized with a start, but then he remembered the hard glare Syran had bidden Tremor when it was revealed that the latter would not be returning to the Nest. It was then that Evert reminded himself it would not be best to underestimate the ferocity with which the Head Phoenix worked. Amused face or no, there was a power within his hand to fell the world several times over, this Evert knew well.

It was why he did his best to temper his shaking hands as he lifted himself atop Vetus once more, and guided her into the sky, slowly following the Creatures on foot south of the Etrian Hills, Syran included.

Chapter Twelve

BAGABILLS

Evian Cross ran a hand through his long black hair, his thoughts once more on Nathanial Vivery and if the Vampire had succeeded in journeying to Lane with Philistia Mastcourt. It was strange that he had not heard from them in the three days that had passed since she'd sent word through way of spell, outlining her fears that they would not be able to stop Equis Equinox.

But Equis was dead, he knew. Everyone knew.

So what kept them from reaching Lane?

He stared around at the remaining rubble of the buildings not yet recovered from the attack by a Giant and Dragons many weeks before. It felt like ages, to him.

Even with magic restored to them in its full power it did not make the clean up any easier. And the Queen, grief-stricken as she was, for both her husband and oldest daughter had died in the attack on London and the Vampire City, seldom left her mansion since then.

It is a quandary we face, he thought, standing from his chair. The observatory where he stood was vacant save his thoughts, all other

Enchanters gone to their homes or rooms created in the building. *The Enchanters Guild of Lane no more.*

The smile lifted his lips but it was quickly dispersed as he stepped past the remaining armchairs, facing the large circle in the center toward the large doorway leading to the room where many of the Head Enchanters of various other Guilds and Wings would meet.

They had not met regularly since the attack, and, he also knew, because there was simply no reason to: Magic had returned to those capable of wielding it. There was no need to discuss the Vampires' and Lycans' hold over their hearts, no need to discuss how best to keep their power down, lest they call the wrath of the very Creatures they were bidden to aid.

All to protect the World.

He scoffed with the thought. *Yet here we are. Scared, despite our prowess returned to us.*

He shook his head, returning his thoughts once more to where Nathanial was, recalling the time he had aided the Vampire in Dracula's training room in studying the maddening ways of magic and spells. A time he had thought amusing. For what Vampire would ever need to learn magic?

He had known then that Dracula had been pushed to fulfill his duties to the Phoenixes, so what could Nathanial accomplish with magic?

Yet once he had learned that Dracula desired the Vampire another tool to keep the beasts at bay, Evian had relaxed slightly. Only slightly.

There was still the ever-present Phoenix fyre burning in his blood, the mark of his task to see Syran's will be done.

Oh, how I've failed, he thought with a sigh.

Somewhere above him a door opened and footsteps trailed overhead. Another door opened and closed and he released a breath.

"For we do the work of the Phoenixes," he whispered after waiting moments longer for anymore sounds above or below to trill through the air.

The fyre engulfed him in the next second, a chaotic heat of black and vibrant blue flame. It stretched across his arms as he extended them straight ahead, swallowing the scream that pressed against his throat, desiring a release.

The heat was immense yes, though he knew he was not burning, was not dying. He was simply being…called.

Tuning into the part of his brain that held the connection to the Nest, he breathed out slowly, letting the fire spread from his lips and lick the air in front of his face, and then he stood in the large golden hall, the sky around him no longer bright and sunlight-filled but dark and thick with dark clouds.

Before him stood a vast number of men and women, large swords, bows, and staffs in their strong hands. They talked amongst themselves, not able to see him yet at all, but he knew they would, and soon.

And surely enough, a terribly tall man with auburn hair down to the middle of his back and numerous daggers across his chest, two long swords at his hips, and a long golden staff in a thick, large hand, stared at him, his dark blue eyes piercing in the dark of the sky.

"Evian Crossus," this man said, his voice deep and thick with impenetrable power, bringing all gazes to it, "nice of you to pay attention to the messages received."

"It…is hard to ignore them," he said, "when they fill our very bodies. What is the matter, Bel?"

Bel smiled, though through his beard it looked cold. "Syran appears to have gone bottom side. He left a letter. He expects retaliation, as I understand it."

"Oh." The word left his lips in a breath, fear collecting in his gut in a steady swirl, no magic able to stamp it down. "And…when will you move?"

"A day should be enough to figure out his location. Caligo's… nature suppresses my brother's light at times," he said, passing the long staff from one large hand to another, though it wasn't thoughtful. The action was quite practiced, and he looked prepared to use it at any moment.

Evian nodded, wishing to be free from the many beautiful men and women's pressing, curious gazes. Their wings were not drawn here, thankfully, but they were all dressed for war: various indiscernible fabrics and metals were draped across their shoulders or secured to their chests, abdomens, and legs, keeping the more vulnerable parts of their sculpted bodies safe from attack. *War isn't necessary*, he thought with a frown. "Well," he managed to say after a time of meeting their gazes, "if I am no longer needed…"

"Oh?" Bel asked, and in two large steps, he'd crossed the vast space between them and stood just before Evian, his glare down at him commanding: Evian felt immensely small, as he should. He hardly reached the man's abdomen. "Leaving so soon, Crossus?"

"I just thought—"

"You forget who you represent when you walk on the dirt?" And the deep voice was no longer any shade of pleasant. It had turned terribly cold, a vicious indignation tainting the words but Evian daren't look up to meet the gaze any longer: it was all he could do to remain upright, indeed. "You wear those robes because we granted you the privilege to do it! We trusted you select…beings with the honor of bearing our flame! Do not *think*, human, and do not talk back to the beings quite capable of destroying all you have built down there," and he felt the heat from the man's breath as Bel bent low to an ear, "with a flick of our fingers."

He could not speak, nor could he bring breath to his lips: all around him burned, though he was not aware of any flame pressing against his skin. It took him far too long to realize it was unadulterated fear he felt, raw and true, as he stood in a room with a god, hundreds of them, and they threatened to end him and the rest of the World unless he moved as he was bidden.

He swallowed the saliva that had collected in his mouth as the man had spoken, and whispered the words, "Y-Yes, o-of course, my Lord, yes—of course. Whatever you need from myself, from the others…it will be done."

"Yes," Bel said, "it will. The others have been called. They are preparing for our arrival. You, Evian Crossus, are the last to let us in. It makes me wonder if you fear your place at our side."

He said nothing, only wishing he was back in his body in Lane, free from the large Creature and free to sort through his scattered thoughts, but there he remained, stuck in the dark-filled air, standing on gold.

Another stepped forward before Bel could say anything more, and it was to this woman everyone's attention turned. Her long blonde hair cascaded down her back, a wavy waterfall, and in the darkness, her blue eyes shined with power, but it was soft, softer than Bel's at any rate. She wore full armor, white along her body, a white thin cape of what looked to be silk flowing behind her as she moved, pressing a slender, bare hand to Bel's shoulder.

"Father," she said, her voice soft, but still ferocious: Evian had the thought she commanded many armies with ease, "what will we use this one for?" And Evian noticed in her other hand was a long sword, the handle and hilt golden, the design of a Phoenix marking where the blade began.

Bel smiled at his daughter, and this smile was kind. "The one known as Philistia Mastcourt moves for him. When she arrives they, together, will move for the place called Shadowhall. Westley Rivers has already moved to secure the Vampire City, as I understand it."

"Shadowhall?" he said, unable to still his confusion. "Why would we move there? Lane has all the tools necessary—"

"Darker magic is needed to quell what has befallen the World. There is one in Shadowhall that will aid you," Bel said, his eyes once more their concentrated gaze, gone from his daughter. "He will aid you where the others will deny you."

"Deny? Why would those in Shadowhall deny—?"

"The World is not the same, Evian."

"I was aware of that when Equis was killed."

"Caligo is my brother's sword. He did what was just. Equis was *greedy*. He had to be put down."

"But he is your family—"

"Again he goes to profess what he does not understand!" The slight hint of humor that had filled his voice was gone. "Get to Shadowhall with the other one, and once you obtain the spells you need, the potions, the herbs, join Westley in the Vampire City. And when we arrive...be prepared to defend us, Crossus."

"Defend—?"

The sky began to swirl with greater darkness and he blinked, staring once more at the stuffy observatory room, surrounded by worn armchairs, though he was no longer alone.

Several Enchanters stood around him, their hands intertwined with one another, their gazes black as they eyed him.

At once, embarrassment flooded what little had remained of his fear when he'd opened his eyes: he had been standing in the center of the room, quite aflame, possibly whispering to himself for…how long had it been?

There were no windows to aid him in his guess, so he turned to Ronaldo, one of the many Enchanters he'd studied with centuries before. "What's the time?"

"Almost daybreak," he said, black mustache bristling as he spoke. He detached himself from the circle of Enchanters and moved to a glowing glass ball atop a circular stand on a low table to the back of the room. Books were littered throughout, in corners, atop chairs, on their shelves and atop bookcases, and it was to these the others moved readily busying themselves, though they still listened, Evian knew.

He stepped to Ronaldo, eager to know how long he and the others had known. The question needn't leave his lips, for Ronaldo said, "We noticed it about a decade ago. The fire about your person. We started the protective circle once we realized who it was you conversed with."

The crystal ball glowed with a purple light and in its depths, he was able to see the wings of fire, the Dragon, and the Ancient Elder that road atop its back.

"And you're…at ease with this?" he asked, hardly daring to believe the others could so readily welcome the fact that their own had been working with the Phoenixes of the Nest.

"Well we pieced it together quite some time before. When you were tasked with aiding Dracula on that Vampire-Enchanter…thing, we knew something was up. It wasn't until you refused to sleep in your home when it was still up that we realized something more was at work."

"I see."

Pages were rustled behind him but he did not turn to look. He'd spent so long watching over Nathanial, nurturing him, protecting him, doing Dracula's bidding, and therefore the Phoenixes' that he did not spare a thought to the others and if they'd notice his prolonged absences at all.

"Don't fret, old friend," Ronaldo said, still staring into the crystal ball, watching the Dragon fly leisurely over trees somewhere to the south, "your secret is safe with us."

For the first time since opening his eyes, he looked out at the room where the others poured over their books. They were all looking at him with slight smiles, a few of them he recognized, others still he had never worked with before but had seen around the building. A tall man with a long, sharp nose who stood at a bookcase pretending to peruse its contents winked at him as footsteps sounded from above.

Ronaldo placed a strong hand on his shoulder, bringing his gaze back around. "Don't worry, Evian," he said as others filed down the stairs, smiling upon him and the others in greeting, while wiping the sleep from their eyes, "we will keep your secret."

*   *   *

Damion grunted as his feet hit ground, the shock from such a fall sending waves through his knees. Looking up, he stared at his brother: The Creature's long wings beat the air, though he hovered, looking—Damion guessed—thoughtfully toward the high mountains they had reached.

He could already hear the Dragons' massive footfalls higher up on another ledge; the one he had landed on was just small enough to hold him. It was still some ways up the mountain, the white snow pressing against him and the hard rock. "You drop me *here*, brother?!" he shouted up at the black-eyed Creature who continued to stare at the mountain seeing things he could not.

Darien snarled then, before pressing downward extending two large clawed hands to Damion's shoulders, pulling him upward with hard sweeps of his wings, until Damion could see the top.

There were scattered caves here and there, terribly large, solid against the swirling snow, and within these caves were the Bagabill Dragons, large Dragons with white glittering scales, red eyes, and silver talons. Their horns curled in spirals high above their heads, silver as well, and they spoke amongst one another through the mind as Dragons did when no other Creatures were present to be spoken to, he knew.

He pressed the Goblet to his chest, mind thick with just why he was there at all when Darien released him. A cry of alarm left his lips as he fell through the air, landing roughly atop the snow, teetering on the balls of his feet, the snow high and thick, burying him at the waist. The Goblet was still in a hand, and checking it was secure, he looked up again, seeing through the brightening sky his brother stretch a black arm straight ahead, a black talon pointed toward the caves.

Damion understood, or he thought he did. The Dragons were guardians, whatever they guarded was what he needed to get to. Remembering the way his brother had led him to the Goblet, he figured this new thing was just as important, perhaps it was Xavier Delacroix, himself, though looking at the black smoke that left the mouths of caves, he could not see how that was possible. The Vampire wouldn't be at the other side of Bagabills, no matter the reason.

And yet...

Darien still had a sharp talon extended toward the Dragons.

Gritting his teeth, Damion trudged onward, the snow forgiving as he moved. Fluffs of power flew into his face as he moved, the wind torrential, here. Stifling curses, fear swirling in his gut as he stepped closer to the nearest cave, he wondered again what remained beyond the mountain and just why his brother had dropped him here.

Looking up into the morning sky, he searched for the darkened figure, a shadow against the sun, but nothing was there. Marveling at how inane it all was, dropping him somewhere, leaving him to his own devices, and in front of Dragons, no less, he continued his trek, almost to the mouth of the first cave, now. Its white rock was indeed snow pressed against translucent, thick ice, and he wondered who had created it—for it seemed man-made more than anything—when a plume of black smoke drifted from the high opening and he froze.

The snow shook around him as the Dragon stepped out of the shadow, massive, its long thickly scaled snout appearing in the sun first, and then Damion saw its eyes, gold in the sunlight, and it spoke:

"I knew I smelled," it snorted more black smoke from the slits at the end of its snout, "an intruder."

Its voice was old, thick with the rumbling of fire as Damion knew a Dragon to hold. This close, he smelled the familiar charcoal, smoke, and blood emanating from the Dragon's mouth, its words roaring through his ears as though the Dragon had not whispered but yelled them.

He bowed, not gazing the Dragon in the face any longer, the Goblet at his knees in his hand. He stared at the black blood as he said to the snow, "Haunting eternal on the sands of the forgotten place. My greetings to you, Belinbol."

"The forgotten place is lost to us, now, strange Vampire," Belinbol said, shifting his wide legs as they were buried in the powdery snow. "Why do you trespass on my ground?"

He looked up, never releasing his back from its forward bend. The Dragon was staring down at him, and through the strands of his black hair, Damion could see Belinbol was surveying him steadily.

Chancing himself, he responded with, "This Vampire...desires passage." He stilled his tongue as thought overtook him: He had no true idea why he was here, and indeed, what could the Bagabills guard that was not the carefully hidden gold buried deep in the tombs of long dead pharaohs?

Belinbol bristled, stepping out of the cave by half, his long wings pressed against his long, large back, glittering in the sunlight just as his long, curving silver horns did. With this sight, Damion knew he spoke to this clan's leader: their horns were always the largest if they held any at all. It was with a shaking breath, the blood in his veins growing colder the more he stood before the Dragon, that he said, "I, Damion Nicodemeus desire passage through your mountains, Belinbol."

"Yes," the Dragon said, his voice somehow colder, "you have said. Yet why, strange Vampire, is what I wish to know."

"Why?" The Goblet fell in his hand drawing the golden eyes to it.

"What is that?"

"A goblet."

"A *goblet*? Do not take me for a foolish lower-*bred* Creature, Damion," the large mouth said, the long sharp teeth shining in the light as he spoke.

Fear pressed against Damion's throat, silencing the words that threatened to rise: that he was not capable of keeping Dracula's secrets, that he was no match for the true power the special blood gave to those that wielded it. Confusion gripping him beneath the Dragon's stare with the odd questions it spurred, he rethought his words quickly. "It is but a mere cup," he said with conviction, despite the smell of the blood wafting up through the snow-filled wind. He cringed: it smelled of strange death, not one he was accustomed to. It was far too unnatural, that smell; it bothered him immensely. Pressing it from his mind as the Dragon stepped from the cave's mouth to fully emerge in the light, pushing him back against the snow, he felt the fear return. *He knows something,* he thought with cold awareness, judging the Dragon's piercing stare.

Indeed, Belinbol had never removed his gaze from him. He'd stretched his massive wings once free from the cave, casting a shadow over Damion and the snow in turn, snorting a plume of black smoke directly into Damion's face.

Damion did not inhale.

"Vampire," he said, and Damion smelled the burning blood that boiled in the Dragon's throat, prepared to be blown out. Damion braced himself, wishing deeply that Dammath was near to aid him. "Vampire, you must rethink what you have been given. You have been blessed, but it is not being recognized for what it is."

Silence passed across the snow as Damion stared up at the Creature that knew more than he, indeed. Yes, he could see it clear in the golden eyes.

And then the Dragon said the words he had been dreading to hear:

"We will guard the Goblet of Existence, Damion Nicodemeus, for the Creature who must drink from it is lost. The black blood is sign of this enough." And he bowed his head low, eyes closing as the bottom of his mouth pressed against the snow, clinging to it.

And Damion understood.

In the world of Dragons, no matter the breed, a lowered head and closed eyes was a sign of peace.

The fear fled promptly, replacing it even more confusion.

As he hesitated, hip deep in the snow, unsure if he should move forward, he lifted the Goblet in his hand, staring once more at the black blood. No sound emanated from its murky depths, and indeed he realized he could not hear the voices that, he was surprised to learn, had become a source of reassurance for him in such a short time. Indeed, the pressing silence, the howl of the icy wind made him feel quite alone.

"Am I not the one that must aid Xavier Delacroix? Am I not the one meant to save the World?" he asked, yet not loud enough to be heard past the howling wind which blew up his hair and made his clothes press against his skin.

Belinbol lifted his head, opening his eyes. "Xavier Delacroix is lost, dark Vampire," he said, and the words reached Damion's ears as entirely strange. "Your part has been done. Now press forward, to the other side of the mountain, and put the Goblet in its place."

"It's place?" he whispered dully, feeling all at once an emptiness pervade him, and it was as though Alexandria Stone's blood, given to him but days before, was being used up by something other than his own body, and he felt remarkably weak.

Belinbol did not seem to see this: he turned with a wave of his long sharp tail, fitted at the end with a silver tip, and began to march past his cave, toward, Damion saw, many more caves that jutted out the mountain's top like stones embedded in a road. "Come Vampire," Belinbol's voice carried back to where he stood, holding the Goblet limply at his side, "we must empower the Goblet which has been tainted. Make it pure once more."

Not understanding a word of it, cursing himself for listening to Dracula at all, for what had it gotten him? Tied up even further in his mess, chased by Etrian Elves, bandied about the Dark World by Darien...

He stifled the sigh of frustration that arose, remembering Darien when he was a normal Vampire, wondering just where the Vampire-turned-monster was, and why on Earth Darien continued to drop him places that only seemed to further the mess he found himself in.

Chapter Thirteen

THE BASE OF THE MOUNTAIN

Philistia pressed a hand to Nathanial's cold cheek, willing him to open his sharp, gray eyes. And still, they would not.

Sighing, for she knew she could not wait any longer, for the sun had risen in the swirling sky, she stood from beside the bed and turned to the others that stood, some bent double, in the low, small bedroom.

"We must leave for Lane at once," she said, remembering Bel's raucous words to her the night before.

"But what about Mister Vivery?" Aciel asked. He, like the others, had ventured upstairs once day broke to watch her attempt to use all sorts of magic to attempt to rouse the Vampire, but nothing, much to their disappointment, had worked.

She looked down at him, feeling all the more despondent. It was her fault, she knew, that he ended up the way he did, blasted with an unnatural spell Xavier couldn't have possibly learned anywhere but Shadowhall, or from a Creature that knew of Shadowhall's spells…

Rubbing away the goosebumps that had appeared beneath the sleeves of her robes, she turned from the others, no longer wishing to gaze upon their fearful faces, their bemused brows. The feeling that she was not as formidable as they seemed to think she was because of her former station beside Equis burned hot in her cheeks. She felt foolish all the more because she had truly believed Xavier Delacroix could be saved, could be redeemed, but Bel's words pounded against her skull, the memory not at all easy to replace:

"*Xavier Delacroix has fallen. The Creatures below need to name a new King, need to prepare the Goblet, lest Syran realize this and unleash his fyre upon the World.*"

"Madame Mastcourt," Lillith Crane said uncertainly, pulling her from scary thoughts. She turned to eye the blonde Vampire who was sandwiched in-between the Caddenhall twins on the other side of the room, her white bow in her hand. "Darien is near Lane."

"*What?*" she breathed, the image of Bel's dark blue eyes quickly overshadowed by Lillith's blazing bright ones. She turned in full to eye the Vampire, so young in face but old in heart. "What do you mean?"

"I can feel him. He is near Lane...somewhere south of it, I believe. He is...eager...for something to happen, I imagine."

Philistia narrowed her eyes. "Miss Crane, you sound as if you are tied to the Creature."

Her uncertainty fled as she said, "I am. When I gave him my blood...I believe he became my charge. I can feel his desires...as animalistic as they are. Once he moves from there, he will venture to a dark place...a terribly dark place. I don't know where it is, but many have died there."

"What does he wish from such a place, Lillith?" she asked.

The blonde brow furrowed in question. "It is hard...to make out," and her hand tightened around the wood of her bow. "But he goes there to gather someone, it is someone with great power but it has been tainted, darkened even more than what Darien now is."

Philistia eyed the others in the room, seeing their gazes light up with recognition just as hers did. "Xavier Delacroix," she said at last, turning her gaze once more to Nathanial, old sheets tucked beneath his arms, red hair pressed to the back of his neck, longer still than it'd been when she'd first laid eyes on him. "He must be moving for Xavier—that place...it must be Eleanor Black's place of rest." She pulled her gaze from Nathanial to eye Lillith once more. "I can only imagine he goes to gather Xavier."

"But what for?" Aciel asked from behind Yaddley. He was hidden by the latter Vampire's tall frame.

"No idea," she said, eyeing Lillith, willing her to say any more.

But she did not, instead, she lifted her bow, tightening her fist around it, and Philistia saw the cracks in the wood the fist caused.

She is angry, she realized.

Without another word, Lillith pushed past Minerva and stepped from the room, her footsteps light despite the quickness with which she moved, and as she rounded the door and began her descent down the old stairs, Philistia saw a flash of red in the Vampire's eyes before she was gone.

Who on Earth bade the girl such a miserable life? Philistia wondered as the others began, steadily, to follow in Lillith's footsteps, leaving the room as well.

She recalled the gaze the quiet Vampire Christopher Black bade Lillith every so often, and how his gaze would linger upon the young Vampire as though pained...

Madness, she thought, blinking in the light of the empty room. The window opposite the bed was unblocked now, the sun shining against the old floorboards and the bed the Vampire lay in. His hand that was not covered by the dirty sleeve of his shirt began to steam, the smell of burning flesh reaching her nose with ease. With a gasp of fright, she waved a hand, sending the light to retreat back against the floorboards where it did not touch the bed.

She stared down at the unconscious Vampire, willing him to rise, remembering his fortitude in sparring with her, in facing Equis alone, the gleam of confusion, of anger in his eyes with the realization that magic, something he had come to rely on, had been taken from him.

She knelt at the side of the bed, clasping a hand in her own, the feel of his cold skin unnerving her: it was as if he were truly dead.

He had the wherewithal, the tenacity, and the power to overcome it all, she knew it, could feel it in his blood. It was why she had believed he would be the one to stop Equis from his ultimate ruling, but the man was dead, and with this gaping hole left in the World, what need was there for Nathanial Igorian Vivery, the first of the Vampire-Enchanter project?

And with these thoughts, the reality hit her with a crushing blow: Equis Equinox was dead.

Thousands of years of magic twisting and expanding through the minds of magically-embedded humans was gone. And Elven magic had the freedom to reign now, but the Earth was no longer pliable, no longer lenient to the Elven touch. Their magic would take and draw and suck from the Earth until there was nothing left.

She gripped Nathanial's hand harder, feeling the Vampire's blood pulse beneath his skin, but the tears fled her eyes, hot and unyielding: all she had lost, all she had fought for—everything she had done to reach her place at Equis's side was gone, and she, bidden to the Phoenixes' hand, had no other recourse but to obey. For the skies were open to them once more, and when they came in full, she knew the World would burn, for it was nothing—*nothing*—like it was before, and that would be their downfall, that would be the reason they would all die.

* * *

Lore had not let up in his run once the free from the blood-filled woods, and in his journeying, he could feel the beating heart of James, the only remaining Lycan left in the World.

A growl leaving his lips, he pressed forward harder, leaving great cracks in the earth beneath his paws.

* * *

She felt the change in the air, but did not take her gaze from Dracula, for the Vampire was staring at the impossibly tall mountain, hesitating, as though he weren't sure he could survive the climb.

The sensation grew even more, and she recognized it as Christian at last...his presence: he was close...he sought her. Yes, she could feel his blood pull her, call her, and she turned from Dracula reluctantly, facing the trees and the ocean beyond...

With a needless breath, she opened her eyes, blinking in the torchlight around the walls, a brighter place she remained in now than where she had just been, lost to her dreams, no, Dracula's memory…

She felt a pressure in the large bed beside her and turned her head, eyes widening at the sight of him beside her, fast asleep atop the comforting sheets. His black hair was pressed behind his head against one of the soft pillows he had managed to wrangle from beneath one of her arms while she'd slept.

The call of his blood had lessened; indeed, it was as though his blood hadn't pulled to hers at all, and in her confusion, the myriad questions teeming in her mind, she pulled the sheets up, covering her chest. "Christian," she breathed, "why are you in my bed?"

He did not stir. Indeed, he seemed quite deceased.

How on Earth can he sleep? she wondered in something like anger now, frustrated he had woken her from Dracula's memory. The Vampire had seemed quite distraught, had ventured through the Merpeople-infested waters, through the unforgiving trees, and toward the lone mountain as though bidden to do it. But before she could understand just what that mountain was, Christian's blood had filled her nose, had distracted her, permeated her every sense, and she'd desired nothing more than to see him. With a snarl, she maneuvered out of the sheets and bracing herself with her hands pressed into the bed, she turned her feet to his side and pushed.

With a cry, he rolled off the bed, his eyes red with his alarm, but she could sense he would not harm her.

He landed upon the floor with a loud thud, a snarl leaving his lips as he jumped to his feet immediately, a brazen wind blowing the soft pink canopy curtains away from their white posts. He stared down at her in bemusement, his brow furrowed, lips curled in a snarl. "What is the meaning of this, woman?"

She'd crossed her legs the moment he'd reached the floor and smiled coyly despite being taken from her grandfather and what he'd tried to show her in her dream. Christian was suddenly much more appealing: He wore no shirt upon his chest, revealing the muscular frame always hidden, at least to her, beneath crisp buttoned up shirts, suit jackets, and thick cloaks. She could not help but stare as she said, a slight smile replacing the snarl now, "What on Earth do you expect a woman to do upon finding a strange man taking residence in her bed?"

"I am no strange man," he said, running a hand exasperatedly through his unbound hair. "I merely sought refuge."

When she lifted a brow in question, he went on, "I took up training with Mister Rivers earlier this morning to better...aid you. The bloody Vampire worked me to the bone. I'm exhausted—I haven't even had blood to sustain me. I merely found the nearest room and—"

"The nearest room just happened to be mine, Mister Delacroix?" she wondered aloud, the smile unable to leave her lips now. Through the curtain's part, he looked downright desirable, his hair wild and strewn across his bare shoulders, his red eyes glaring down upon her but with no false anger now, but something else she had recognized in his gaze for weeks.

His voice lowered as he sank onto the bed, pressing a hand atop her leg, moving it aside, "As it always seems to be."

The touch sent a brazen spark through her blood, banishing all thought of Dracula, of where he'd stood: It was unlike anything she'd ever felt before. And she'd been touched by Vampires previously, indeed; her date after their impromptu training had ended had been lackluster at best. The Vampire had gone for a kiss and she'd relented, remembering how dull it was, their fangs all but getting in the way: his tongue had proceeded to lick against them as though he desired the taste of his own blood, for every sharp cut made his blood would spill and he would suck it up in his frenzy.

It had not helped that he had been one for dull conversation as well. He had only preened on about her beauty and his own, referring to his home somewhere farther up north, and how he had only attended the Winter Ball this year because he desired to meet other 'rare' beauties he had not been privy to in his homeland.

She found herself rolling her eyes, ultimately desiring the company of Christian so that they could share more stories of their pasts as she had enjoyed it immensely once they'd left the training room. She had not expected him to appear in her bed, nonetheless, and however secretly she was thrilled he did, she had no intention of letting him know this: she wasn't quite sure what she felt about him, besides the fact that she was beginning to enjoy his company.

"I was pulled to your blood," he admitted staring at her with much more tenderness than she ever thought him to hold. He sat up against the pillows, turned slightly so that he stared at her in full. "With my lack of sustenance, my exertion, my mind sought out the blood I have come accustomed to tasting when near death."

"As you always seem to be," she said dryly, finding it difficult to keep herself pressed against her own pillows. She desired nothing more, suddenly, than to feel his lips against her own, but how brazen the thought was, no matter if she had thought it many a time before...

His gaze roved across her body and she was reminded of when it pressed into her back in that cozy office and she'd felt the strongest desire to remove her clothes—

Ah. So that was *him.*

She'd had the thought that it could have been him inspiring that desire, but she'd dismissed it outright. It was not until she'd pressed her red light around him, protecting him, feeling his desire to protect her in the training room that she'd understood the connection they shared.

"Something interest you, Christian?" she asked, knowing full-well what he wished.

He sighed, but not before licking his lips sending a thrill of cold heat through her. She was surprised at how much yearning he elicited from her, indeed, she remembered the way his gaze was held on her when she'd awoken as a Vampire. *Even then*, she realized with a start, *he wanted me. And not just for my blood or what I could do, surely*, she thought, recognizing the heady gaze his red eyes held.

"Many things interest me, Alexandria," he said lowly, as though the words were a struggle to leave his lips. His stare was pressed to where the chemise dipped at her chest, revealing the tops of her breasts.

"Like my blood," she said, still smiling.

He blinked, his gaze moving to her eyes. She had not known when her own gaze had reddened, everything was a reddish hue, indeed, and she could see the weakness that permeated his blood, a neediness, and yes, she could feel it now—he *did* need her blood.

Without another word, she sat up in the bed, pressing a fingernail to her wrist. Steadily she pressed down, watching her blood appear atop her skin. "Quickly," she said, looking up at him, "before it heals."

His gaze was transfixed on the blood, so much so, he did not seem to realize he reached out a hand for her wrist while saying, "Alexandria...I couldn't." Yet he'd pulled her wrist to his lips all the same and opened his mouth.

As his tongue licked against the blood, she felt a flicker of unadulterated pleasure course through her, swirling between her legs. Unable to do anything more, she caught his gaze as he sucked in full now, and she could see it plain in his eyes: Lust. Need. Indeed, there was no flicker of care in that gaze, the tenderness all but gone, now. He was unguarded, feral, needing, and her blood was the antidote to his disease.

He released her wrist with a deep sigh, and she reclaimed it, pressing a hand to where he had sucked as it healed. She could no longer reach his gaze, the feeling of shame replacing whatever desire had coursed through her so readily. *He wanted nothing more than my blood*, she reminded herself, feeling immensely foolish at his side, now.

"Alexandria," he said, his voice uncertain in the room.

She turned from him more, swinging her legs off the bed, and when the fingers grazed a shoulder, she stood, the shame growing. *He only desired my blood, only wished for my blood, it was why he found himself in my bed; he did not want me—not at all—*

"Alexandria," he said again, and despite herself she eyed him. He was staring at her from the same position, his eyes still red, but wide as though he could see into her very soul, what remained of it, anyway. "You are troubled."

"I," she said, turning from him again, "am merely reminded of what is...right. I am Dracula's granddaughter—this existence I lead was never mine to misuse."

"Misuse?" his voice was incredulous but she did not turn to eye him this time.

"Yes, misuse," she clarified, unable to keep the venom out of her voice. "I cannot get...sidetracked by—by—"

"By what?"

She stared, frustration fueling her more than anything else she felt at the moment. "By you and your...desires, Christian."

His eyes widened in disbelief and he stood from the bed as well, pushing the curtains aside to better eye her across the ruffled sheets, his eyes black in the torchlight. "I cannot help my feelings for you, Miss Stone," he said coolly, and she blinked, unsure if she were seeing him correctly.

"You mean you cannot help what Dracula desires you do for me. You cannot help what you are *compelled* to do, by his blood coursing through your veins—and when you hold the sword," she corrected.

He shook his head fretfully, and it was as though he was attempting to shake off miserable thoughts. The shaking tousled his once pristinely-kept hair even more so that several black strands shook across his chest and her gaze moved there. She swallowed.

"I cannot help what I feel for you," he clarified. "And if it is because of my turning you or what, it has only grown with your Vampire state. I want you...I want all of you. I want—no, *need*—to know all I can about you. Not because Westley told me to, and most certainly not because Dracula's voice screams in my mind demanding I protect you. I want to know you because you intrigue me—you came back for me, *me*, a bloody outsider to his own kind; you did not leave me to die in the sun like so many a human or hell even another Vampire would have done.

"You showed me a kindness only my brother has ever shown me, and you have helped me remember that humans are more than blood and flesh, that they have lives, have fears, and to play off them, use them, kill them as I once did for my selfish gain was more destructive than anything I've ever done as a human boy."

She merely stared, his own gaze so earnest, so raw, so true she could not find the words to doubt him, but the wall in her heart was thicker than his monologue, made colder by her current state, and she snarled despite wanting to jump across the bed straight into his arms.

A foolish thought.

"Pretty words meant to placate shall not get the better of me, Vampire," she said, remembering in full—because she needed to, lest she forget herself completely and fall into his well-toned arms—the sight of Dracula standing at the base of a mountain that held great importance for him, for them all. "You helped make me this...thing because Dracula desired it. I cannot allow myself to get...thrown in with your...needs. You don't need me," she said, the words pouring from her before she could stop them, the anger at Dracula, at her mother, at her grandmother filling her cold heart forming an invisible dagger she wished to place into Christian's heart for furthering their plans, "you need to do your duty. It is why I was taken from my home, bandied about this World with you at my back—to do what Dracula desired be done. And with the state of the World, Christian, we cannot allow ourselves to get...sidetracked by any erroneous desires we may believe we feel. We cannot...we can't—all the men in my life were turned into Vampires before I could get to know their full names... Dracula has stained my life in more ways than I can even remember, and even with the memories as they return, I cannot find one instance of my life where he was not present."

She crossed her arms under her breasts, silently daring him to look there. He did not, much to her surprise: his gaze was held, austerely, on her own. "Now," she went on, slightly miffed that he did not eye her, desire her as she did him, "if Westley Rivers says we must train to defend the World—protect it—that is what we must do."

His stare was incredulous. "But you went on a date with that duke—"

"A mistake," she countered simply, "won't happen again."

An eyebrow rose, but she thought she saw a twitch of his lips. "You asked me to the Winter Ball—" he tried again.

"Under the pretense that you would protect me. What sense would it make if you and the Ares were not by my side able to defend me should I need it?"

"You don't *need* defending!" he said cruelly, the snarl vicious as it left his lips, stunning her into silence. "Your bloody red light can reduce *all* to ash if you so desire it, Alexandria! What game do you mean to play with my heart? You joke with me last night, tell me of a shared past, you console me when I learn that it is my duty to replace my brother as King of All Dark Creatures, and you give me the slightest hope that—that there can be something between us. Something more than just Dracula standing in the middle!"

He truly believed it, she thought with a start, releasing her arms. The urge to press herself against his bare chest was insurmountable now, for she knew, somewhere deep in her mind that she wanted Christian in the same way he wanted her—needed him, even, but it would not do to give in to that urge, she knew.

Dracula is the only reason we are bound to each other, she reminded herself hastily, looking around the room, looking anywhere but his pained gaze. *There was no point in feeding into these urges that were just that, urges. I'm a woman, he's a man, throw in the art of blood, the nature of a Vampire, and there was bound to be some attraction. But that was all it was, indeed, all it could ever be.*

"I'm sorry, Christian," she said at last, returning her gaze to his. His stare was heavy, barreling into her with great pain, pain she could feel in her cold heart. She almost let out a cry it was so strong she felt her dead heart squeezed as though gripped by a Lycan's claws, but the words left her lips all the same, and the moment she said them, she wished she could put them back: "There cannot be anything more between us."

He grew still as though he'd slammed into a wall, and she thought, for the briefest of moments that tears would flood his black eyes, but he merely nodded once, then again, and again, as though repeating the words to himself, drilling in their meaning.

"I see," he whispered at last. "Well, my Lady...my Queen...my," and he paused on the word, eyeing her coldly, "*charge,* I shall not let my...need of your *blood* get in the way of my place at your side. I will merely...defend you as best I can. Nothing more. Forgive me... for ever...wishing—forgive me for ever thinking..." But his voice trailed, the vast pain that ripped at his throat causing his words to dip and rise, his breaths needless and quick. And before she could say a word to him, he'd bowed, a hand over his heart, and stepped from the room, blowing the torches out in turn.

She stood in the dark, a hand over her own heart, a hand clawing at her chemise, feeling the most painful need to sob but it was as though her mind, colder with her dead state, would not allow her the pleasure. With him gone, the coldness of the room was suffocating where before it did not encroach upon her blood like an unwanted worm. Tearing at her chemise, she was aware a grand sensation of anger flooded her veins, burning white hot beneath her skin, and suddenly she smelled Christian's blood as though he still stood before her, the snarl at the flare of desire the smell caused leaving her lips harshly.

She glared around at the corners of the modest room, only able to see Christian's eyes, his smile, taste his blood on her tongue when he'd fed her upon her awakening as though it happened again—

The gray statue of a woman with long hair and sharp ears atop her bedside table caught her eye, and she glared at it for a moment, not understanding why anyone in the Vampire City would have a statue of an Elf near their bed. The anger flared with greater tenacity in her veins, and with a vicious snarl she lifted it from its place and felt it fly from her fingers, through the pink curtains, watching it crash against the floor, just feet from where he'd just stood. The cold, gray stone splintered across the smooth marble floor, a chunk of the woman's head sliding to the wall where it cracked in two.

She stared at it, an odd sensation of grief flooding her core, the anger, the flashes of Christian fading fast. "I'm," she stammered to the pink curtains that still billowed in the cold wind she'd conjured in her anger, "I'm...dead—a Vampire..." *And I need him.*

She could not deny it, now, no matter what she'd said. She regretted it even more, the words that had fled her lips. She had seen the pain she'd caused in him, how it had struck him to his core, and she thought of calling him back when the coldness of his gaze returned to her in a harsh wave. And she remembered when that gaze would find her, cold and calculating, when she was alive, and how she'd wished it would go away. And yes, she felt that same desire now, that it would fade, but it was for an entirely different reason.

She desired his cold stare gone from his countenance when he eyed her now, but she knew it would be a long time—if ever—before she was granted the softer gaze he had bade her whilst here.

"I'm dead and he's the only thing I have," she admitted aloud. And saying it to the room, the pink curtains, the torchlight made it real. She'd had no one else since journeying to London to meet the lie that was Count Dracula, save Dracula's presence in dreams and visions, but it was not the same as a reassuring hand on a shoulder or a kiss planted on unsuspecting lips...

"What the Devil is wrong with me?" she asked the room, knowing she had seen his truth in his gaze and she had broken it without a second thought. Pushed away the only person she had that wished to aid her, never mind the confliction of feelings she felt toward him; he was constant, unlike the others...

"You are troubled," the voice said from the doorway, "by your new state."

"Westley," she breathed, collecting herself, hiding her thin chemise beneath a, perhaps, even thinner slip of curtain. "You surprised me."

She watched him step into the room, and beyond the flickering orange light she could see his once-black eyes were now a light brown, lighter than his skin. His lips curled up in a knowing smile. His black shoulder-length hair was swept back against his face, and he wore the clothes of a soldier, waistcoat black, still with splatters of dried blood, and he had his only dark hand on the handle of his sword, snug at his waist.

He stepped to a dark armoire to the back of the room and opened it, sorting through the slips, the colorful dresses, and the matching whale-bone bodices that hung within its dark wood.

It was then, mind clearer with the smell of Westley's blood, that she realized she must have stayed in a guest room for one of the many royal dignitaries that roamed through the mansion. She looked back over at the broken statue of the Elven women against the floor, wondering if an Elf had ever laid their head here when Westley's voice rang right next to an ear, "For you, Miss Stone."

Draped over his arm was a brilliant red slip, day dress, black bodice, and many black and red skirts she was to place atop a wire bustle. It hung, she saw, glancing briefly over his shoulder, against the wall near the armoire, near a painting of a very beautiful woman with pale blonde hair in a hold high atop her head, and piercing, but somehow kind orange eyes. The tips of her ears, Alexandria saw, were pointed.

Blinking back upon Westley, she took the garments, laying them out on the bed, mind still fresh on Christian's words: *"I will merely... defend you as best I can. Nothing more..."* To the Gods, he hated me, she thought with a fresh realization, and pressing her hands into the silk of the red slip, she wondered just how she could correct what she had done. She had not meant to anger him, further, his declaration merely…frightened her, is all. It was the last thing she'd expected. The last thing she'd ever expect from anyone, let alone him.

She felt the eyes burrowing into her back and remembered where she was, the desire to be near Christian subsiding into a miniscule ebb, but still, as it ever was, there. Straightening, she turned to Westley, no longer hiding herself behind a flimsy curtain, and said, remembering herself, "Was there something you wished to discuss, Mister Ri—?"

He'd lifted the sword from its sheath before she could see it and sent it straight into her abdomen, the cold from the blade unforgiving, somehow colder than the air against her skin, and she could feel her blood seep past its coldness, pooling around his hand as he drove the sword to the hilt, pushing a quiet scream out from the depths of her throat.

He'd stepped to her between all of this, and in the proximity of their closeness, she could smell the fire on his clothes, in his hair, the thick smoke akin to a burning building on his skin. She felt stuck, forbidden movement at all, and bending double despite the closeness of him, she rested her forehead against his shoulder, lifting a hand to his other, determined to push him away: the anger burning in what blood remained within her veins. But much to her surprise, she found she was quite unable to do much of anything at all; she felt entirely drained of power, indeed.

Cursing her distracted mind, cursing her inability to smell the strange fire, and yes, the strange blood that filled Westley's skin, she snarled, her head still against his shoulder, as, with a start, she realized she could not move.

Christian, she thought frantically, her vision beginning to blacken, *Christian—help.*

Yet what met her was silence—a pressing, resolute, silence.

Has he cut all connection to me? she wondered, a panic clouding her mind that had already begun to soften to a satisfying dullness… *Is that possible? Can he disconnect from me? Aren't we connected through the blood?*

Blood.

Mine is leaving me, she realized with a horrified groan, and still Westley would not move an inch, would not release the sword, would not move his shoulder so that she slumped all the way forward, no, he remained resolute, and she almost thought him a statue of smoke and faint fire, when he was suddenly lit up with flame, and she was as well.

What in the World? she thought as the sword was released at last and she fell to her knees, aflame in the blue fire, yet not burning.

He was looking down at her, his expression apologetic as the orange torchlight flickered against the electric blue flames, and then he whispered, his sword pointed toward the floor, partly clean as it'd slid through her in its exit, *"May we do the work of the Phoenixes."*

And Alexandria could see no more.

* * *

Reject me?! Reject—*me!* he thought, incredulous, the anger burning in his blood. He marched blindly, no mind at all in where his feet led him. *But she is another breed*, another voice whispered in response though he hadn't asked its opinion, *she is higher than you— better—she does her duty to the World, as should you.*

*Yet I just wanted...I wanted...*Yet he could not form the thought, not any longer. Where before he knew he desired to know about her, *of* her, who she truly was beyond the scared human she had been, with her coldness to him just moments ago all notion of desiring anything more than to be as far away from her as possible was dismissed outright.

She's a simpering Vampire, blind to her duties just like Xavier had been. He hadn't had time for me and she—

"She's made her decision," he said aloud, drawing confused stares from those that walked past. Ignoring them, he squared his shoulders, the familiar coldness she had all but melted away with her presence, her kind words before the angry ones, returned with a greater flare, and he fought—with a vengeance, the burning seed of grief, of humiliation just begging to be watered in his dead heart.

The taste of her blood returned to his memory and the snarl escaped him as he cursed it, cursed the brilliant taste. A part of him yearned for the days when she was nothing more than a human he was bidden to watch, no better than he, both of them unaware of their true natures—

No, that wasn't true, he decided at once. *I knew who I was. I knew what I did. Before her everything made sense—before her everything was perfectly fine.*

And it shall be once again.

I needn't tether myself to someone that doesn't want me.

So what if I gave her my blood? She is as much mine as a Lycan is a precious puppy adored by children.

He blinked away disturbing thought to find himself standing before a row of doors he had never seen before in his previous perusal the mansion. "The rooms of the royal guests from across the World," a voice, thick with a foreign tongue said from behind him.

He turned to see a rather handsome couple clad in high black fur hats, their thick fur coats hiding their frames, yet he could tell from the sanctimonious glare both Vampires bade him that they were two of these royal guests.

He said nothing, feeling whatever would leave his tongue next would betray the anger he still felt. Instead, he turned his thoughts to what the woman had said, feeling as though he should say something in response.

"I did not realize guests could take up residence in the mansion as well," he offered after a time, remembering the large buildings he had seen when he first entered the city. Their guide had told them these buildings housed the Vampire royalty from all over the World—they were called the Secondary Houses.

"Ah, but of course!" she said while her companion, a stoic-looking gentleman with a brutish jaw, a tuft of blonde hair peeking out from beneath his black fur hat merely nodded as though she spoke nothing but fervent truth. "Yet, this was not done when…Tremor rest his soul…*Dracula*," this name a whisper, "still walked the Earth, but now that *Gospòdin* Rivers is in charge as I understand it—well—things have changed, haven't they Dimitri?"

Dimitri's lips did not curl in an acquiescing smile but merely twitched, before he said, his accent, perhaps, thicker than hers, "It is good thing, this happened. Bring many *Vampir* together, under one *krov.*" He then eyed her expectantly as if to receive praise based on how good his English was received.

She did not meet his stare; hers, Christian realized with a jolt of alarm, was placed steadily upon him, had been since he'd turned to face them. As other Vampires passed, whispering behind their hands and pointing directly at him, he realized, with a start, that he had had no shirt to cover his chest. It lay, he realized with a grimace, on the floor of the training room he'd frequented with Westley but hours before.

Amazed at how twisted into anger and humiliation Alexandria could make him feel so that he would storm out of a room half-naked, his eyes widened in his astonishment and the woman must have taken this for interest on his part for she dislodged her arm from her companion and stretched out a darkly gloved hand.

"Katrina Asimov," she said gently, the invitation on her dark red lips one he could not ignore.

He took her hand, shaking it gently, all too aware of his nakedness. "Christian," he said in greeting, mind still caught on the coldness of Alexandria's eyes as she'd spat the words he still couldn't believe had left her lips, "Christian Delacroix."

At his name, Katrina and Dimitri balked, a hand sliding to Katrina's throat in feigned surprise, her dark red lips forming a perfect "O."

"*Kakaya udacha!*" she whispered, slapping her gloved hand against Dimitri's furred arm as though pleased with an outlandish joke. "*The* Christian Delacroix! My, Dimitri, our luck is good, yes? Ah, *Gospòdin* Delacroix! You must allow us to give you a tour of the mansion, yes? Have you seen the Hall of…oh how you say," and she eyed Dimitri for a moment, "Hall of Death, *Gospòdin* Delacroix?"

"Hall of Death?" he repeated, despite himself, interest certainly piqued.

She ran a gloved hand against Christian's arm, and he was disheartened when he realized he could not feel it. *But there is someone whose touch you can feel*, the voice returned, shocking him even further.

Her gray eyes were mischievous as she dislodged herself from a disproving Dimitri and stepped up to him, parting her large fur coat to reveal skintight material upon her legs and hiding her breasts nothing but a black vest. Around her throat was a large necklace that stopped at the beginning of her breasts, bejeweled with red rubies.

Surprised at her rather unbecoming outfit, he gasped as a gloved hand found the steadily growing bulge between his legs and squeezed it.

That he felt.

He stepped away at once.

A coy smile was on her dark lips, and he stared upon her more seriously.

"You," he said once his voice returned to his throat, "are quite the bold Vampire, Lady Asimov."

She laughed and it sounded to Christian a snarl. She did not turn her gaze to Dimitri as she said, "But can this be? The tales of you are numerous, *Gospòdin* Delacroix. Surely the Ripper of London— *Potroshitel'*—is not afraid of a little fun? I admit, I am disappointed." And she purred in distaste.

The what? "The Ripper?" he repeated, dumbfounded.

At this Dimitri folded his expansive arms over his chest. "He does not know he is *Potroshitel'*," he said, and it was as though he found it amusing.

Katrina took up the torch where question fogged Christian's mind, much to his relief: "The Ripper of London—Christian Delacroix—are these not the same? The one who drains the blood of all the pretty women in town leaving them dead on the streets."

"There were men as well," he said in lieu of anything else: he found it amazing he could not think of the proper words to display the wonder, the disbelief he felt. He was known…known in a foreign country at that. *Unbelievable.*

"But the papers—the letters—did not say this," she went on, emboldened by his silence; "I suppose it is a prettier picture—the one who kills so completely to only kill the women of the town." She dusted her hands as if she'd picked up something distasteful. "But enough, I grow wanting and the Hall of Death need not wait for us. Coming, *Gospòdin* Delacroix?" And she made to move around him, Dimitri at her heels, when he blinked, still caught in the title bestowed to him by Vampires—Creatures—humans he would never meet.

I was known.

A swell of pride filled him, but he found it lessened as the humiliation bestowed to him by Alexandria, still so fresh in his dead heart, returned. But with this memory the anger returned, and he stared at Katrina anew, seeing the fresh seductive gaze she had bade him since they locked eyes.

The flash of Alexandria's brown-green gaze filled his mind and with it his anger flared. With a smile, he offered Katrina his arm, and pleased, she took it, and together, the three of them walked down the long hall, past Vampires that stared at them in bewilderment and envy, Christian doing his best to cast all thought of the maddening woman aside.

* * *

Westley stood before the ocean, perched at its end as though prepared to step forward and walk into it, but he would do no such thing. The Merpeople within its depths were cruel and cold, mostly because of their proximity to the mountains of Shadowhall: a place enshrouded in darkness because of the dismal magic that took place there. The spells performed there were of the dark and cruel variety, thickening the air with a deadly tinge. But the sky was already darkened despite it being morning, since Eleanor Black's reappearance, yet that did not diminish the effect the Enchanters in Shadowhall had over their small part of the World.

"Wh-why are we back here?" she whispered from behind him.

He turned to eye her and saw her eyes wide in their confusion, anger, and fear. She cradled the place he had struck with a hand, though it did not bleed, at least not here.

Here.

He looked out again across the still waters, trying his best to focus on what Dracula had shown her. He had only known she dreamed of him when it was far too late: he had lost the scent of Dracula when she'd awoken from her slumber and he'd immediately reached out to Bel to see what, if anything, had changed.

All was to proceed as normal. He was to ensure Alexandria Stone and Christian Delacroix were prepared to take their place as the leaders of the World—to stand before Syran and stop the rampage that would surely ensue, and to remind Syran of the oath he had taken for Dracula to allow his kind to become human.

Yet Westley got the distinct sense the Phoenixes were growing restless: Bel would rarely reach his gaze and shifted his large footing far too many a time as they shared terse words.

It was quickly that he returned to his body in his office and moved for her, using the hidden passageways throughout the mansion that only he, the other Chairs, and Dracula had known. He had seen the quickly retreating back of Christian Delacroix as he'd approached her bedroom door, smelled the anger on the Vampire's blood in the air, but he figured the Vampire were merely at odds with the woman for the moment.

He eyed her once more, her brown-green eyes scanning the water with great fear, and he furrowed his brow. "Alexandria," he said, turning his back on the water to eye her fully, "were you here with Dracula? In your dream?"

"I…yes," she said absently, her gaze held on the water, transfixed.

"Alexandria…did you swim with him within these waters?" he asked tentatively, not wishing to cause her greater fear but needing answers, and fast.

"Y-Yes," she said, stepping closer to him. She too seemed to feel the forbidding energy in the air: she drew her arms across her body, across the thin chemise she still wore. It was not stained with her blood here, and he thought if she could shiver, she would.

The high mountain in the distance where the castle of Shadowhall sat lingered miles behind her, a black foreboding mass of dark stone, its base hidden behind thickets of green leaves, their trees' bark as black as the ground at the thick roots.

He turned his gaze from the black castle that was obscured by dark clouds to eye her interesting gaze once more: still it was trained on the still waters behind him. He stepped toward her, glad when she did not flinch, only sure it was safe to grasp her arm when he stepped directly in front of her, drawing her gaze to his face.

"Why did you bring me here?" she asked again, torment clear in her eyes.

Poor girl, he thought, despair clawing at his brain, but as a torrential wind blew carrying with it the distinct air of dark magic, blood spells, and forbidden herbs, he squared his shoulders, remembering why he was here.

"This is where Dracula took you in your vision," he said quickly, "what did he deem to show you?"

"He s-stopped," she said, her lips trembling, and he thought it odd they seemed to hold the color of life, "just there, before the mountain on the other s-side."

Her gaze had passed him by, eyeing the vast expanse of the water, and he followed it. Yes, in the distance he could make out the tall mountain: a faint outline against a fog that had begun to roll across the water.

"The Nest," he said at long last. He blinked back upon her, not understanding it at all, but how thick the dread was beginning to press against his back…Licking his lips, he tried again, the thoughts that filled his mind not making sense at all. "He took you there?"

"He did not climb it," she whispered, and how interesting it was that color was steadily returning to her face in the darkened light of the morning.

"But he took you?" urgency pushing his voice. If it were not a vision but a memory then they had less time than he had hoped.

He snarled, the frustration pulling at him the more she stared upon him in bemused fear. "Alexandria," he almost roared, "did he acknowledge your presence? Were you being led or did you follow him?"

"I," she began, when her gaze moved behind him once more and she gasped, stumbling back against the gritty sand with bare feet. A hand had risen to her mouth, and it was shaking, pale, yes, but definitely darker than it had been just moments before.

He blinked upon her, not wishing to understand it, for it did not make sense.

He'd run to her room because of what he'd felt, quite sure it meant that she was the true replacement for Xavier Delacroix. He had previously wished it were Christian that could be King, as that Vampire held Dracula's sword, yes, but when Dracula's scent drifted through the manor, he had begun to doubt his guess.

But staring at her now…it was impossible that she not be the one. He had been sure—*sure*—that because she held the vision…dream…

whatever, that Dracula had seen in her, had chosen her, through the blood, to lead the Dark World, but here she was, shivering, full of life—human.

The true King—or Queen—would have been a Vampire when driven on the air, driven through the mind by the Phoenixes. That she was human now...he blinked again upon her, the fear returning in full.

So could it be? Was Christian Delacroix truly the King of all Dark Creatures? If so, why was it not he that Dracula visited in his sleep? Taken to the Nest in a vision?

"Mister Rivers," she breathed, and he could smell her breath—the blood that trailed on it—in the strange air. Blinking back the urge to step to her and sink his fangs into her neck, he furrowed his brow upon her in question, only just realizing he had been staring upon her incredulously.

"What is it, Miss Stone?"

She lifted a shaking hand to the water and he followed its point, a gasp leaving his lips, for there in the water were the many slick heads of the Merpeople now emerging from the dark depths, their eyes all an all-consuming black within the thick of the fog.

The fear could not be quelled now.

Reaching out behind himself blindly, he whispered, "We must go—now, now! Take my hand, Alexandria—take it!" But he grasped air.

Tearing his gaze from the waiting Merpeople, he turned back to her, blinking when he found nothing there, but as he'd turned his head he smelled her blood, fresh on the cool air, and looked toward the sand.

"Alexandria!" he cried, where he'd struck beneath her breasts bleeding through the white fabric with an alarming quickness. "No," he whispered, dropping to his knees at her side, willing his mind to return to his body in the Vampire City, but all he conjured was black.

"Damn, damn!" Panic flooded his senses and without thought he grasped her abdomen where she bled, holding her close to him. "Bel!" he shouted to the darkened heavens, though he knew it should have been morning. "Bel, release me! Let me go back! I must go back! I will find your King! I will!"

And the large shadow flew directly overhead just then, its wings large and wide, curving against its body as it flew, and he gasped in relief, though he needn't spare the breath.

Chapter Fourteen

THE ROOM

Aurora breathed in cold morning air, reinforcing the spell with an exhale, her arm more than sore from being held aloft but she dared not lower it.

The sheer energy the Phoenixes exuded was overpowering to her magical sensibilities, but still she did not waver: It was the dark-skinned one, black wings settled against his large back that scared her more than anything. She had heard of the Phoenixes, felt their power burn in the medallion, but she had never seen one. And when finally placed with their otherworldly glares she had felt remarkably small.

Now they trekked to where it was believed Eleanor Black remained and Aurora didn't know what scared her more, that they were going to see Eleanor Black, or what exactly Aleister would do once he saw his son at her side.

For the healed Vampire looked quite angry still, and it seemed to Aurora anger that he had been forced to move—once again—at the behest of Creatures greater than himself, not able to move for his son like he *wanted*. Move for his son and protect him, where it seemed these great Creatures wanted to kill him were he not…what

176

they wanted. And Aurora knew Xavier wasn't if Philistia Mastcourt's words in the cottage were true.

She shivered despite the steady glare of the strengthening sun: the cold from the Vampires and the colder air penetrated her robes and she felt as if she wore nothing at all, the cold able to press rudely against her bones—

"The darkness of this World is troubling…" she heard the dark Phoenix whisper to the brighter one.

"Enough," the brighter one whispered back harshly, a hand held solidly in the air to silence him.

The dark one drew silent, though by the rigidness of his broad shoulders behind his black wings of flame, she knew whatever it was he desired was still burning beneath his dark skin, in his completely black, cold eyes—

The heavy hand pressed against her shoulder and despite herself, she jumped. "Aleister," she breathed, turning to eye him, "you startled me."

"No," he said, smiling, much to her surprise, "I did not. You're just preoccupied."

She stared, relenting after a time. "Of course," she said, the hand holding up the rod lowering slightly, the words embedded in the smooth wood glowing with her focus to keep the spell aloft, "but how can I not be?"

"It is a troublesome lot we've been cast, no?" he said consolingly, his boots not making a sound against the dried leaves as they entered the slew of high trees south of the Etrian Fields.

"Hasn't it always been?"

"Yes, of course but now—"

"Now," Peroneous's harsh voice interrupted as he stepped up to match their stride, "we're chained even more to these…Creatures."

Aurora's brow furrowed. "Keep your voice down, Peroneous!" But by the twitch of the dark Phoenix's wings, she knew he had heard.

Fear swept over her in a tighter wave. She could not name it, but whatever that dark Phoenix held in him quite reminded her of what she'd felt when she'd first laid eyes on Dracula's true form, bat-like wings and all. Yes, the more she stared at the broad back, the black wings flickering in the scattered sunlight, she knew, somehow, that he was the cause of the Vampires' true forms being what they were...

"Why should I silence myself so the Creatures can feel more superior? They've already taken magic from us, given it back to the Elves—been conspiring with the Elves this entire time—why should I—?"

But Caligo turned fully whilst stepping backwards, his defined chest gleaming from sweat in both the shade and specks of light, and his gaze, black oddly blank appeared to rove across them all before a smirk turned up a corner of his lips.

The feeling returned in a harsher wave and Aurora swallowed the acidic bile that had gathered at the back of her throat, and with a shaking hand wiped her damp brow. All others beside her were silent with Caligo's gaze, and only when he turned back, walking alongside Syran once more did anyone speak, and it was Peroneous to do so:

"Still," he said, his voice a whisper now as he bent his head toward them to share his words, "we're chained to them—and these chains aren't ever coming off."

* * *

Victor Vonderheide is dead.

The thought pressed against his mind as though foreign, let in by a welcoming host, though he weren't sure it were from himself.

He stared from his place beyond the door at the broken man that was once a Vampire, his silver hair darkened to brown in some places as he'd turned back into a human, but the paleness of absolute death blanketed his skin. He stared up, unseeingly at a peeling ceiling, the face once so sharp and knowing now slack and dull.

Thomas could not believe it. He had crept from the blood-filled hall after the retreating pair, keeping a safe distance so as to not be seen, and had heard Victor whisper the words Eleanor had wanted to hear. Her sigh of contentment told him that much. And he had waited beyond the door when they had entered the room and eerie silence greeted him with a familiar coldness.

And he had waited, only retreating to safety once more when the door opened and out she stepped, completely naked, red eyes glassy with the oncoming of tears he knew would never fall.

And now he saw.

Victor Vonderheide is dead.

A Vampire he had known throughout his adult life, someone he had even been cordial to whilst amongst humans but never had the pleasure of fighting as a Lycan had defied her. For that was what he knew must happen for Victor to appear as he did, but to die while human?

He had never known it possible for a Dark Creature.

It was then that he wondered how soon it had been for the Vampire to call for Dracula, for they had only frequented the room for about forty minutes.

Now he stepped through the broken, withered doorway, abused from its use and the strain of the energy that filled this place when it was closed. The old wood groaned in protest beneath his boots, quite prepared to break away, but he remained, stepping gingerly until he reached just beside Victor's upturned boots.

He stared at the man up close now, unnerved by the suddenness with which his death seemed to have reached him: he looked as though he would spring from the floor at any moment, staring at all things in distaste, silver brow creased in rumination...

The stone, the voice called, and he followed its sweetness, bending to a knee beside the corpse, running a hand against the outline of the Vampire's cloak and breeches. No circular protrusion reached him anywhere on Victor's person, and confusion struck, for he was sure the Vampire had had it when in the large hall...

Horror quickly replaced the bewilderment:

Had Eleanor Black gotten her hands on the stone?

No, he calmed himself, that could not be—she held nothing when she left the room.

So where, where was it?

And that was when he turned on his knee, his tired eyes beholding the dull, black stone just feet from the door. It rested against an old over-turned armchair. Inspiration springing him, he jumped to his feet, stepping to it with absolute joy, for here was the key to regaining some sort of control over his miserable life, here was a key back to Mara—

He'd made it but three steps toward the stone when it unleashed a burst of horrid heat: it felt quite like a scorching lake of fire, and he recoiled, falling back against Victor's cloak, stumbling over the Vampire's body as he moved on his hands and heels away from the fire. It was now licking the old wood, the peeling ceiling, the dusty, forgotten furniture of this damned place, threatening to reach him next.

It was far too late when he realized he was being pushed away from the open door, away from the cool, cold air greatly tinged with Eleanor's dread, away from safety. Instead he moved back against the yet un-burned floorboards toward a place he could not see. He kept his gaze on the ever-growing barrier of flame that moved as though sentient, filling the cabin as though a wall, and it was moving, moving toward him as he scrambled ever backwards, never stopping—

The back of his head bumped against a hard surface, and blinking back tears from the pain, he turned atop the floor, tearing his gaze from the sight of Victor's body, gone up in the wall of flame, charred now, surely, and squinted his eyes upon what looked to be a handle hanging precariously above him from a more resilient-looking rectangle of wood.

A door, he thought in relief, equal fear. And wasting no time, he lifted a hand, able to feel the burning heat draw so much closer now, and for a brief wild moment, he thought it the heat of the Lycan within, but he pulled down on the hot silver handle and pressed his head and chest against the door.

A burst of cold pierced his skin, and he fell forward face-first into freezing cold water as, above him, the fire burst into the new room, passing across the back of his head and clothes, their heat unbearable.

He thought he'd caught fire it was so hot it pierced his skin beneath his clothes, but then, miraculously it was gone, and he threw back his head, gasping for air. Shaking the water out of his eyes and nose as he stared around, he blinked, regaining himself as he gazed in bewilderment on the lake before him. Darkness blanketed the sky, rendering the lake's surface the same. He shakily rose to his knees, turning his head to eye the cabin, quite confused when nothing was there. Yes, he kneeled in a charred wooden doorway, clutching the wooden frame with white hands for support, afraid he would fall forward or backward, unsure which was safest, for he felt quite suddenly ill.

The stone, he thought, rising on unsteady legs. It was gone. Defeat replaced the fear, for he felt quite misplaced, unsure what more to do now. He had lost Mara for the millionth time of that he was sure, and yet the invitation to merely step off the door's frame and dive into the unfathomable lake would not greet him with anything more than disdain.

I am not that far gone that I wish to kill myself, he reasoned with the black water, thinking only of Merpeople within it. The thought further dispelled him of the notion and he turned his gaze to the sky, wondering what had happened to Victor, what Eleanor would now do, where she now was at all. He was quite sure he had left her tunnels, left, perhaps the Dark World entirely, for this strange place seemed bathed in a glow of eerie strangeness.

Nothing filled the black sky, no stars, no winged monsters. No Vampires in human form flew past, no Dragons; all was remarkably quiet. He stifled a sob.

Knowing there was nothing else to do, he pressed a boot against the dark water, surprised to find that, where his face had broken its surface just moments ago, now his boot pressed against resolute flooring that seemed to be the water itself.

Intrigued more than anything, he stepped forward, surprised when nothing more than a ripple danced across the water's surface, its contents still black beneath him. He stepped cautiously moving further and further away from the door's frame, not stopping until he reached the moonlit grass that was littered with droplets of water as his boots pressed upon them.

Breathing a sigh of relief, for no slick-haired Merpeople had broken the dark water's surface to eye him with severe coldness and for this he was grateful. He did not desire to be pulled beneath the still depths, nor did he desire the uncomfortable conversation that would ensue should their leader decide to accost him about his ability to walk upon the water's surface. He, himself, had no idea how it was possible. Indeed, he thought looking around with greater confusion, nothing seemed possible, here, wherever here was.

He stood before the water a moment, staring at the outline of trees in the distance, which reminded him of those most near that small village guarded by Dragons. Cedar something or another. But how curious. Why would the room lead me here?

He eyed the sky, searching the silk-like blackness, looking for any outline, any dense shadow of mountain in the distance. There was none.

Incensed now, for it truly seemed he was no longer in the World, the real World at any rate, he stepped forward, away from the lake, his thoughts, tied as they often were, on his late wife—

"Thomas," the voice called, causing him to stop dead in his tracks.

He turned slowly, heart racing in its cage, a tumultuous drum that echoed in his ears. There she stood, directly atop the water, her bare feet almost touching the still surface. Her eyes were penetrating, just as he remembered, a soft gray, kind and yielding, her hair its usual frazzled brown cascade.

"Mara," he breathed.

"Thomas," she whispered, her red lips parting and it screamed an invitation he could not ignore. Immediately he started back toward the lake, gasping in surprise as he pressed his boot against the black only to have it descend into the water up to his ankle.

What on Earth? He blinked, wiping tears from his eyes, doing his best to keep her in his sights, though it weren't too hard: she wore a white, flowing dress, its fabric possibly silk, and though no bodice squeezed her torso, he could see her lovely shape just beneath it as a gentle wind blew past.

"Mara—what is this?" he asked, disturbed that the door had disappeared behind her, leaving nothing but a vast valley blanketed in darkness.

She spread two pale arms wide as though welcoming him forward but he did not move, his waterlogged boot a painful reminder that he could not. "It is your wish," she said in the same soft whisper he had been accustomed to her using whilst in their bed. "Your wish to be with me—always."

He blinked. "But…the ring…the stone…the power they hold to help me be with you forever?" He found his words rushed, a dizzying heat beginning to fill his mind making it quite hard to hear what she said next:

"All useful but not…all that…needed was us…desire…the power…Dracula's…"

He blinked hard in the heat that claimed his face now, not understanding from where or whence it came, and Mara's voice continued on, the more it did, the more she was repeating the same words again and again, harder and harder to hear with every utterance:

"All…not…all…needed…us…power…Dracu…"

The words weaved and waned through his burning ears, the white of her dress blurring with the dark of the lake that was now no longer still—

He blinked hard as his knees gave way beneath him, and now much closer to the ground he smelled the scent of old water, death, and, curiously, Lycan anger…

Completely black eyes, wide and round appeared just feet from his bleary gaze in the next moment and then the webbed hands pressed against the sides of his face, blisteringly cold frost sinking deeply into his skin. He jerked away, though the hands pressed harder against him, the nails finished at the end of the black, webbed fingers digging into his ears as they pulled him toward the water.

"No," he groaned, pulling himself painfully from the water's edge despite the strength with which the Mermaid pulled. "No!"

The blurry vision of Mara overhead pulled him from the terrifying black eyes, and he felt the warm blood slide down his neck as he struggled against the Mermaid who screeched madly, the only other thing piercing his ears.

"Mara," he screamed though he could no longer hear his voice. "Mara, help me!"

Her gaze was no longer serene: her eyes were red, darkened with what seemed anger or bloodlust, he could not be sure. The sight frightened him immensely, so much so he momentarily forgot where he was, and with whom, allowing the Mermaid the upper hand. With a hard, quick tug she pulled hard, ripping a jagged, painful line from his ears to his cheekbones. Blinding pain flashed before his eyes, though his mind only found, somehow the vision of Mara, her cruel unforgiving gaze. And through the pain, the grand feeling of despair, of loss, flared in full, and he remembered his dead wife with startling clarity:

The lust in her eyes whilst she was human, the desire she held to be like him had been overwhelming in her gray jewels of need. Not a need for him, no, he realized as the Mermaid's black tail swished strongly through the dark water, but a need to enter his World, become a Lycan. Was it so farfetched then, to assume she had not gotten what she desired, turning into an Elite, that she was pleased, even in death, to be what she was? That these phantoms of her, of Alexandria Stone that played a horrible record in his mind's eye were merely creations of his grief-stricken, damned imagination? Was it possible, truly, that Mara Montague—no, Mara Clarke, merely wished to escape the lavishness of her human home and become a Creature of the Dark, of her own free will, save his admonishments on the topic?

As the Mermaid drove him deeper down where the silver light of the moon could not reach, he blinked in the absolute dark, not surprised at all that the desire to save himself, to turn and swim upward had gone just as the pain, a piercing cold replacing all else despite the breaking of his already damaged heart.

*　*　*

Xavier Delacroix, exhausted slightly from his few-day-entanglement with Eleanor Black, strode the stone tunnels this morning attempting to understand the source of strange energy in the air. Eleanor had, begrudgingly, left his side once someone had called through the door to tell them the sun had finally risen if only to begin to set about their plans to see Christian dead.

When he had suggested she call another to take her place and get information, she wrinkled her nose and said, "And let any of them know we've a threat in the World? Never." And then she had dressed quickly, throwing on a black ruffled blouse, breeches, and his riding boots, and set off with a wave of her long black hair over a shoulder.

And now he stepped gingerly where he used to walk calmly; it was the energy, the nature of the tunnel that had changed, he'd noticed, sometime in the night. It rattled him, though he wasn't sure it should have, after all, he was in new territory. The four or so days he had been in her hallways had not been enough to acclimate himself to the Elite Creatures' energy until he became one himself. But despite this thought, he walked on, not sure that were entirely true, not sure he could merely remain in her bed, snarling away dreams in which he slit his brother's throat or broke Alexandria's neck.

He wouldn't allow himself the thought that the dreams disturbed him, for they did, but it was better, he found, when in Eleanor's presence to embrace them as good things, signs of what must be done. He merely felt it were his mind working out the fantasy world he had lived in whilst unconscious those weeks before, and he didn't quite like the idea that he need kill Christian. He was family, the only family he had left besides Aleister who didn't quite count since Xavier had believed the Vampire dead for the majority of his human life.

And just as the unease, the doubt creeped in that he need kill Christian and Alexandria at all, her essence wrapped itself around him like a cloak clasped tight at the neck, and he breathed a sigh, allowing it to fill his cold blood.

At once, his thoughts changed. They were no longer doubtful nor pensive but assured, just. It was right that they kill Christian if the Vampire had taken Alexandria's blood...was equal in power to him. *No one should be equal in power to me*, the thought came, and he did not push it down, so lost was he in thoughts of Eleanor's skin beneath his hands, *I should be able to rule unopposed, able to feel all sensations, understand all things.*

He had reached the end of a sloping hallway, intrigued by the apparent newness of the wall here, and stopped dead. Though it seemed nothing but regular wall...and yet, the energy of the tunnels swarmed his senses with a marked, strange difference.

Intrigued, he stepped forward, pressing a flat hand against the stone, the dampness of it clinging to his skin. *A door*, he thought, *has to be*.

And despite the solid stone that stood resilient before him, he felt something press against the other side of the wall. Almost...yes, he pressed an ear against the stone, a low whistling sounding beyond it. *A door indeed.* Stepping back, the mud squishing between his toes, he appraised the wall, folding his arms against his bare chest, and yes, there was Eleanor's call again, alluring, comforting...desiring...

As if on cue her voice entered his mind as though it belonged there: *"You called, my love?"*

"I've found...a wall."

"A wall?"

"But there's something beyond it, I'm sure of it—"

"Ah you found the wall. Just think of me and it will open."

"Oh?"

"Yes, now I must run, there's something...nasty heading toward the tunnels. I'm going to check it out. Talk later. Oh, and my love?"

"Yes, Eleanor?"

"Have fun."

Have fun? he thought, incredulous. *What the Devil did that mean?*

And before he could say another word, the door appeared within the stone and he stared in bewilderment. Before long however, he whispered a thank you to Eleanor, and moved a hand to the jagged, old handle. Yet before he could press down on it, a burst of wind greeted him, blowing his hair forward and pushing the door open in turn.

Once it settled, he blinked upon the darkness that greeted him, and as his eyes adjusted, he stared around at the dark, peeling wood, the blood that splattered it, the overturned armchairs, broken lamps, and smelled it.

The blood of a man.

It was quite familiar, that blood, but it was changed. He could not place it, but still it drew him further. He left the soft mud and pressed a bare foot against the cold wood of what appeared to be a cabin, and in the darkness of this new place, he eyed the man that lay just feet from the door, hands limp as his sides, his chest pressing upward beneath his clothes, face pale with permanent death, eyes staring up at the ceiling, unseeing.

He couldn't place the man, not at first. It was not until he stepped closer, kicking aside a stone ball with his toe that he gasped and staggered backwards, fear gripping his cold heart. "Victor," he breathed, a shaking hand rising to his lips, "Victor—what—*what did she do?*"

He hesitated greatly, unsure if he should step forward again and kneel at the Vampire—man's—side for a better look or remain where he was: He wasn't quite sure he wanted a closer look.

The back was broken, that much he could tell by the unnatural way the middle of the man pressed upward toward the ceiling. The smell of human death was far too prevalent as well. *Human—but how could he be?*

A greater numbness than the cold he always felt pressed against him, and he sank to a knee with the crushing realization that Eleanor had killed Victor Vonderheide and hadn't told he, Xavier about it. Indeed, she'd returned to the room naked and with a smile, only raving about how she had been right, that Christian Delacroix had turned Alexandria Stone into a Vampire and that they must be killed.

Of course, of course she would say that, he thought, anger replacing the numbness, she only wanted what she wanted and she would kill Victor Vonderheide to get it. He thought of her, perhaps in her new horrid form, perhaps wrapping her large clawed hands around the old Vampire's throat because he would not submit, would not turn into an Elite at her constant behest...

Turned.

He stared around at the cabin with greater insight now, this place that did not exist until he thought of her, until she gave him permission to enter it—

Could it be?

Figuring he had nothing else to lose, his mind a scramble of confused thought, grief, and anger due to all her secrets, he thought of the Vampire he had trusted until it became apparent all Creatures were simply pawns in a maddening game.

There was a burst of light and he stared up at Dracula, feeling nothing as he stared at him. "Vampire," Xavier said in greeting, rising from his knee, preparing himself for a yell or an attack.

Neither came. "Hello," was all the Vampire said, his brown eyes piercing with a distant coldness. He was shrouded in a black cloak, what he wore beneath obscured, and even still Xavier could not see any protrusion of weapon upon his person.

Xavier had the distinct impression he was no longer favored by the Vampire though he wasn't sure he favored *him* anymore at any rate.

Dracula eyed Victor's body at his side, his expression darkening as though he smelled something horrid. "Oh, Victor," he said softly as though talking to a child, "Victor, Victor, Victor. You did not choose wisely did you?"

"What?" Xavier asked immediately. "What choice did he make?"

"He chose," Dracula said, white hair hiding his face as he still stared down at Victor's body, "fear."

"And his choices were what? You or Eleanor?"

"Aren't they always?"

"I wouldn't know, would I? I had no choice when I entered *The Immortal's Guide*, Dracula."

At this, Dracula stared at him, his expression cruel in the darkness. He did not show his hands, clasped as they were at his back. "Haha," though it sounded immeasurably strained. "You always had a choice, Vampire. Do not blame your decisions on my...signs. Yes, signs," he said harshly for Xavier opened his mouth to retort, "only meant to push you in the right direction but at every turn, Xavier, you chose *her*."

"Would you blame me Dracula?!" he was shouting before he could stop it. "With her there are answers, there are truths she would never keep from me—with you I had been coddled while sent across the Dark World to die! The choice was the easiest I've ever had to make!"

He snarled viciously, but Xavier, not a human man in this room, not anymore, did not flinch. He snarled back, wishing only that he had the damned sword if only to cut off the Vampire's head.

Dracula did not flinch either. "I see it now," he said coldly. "I see it—your weakness. Your lust for power. You kept it hidden so wonderfully, didn't you, Xavier? Yes, you had me fooled. You weren't as strong-headed as Eleanor, bandying about the Vampire City about your desire for knowledge, but it was in there, wasn't it? Burning in your cold blood as you soaked up all I showed you. Biding your time so you could be the one to take over—"

"You gave it to me! I didn't want it, not like that!" he yelled. "You threw me the crown without telling me a damned thing about how to wield it! Fighting that bloody Elite Creature, Michael, calling us 'tools'—we're *not* tools—we should be led by a just leader! And she is that leader! She—"

"Lied to you!

"How?! Tell me that!"

He pointed a pale, sharp finger to Victor's body, his mouth a thin line.

Xavier stared at Victor, then Dracula and back, understanding. "He didn't make his choice," he said, mirroring the words Dracula just said, "if she had reason to kill him, I'm sure she would have told me when she was ready." Though, as he said it, the doubt grew.

"You're deluded," Dracula said harshly, "mad and spiraling! You're selfish, unworthy to be King of anything, so why, why did you call me if you already decided what you would become?"

His brow furrowed. "What I would—what?"

"Become—become! You enter *The Immortal's Guide*, you better be prepared for the consequences! Though this you should already know! You traversed it—survived it—before! And only because of me!"

And with the words, he found sense. "This—is *The Immortal's Guide*?"

"It is only a page but it is no less powerful. She corrupted it, of course, with her...ways, but here she has the power to turn those who choose her, who accept death and embrace rage, into her damnable Creatures. And you Xavier, you entered the room, you must decide, and you cannot leave until you have."

He blinked in the dark. "And you have only come because I have called you?"

Dracula nodded.

"And if I call Eleanor, what will happen?"

A cold smile lifted his lips, but a shadow crossed his eyes. "You're no stranger to doing things yourself."

And with that, he began to fade, a darkness engulfing his image until at last he was gone and Xavier stared upon the destroyed cabin, mind blank.

He hesitated for the briefest of moments, remembering when he had called the Phoenixes to him when first he traversed *The Immortal's Guide*. He wondered if he dared call her now but question kept him from the action. What would she do now? Would she deem to kill him because he was still a Vampire? Indeed, he knew nothing of how the process worked, but the image of Dracula, annoyingly smug and berating returned and he exhaled a breath he did not need, driven by rage more than anything else, and thought of her.

At once all went dark, the cabin floor and walls falling away, and startled he was, a cry left his lips, but he relaxed as he realized he was not falling along with them but remained standing in darkness.

And then, as if he had always been there, a man appeared, his green eyes cool and knowing, his hardened brow cut into an elegant slope, his jaw square and equally hardened, a knowing smirk upon his lips.

He wore an elegant cape finished at the ends with what looked the scales of a black Dragon. They glimmered though there was no light to cast a shine upon them. Covering his chest and arms was a darkened metal pauldron, flared out at his shoulders and neck so that he looked to be wearing a high metal collar. His long black hair rested freely behind him, and upon his legs were not breeches but equally flared darkened metal armor, and at his waist, surprisingly Xavier saw, was the Ascalon though it was no longer a normal silver blade; the blade was now black, held in place by a single black leather strap around his hips.

Xavier stared at the man for quite a long time before he realized he was staring upon himself.

No, the man held his features, but there was heavily something different, stronger, more resilient in his stance, his eyes. Yes, he held knowledge, had seen it all, and was not scared or hesitant in the least to use the knowledge he'd obtained.

Xavier sniffed the air. He was also an Elite Creature.

"I take it this is what I will become when I transform?" he asked the better-version of himself.

The better-version's smile never left. "If you can survive," he said and Xavier shook his head with the voice: it was equally as alluring as Eleanor's.

"What do you mean?" he asked. "What do I have to do?"

"Like I said," the better-version said, the smile gone. He shook violently then, the pauldron and armor falling away from him as he grew and lengthened, his wings forming beneath the strands of black hair that still clung to his head as his chin grew and sharpened, his ears as well. The screech was horrific as he opened his many-fanged mouth and the word entered Xavier's head before the better-version lifted from the floor and darted for him: *"Survive."*

Chapter Fifteen

THE CHOICE

James lifted a balled fist from the floor, straining once more against the wide cuffs that held him against the cold stone. The floors were not marble here as they were in the main parts of the mansion; indeed, he felt he'd been put in a dungeon rather than any chamber he'd ever seen.

He snorted the stench of Vampire out of his nostrils, sickened by their blood. *Always, Vampires and their blood.* He was tired of being surrounded by them, being revived by them, forced to stick by their selfish sides. Indeed, he didn't know a Vampire that wasn't out for themselves or their *precious*, lofty goals.

Bind the blood, he thought, spitting out what little Unicorn Blood remained on his tongue, *ha! Dracula and his damned schemes. Keeping me in the house of Vampires, forcing me to exist alongside them, cater to them, knowing—knowing I was always a Lycan. What did he expect? For me to one day face Lore and get bitten, starting my transformation? He can't have known—*

"Wonder if Xavier's brother will take that woman to the Ball tonight?" a voice beyond the reinforced steel door said, muffled though it was.

The guards behind the door had been sharing words since they'd arrived at the door for their post, but it was the first time James ever had the mind to listen.

"I've heard she's gotten a number of offers since they showed up. Jonathan in the 2nd Army even asked," the other soldier said.

"Rebuffed?"

"Of course. She doesn't seem the type to have her dalliances. But she was seen with a duke from Tiran yesterday. Someone caught them deep in tongues and fangs behind a pillar deeper in the mansion."

There was a gasp. "No? A bloody duke? Of course—royalty'll get the good ones."

"Hold your horses, now," the other said smoothly, "she was also seen running away from him shortly after. Didn't seem to like his affinity for blood-tasting."

"Gah, the royalty's always into the dirty stuff. What's wrong with plain old embracing? Kissing? Why do they have to taste the other's blood, drink it even?" There was an audible shiver. "I've only been a Vampire for a little less than a hundred years but by the birds if I wasn't disgusted by the state of things—I've even heard whispers that *Xavier Delacroix* was apt to share his blood with others—especially Eleanor Black when she was a member of these halls. I mean, what's the point of it? Didn't Dracula set up these rules for reasons? No Vampire is ever—*ever* to drink the blood of another!"

Never to drink the blood of another? James thought, intrigued. *Why on Earth was that?*

"At any rate, she didn't take kindly to it and hasn't been seen since. Christian Delacroix, however, has been seen going in and out of her room," the other went on, a slight hint of exasperation on his words.

"Ah," the other sighed knowingly, "she *is* of new blood. You don't think *Christian* was the one to turn her?"

"Not a damn thing surprises me anymore."

"But you don't think she and Christian…"

"Together? I'd be terribly sad if that were the case, but not inclined to believe it—isn't Christian the connoisseur of using others for his needs and discarding them?"

"That's what I've heard as well but seeing him...well, to be honest, there wasn't a way to get a read on him right off—he does exude similar...blood-chilling qualities to his brother. I didn't think it possible, but passing him in the hall, it's hard not to feel as though he could...well, replace his brother as King."

"Bite your tongue!"

"But we've no proper idea *where* Xavier Delacroix is, do we? And if he won't show his face why shouldn't I think he has abandoned us? And Christian...he seems to have a better head on his shoulders—I say we give him the chance—"

"But didn't you hear?"

"What?"

"Xavier has supposedly...and I say this lightly, mind you— switched sides."

There was a moment of silent incomprehension, and then, "You don't mean—*Eleanor Black*?"

James assumed the other soldier nodded or some other gesture of affirmation, for the soldier went on, aghast, "But he wouldn't—that is to say he *couldn't*—where'd you hear *this*?"

"Slew of Vampires—late-comers. Swear by Tremor the Great... say it's passed across the Dark World entirely by now, though it's only a case of believing it, which many—*many* are starting to."

"Well what do you believe?"

"What does it matter? The World's going to shit regardless of my thoughts on the matter. Did you know the bloody Elves of Etria have their *weapons* back?"

James withdrew his focus. *Xavier, joining Eleanor?* Would the Vampire truly leave Christian behind and join the woman that was making it difficult to survive. Lore's dwindling number of Lycan Creatures were proof enough of this. *But why would Xavier join her?*

The thunderous heat within his heart burned in his chest, then, and he exhaled, breathing the rage back. He had first tried to transform before when dragged to this place, finding it rather painful:

The chains at his wrists and ankles burned white hot, keeping his larger form at bay.

Continuing his deep breaths, feeling the sweat drip down his brow and nose, he focused on the thundering in his chest, his heart. Lore was getting closer. *Would be here by midday at least if not deterred. And he would not be,* James knew.

And then we can rip apart the Vampires and I can take my rightful place alongside my true creator, he thought, the burning within leaving his throat in smoke. He was excited, quite, to see the Lycan again, and though Lore had left him for a time, he found it an easier place to be, by the Lycan's side, rather than a Vampire's.

Anything of Alexandria Stone's blood was a distant memory, whatever magic she'd worked to bring him back to life not tying him to her as much as they had all thought it would. *Lore had found it easy to break that connection,* he thought, breathing back the Lycan blood despite the joy that filled his heart. The heart that strained against his chest, eager to grow larger, to help aid his Lycan form…

Patience, young one, Lore's voice said, jarring him where he lay.

He went still for a moment, the shock of the voice washing over him, his sweat now cold, but he relaxed after a while, reassured when he felt the warmth return. It was a far cry from the cold, the stench that drifted off the Vampires…

Keep the rage back until I get there, Lore said knowingly.

James smiled against the cold stone, against the puddle of his sweat that had formed. He focused his best on keeping the rage of the Lycan back, for it was all he could feel now, Dracula's plans, Alexandria's blood gone to him in this room where they—the bloody Vampires—kept him down.

* * *

Westley Rivers had returned to his body to find that quite a few hours had passed: Alexandria Stone still bled from her wound, and what was worse, all could smell her blood.

He'd blinked from his knees upon the number of royal Vampires that filled the room to capacity all whispering words of confusion, though there were, thankfully, a few soldiers who had bravely entered the room as well and held the crowd away from the bed.

And now that he had recovered, Alexandria had been cleaned and fed Unicorn Blood, resting beneath her sheets, he thought on Christian Delacroix.

He'd expected the Vampire be the very first to see what the matter was, for surely—*surely*—he'd smelled the woman's blood, and smelled it far more than any other Vampire, due to their connection of Vampire and charge.

And yet Westley never rose from a chair he had requested hours before, quite displeased to find that Christian had never showed.

Which is why Westley was quite surprised when the very Vampire swung open the door at last, his eyes ablaze with terror and confusion. The buttons of his breeches were not fully clasped, part of his manhood was slightly visible through the open slit, and the stream of questions that left his blood-stained lips as he entered the room made Westley rise from his chair: "What happened? Why wasn't I called?"

"First," he began, raising his hand to keep Christian away from the bed, "cover yourself completely before you talk to me, Delacroix. Secondly, I see you don't take your place as her Vampire seriously, for you didn't heed the numerous, overwhelming callings you must have felt as she suffered and called for you."

He did not look away as Christian hastily buttoned his pants and then looked up once more, angry burning in his red eyes. "Suffered? Why would she suffer? What—what did you do?"

Westley eyed the Vampire, recognizing now the scent of sex and numerous cold blood that covered him like sweat. Westley frowned. "I followed a hunch. It didn't pan out. Though staring at you now, I'm hard pressed to really believe *you* are the King of All Creatures."

The Vampire's affronted gaze said it all. The shame and ridicule seeped through his eyes now black and then righteous anger replaced all. "You attacked her to prove to yourself that she could rule?!"

"I did what I felt was best, I just told you," Westley said, exhausted: he hadn't had blood since he'd returned to his body. "But you, Christian Delacroix, lothario-at-large, have a lot to prove to yourself that you can be King."

"What do you—?"

He waved his hand, silencing the Vampire. "Going off and fucking the first thing you see after a little tiff with the woman, Christian," he said, unable to keep the bite out of his voice, "is hardly what any reasonable *King* would do. How on Earth do you expect me to believe—hell, have the *Phoenixes* believe—that you of all Vampires can *possibly* be King when you leave your bloody charge at the first sign that she couldn't possibly share your affections? Instead of sulking and taking it out on the nearest wet hole you can find, why not, oh, I don't know, respect her wishes and be there for her as her confidante and friend, instead?"

He was stunned, his mouth opening and closing as though his jaw was weakly hinged. And when at last he could gather his tongue, Westley snarled, shaking his head. "Save it, Delacroix. I need a blood pack. I can't deal with your mess right now. I've work to do—a proper King to find." And he stormed past the speechless Vampire, closing the door with a slam behind him, exhaustion and fear tearing his mind in two as he moved.

* * *

He did not know what to do with his hands. They opened and closed into fists as he stared at her past the pink curtains. Her eyes were still closed, her heart-shaped face as peaceful as ever.

He knew it would not remain so when she awoke, when she laid eyes upon him, perhaps still with anger, and when he told her of his excursion...

For he knew he had to tell her, whether it be out of shame or a need for her to know what he'd undergone.

But that was foolish, a voice said, *you weren't tied together in earnest. Just shared blood. And she's made it perfectly clear she wants nothing to do with you romantically. Keep your time to yourself, and if ever she expresses interest, then tell her. There's not a need to stir the pot needlessly.*

Yes, he agreed. *Yes, that is what I will do. Keep my memory to myself and if ever—who am I kidding? I never came to her while she called for me—I didn't feel her call for me—why would she ever see me as more than a reckless Vampire that was compelled beyond rational thought to turn her?*

With a sigh, he moved around the bed, dropping into a chair, knowing he could—should—do nothing more until she awoke.

* * *

The late morning air pressed against her face as she stepped for the hills, the band of Creatures at her back whispering nervously to themselves, questioning what Lane held, for she wouldn't tell them. Wouldn't tell them until she saw it for herself. Evian safe, Lane rebuilt, the plan moving forward.

She pushed down the nervous twinge in her gut that Nathanial would not make it to Lane, but with the small spell she'd placed upon the Vampire's body, she could feel he was still alive...as alive as a Vampire could be at any rate, and that was enough.

And she vowed once Xavier was found she would teach Nathanial Vivery how best to really aid himself against the magic of the World, for if anyone could do it, she maintained that he could, indeed.

* * *

Alexandria Stone pressed a hand to the cold, dark stone most near her and stepped down the familiar tunnel. She let her hand canvas the wall for she did not know how she had come to be here again, and what unnerved her more than her appearance here, was the fact that she was terribly scared.

Yes, it was a fear that stretched against her blood, freezing in her veins, the soft fabric of the black dress she wore, felt like a cold wisp of wind against her legs as she moved.

She walked on despite her mind, frantic with thought as it was, listening intently for any sign of another to round a corner and accost her...No one came.

She turned corners, finding herself lost in a deliberate black haze that seemed to have lingered in this place, seeped into its walls since she'd last been here. And the memory of Christian dragged away, of Eleanor Black's blade stabbed into her skin over and over, of the woman's eyes of rage, of fear returned, and Alexandria knew something important had pulled her here...

"...haven't seen him since yesterday when he went off Eleanor," a voice said suddenly farther down the hall.

She stopped, the same hand bracing the wall, for the torchlight in these tunnels did nothing to dim the shadow that hung low over their fires, causing the torches to flicker what seemed darkness, not light.

She narrowed her eyes through the dim, able to see two figures further down the hall, heads bent low together, hoods hiding their faces.

"But do you think..." the other began, unable to go on.

"Wouldn't surprise me," the other finished knowingly.

"Well...what are we to do now? We cannot move as we are— bound to her even further—and...well I feel she's left the tunnels, don't you?"

"Ah! Now that you mention it—yes—yes, she's gone. But why— why would she leave her beloved king here all by himself?"

"Percival told me he saw the Vampire wandering about earlier..."

"Really? He left her sacred bed? Come up for air, has he? Well, any idea where he went?"

"What do you have in mind, Randall?"

"Oh nothing, nothing—I just wish to meet the man up close and all that. If we're gonna be under *his* rule as well, might as well make sure he knows my name."

"Ingenious. I'll come with you."

"Excellent. You'll help to settle my nerves..."

And off they set, their traveling cloaks, tattered heavily, resembling more ripped fabric than actual cloaks, swayed as they walked quickly.

Without another thought she followed their silhouettes, not stopping until they rounded a corner for they were suddenly gone. The tunnel stretched onward into darkness, the dirt ground littered with boot prints leading back and forth but none new, none detailing where the two Elite Creatures had gone.

Had I made a mistake? she thought, trying to decide if she had erred in following them, or gotten herself mixed up and followed another pair of Creatures, and yet, she had not seen any other Creatures at all.

The question she had not asked since she appeared here stabbed at her mind with repeated need, the answer not finding her the more she thought on it: *Why am I here?* She could not remember anything more than appearing in the tunnel, a hand on a wall to steady its trembling.

"*Pretty little thing in my walls...pretty little thing walking my floors...*" The voice was cold, a mocking lilt to the familiar cruelness, a pulling call that, if it wanted to, Alexandria knew would lull her in with its sultriness, however false...

She turned in the encroaching darkness only to find nothing behind her as well, but when she turned back, she was quite surprised to find that the long tunnel had disappeared entirely, nothing but the small patch of dirt she stood on the only thing there.

What on Earth?

And then the voice returned, a menacing edge there that was not present before: "*How interesting things get when I leave my home for but a moment. But you are not really there, are you? You merely trespass in spirit. How brilliant you must be to master such magic without even knowing it...*"

Eleanor. The wave of fear that had subsided as she'd followed the Elite Creatures returned with a vengeance, clawing through her just as the voice that continued now, almost a scream in her ears, pounding against her mind:

"*What's the matter foolish woman? Confused? Lost? Scared? You've every right to be. Even now, Xavier undergoes his transformation into my Creature. Even now you and Christian Delacroix shall lose everything and I can finally have my rightful King...*"

"Xavier?" she said aloud to cold air, remembering what Westley had said, that Christian could be the new King of All Creatures... *Would Eleanor come for us? That was what she seemed to imply... and if she was not here then where was she? Searching for Christian and myself?*

A harsh burst of cold wind pressed against her from all sides and she covered her eyes with an arm, as the barrage of decidedly dreadful energy pierced her clothes, her skin, and seeped through her blood—

She felt the warmth of the red light swarm upward through her, pushing aside the horrible dread, but the dread was thick, so much so she thought she would be sick with its presence...

Once the wind died she stepped forward, not knowing in which direction she was going (all was still black), but she stepped through the dark, walking carefully for she knew not whether her next step were more ground or nothingness upon which to fall...

When at last she thought she would walk endlessly, feel and smell the horrid dread press all around her, she saw the door through the haze of black, ordinary-looking yet haphazardly placed within its frame. The minor slits within the door's frame allowed the strong dread to pass through, reaching her as impenetrable the closer she moved.

She hesitated in reaching out a hand for the plain, old handle, but then she heard it, the grunts and groans beyond the old wood, and she dropped her hand, stepped forward, and listened.

* * *

Xavier wiped the blood from his eye, struggling to his feet for the seventieth time, finding it a tiresome ordeal. The more he fought the... Creature before him, the stronger the Creature seemed to become. He had wondered more often than not whether he had made a mistake in calling for her, in being quite rude to Dracula before, for the anger he held toward the particular Vampire had waned greatly in the haze of the repeated slashes and bumps the winged monster continuously assailed him with.

"Hold!" he called angrily, holding out a hand to keep the thing at bay.

It relented for the first time since he had cried out for it to stop some many times before, and in his relief and wonder, he almost forgot what he'd wanted to say. Almost.

"What is the point of this? Is this how you turn me into one of her Creatures? Making me face...an obviously better version of myself? One already versed in her...darkened ways?"

The Creature tilted its head to the side as though a dog confused at a command, and then the voice quite similar to his own entered his mind:

"Turn you? Into one of hers?" It laughed cruelly, a sound that chilled Xavier to the bone. *"Don't you see Xavier? You already are*

one of hers. Think. Every time her energy entered you what did you feel?"

He thought, though not long. "As though…I could not get enough. I felt stronger…more capable…not confused like I was at Dracula's behest…"

"And do you not see why this is?"

He could not.

The Creature went on before he could conjure an excuse as to why: *"You already hold her energy within you. You already are an Elite Creature. Do you think all Creatures who enter this space are greeted with an Elite-form of themselves? They are met with Eleanor…in her true form. Many don't remember it, but once they face it and survive they are granted the lessons needed to embrace death, to withstand their inner rage. But you need not face the Elite-form of Eleanor because you and she are the same. You always have been."*

At this, only confusion could enter his mind. "But…I know not how to take the form of a Lycan…I don't know how you all take the forms you hold…"

At this the Creature waved a sharp-nailed claw as though to silence him. *"You began your true transformation in the cabin those months ago. When you faced her, when you cut her down, when you journeyed to Dracula…when the doubt set in. You were already tied to her; you had already shared your blood with her. You gave her the ability to be birthed into a full Elite, to hold the blood of the Lycan as well as Vampire. You helped her get one step closer to her true goal."* It spread wide its long gray arms tinged with gray fur. *"To be this."*

He opened his mouth to retort when it went on.

"You denied Dracula at every turn after she came to you in the woods for the first time. You doubted him, and doubt, Xavier, is the key to greater understanding of truth. Inner truth. You cannot grow if you do not doubt what you have been told for years. After that, with Dracula's Creatures about you, you succumbed to her will—your will much easier. It was only a matter of time before you transformed—"

"My arm" he gasped, remembering when he had been met with a blinding pain atop the rocks before Merriwall Mountain, when he had begun to transform in earnest.

The large Creature nodded, and Xavier thought he could see himself in those completely black eyes.

"So all this time..." he began, unsure of what he desired to say.

"*Yes,*" was all the Creature said.

"So why go through this," he waved a hand toward the Creature, "why fight me at all?"

"*I said when you first called me, didn't I? You had to make your choice. Make a conscious choice. All your choices up until now have been subconscious ones. Your blood knew what it was, what you had accessed when you gave Eleanor your blood, but your waking mind continued to fight it. Here, now, seeing your truth, you can accept it, or die for good. It is why you could go longer in your desire for blood. It is why you have gotten lost in dreams, fantasies, truths of you and Eleanor's purpose—why you slashed Damion Nicodemeus's neck, why you continue to dream of killing your brother, ruining Alexandria Stone—*"

"I get it," he interrupted coldly, remorse filling him as the Creature spoke. "I know what I did...I wish I hadn't...but is this truly the way it must be? I must...embrace the dread—the energy—allow it to—to fill me entirely—and embrace how powerful I feel when it does—and—and—finally become King of her—my Creatures? For good?"

"*And you must kill Christian Delacroix and Alexandria Stone to ensure your place as the rulers of the Dark World are secured.*"

And suddenly the thought of Christian dead at his feet, Alexandria a bloodied mess beside him did not seem so wrong. It *was* Christian's fault he had become a Vampire anyway—no, it was Dracula's, for the Great Vampire had seen to it that they become Vampires at all, hadn't he? And all of Dracula's plans? And wasn't he, Xavier, always destined for something more? Something greater? Was this not it?

He had not realized the Elite Creature had shed its horrid form and now stood, similar to him in face but so much more assured. He was completely naked and had stretched out a strong hand expectantly.

Xavier stared at it for quite some time, remembering, as he held Dracula down, demanding he be told about Aleister, how Dracula had laughed in his face. He stared at the waiting hand remembering when Christian had shouted at him from his knees, and he, Xavier had planted a boot to Christian's face. He stared at the hand quite like his and remembered when Eleanor would come to him, beautiful, yearning, brilliant, the gleam of promise always in her eyes. And he knew then, knew it well, that they had always been more, that they had always promised to themselves to strive for more, to be better than Dracula had ever desired for them. Though they had never said it aloud, they didn't need to—it was embedded in their blood, it was written in their veins, in all they had done to reach this point.

It was the only place he belonged, he knew.

It was why it was quite easy to extend his own hand and grasp the Elite Creature's, squeezing it tight as they shook.

Chapter Sixteen

THE UNINVITED GUEST

Xavier Delacroix was prepared for the blast of energy that filled him next, welcomed it even: He closed his eyes as he the hand within his own faded away, and felt his power, his truth return to him. The doubt was gone now, never to return. All matter of Dracula, of his lies, his secrets did not seem quite as important anymore, indeed, all he had gone through until now seemed beyond all things, quite trivial. Yes, he was above it all.

He opened his eyes, not surprised to find he stood again in the old cabin. All was as it was when he first entered, the armchairs overturned, the old wood peeling...

He looked down and stared at the corpse of Victor, wondering why it was still there, when the door opened and he turned, smelling Dracula's blood.

Her eyes were wide and fear-filled; he figured there should have been tears there—*would* have been tears if she were still human—but all he saw was anger in her brown-green eyes. She held a hand on the door's old knob and did not move it as the silver handle fell away and rolled across the floor.

Her mouth opened and closed as she grasped for the words that eluded her, but with all her anger she did not take a step into the room. It was something he thought she would like to do.

Cracking his neck, though it did not need it, he smiled his best welcoming smile. "Alexandria," and even he noticed the difference his voice held, "what a surprise."

Her lips formed a line and he could hear her heart beat, though how dull it was. That it beat at all betrayed her fear, her anger, indeed. His smile widened.

"I'd offer you some blood but we're fresh out just now. But I'm sure if you wait around you'll run into some human we haven't converted yet."

Her red light flared and with it he felt himself repulsed: he was pushed back two steps, and her blood, once undeniably curious to him, now smelled vile, much like that of a Lycan's...but with the memory now, he found even the beast's blood to not smell as bad as it once did.

"Angry, are we?" he said, recovering from her red light. "That cannot be helped. If you'd come but minutes earlier you may have been able to stop me. That is what you wanted isn't it? Why you are here?"

The look of confusion upon her face confirmed the truth.

He laughed despite himself, and it was full of joy, a joy he could actually *feel*. "You don't even *know*, do you?"

"Know what?" she said at last, and with her voice he could feel Dracula's presence as though he were in the room, an annoyance more than anything else.

"Know why you are here, you stupid girl," he spat unable to hold himself back.

She did not flinch with his words. Instead her gaze left him at last and roved around the old cabin, before falling across Victor. She gasped, her eyes widened in disbelief, and before either of them could do a thing, her red light moved for the dead human, covering him in its fiery glow, a heat Xavier could feel.

Before he could rejoice further, he noticed the red light also found a small circular stone mere feet from Victor and was lighting it up as well.

Confused more than anything, he stepped forward to better to see what it was and why it called her light as well, but before he could make it very far, the red light flared, pushing his hand away, a terrible burning sensation pressing against his palm. He stifled a scream surprised at the feel of it, and gripped his wrist with his other hand, holding it close to his chest as he stepped away, glaring at her.

Her eyes were completely red; she didn't seem to be here at all but a mere conduit for the red light to charge up the body of the Vampire and the stone. It was why he gasped when the red light finally died, revealing red irises shining amidst white.

She was staring at him, her gaze cold, enraged, and in the haze of her terrible anger, she said, "Whatever you hope to accomplish by forgoing my grandfather's blood...it will not work." And she was gone.

He stared at the empty, broken doorway for a long moment, the implications of her words not lost on him at all, but what could he do about it now?

She was a far-away concern, one not to be tampered with, for there it was—the righteous, the exactness of power that flowed through his veins. Yes, all was right again, and it was with relief that he began to step forward, leave the room, seek out the others, and prepare them for war.

For war *was* coming, this much he was aware. And he knew he and Eleanor had little time before the vision of Alexandria returned to wherever she resided and told Christian Delacroix all she had seen. For she was stronger now, much stronger than he'd ever thought she'd be as a Vampire, and with the little display of power she had shown, he was certain Eleanor would be caught off guard if indeed she ventured to stop them from gaining in any more power.

He focused his thoughts on Eleanor, attempting to get a warning out when he felt the strange heat burn at his legs.

He looked down.

Victor's corpse was glowing faintly with the red light, and the sight caused him a sliver of alarm, for whatever the woman had come here for was tied to Dracula and his never-ending plans, surely.

But why Victor?

The Vampire was dead for good that could not be denied…and yet, Xavier could not help but feel the corpse would open his eyes at any moment, glare at him with all the contempt he could muster and ask for a hand up or else Xavier would love to stare at him all day.

But Victor remained; eyes closed, mouth slack, hair slightly silver, slightly browned in places from returning to humanity, it seemed

Dracula's favored anomaly, he thought, sighing. Kicking aside the stone as he stepped out of the room, he focused, with resolve, on the love of his life, and wondered what she had discovered beyond the cave.

* * *

Eleanor Black could not move. She'd smelled the overwhelming scent of smoke and magic in the air once she'd left the cave and moved toward the trees that changed since she'd last seen them. They were taller, thicker, no longer gnarled and black, but straighter, a healthier brown to their bark.

Thinking it all strange, she continued on, not stopping until she felt the immense energy of Dracula and another energy she had never felt before.

That was when she saw them, just barely through the trees, the wings of brilliant flame, orange and black, and then the slew of Creatures behind them that marched, fear on their faces. The Dragon above that carried an Ancient Creature swooped low overhead, and in her own fear she found she could not form proper thought.

How could they have found my home? How could I not have felt them approach? But the moment she'd asked herself this, she released the thought, for was it not clear? *Xavier. It was always Xavier.*

She had never stopped to think that a greater threat than Dracula and his family could ever appear in the World, but here they were, and they had not seen her yet.

She could still escape; she could still move, appear back by the mouth of her caves and find solace in her Creatures' power, in Xavier's arms…

A pressure appeared at her throat, and she found it hard to breathe, the restriction rising up to greet her as though an old friend, one that had lingered within her for quite some time, undisturbed until something had called it awake...

"There is something there," a deep, inhuman voice boomed, "through the trees."

A breath drifted through the morning air and though it was soft, Eleanor could still detect it on the wind. "What is it?" the new voice asked. It held great command, and though she could not see the winged Creatures beyond the tree she hid behind now, she knew it belonged to the lighter one.

A Phoenix, she thought in dismay. *I refuse to meet my end because of a bloody bird!*

And with her shoulders squared, she stepped around the tree, the sight of them several feet away clear through the shade of trees. She could not speak, the heaviness within her throat keeping her words at bay. She merely eyed them until they took notice, and it was the dark Phoenix to do so.

"Eleanor Black?" he asked, his voice trailing through the shadows cast with great power, perhaps greater than her own...

All Creatures behind the two watching Phoenixes stared over the wings with a mixture of fear and contempt and she blinked hard when she eyed Xavier amongst the crowd. But no, upon second glance it wasn't Xavier, it was the Vampire that had charged for her back on the path to Merriwall Mountain...but changed so completely? Gone were the numerous scars that blanketed his skin; he looked ever the picture of Xavier, if only older in face, kinder, perhaps in the eyes...

And that was when she noticed the glowing sword in the Vampire's hand. It glowed brilliantly with a golden light, just as the other weapons in all their hands did, save a large, black crossbow held by a Vampire she had never seen before. His weapon emitted black smoke, much like the smoke that left her and her Creatures.

Staring at this Creature, wondering who on Earth he was, she was taken aback when the blue-eyed Phoenix sighed as though quite tired, and then took a single step forward, all the while waving a hand through the dark. "Eleanor Black?"

She gasped as the ability to speak was given to her. "Creatures," she said, mustering all the authority she could, yet how hard it was to feel strong beneath their gazes, "I should have welcomed you to my home with the usual fanfare set aside for guests, but you've caught me quite unaware. What a pleasant surprise!" She stepped forward, extending a hand to greet them, refusing to be intimidated by any Creature, no matter what they were. But she had only made it a few steps when she felt it in full: the wall of buzzing brilliance that exuded from these winged beings, keeping her own power at bay. She dropped her hand in defeat, staring with wide eyes upon them all, a great fear replacing the curiosity she had previously felt.

"It's no more pleasant than it is necessary that we be here," the orange-flamed Phoenix said. "You are Eleanor Black, the reason the World has suffered even more under the darkness the so-called Vampires and Lycans spread across the land? If you are, then you hold the chosen King of All Creatures, do you not?"

"If you mean Xavier," she said, hiding her shaking hands behind her back, "then yes, the King of the Elite Creatures is at my side."

At this both Phoenixes glanced at each other. "So he has become... like you?" the blonde one asked after a time, returning his calm gaze to her.

She raised an eyebrow, wondering why this Creature could be so still, indeed, why he didn't seem the slightest bit perturbed that he stood before her, the one Creature that had taken Dracula's lies and fashioned out of them a greater truth. It upset her heavily that he would not show the slightest bit of fear, or even curiosity as to her greatness, for it was apparent, surely. *Wasn't it?*

Pushing aside the doubt with a cold breath, she focused instead on his question. She turned her focus, briefly, to her home and the Vampire within that should no longer be as such...

And the rush of power greeted her, a match for her own, and she exhaled a needless breath, for she could smell it on the air, taste it along her tongue, feel his hands around her waist...

She opened her eyes, staring with greater clarity upon the tall men with wings of fire, the scared Creatures behind them, and all fear fled. "He has become a greater Creature," she said simply, willing him to her side, eager to show them all his truth.

And in the next second, indeed, a strong hand clasped around her own; she breathed a sigh of relief as she turned to eye him.

He wore a black shirt, buttoned to the collar, a decidedly cool nature to his green gaze, his unbothered expression. His long black hair was unbound, giving her the greater impression that he was completely comfortable in his new power.

And what a power it was. She could feel it radiate off him in droves, strong and assured, and it bolstered her all the more; she felt herself stand taller at his side, felt reassured with the blood that flowed through his veins though he was not in the Vampire form: he held a human face but was no less impressive, indeed.

"You needed me, my love?" he asked, his voice sending a shiver of need to descend her spine.

"Yes," she said, swallowing hard, "these Creatures here wished to know if you were...like me."

"Did they now?" and Eleanor could hear the hint of amusement on his voice. "Well I think they can see for themselves that I am every bit what I was meant to be. What I always was."

The blonde Phoenix took another step against the ground, and Eleanor felt herself being pushed back by the invisible wall once again. Xavier, still in hand, stepped back as well. "You...were the one chosen to lead this World back to brilliance, Xavier Delacroix," he said, his voice cold for the first time since Eleanor had seen him. "But you have...sided with lesser, destructive...beings...forgone all your predecessor has worked so terribly hard to grant you and these other Creatures in his stead. What do you have to say for yourself?"

She stared at the man at her side, watching in amazement as his skin paled, his irises gleamed red, and his brow furrowed with indignation. "Excuse me?" he whispered, the harsh wind conjured from his fluid transformation sending his hair to blow across his shoulders. Eleanor squeezed his hand, doing her best to keep her feet planted on the ground. "Dracula never gave me a choice, merely thrust his title upon my shoulders and demanded I trek across the Dark World at his behest. Here," and he squeezed her hand back much to her pleasure, "I have a choice. I made it."

The blonde Phoenix seemed to look regretful for a moment, and then his shoulders squared, his blue eyes appeared to brighten, and he lifted a hand. As he did, the many weapons the Creatures behind him held began to glow tremendously, so much so Eleanor found her eyesight taken from her, and then the many Creatures were in the air, jumping over the heads of the Phoenixes heading straight toward them.

Xavier moved before she could: He swung the arm he held her hand with behind himself, pushing her there before releasing her, lifting off the ground with fluidity, no sword in his hand, but that did not seem to matter:

He met the closest Creature, the reinvigorated Aleister in midair pressing both hands to the glowing silver sword the Vampire held. They remained in the air, their hair and clothes billowing around them in a brilliant haze of pure power. Eleanor had barely blinked away the wind when the female Enchanter appeared before her, whispering words she could not catch, holding a small rod with glowing words upon its body.

Before she could know it, a great encumbering force pressed against her driving her to her knees; vines stretched up from the earth to wrap around her legs, snaking their way up her torso, wrapping around her chest, holding her fists immovable against the dirt...

Xavier shouted unintelligible words to the Vampire he kept in the air, words she could not hear over the shouts of the many Creatures that encircled her now, all pointing their staffs or swords or arrows at her face. She snarled in frustration, struggling against the squeezing vines, desperate to rip free for it seemed that Xavier was being shouted at by the Vampire that looked so similar to him, anger clear on that face so similar, desperation, regret, sadness...

No, she thought frantically, struggling harder against her binds. She could feel one weaken, indeed, it was almost—

"Don't you dare!" a voice shouted from behind her.

She turned her head as best she could against the vines that had begun to slither around her neck, and glared upon the Elf that held a white cane pointed at her back. "Arminius," she breathed, not at all surprised, "you truly think your magic can keep me down?" She winced as the broken vine regrew itself stronger, doubling itself around her just free arm.

"It seems to be doing the job well enough, Eleanor," he spat, the continual hiss of his voice trailing on the power-filled air long after he'd spoken.

"No," she snarled, focusing on the darkness within, "not well enough at all." She felt the pull of the darkness swirl in her gut, let it ascend to her throat, and with a scream of desperation, the black smoke left her lips and filled the morning air.

As her sight darkened, her spine lengthened and grew, her arms thickened, breaking the vines with ease. She was aware a great shadow covered the sky and great flapping wings beat a joyful song to her now large ears.

She ripped free of the vines, blowing all Creatures around her away as she lifted into the sky, searching for Xavier: he and the Vampire he fought had been blown away as well during her transformation. And indeed, amidst the darkness she and her Creatures cast against the sky, the Phoenixes' brilliance seemed dimmer, duller, though they never lifted hands or weapons to protect themselves.

She glared down at the blonde Phoenix that merely stared back at her as though judging her prowess, and then the dark one roared in anger, before lifting himself into the air, his black wings beating hard as he zoomed to reach her—

He was thrown out of the sky by an Elite with gray skin and tufts of black fur who then straightened in mid-air, screeching in defiance at the ground where the dark Phoenix had landed hard. And Eleanor realized, with a part of her brain that was still able to hold the transformation back into Vampire, Lycan, or human, that this Elite was Xavier.

My love, she thought, *you're brilliant.*

He looked up, his completely black eyes searching her, and for a moment she thought he did not recognize her, but then: *"It is you who are the brilliant one, Eleanor."*

She let out a screech of joy, but recovered quickly, for the dark Phoenix was rising to his feet. Throwing up a hand, she called for her Creatures, not liking at all the calm, concentrated gaze the blonde Phoenix gave from his place on the ground. It was as though he could not believe what he stared upon.

Unnerved, she allowed the darkness to cover them all, pulling them to the first place her mind could conjure. As she and the others were blanketed in encroaching darkness, she felt the shock of pain throughout her body and gasped, the blue eyes never once leaving her as she disappeared and the others disappeared.

* * *

Aleister Delacroix reached a trembling hand for his glowing sword, casting his gaze toward the sky, searching blearily for any sign of them, any at all. For it couldn't be possible. That couldn't have been Xavier. It couldn't have been his boy. No. He wouldn't believe it. He wouldn't condone it. He wouldn't allow it.

The hand was on his shoulder in the next second and he shoved it away, wishing greatly for the tears to fall, but they wouldn't. Cursing his existence as a Vampire for the millionth time since he'd allowed himself to be turned by Victor Vonderheide, he stabbed the sword into the dirt and cursed loudly.

"Leave him, Aurora," Peroneous's voice said from a few feet away, "he's just lost his son. We've just lost a King."

"There's no time for mourning, Creatures," the dark Phoenix said coldly, and at his voice, Aleister looked up from his pain. The Knights of the Order were rising from their backs or walking over to where Syran stood still staring up at the sky. He stared where Eleanor had been as though she was still there. Once all encircled him, their weapons placed more comfortably in their hands, Aleister stood, but he did not step forward, nor did he eye Aurora whose eyes he could feel boring holes into his back.

"You have failed in your duties as Hands of the Order," Caligo went on, "you must be prepared to face the consequences."

He raised two dark hands into the air, a swarm of black leaving his fingertips, and at once, Aleister felt his will to live recede until he found himself staring at the tip of his glowing sword, quite prepared to plant it through his forehead, no other thought reaching him.

"Not quite," Syran said, and with his voice, Aleister blinked, lowering the sword. He stared around at the others, all of whom had their weapons pointed at various parts of their own bodies. "What we've just seen is greater than I thought."

"Excuse me?" Caligo said, Aleister watching with incomprehension as the dark Phoenix moved to stand directly in front of Syran, matching him in height. "What we've seen is exactly what we must end! We have let these lesser Creatures do what they will for far too long, father! We must act! We must end them!"

Syran merely stared at this dark Phoenix that Aleister thought no longer looked anything remotely like a man. He was a consummate warrior, something darker in his gaze, far more than his appearance, and Aleister suddenly respected Syran for being able to stand there and face it as though it were normal. "We must uncover the source of my power on the Earth. It is still here, even if Xavier Delacroix is not."

Caligo sighed in exasperation, throwing up his hands. "Where is it then? In her caves?"

Syran ignored him, instead focusing on the sky. "Evert!" he called.

All watched as Vetus lowered herself to the tops of the trees and the tall white bundle of robes came flying off her white back, the man within them landing gently on the dirt ground before the Phoenix. "Yes, Syran?"

"The wisp of fyre one of my own sent down a while ago, I feel it is here."

"Oh?" he whispered in response, a look of concern etched into his old face.

"We must find it. It has solidified—someone has taken it. We must find out what they have been allowed..." And he turned and walked through the trees toward a direction Aleister knew he did not wish to travel at all. As the others bade each other wary looks, placing their glowing weapons at their sides, beginning to follow in Syran and Caligo's steps, Aleister groaned.

The sight of Xavier, the words he'd shouted over the sword, would not leave his mind, but Aleister did not wish to think it true: That his son hated him that much, that he truly chose Eleanor, truly wanted to become the horrid monster he was now. For he was no longer a Vampire, let alone anyone's child, this Aleister saw firsthand, had seen it, indeed, when Xavier had appeared at his doorstep, slung over the back of Nathanial Vivery. But he did not wish to believe...no, he would never believe it. *Xavier is still in there. My boy is still there.*

"Aleister," the voice said, uncertain, but still kind.

He blinked, looking around. Aurora held her rod limply at her side, her eyes watering with oncoming tears, and in her gaze he saw his own pain mirrored back at him. The tears he could not shed, she would. He moved to her at once, running a hand through her long black hair. "I'm sorry, I'm so sorry," he said, feeing terrible, indeed, for brushing her aside, for even in his anger, in his grief, he should have never brushed her off. Not her. She, who had been there through it all with him...

"It's quite alright, Aleister," she whispered, pulling away. She ran a shaking hand across his cheek and he imagined the feel of it, doing his best to remember when he could feel anything but grief and bloodlust at all. "*I'm* sorry about Xavier. He's...he truly chose her after all this time."

"I haven't given up," he said, remembering the sight of Xavier's eyes when he, Aleister, had told him that he could fight this, could fight her, that he did not have to be tied to her. Call him crazy, but he had the strongest feeling Xavier was lost inside his own mind, putting on a brave face, but that he was scared, still unsure. It was Eleanor's... madness getting to him as it had the moment he'd left the Vampire City. "It's her dread. It's poisoned him. I believe we can still reach him, Aurora. We can still..." But he saw the sadness in her dark gaze and felt his words drift on the morning air.

She wiped away a tear as she said, "Aleister...it'sit's over. Even if Xavier is lost, even if he is really in there—controlled by Eleanor...it's over. He's *chosen* her. Be it her madness doing it or his own mind—he chose her. He attacked Philistia Mastcourt and Nathanial Vivery, he slit Damion Nicodemeus's throat, he drew a sword on you, and he's been lost to her dread ever since he felt it grace the air." Sobs wretched her throat as she shakily went on, "It's done. Over. Syran is...he's seen him, now. Xavier is not our King...he's hers. And Syran...if not Syran, then that darker one—they'll kill him. And perhaps...maybe it is best—"

He tore away before she could say any more, grabbing his sword as he went. *It is best. It is best what? That Xavier be killed? Put down like a common criminal? He's my bloody son. He's the reason I'm even a Vampire—he's the reason I locked myself away from the World—he's the reason I jumped back in. He's the reason I fight, the reason I go on—it is best! Bah!*

I won't see him dead. No, he's still in there—he is!

He ignored her shouts of his name, ignored the power teeming from the sword in his hand, from the rod at his back as he moved further and further away from her. Mind gone on the image of his son, fluidly shedding his clothes, his Vampire form, to bear bat-like wings, completely black eyes...

He shuddered, stifling the flood of fear that he'd truly lost Xavier in full as he stepped in the footsteps of the Creatures ahead of him, desiring nothing more than to run in the opposite direction.

Chapter Seventeen

BETRAYALS

She tumbled through darkness, falling sometimes, stumbling others, hitting unseen objects as she went, sometimes soft things, sometimes hard, all smacking against her shoulders and hips; sharp unknowable things that tore at her clothes, her arms, her legs.

And all the while the image of Xavier Delacroix and Eleanor Black would not leave her mind's eye. How they gloated and laughed at her retreating back and nowhere was Dracula to be found.

"Christian!" she called instead, the fingers squeezing around an arm.

She blinked hard in the dancing light of the many candles around the room, surprised to find Westley Rivers staring down at her with concern.

She sat up at once, shrinking away from him as though burned. "You stabbed me!" she cried, remembering with a swell of fury that he had indeed entered the room some time before and placed his sword into her midsection. Her hands instinctively moved there, and to her surprise she felt a softer fabric at her touch but she did not look down: Westley was staring at her with subtle hints of anger and sadness.

He held up both hands in surrender. "It was a test," he said, "and you failed." Before she could ask what test, he went on, "You are not the Queen of the Dark World."

Her brow furrowed. "I thought Christian was—"

"It seems I'm not a candidate for royalty either, Miss Stone," Christian said, stepping into the room. She blinked upon him, realizing he had been standing beyond the door's frame the entire time, perhaps called to her shouts just as Westley had been. He wore a fresh, white shirt, though it was not buttoned at all, leaving his chest and abdomen to be seen through the opening, and on his legs were very fashionable pants Alexandria had never seen him in before, as dark as the freshly polished shoes he wore.

She found his state of dress curious, but opting to ignore it for the moment, for she was quite interested in whatever this test happened to be, she opened her mouth to question him when a woman filled the doorway. Her black hair was held up in an unfathomable creation, her eyes gray, a seductive smile upon her red lips, and the large black fur coat she wore hid her clothes from view, but Alexandria had the greatest suspicion she wore something quite unbecoming beneath it. *She was immensely attractive*, she thought, all question of Westley's betrayal gone now.

"Christian," this woman said with a heavy foreign tongue, "shall I see you at the Ball tonight?"

He looked as though he wished to sink into the floor and disappear, but he turned to her, smiling far too politely, gesturing a hand toward the bed. "I am to accompany Miss Stone, Lady Asimov, but I suspect I shall see you and Dimtri there?"

Lady Asimov gave Alexandria a quick once-over before smiling. It was quite cold. "But of course, Delacroix," she said, returning her gaze to Christian with far too great a familiarity, "I shall save you several dances." And with a wave of a gloved hand to all in the room, she turned and disappeared through the doorway.

An uncomfortable silence stretched across the stifled air, the implication of the woman's very presence clear to Alexandria, if ever she could grasp one. But before she could process what little she could feel, Westley cleared his throat.

"Alexandria," he said, bringing all eyes to him, "you called for Xavier and Christian while you slept. What did you dream?"

She tore her gaze from the dark Vampire to eye her hands, quite surprised to find she now wore a white gown, but she could not think on it further before the memories returned, the fear growing anew.

Xavier stared at her with cold, hateful green eyes, a sense of superiority within them that suggested he was above it all, knew more than she, indeed.

She clasped a hand to her neck as the fear bubbled there, a scream threatening to leave her lips, but she swallowed it down, eyeing Christian, sorry she would have to say it before he could see it with his own eyes.

"Xavier," she managed, suddenly desiring a vast amount of blood. "Xavier's one of hers. He's an Elite Creature."

Christian did not move, nor did she expect him to. She did not know what she expected from the Vampire, but Westley's cry of alarm pulled her gaze from him. "Are you certain? What did you see?"

"I was in Eleanor's…home. I walked the halls as though I was there," she began, aware Christian was listening: she could feel his eyes on her, "and I came upon a door. It held…such powerful energy… and when it opened…he was there…different. Cruel."

At this Westley's gaze darkened. "Damn. Then we've no time at all. If Syran sees what he's become, he will kill us all. But without a King to replace Xavier we're as good as dead regardless—"

"But Christian—you said he was as good as King, Westley," she said, her thoughts jumping to her tongue before she could stop them.

Westley's stare to Christian held much more words than he would say aloud, and Alexandria had the distinct impression she missed quite a bit while she was under. Before she could question it however, Christian finally spoke.

"Westley does not seem to hold confidence in my ability to… protect the things necessary. To focus," he sighed, "on the things that matter most."

"Quite," Westley agreed, "which is why I must find the *proper* candidate before Syran gets wind that I don't have one lest we all suffer a fiery, permanent death. Excuse me." He bowed to them both, a dark-skinned hand over his heart, and left the room, the tail of his cloak swaying around his boots as he went.

Once gone, Christian waved a hand and the door closed, but he did not move from his place beside the portrait of the Elf.

Desiring to end the silence, desiring to apologize for her words to him earlier, she opened her mouth, but was rebuffed

"Westley is right," he said, his voice quiet in the punctured dark. "I am no King. I did not even know you were injured—I was too selfish…embroiled in my own anger…" He sighed, dropping his arms from their position across his chest, and how it seemed all the fight left him. "I am still a coward, no matter the blood I drink, the swords I wield, the Creatures I run alongside. I am not good enough for this… to be your protector. How can I when I let simple things like emotions get the better of me?"

She threw the sheets off her, settling the hem of her dress across her legs as she swung them over the side of the bed, staring at him more seriously. "You're being quite hard on yourself, Christian" she said softly, "you've done what any Vampire would have done if given a woman with Dracula's blood and told to protect her. You needn't beat yourself up."

He stepped to her, sinking into a wooden chair most near the bed, eye-level to her now. And here she could see the regret, the sadness in his gaze, remembered her words to him yesterday, a fresh pang of regret tearing at her own cold heart. "I am a fool," he whispered, the words leaving his lips in a rush, "I am a selfish, cowardly fool who should have never stumbled upon you that night. If I had stayed in Damion's home, received my training, perhaps it would be Damion in my place right now doing a far better job than I ever could.

"I was never meant to wield the sword of Dracula. Never meant to be here, by your side, never meant to turn you—by God I was never meant to turn you—"

She grasped his hand, ignoring the raise of his eyebrows, the confusion in his black eyes. "No Christian," she said, "these are all choices you made on your own. You talked Xavier down when you all were trying to figure out what to do with me. He was…unaware of my fear, even then. But you, Christian," and she ran her thumbs across the backs of his hands desiring the regret and sorrow to leave his stare, "you saw my fear—you held me whilst in Victor's room, consoled me when I learned what you were—you saved me from Thomas and Lore at every turn—"

"And you came back for me in those woods," he said, gratitude radiating off him in droves. "Never had I had anyone...that cared. And saying that, earlier...I should not have...plied all of my desires on you...expected you to accept them outright—"

"Christian," she began, unsure of how to proceed, "immediately after you left the room I'd regretted what I said to you. Dracula's... commands be damned, there is something between us...something beyond his blood flowing through our veins, and I would be the fool, Christian, if I did not admit it to myself, and to you."

His stare was one of disbelief but the corners of his mouth turned up ever so slightly, and he dared himself to show a fang. "And what do you feel between us, Alexandria?" he asked after a time of staring at her hand within his own.

She stared at him, unsure of what she felt exactly, but quite sure she wanted his peace, wanted him to see the Vampire she had seen, the one that had been there when she had opened her eyes after the cold air of death had filled her lungs, settled there, and never left.

"Christian," she said when his gaze would not meet her own, "you are strong—perhaps stronger than your brother. He is...he is corrupted...he isn't in his right mind. And I know no one else—no one dragged into this...this madness should be expected to easily rise to it all. My grandfather—Dracula—he was mad—driven to madness but he sought peace. Everything he did was for peace. His peace of mind. What we're working for—what Westley is working for is for peace. And I truly believe you can be the King we need because Xavier—I'm sorry, but he is not it."

As she spoke, his black eyes flashed upon her with sorrow. "My brother...what is he like now?"

"Cruel. Quite rude, honestly. Powerful. But definitely corrupted."

"Damn. I should have been there—I should have been by his side. Helped him better—"

"You can help him by helping me, by helping Westley—be the King he needs you to be. Because out of all the 'pure' Vampires in the World, you are the only one with Dracula's sword and his granddaughter at your side; you are the only one already poised to defend the World from Eleanor Black...from Xavier."

He was quiet for a long time, and it was not until he exhaled a terribly cold breath that he said, "You truly think I can be the King, Alexandria?"

I've no other options, frankly, and neither do you. "I know you can, Christian," she whispered, giving his hand a squeeze.

"Then that is what I'll do," he said, straightening in the chair. "I'll prove myself worthy of the throne."

"Even if it means facing your brother?" she asked, confused when his grip strengthened around her hand, reassuring yet firm.

His black gaze darkened to a vibrant red for a moment before retreating to its unfathomable darkness, and she thought she saw a hint of sadness but then he said, "Even if it means destroying what he's become. There's too much at stake to allow him to continue to get lost in his mind."

She nodded, managing a smile, the twinge of pain in her cold heart deepening as she stared at him, the sacrifice clear in his gaze.

A necessary sacrifice, the voice in her mind whispered suddenly, and she felt the weight of Dracula's decisions fall heavy on her shoulders in full.

* * *

Evian Cross waved a hand against the crystal ball, eyeing the many figures that appeared within, their cloaks trailing around their worn, bloodied boots as they marched over the grass.

"What's the next step?" Ronaldo asked, spreading his tan hands wide across the book that lay open in midair before him. A subtle red glow left his fingers, and his normally brown eyes glowed a vibrant gold.

Evian turned from his friend and regained his focus, willing the image to reappear. "We wait for Philistia Mastcourt to arrive, then we head to Shadowhall to gather the necessary tools."

"And what tools would these be?" Ronaldo asked, the glow from his work subsiding slightly. Evian could tell he was paying attention.

"What the Phoenixes desire to help prepare for their arrival," he said, not turning to eye them, gaze held on the familiar shoulders of Philistia shrouded in her cloak as they were.

At this, the red light died immediately, the book was thrown to the floor, and Evian heard the hurried footsteps moving to reach him. He did not look up as Ronaldo drew level, saying, "Their arrival?! Evian, what on Earth are you talking about? They cannot land here!"

"They already have, Ronaldo," he said crossly, not looking up from the wind-stricken Creatures within the sphere. "The Head Phoenix walks the Earth to find the chosen King, but we've all heard the reports—Xavier is no longer on the side of his Vampires, he's no longer on the side of any Dark Creature—he's chosen Eleanor Black."

"But what will the Phoenixes do?" the fear in the voice palpable, urgent.

"They will kill him, save Syran from killing us all, perhaps. It was courageous to make we humans once upon a time, but now... it has become far too dangerous, too difficult. For all the gifts the Ancient Elders bequeathed unto us, abuse of power was not the one he wished we settle on."

Ronaldo grabbed his shoulders, swinging him around to face him. The man's eyes were wide with his fear, though still tinged with slight gold. "But that is not on us, surely! That's the will of the Vampires, the Lycans, the Elite Creatures. They abused their power! We Enchanters merely did as we were told by the ones in power, we never stepped out of line!"

He sighed as the fear took greater hold in his gut. "Do you truly think Syran will stop at the Vampires, Lycans—Eleanor Black's Creatures? I've seen them, Ronaldo, they are dressed for war. We are all their creation—all of us burdened with the sins of the few! Do you truly believe we will get out of this...purge unscathed? Do you truly think Syran will allow us to keep the arts for ourselves after seeing what can be created—twisted—under its hand?

"I helped a Vampire learn the art, Ronaldo. I took the arts once so pure and gave it to the Vampire to better Dracula's...myriad schemes—!"

"But you didn't do that! Dracula forced you to! It wasn't your fault!"

"Yes, but once it was done, the Phoenixes contacted me—had been watching me, saw my 'creative mind,' they called it. Wanted me to help the King further his plans, but also prepare in case he would fail. He has. And now Equis is dead because he grew greedy, and I heard another Vampire who met with the Phoenixes is dead because he did not live up to his word. They are a noble race of being, Ronaldo. Lies and half-truths—doubt—it doesn't mean the same things to them. If you do not fulfill your end of the deal with them—you die, simple as. And if they're going to kill me anyway, I'd rather go down helping this World regain a little bit of its natural face before I go."

Ronaldo stepped away, whispering words of disbelief in his native tongue, his slightly glowing gaze held on Evian as if he couldn't believe he existed, and Evian did not blame him. He'd looked at himself in the mirror after his very first meeting with the birds, not able to stomach himself, nor the severity with which the fate of the World rested upon the shoulders of those chosen to save it. Those that would eventually fail…

He resumed his gaze upon the crystal ball, though the image of the walking Creatures did not resurface: His mind had fled him, lost on the treacherous climb to the Nest, and the terrifying, powerful Creatures that always greeted him there, tying him with a symbol of a sword encased in fire, at their feet.

Chapter Eighteen

STORMING THE GATES

The afternoon sun pressed against the clearing before the black, rusted gates and the seven Vampires that stood guard beyond it were focused.

For they knew having the brother of Xavier Delacroix in the Vampire City was a matter most important for all Vampires, hell, even all Dark Creatures, and they, the ones chosen for their special task, were determined not to mess it up. A command like this, if executed well, meant a promotion or other means of advancement, or perhaps scores of the special blood *Anima* at their request for years on end.

Yes, it was a gig many would be a fool to pass up or deny, so they stood before the gates, an impenetrable line against all who would dare attempt to enter the Vampire City that was not a royal guest or Creature with direct ties to Xavier Delacroix or his brother.

Which was why when the smell entered their noses and drifted past their skin in a brazen breeze foretelling of the battle to come, they released their snarls, withdrew their swords, and raised their shields, prepared to defend the haven for all Vampires without another thought.

* * *

Lore slowed his gallop to a steady trot, smelling the Vampires some ways up ahead. He knew he was close, but the presence of Vampires was not welcome. More of them anyway.

He still stank with the blood of the ones he'd killed on his way here, and what was worse, he still tremored with the painful pulses of magic that pressed against him, no matter the form he held, and he was severely doubting his ability to fight once more.

Seven of them, he thought, slowing to a crawl, padding the dirt beneath his large paws uncertainly. *Seven of them. One of me. Not fair odds.*

He took a step back before bracing himself to push forward, the sudden voice holding him at bay: *"Lore?"*

James.

"The Vampires have me chained like an animal in their dungeon," and Lore could hear the anger in the man's voice. *"What is your plan, my King? There are far too many bloodsuckers here for us to take on, on our own..."*

He lifted his snout into the air and inhaled deeply. Yes, there were numerous Vampires below his paws, beneath the dirt, but he only wished to kill the woman. Regaining himself, he returned his nose to the ground. *Where is the woman? Alexandria Stone?*

"What? What of her?"

She must die, James. She must be strung up with the others, held by their necks until their heads are removed from their bodies—

"Is that why you came? Because of her?"

I could feel you, James. I knew you were not dead...but I felt her as well, felt her blood tied to yours...where she would be, you would be...I must end her. You can help.

Silence met him in an uncomfortable rush of wind, but he stayed, listening, waiting for the connection to reopen. It did not.

Growling in frustration, he stepped forward, reminding himself that though he was injured, weary, he was still the King of the Lycans, still here, and there was one more of his kind, bitten *by* him beyond the gates. Bidden to do the King's will no matter whose blood encased his scent, now.

He would fall in line, he thought, stepping forward, preparing himself as best he could to enter the place he had never been before. Desperation, as it had since he thought he'd lost James for good, clawing at his frazzled mind.

* * *

Christopher Black followed the Creatures as they traversed the deserted hallways, all of her Creatures pulled to her side during the battle. And no one knew where she or Xavier had gone and all the Phoenixes seemed to care about was something they would only whisper about while they led the group. And Christopher, though the medallion at his chest blared brighter than ever before, did not desire any longer to be a part of this madness.

For he had seen what his sister, what Xavier had become—it was what Darien had become, a winged monster unable to speak words, but force guttural, screeching sounds to scrape against their long throats.

And he blinked in the light of a nearby torch as he remembered Dracula. How the Vampire had never mentioned—never uttered a word as to the truth to his power. Christopher had seen shades of it in the Great Vampire's demeanor, the darkness of the eyes so cold when the Vampire would pay him the sparse visit, but he never thought—a monster. *And he had us all chained as a monster would.*

What the devil am I doing with these Creatures? I didn't pay a mind to their goals as long as I could speak to Lillith, get her see I was kept a prisoner just as I made her...but now...I am kept from her—stuck with these Creatures...these Phoenixes that merely want their odds and ends settled. But what of mine? What of Lillith?

"There is greater energy down here," Caligo's rough voice said, cutting through Christopher's reverie.

It was with a start that he stepped with the others who had already rounded the corner, a long tunnel, narrowing into a smaller one several miles down greeting him when he reached their backs.

An old door barely hanging on its hinges ended the hallway, and the blonde Phoenix's broad shoulders were already taking up view of the doors, whatever lay beyond it.

Caligo followed shortly after, and with slight snarls of protest from Aleister, the rest followed suit.

Christopher, however, stayed staring after them, unsure whether he wanted to move further, wanted to be dragged even deeper into a mess that was no sign closer to Lillith Elizabeth Crane.

"There's nothing here but a dead…human," Syran said, his voice reaching Christopher's ears beyond the heads of the others. Christopher noticed the Phoenix never stepped past the threshold of the door.

"Former Vampire, you mean," Caligo said over Syran's shoulder.

The others attempted to peer over their broad backs, and the ones that did immediately shrunk away in disbelief and horror, whispering a name Christopher did not care to catch.

It was not until Dragor, the Creature closest to him received the name that he knew who the commotion was about at all.

"Victor Vonderheide?! No. I don't believe—out of my way!"

And the Vampire pressed past the Order of the Dragon, even throwing aside the Phoenixes who had moved from their places just in front of it, a cry of greater disbelief leaving his lips as he stared into the room.

As Christopher watched, Dragor made to step into the room, but Syran placed a hand on his shoulder holding him back.

"No, Vampire, you don't want to enter this room."

"But why on Earth not? That's Victor bloody Vonderheide on the floor! Dead!"

"Because Vampire," and even from where he stood Christopher could see Syran's bright blue eye as he turned his head to eye Dragor, "this room doesn't exist. Its power is fading. All within it are as good as dead. She has corrupted the sanctity of *The Immortal's Guide* far too much as it is. This last remaining…vestige of that great work has been tarnished. And with the original work destroyed, its task done, it was only a matter of time before this page," he waved a hand toward the room, "was destroyed as well. The Vampire there is as good as dead. There is nothing we can do for it…but…" And his voice trailed as he gave them all the back of his head, staring, what Christopher guessed, was thoughtfully into the room.

Dragor blinked in awe upon the Creature before finally saying, "Well? What is it?"

And Syran stepped forward, into the room, eliciting gasps for all the Creatures, save Caligo who merely stared.

Dragor snarled. "You just said no one could enter the room!"

Syran did not turn to eye him as he stepped across the old wooden floors; his golden glow seeming to ripple through the air of the place, sending the strange blackness to shrink away from him with sparks of orange fire.

He walked further, so that Christopher could no longer see him in view of the doorway, and then a brilliant flash of light pressed against the old wooden frame, blinding all who stood in the hallway.

There was a wave of heat Christopher could feel against his front, and he almost thought he were being burned alive it was so strong, but then it died and he opened his eyes.

Syran had reappeared in the doorway, in a hand a burning stone ball that did not scar his palm as he held it. "I found the source of my power on the Earth," he said as the ball crumbled into black ash, the flames dying; "now we locate the King."

"But Xavier is not—!" Aleister began, his shoulders trembling.

"Not that Vampire," Syran interjected, his blue eyes held on Aleister, now, "he is not the King. There is another…"

"Another?" Aurora and Peroneous asked together.

Syran began to step past them, heading toward the beginning of the hallway where Christopher still stood, mind blank. And as Syran reached him, he thought he saw a flicker of contempt in the Phoenix's glowing gaze.

It jarred him where he stood, that stare, and he felt the chain at his neck grow hot, the cold of a Vampire fleeing him at once.

And as the Phoenix brushed past him, he exhaled a cold breath, unsure if there were another who could take the title of King, unsure if they, the Creatures bidden to the King's side, could survive the wrath of the Phoenix that burned within.

* * *

Damion had traveled with Belinbol past the mountain, the Goblet in his dark hands, the blood bubbling within its golden body. "There

Vampire," Belinbol said, his eyes trained on something in the distance, "place the Goblet there."

He eyed where the Dragon looked, a gasp leaving him with the sight.

There, several, several yards ahead of the where they stood, mostly hidden behind high trees, was what looked to be a high stone enclosure rising out of the snow-covered ground. The stone rose on either side of an opening in its middle, which appeared a small table made of what looked to be charred rock.

The moment he saw it, he stepped forward, leaving the snowy opening to traverse the trees. As he walked, he realized he moved alone, and he turned, eyeing the Dragon. "Are you not coming?"

A large plume of gray smoke left the long, white snout. "I cannot enter the trees, Damion Nicodemeus. You will make this journey alone."

Alone. He faltered for a second, the Goblet slipping in his grasp, but regaining himself, he held it tight, squaring his shoulders. *I've always been alone. What difference does this make?*

Giving Belinbol a curt nod of thanks, he turned, stepping deeper past the trees, hearing the large Dragon's wings press against the cold air as he lifted back toward the top of the mountain.

The strong breeze followed shortly after, buffeted by the hard bark of the trees at his back, but he never turned to eye the Dragon's departure, he kept his gaze on the ever-growing stone enclosure before him.

Yes, he was almost to the edge of the trees when the Goblet grew scalding hot, a painful burning pressing against his palms, the cry of pain leaving his lips before long.

The Goblet flew from his hands, hitting the ground brusquely, a sizzling sound pressing against his ears as the snow melted where the Goblet landed.

The hard, round object pressed against his back and he lifted both burning hands in surrender.

"Who gives you permission to trespass on sacred ground, Vampire?" the strange voice said from behind him.

"Belinbol of the Bagabill Dragons!" he shouted, confusion filling him. "I'm on special task from Dracula, himself!"

"Dracula's good and dead, Vampire. Every Creature knows it— what mission do you presume to have from him?" And the object was jabbed harder into his back.

He eyed the Goblet at his feet, the grass around it dark with melted snow. "I'm to bring this Goblet to that place just there! It must be purified before the King's to drink from it!"

At this the object was removed, and he exhaled a needless breath, surprised when the sound of hooves crunching against the snow entered his ears. Before long he stared into the hard, black eyes of a Centaur, its long black hair unbound against its shoulders and back.

"Damion Nicodemeus, is that you?" the Centaur asked, a quizzical expression upon the serious face.

He blinked in question upon the Centaur, the bare tan chest gleaming against the evening sun that managed to pass through leaves.

"I'm sorry, do I know you?" he asked, figuring the Centaur someone he'd crossed paths with many years ago.

"Vimic, Damion," he said, "Vimic of the Rein Clan."

He relaxed with the memory of the Centaur that he had met in his many travels, indeed, he still heard the roar of the Giants as he and Vimic escaped their terribly large grasp one foolish night. "Vimic, what on Earth are you doing here?" he asked, stooping to reclaim the Goblet. It still sweltered with a swarming heat but he grasped it all the same, unsure he should leave it on the ground for the Centaur to claim.

Vimic lifted the long wooden staff he held in a hand, his black tail swishing in a breeze. "Additional protection for the Goblet's home," he said, eyeing the Goblet now, "quite surprised you're the one holding it. I would've thought Nathanial or even Christian would have—"

"But it's me," he said, unable to keep the bite out of his voice. Looked over, even if he was here, standing with the very object that would turn the tide of war, indeed! "I'm the one here! At the gate! I'm the one Dracula told to protect the World! To save it!"

"And I do not doubt your ability to do any of those things, I assure you, Damion, I just never thought you much…involved in Dracula's affairs."

"A lot has changed since he died."

"Indeed."

Damion stared, wondering if the Centaur was telling the truth. And after a moment, deciding it didn't matter, for he *was* the one holding the Goblet, after all, he stepped past Vimic, moving for the stone stand—

The large figure appeared just before it in the next second, its large gray wings spread wide. It stared down at the stone stand where the Goblet should have been.

And indeed, the black blood was bubbling intensely now, the heat grand within Damion's hands, but he kept his gaze on the large-winged...thing that was hovering several feet off the ground.

"Darien?" he whispered, Vimic clasping a hand over his mouth, stilling his question at once.

He eyed Vimic in wonder, surprised to see a grand look of fear and bewilderment on the normally stoic face.

Turning his gaze back to the strange figure, he eyed the large wings as best he could given the distance, seeing that it was not Darien, indeed: the thin skin was gray, not black, and the ends of his wings curved slightly more than Darien's, so who was this?

"*Eleanor, it is not here,*" the new voice whispered through his mind, and how familiar it sounded...

"*No matter,*" the other voice responded, though this one sounded farther away, indeed. "*We take the Vampire City. Now.*"

"*Yes, my love,*" the Creature in front of them answered, and then with a grand burst of horrible wind that reached them even where they stood in the trees, it rose into the air. "*We take what is ours.*"

Damion watched with a stunned Vimic as it disappeared back over the mountain, fear full in his cold heart.

Eleanor. That must have been...Xavier? It could not have been. Xavier was King. But hadn't Belinbol told me Xavier was lost? Lost to her? One of her Creatures? It couldn't be—that couldn't have been him—

Vimic removed his hand from Damion's mouth and Damion licked his lips, despite their trembling.

The Goblet suddenly felt like lead in his hands, and it was all he could do to keep from dropping it, the blood within continuing the bubble, to boil with urgency. Yes, he could feel it, the World was compromised, the blood needed to be pure. But what did it matter if

Xavier was no longer pure, himself? If he had left Dracula for good? Become one of those...Creatures.

Eleanor...yes, my love.

He blinked upon the blood, remembering when he felt so pulled to Eleanor, enraptured by her, the attention she showed. He thought of Xavier's bat-like wings and shuddered; glad he had not pursued her beyond what they had shared. Perhaps somewhere in the back of his mind he knew it fruitless, knew it dangerous. Knew she would always choose Xavier Delacroix...

The hand was on his shoulder. "Put it there now," Vimic said urgently, fear in his voice. "They won't look here again."

He hesitated, the blood churning thickly within the golden rim. "What's the point?" he asked the blood.

"What's the point? You're saving the World if you restore the blood!" Vimic said, incredulously.

"What's the point? *The point?!* Xavier is no longer King of anything but Eleanor's...madness, there's no replacement in line, is there?!"

Vimic was silent for a moment, and then, "*You* are pure of blood, aren't you Damion?"

He looked up into the black eyes, unsure what was being asked. "I...am, but could I ever...?"

He stared back down at the blood, finding it strange it never called to him, never pulled him to drink from it, indeed he wasn't certain he could. Not at all. But if all it needed was one pure of blood, who's to say it couldn't be him? *Shouldn't* be him?

Driven with greater desire now, for why should it always be Xavier, he lifted the Goblet to his lips, the black blood still bubbling, still hot—

Vimic smacked the Goblet from his lips, using only the staff. Before Damion could say a word, Vimic began, "It needs to be pure before it can be taken! You'll meet your death if it isn't calm! Unburdened with the heat of change!"

Seeing sense in the Centaur's words, Damion moved forward with whatever ungainly speed he could muster, urgency clawing at his mind, the desire for power, power that had been kept from him for years while he plotted and schemed, worked and worked hard was suddenly before him. In his hands, in this burning cup—

He placed the round bottom atop the charred stone which, closer now, he realized was not charred stone but darkened gold. Tiny flecks of it shone through where the rest was not darkened—with what he could not know—and at once the Goblet began to glow with a brilliant, golden light.

The blood calmed, regaining its red color, vibrant against the glow, but never once did the desire for it reach him. And how strange he thought it, this lack of desire reaching him. He remembered the brown-green gaze of the human Christian had found those months before. How he could find no pressing desire to bite her at all...

"What are you waiting for, Damion? Take it! Finish what Dracula started so many years before!" Vimic shouted.

He stared at the blood, unable to grasp the Goblet. *Dracula*. There it was. *Dracula* was the reason he could not grab it, could not drink from it, could not be King, and could not have any sort of power.

He, Damion, was never *chosen*, never in the know; never the one Dracula had *desired* to take his place.

And he remembered the meeting, so many moons ago, where it was decided that Christian would train with he, Damion. Christian, chosen for training by the Vampire best for the job. Christian, the one who had found the woman, had moved courageously, foolishly, to save her. Christian, the obvious choice if Xavier should ever fail. Christian, the one who had seemed so drawn to the mysterious woman, who had kept to himself, not desperate for power, or desperate to uncover Dracula's secrets. Christian the one who had watched her without fail...

"The one in line to rule us all," he whispered, understanding his place in all things at last.

It was always to prepare the one chosen. The ones with special blood. And though he and his brother had taken Dracula's blood as well, he knew it was only those Dracula had readily placed in his mind, a *conscious* choice, that would be able to rule the Dark World. That would be able to do what must be done.

And that was not him.

It was never him.

235

"Christian bloody Delacroix," he whispered, a chuckle escaping him.

"What? What was that?" Vimic asked closer now than before.

Damion turned, the Centaur was still near the line of trees but slightly farther now. He bowed to the Creature, a smile on his lips. "I said Christian Delacroix is your King, Vimic," he called over the distance, "I daresay, he has always been."

"What on Earth are you——?"

"It would do neither of us any good if I drank from the Goblet, Vimic. Christian Delacroix is the King of the Dark World. And wherever he may be, Tremor bless his soul, may he be a better King than I or Xavier Delacroix ever could."

Chapter Nineteen

THE WINTER BALL

Christian placed a comforting hand on the leather handle of the Ares, the clothes he wore, as Westley had told him, were those fit for a King.

He wasn't sure if that were true, but he did feel more regal, if only because he would be attending this Ball with Vampire bloody royalty at his side.

He'd been pinching himself since he was dragged from the room to allow her to get ready, unable to believe that he would dance, waltz, and sway with the woman at all. The woman that had, in a matter of minutes, reduced his feelings of inadequacy to a standstill, allowing thoughts of power, passion, and good things to flourish.

Good things. Heh. He never thought he'd think himself capable of it.

He readjusted the black collar of his suit jacket, the white buttoned up shirt underneath, eyeing the white gloves upon his hands, unable to recall when he'd ever been quite so dressed up. Even the shoes upon his feet were new, foreign to his body. Polished heavily though, pointed sharply at the toe, the slight heel clicking loudly against the ground as he paced his room to and fro, waiting on pins and needles until he could leave and see her.

The loud knock at his doors snapped him from his reverie, and inhaling sharply, he stepped for them, releasing a hand from the Ares, pulling them open.

"Christian," Westley said, eyeing him up and down, nodding appreciatively, "I see you've decided to wear your hair down as opposed to in a hold."

"There's only so much of your damn rules I'll abide by, Mister Rivers."

"Fair enough."

He stepped aside, allowing Christian to enter the hallway, and as they ventured down the hall, toward Alexandria's room, Christian found himself incredibly nervous, suddenly finding the lapel of his suit jacket far too high, not folded quite enough, the buttons of his shirt beneath pressing hard against his front—

"And Lord Delcroix, your date, Misses Alexandria Patricia Stone," Westley was saying, throwing open the familiar door that Christian had not realized they'd stopped in front of.

He blinked in the torchlight of the room, unsure where Alexandria was, for the woman that stood in front of him now could not have been her. Her dark brown hair was up in what looked to him a bird's nest, golden leaves placed and pinned within its folds and tendrils, giving her quite an earthy look. But much more practiced and refined, unlike the quite literal earthy look she'd held since he'd known her, being chased through woods, across fields, and up mountains. Her lips were a deep red that reminded him completely of the blood that had spilled from her neck when he'd bitten her at last, her eyelids dark with a smokiness that drew out the vibrancy of her brown-green eyes much in a way the red from tiredness, from fear had never done.

She smiled, showing her fangs, and in the orange light of the torch, he had to keep from moving to her and kissing her deeply.

"Am I a worthy 'date,' my Lord?" she asked, playfully.

The collar was indeed far too tight: if he needed to breathe, he surely wouldn't be able to manage it. "It is I who am wondering my worth this night, Miss Stone," he whispered, unable to do anything more.

She stepped forward, taking Westley's hand, and as he closed the door behind her, Christian took in the rest of her eagerly.

She wore a dark red dress, her many skirts flowing around her legs, hiding them from view. The neckline was low, pulled down around her shoulders, and it was here he stared the most, eager to taste her blood again, for it was so delicious she looked, so alluring a Vampire, a Dark Creature, she was.

There were leaves, golden as they shimmered in the torchlight, stitched into the red fabric, expertly woven all across the dress, and at its hem and neckline, golden thread held and finished it.

"You look stunning," he offered lamely, unsure of what more to say, what more to do in a situation such as this, for although they'd gone together to Victor's ball those months before, he had hardly known her, he had not thought it anything special, a simple outing he'd been invited to. She was a human to be watched.

But now. Yes, everything was different.

"You look quite smart, yourself," she offered, giving him a dark red gloved hand.

He took it in his own, and he nodded to Westley who nodded in return. Christian walked with her toward the end of the hall and did not turn to look back as they ventured down the stairs. It was where he had heard the Winter Ball was to be held: in the basement of Dracula's mansion where it had been held every year, as he'd learned.

He was unsure of what to say, what to do, indeed, the more they walked, descending more and more flights of stairs. They'd descended nearly six of them when he remarked, "There must be magic holding these walls up. This building isn't large enough from the outside to warrant these many floors."

"I was thinking the very same," she offered, the golden gem around her neck glistening in the torchlight as they moved deeper and deeper into the less known parts of the manor.

Indeed, Christian had never seen these walls before. Unlike the silver walls of the floors above, these were all stone, gray with age, but smooth as though they'd been crafted painstakingly by hand. *Or magic*, he thought wryly.

And when at last there were no more stairwells to traverse, Christian found himself staring upon two terribly tall, large doors, silver, made of some strange material he did not recognize. It shimmered in the white light of two silver torches on either side of the doors in black holders, and he stepped forward, lifting a hand for a white handle.

Pushing it down, he pulled the large door toward himself, eyeing the impossibly high ballroom that opened up before him. There were balconies as high as the never-ending ceiling where Vampires mingled, kissed, and sipped blood from clear goblets in gloved hands.

Candles hovered all throughout the air while large silver torches clung to fixtures against the white walls. And here and there along the walls were golden decorations, some of winged beings, others of Vampires in elegant battle with Lycans.

He stepped in, feeling the touch of her gloved fingers on his back, but he did not turn to eye her: The golden words

Protection, Preservation, and Peace. Always.

were emblazoned in the air, shimmering as though they belonged there, high above the heads of the Vampires that danced beneath them. Their gloved hands intertwined, their bodies close, their skirts and tails of suit jackets twirling as they swirled and dipped and stepped to the music the live band played toward the back of the terribly large room.

And though they were quite far from where Christian stood, he could not mistake the sound, for it was clear even where he stood in the doorway.

"This is what I've missed? All these years?" he whispered to the clean, lavish air, feeling quite foolish to hate his brother, hate Dracula, and hate all he had not been told. He saw it now, in the proud way the Vampires walked about on the edges of the dance floor, many mingling at one of the two long, large, golden bars where bartenders were dishing out fresh goblets of blood with smiles, just what he had missed.

Ease, access, *pleasure*—indeed, he'd stalked about the night for years searching for his next prey, his next play, and here—here one merely had to snap their fingers and it would be given freely.

He thought then of the seductive Lady Asimov and how easily she'd pulled him to that orgiastic display in that room well-hidden unless one knew where to look.

Sex, lust, blood, all at one's behest.
And I've had to fight for it.

He could have smacked himself, he felt quite out of the loop, quite disregarded, indeed, but then she was by his side, eyeing him with concern and he righted himself at once.

"What's wrong?" she asked, a delicate hand placed comfortingly on his arm.

"Nothing," he said, smiling, "I'm just berating a younger version of myself for daring to go so long without seeing such splendor."

She smiled knowingly. "Just think. As King, you shall never go long without such splendor if you so wish it."

"If I so wish it," he countered smoothly, "you shall never leave my side."

She said nothing, but the smile never fled her lips.

They walked to the center of the dance floor, Christian unsure who was leading who, for he was quite sure he didn't quite want to dance yet. He wanted blood. Would need it, even, to get through tonight, but there they were, in the center of the dance floor, the Vampires around them not pulled from their steps, but watching them with interest all the same.

She slipped gloved fingers through his own, smiling widely upon him, and he pressed a gloved hand against her waist, and with great grace and swiftness, she turned him around so that he spun on his heels, stopping just before her again.

As others most nearby laughed, Christian stared at her through red eyes. "Attempting a little humor, Miss Stone?" he asked, not used to anyone, let alone a Vampire woman, moving him about as they pleased.

"What better to ease your troubled mind, I figure," she said nicely, though there was a concentrated way her gaze would not leave his that made him far more nervous than he'd been prior to seeing her.

They moved together, swaying and stepping as the dance dictated, but still her gaze would not leave his own. And when he could stand it no more, he said, "What makes you think my mind is troubled, Miss Stone?"

"Alexandria, Christian," she corrected, as she dipped and he bowed, "and its plain to see really. You doubt your place in all of this.

You doubt what Dracula has chosen you for. You doubt...well, my affection for you, quite honestly, don't you?"

"I wasn't aware there was affection there, Alexandria," he said seriously. *Though I had hoped.*

"I daresay it, I can't deny it. To do so would be foolish, wouldn't it? I care for you beyond this connection Dracula has instilled in my blood...in your blade. And by care, I mean I care if you were hurt, I care if you were beating yourself up about things you can no longer control, like now. I'd care...if your brother tried to kill you...and succeeded, Christian. In the short months I have known you, I have grown to care what happens to my maddening, Vampire protector." And she smiled.

He could say nothing, all thought, all things fled his mind, his voice left him, and he wondered where this was coming from. He could only ask as much.

She closed her eyes for a moment as though in thought but opened them long enough to twirl in his hand. "I told you earlier, the moment I told you you were nothing more to me than a job Dracula needed us to do, I regretted it. I regretted pushing you away. I knew what I had said was not the truth—to be quite fair, I was scared of the truth."

He braced himself for the answer his question would yield. "And what is this truth, Alexandria?"

"Please, Alexi," she corrected again. "And the truth," she said stopping the dance, keeping her fingers intertwined with his own, wrapping a hand around his waist, pulling him close, "is that I care for you greatly, Christian Delacroix. And I would be...pained, greatly, I believe, if you were...no longer by my side."

"Are you sure you are not just used to my presence? We have been stuck together in close quarters for the better of a few months, Alexi...are you not sure—?"

Her lips were against his before he could realize it, and then her tongue slithered past and he tasted her sweet blood upon her tongue. He pressed her against him hard, not daring to believe she had granted him such a wonderful gift, such a beautiful, pure, incredible gift—

"CHRISTIAN!" the terribly loud voice of Civil Certance drilled through his ears, pulling him from her regrettably.

He looked around, not daring to release her, stunned to find a blood-splattered Civil stalking toward them through the crowd, brown eyes wide with fear and something else Christian could not place.

"What's happened?" he asked, turning to the Vampire fully as others stopped their dancing, crowding around them with equal confusion.

"Can you not smell it?" he said, waving two long-fingered hands through the air. "LORE—LORE IS HERE! IN THE VAMPIRE CITY!"

"*What?*" he snarled, withdrawing the Ascalon immediately, pulling his focus from Alexandria to find the scent of Lycan blood... yes, there it was. Stronger than James, but not by much.

He eyed Alexandria who was already ripping at her many skirts, undoing the bustle beneath, her bloomers apparent to all who desired see them, but now was not the time for modesty and Christian admired her courage for it.

A woman after my own heart, he thought fondly, watching as she released her red light, letting it bathe her, him, and the sword in its glow.

"Miss Stone, what on Earth are you—?" Civil began when she snarled at him, her red eyes trained on him coldly.

"Where is Westley?" she asked, snarling. "Where are the Armies?"

"Th-they are—they are holding him back," he offered weakly.

Christian's hand twitched with the sword, sensing the reluctance in the Vampire's voice. "Where is Westley, Civil?" he tried.

"He—he is in battle," he stammered.

"Is he hurt?" someone asked.

"Yes, where is Westley?"

"He is badly hurt, yes," Civil admitted at last. "It was why I came for you, Lord Delacroix."

He snarled, frustration tearing at his mind. *The Vampire could not meet his end, not now, not like this. He had tried to warn us. He tried to move to save us. And we didn't listen!*

"Take us to him! Now!" Christian shouted, pushing the Vampire forward. "Quickly!"

Civil whimpered but turned on a heel, running through the crowd as though fire was at his heels, but he did not get far before screams of fright left the Vampires most near the doors.

Before anyone could say or do anything else, the crowd parted and the Lycan growled in the damaged doorway, his black eyes searching the grand hall as though eager.

Many snarls left the Vampires around them, but Christian tensed, training his red gaze on the Lycan, wondering how on Earth James had gotten free.

And then Alexandria Stone had pulled herself from his hand and was running toward James, a snarl leaving her throat, and for a moment, Christian felt her guilt, her anger. For if she had not revived him for Dracula's schemes, he would not be here, he would not have killed the Vampires he had in order to stand here now, and do who knows what to them.

"Alexandria!" he called. "It's not your fault!"

But it was no use, indeed. She crashed against the Lycan with a brilliant burst of red light, successfully taking him down. And at the sight, the many Vampires that had merely watched in awe, finally moved into action, all moving to slash and tear at the Lycan with daggers brandished from their stockings or suit pockets.

"Alexandria!" he called, the sword burning in his grip.

She was not listening, was not pulling her long-nailed hands from the Lycan's chest. It was then that Christian realized what she was attempting to do.

She means to rip out his heart.

"Alexandria!" he called again when there was a thunderous boom from above. All Creatures stopped their snarling or thrashing immediately.

"What the devil was that?" someone asked.

The high ceiling began to shake, and the far-away candelabra hanging from it began to shake as well with whatever was above it.

"Is that Lore?" another asked as sniffs filled the air.

No, Christian thought, unable to smell Lycan at all. *No. It's not Lore.*

He braced himself as the ceiling cracked, the candelabra dislodged from its place, and began falling through the air. It reached the hovering, golden words, reducing them to wisps of golden smoke just before all torches and candles went out, darkness claiming all.

Chapter Twenty

THE BROTHERS DELACROIX

Eleanor Sindell Black looked around at the scared Vampires, the ones not crushed by the heavy ceiling, that is, and laughed.

Her hand stretched out for the Creature at her side, quite glad when it clasped around hers, squeezing it tight.

"Shall you do the honors, my love?" she asked him.

And he smiled, stepping forward, his bare chest gleaming in the white light of the silver torches that still clung to whatever wall remained. They'd sparked them to life when they'd arrived on the ballroom floor without a sound. Above their heads, a cold breeze from the remaining mansion and Vampire City beyond it blew into the hall, and with it he regained a Vampire form.

"Vampires," he said, his voice commanding through the cold air, "I am sorry I have been kept from you for so long."

The Vampires that remained upright stared at them in alarm, but it was the Vampire who had dislodged herself from a felled beast that caught and held Eleanor's attention.

The woman was glowing with her red light, her red gaze vivid through the dark, her hair undone from her hold. The dark brown tresses fell across her shoulders, and Eleanor could at last see the power Dracula had imbued her with.

Slight fear filled Eleanor with the sight, the memory of Dracula, but she regained her composure, reminding herself who it was that she'd gained as her King.

"Christian?!" Alexandria called, her red eyes searching the rubble for the Vampire she wished.

At her voice, Xavier eyed her, his long black hair rippling greatly in a darker breeze conjured from his blood, alone. "You!" he called. "The great one of Dracula's myriad schemes, the one to 'keep the Lycan's at bay' while the King would drink from the Goblet, render us all…disgusting humans." And he marched toward her, stepping easily over the rubble and bodies beneath his bare feet, but he had not made it several steps from her when someone lifted from the rubble behind him, sword glowing with the same red light.

Eleanor narrowed her eyes on him.

It couldn't be Christian. Why, he looks so…different.

"Brother," Christian said to Xavier's back, dust and pieces of ceiling clinging to his shoulders and hair, "if you take another step toward her, I will ram this sword through what remains of your heart."

Xavier stilled as though struck, but turned before long, a wide, mocking smile on his lips. "My, my. Look at *you*, brother. All high and mighty with your pretty little sword, aren't you? What is it? Why do you look at me as though you hate me? Are you not overjoyed? Are you not thrilled to see your brother after…well how long has it been? We've been apart for far too long, haven't we? Far too long. Can you not see? You, tied with your…concubine, me, with my Queen. Each of us given something in our…love that we previously would have never known if we had not been…lost in their embrace.

"But there is something different in what Eleanor gives me than what your dear, sweet, Alexandria Stone could ever think to give you." At his look of what Eleanor guessed was incomprehension, Xavier smiled. "Brother. A real woman will give you power, truth, the sensations of the flesh we greater Creatures are cursed to feel as lesser. But that is not me any longer brother, let me show you."

And Eleanor watched with glee as he took the form of a human man, his pale skin tinged with life, his green eyes duller in their vibrancy, yet still foreboding, and Eleanor heard all Creatures gasp.

"You really did it—you truly joined her?!" Christian yelled, his disbelief echoing off the crumbled walls, their ears.

"What were my other options, Vampire?" Xavier asked cruelly, regaining his red eyes. "Grovel at the feet of a dead Vampire, haunted with only visions and whispers of a truth he would never freely spill? Bidden to carry you weak, pathetic, Vampires on my back while I carted a useless dagger duller than my Vampire heart? You think too small, Christian! You always have! If you had only stepped up with me, if you had only ventured to this godforsaken city with me years ago, you would be on the side of the winners, of the ones in true power! But you chose to remain upon the surface, stuck in your blood ways, not desiring to gain better truth, gain better power!"

"What the devil are you talking about, Xavier?" Christian countered coldly. "You weren't at her hand back then! You weren't mad with power as you are now! It's the dread that's doing this to you! It's the absence of Dracula's truth that's doing this to you!"

"Oh, but that is where you are wrong you simple fool. I was always tied to Eleanor, to greater power. And I have it now where Dracula would never give it."

"Can't you see she's tricked you! Used her siren ways to lure you to falsehood?!"

"She's done no such thing! And you will understand what it is I have gained, Christian!"

And as if on cue, the large Lycan at her side began to stir, slowly lifting from the cracked ceiling he lay upon, his black eyes wide but bleary, the green spell placed upon him keeping him weak.

"Yes, see!" Xavier shouted, waving a hand to Lore. All eyes stared at the beast, even more snarls leaving the Vampires' throats. "Exhibit A. Lore. My enemy of many a year, a thorn in my backside, a damned beast always to be killed, but never to be found, or never to stick around long enough to get killed." And he moved swiftly from before Alexandria to stand before Lore, who had only just staggered to his large hind legs.

Lore merely growled at the sight of him, blood matting his fur here and there where he'd been struck within the Vampire City. But he could do little more before Xavier pressed a hand straight through Lore's chest, Eleanor gasping as the large heart beat on the other side tight in Xavier's hand.

"NO!" the Lycan near the doors and Alexandria shouted.

Eleanor watched in slight amusement as the other Lycan began to rip up the floor to reach Xavier who had removed his arm from Lore. He stared down at Lore's large, still heart as though unsure of what he held. "I had no idea it would be so easy," Eleanor heard him whisper.

And just before the Lycan could reach Xavier, someone appeared in front of Xavier, waving a hand, sending the Lycan flying back through the air.

Eleanor smiled at the Enchanter who had appeared, his old hands finding the pockets of his long black robes. With an old, withering breath, the Enchanter said to her, "Apologies, my Queen, but those Phoenixes are at what remains of the gates. We're doing our best to hold them off but it looks as though they're to break through at any moment—I thought it best to tell you, myself before they surprised you."

"Indeed," she whispered, anger burning through her, "thank you, Enchanter." Turning to Xavier, who still stared upon the large Lycan heart as though in disbelief, she said, "My love, those birds are here. We must do it quickly."

At her voice, he looked up, dropping the heart beside Lore, and blinking in the dark, for it seemed he realized where he was, he wiped the blood on a leg of his dark breeches, squared his shoulders, and turned to the room at large.

And as they watched, she clasped a hand within his own, allowing the darkness to take them.

* * *

Syran felt it pull him deeper into the dark, and though he may have admired the crude craftsmanship of Dracula's place of rest, he found it ruined by the Lycan that had run through this place, destroying things as he'd went.

The white doors to the entrance of the city were blown off their hinges, the number of Vampire bodies here prevalent in number; it was apparent they were unaware what was to come.

He flew through the first building he'd seen, a low building, ransacked from ceiling to floor, piles of ash everywhere along the bottom. He did not stop even as he pressed through the doors leading to the rest of the Vampire City.

It opened up before him, a large sprawling place, and even here there was more death, more darkness.

But it was the large gaping hole in the center of the mansion at the end of the terribly long street that drew his attention most and it was here he flew, sprinkling his golden dust across the ground as he moved.

Once he reached it, he withdrew his wings and peered down at the madness below, amused more than anything:

A Vampire quite similar to the chosen successor was fighting one of Eleanor's Creatures while Eleanor herself fought a female Vampire. Neither Creature was letting up, though Eleanor surpassed the woman in size for she took her monstrous form.

The Vampire wielding the glowing red sword parried Xavier's large, dark claws with desperation, anguish, and what Syran could also smell as guilt. It was a battle of need for both Creatures, he knew. The need to prove to the other that they had been chosen, had been pushed onto the better path.

Poetic, he thought, not seeing Dracula's preferred King here, anywhere at all.

With a sigh of frustration, he vaulted himself into the large hall, landing roughly atop the rubble directly in the middle of the once grand hall, sending all Creatures to topple over themselves or dislodge themselves from battle. He spread his fyre wide, searching for the true King, surprised when his fyre latched onto the woman the monstrous Eleanor had fought. He could barely eye her before his bright flames moved to the Vampire that wielded the glowing red sword.

The fyre turned green as it touched them, neither burning in truth. And it was here he sought their truths, the essence of what remained of their souls— *"How dare you?!"* the angry voice entered his mind and he turned his attention to the Creature that had uttered it.

Xavier Delacroix. Of course. "All of your indignation is better served kneeling at my feet, foolish Creature," he said crossly. "You will no longer hinder these Vampires from fulfilling their mission—they so nobly try to right the wrongs of their creator and you would stop them. How can you not see that you are not meant to exist?"

The large wings flapped as Xavier hovered in the air, staring down at him with great disdain. *"We are meant to exist just as much—even more—than you pitiful Creatures. We are the rightful ones meant to rule! We do not hide! We show our faces! We exist!"*

"You ruin and decay all you touch!" he roared, sick of the defiance. He lifted himself into the air, face to face with the Creature's cold, black eyes. "You, abomination, are a plague upon this Earth. And you shall fall where you stand. It is necessary."

At that the Creature extended a hand, but before it could get very far at all, Syran allowed his fyre to surge, engulfing him completely, and Xavier shrank away, a cry of pain leaving his large mouth.

Syran moved quickly, focusing on his fyre as it bathed the two Creatures doused in Dracula's power. He thought only of the Goblet, where it could be, for he did not know if he had the strength to kill the Elite Creatures and he didn't want to chance it if he could help it. *Better to just move on with the plan, rather than succumb to needless death.*

He searched the World at large in mind's eye, letting out a sigh of relief as he happened upon the glowing golden cup. And with a surge of power aimed straight for it, strengthening his focus on it, he began to pull himself and the two Vampires there.

But he had not made it far before the clawed hands were at his back, slashing against his skin. His cry of pain echoed in the haze of his fyre as he left the destroyed place and traveled through the flames, doing his best to hold onto the two Vampires as he went.

Chapter Twenty-One

THE GOBLET OF EXISTENCE

C hristian shuddered as the strange fire left him, a grand cold replacing it. It was a cold he had not truly felt in quite some time: The cold of a Vampire which was no longer tinged with the strange heat of red light, or the fire of a man with wings of fire. He wasn't sure what scared him more.

"Christian," she gasped, shock clear in her gaze as she stared around at the trees that surrounded them now, "where did he drop us?"

Confusion gripping his senses, for he was just in the Vampire City facing his brother, he tried his best to get his bearings when a loud swish like the air being split, sounded from behind him and in a great burst of flame his father appeared, though he held no scars on his face. A slew of other Creatures were appearing as well and he did not have to look twice to know them as the Order of the Dragon.

He withdrew from Alexandria immediately and ran to his father, embracing him in a crushing hug despite the Ares heavy in his grip. He was quite pleased when the Vampire met him with equal joy.

"Father," he whispered, pulling himself from the strong arms to stare into his eyes. The glow of the sword the Vampire held cast relief across his unscarred face. "Your face—where are your scars?"

"Healed," he said with a smile, "better than ever."

"We've all been healed," an Elf said from his side, looking around at the woods wearily. "But we were just fighting Eleanor's Creatures…why were we placed here?"

"I fought Xavier," Christian said quickly, "then this man with wings of fire appeared—"

A plume of dark smoke appeared at Aurora's back and a terribly dark-skinned man appeared, his completely black eyes glistening in the night though Christian was not sure how it was possible. This Creature marched past them all, shoving them aside rudely, stepped right up to Christian, and pointed somewhere past him, over his shoulder. "Go. Now. Drink from the damned cup and we can finally be done with this," he said, his voice holding a sliver of something wicked on his tongue.

Christian blinked, fear spiraling through him as he glanced at his father who merely nodded his assurance. But Christian could not turn to eye where he had to go, for a loud explosion sounded just then, far behind where the Order stood, and as snow and smoke flew through the dark, the Order raised their glowing weapons prepared to use them.

He felt the hand pull at his arm, and he stared at it. Slender, curt, but strong in its grip.

And then he was able to hear her voice yell in his ear:

"Christian! Let's go! Now! The Goblet—I see it! It's there! We must move! Now!"

It was not until the Elite Creatures appeared over the Order's shoulders in their Vampire forms, naked save the black wisps of smoke that covered their indecent parts that he realized why he should move—

He was pulled against the snow before they could land, the woman who pulled him never slowing in her steps, her feet bare against the snow. He could feel the growing dread at his back, and daring to turn his head, he saw his brother and Eleanor Black running after him, their dread reaching out for his him like grotesque, smoky claws. Beyond them was the dark Creature, beyond him the remaining members of the Order, and beyond them, the anxious blonde man who had appeared in the Vampire City amidst the destruction.

"Christian, use your legs!" Alexandria yelled, her hair freeing itself from its binds, flowing behind her. Snow flew up as her feet pressed against snow only to lift into the air once more.

He regained himself, amazed at her ability to move, and so effortlessly, running alongside her now through the cold, their destination unclear to him until he forced himself to stare ahead where the plain-looking Goblet sat upon the stone stand. It was plain except for the glowing white light that surrounded it.

Is that really it? he thought, the dread's claws scraping against his back attempting to pull him in.

But still he ran, and how far away the Goblet seemed.

"Don't be a fool, brother!" Xavier's voice, distorted so that it was almost unfamiliar, sounded from behind him. "Don't destroy what I have built!"

"Run, Christian" Aleister's voice shouted next, "don't listen to him!"

And there it was, just before him, just there—all he had to do was reach out for it—

A sound much like a cross between a gasp and a gargle reached his ears and beside himself, he turned.

All Creatures had stopped their run, staring in alarm at Eleanor who had sunk to her knees in the snow, a look of surprise on her face.

Christian stared, unsure what had happened, when Xavier pulled the dagger out of her back, its metal black. He stared at it as though not seeing it, and then he eyed the Creature who still had his hand poised, his dark fingers still releasing the blade.

"You..." Xavier whispered, staring at this Creature, but not leaving Eleanor's side. Indeed, she had darkened herself, as she kneeled there, her skin becoming hardened, gray stone. Her mouth lay open, a hand outstretched toward he, Christian, her brow furrowed as though she did not understand what had happened.

Xavier kneeled at her side, tearing his gaze from the dark Phoenix to stare upon Eleanor, who suddenly resembled a statue, hand still outstretched to grasp what could not be grasped.

And it did not take Christian long to realize that she was dead, that there was no coming back from this kind of sorcery, no matter her claim of great power.

Xavier seemed to realize this as well, for a grand sob left his throat, and he held the back of her head with a trembling hand and placed another on her face. *"No, no—nothing could touch you. Nothing could—we were strong—so strong—you cannot be—we had power,"* he whispered, though how strange the words sounded.

Never had he seen Xavier like this, never had he witnessed the Vampire once so stoic and self-assured reduced to a blubbering mess, and yes, those were tears leaving the Vampire's red eyes.

"He's lost," Alexandria said from his side, and Christian stared at her.

Her brown-green gaze was held, as was everyone else's on the scene before them. Sympathy blanketed her gaze however. "Without her," she went on, purely for his benefit, he knew, "he does not know what to do. She gave him the power. She imparted upon him the knowledge. She gave him the freedom, whatever freedom he thought he needed, to make his own rules, where my grandfather's hand could not touch him. But he's lost. He cannot go on—"

"Aleister!" Aurora Borealis shouted then, and Christian looked away from Alexandria, toward the Vampire that had left the line of Creatures. His sword glowed a vivid gold color as he marched up to Xavier who still held the woman in a hard embrace.

Aleister said nothing as he lifted the sword, bringing it down through Xavier's back until it pierced through his chest. He said nothing as he pressed his boot to Xavier's back, sliding the sword out and there was a brief moment where Christian thought Xavier would rise from his knees, moving with madness to slash at his father, but he did not, he merely slumped forward, Eleanor still in his arms, and slowly, but surely, turned to stone.

No one said a word.

Indeed, Christian did not understand how anyone could form words.

He had not realized he'd sunken to his own knees until Alexandria was in his face, looking terribly concerned, and it was quite some time before he realized she had been speaking, that they all had been speaking:

"Christian, are you alright? You must get up!"

"Aleister, what were you thinking?! He could have been saved!"

"How were they able to turn to stone like that? What magic was that?"

"Christian, please—"

She pulled at his arms, and begrudgingly he rose to his feet, unable to take his gaze from the statue both Creatures formed in the snow just steps from him.

His mind rang with images of Xavier, green eyes hard as they'd believed their parents dead, Xavier, forbidding him to journey to Aleister's home, Xavier rising from the ground a Vampire, Xavier a young boy wooing the skirts off any woman who'd listen, Xavier the Vampire who had left his home to train with Dracula, Xavier, a Vampire who had been madly in love with a woman named Eleanor Black, Xavier, a Vampire who had left her scared he could never truly love the way his father had done…Xavier, stone before him, the boy who had never cried in his life or death, forever immortalized with grand tears leaving his eyes.

He opened and closed his mouth, unsure of what to say, for how strange the world seemed now, how dark the sky seemed, how foreign everything was.

Even the man who still stood over Xavier's body seemed, somehow different, indeed.

It took Christian longer still to realize this man was pointing the blood-laden sword toward him, telling him to drink something Christian did not know.

"Christian, please! You must drink from the Goblet or all of this will be for naught!" Alexandria pleaded in his ear.

With her voice, he turned to eye her, a shaking hand in her own steady one.

How can it be steady? he wondered dully, turning to eye the golden Goblet that had not changed at all with Eleanor and Xavier's—

No, no, I cannot think of it now, he urged himself. *I shall merely drink from this and it will be all over. I'll wake up and this will be easier to bear.*

He eyed her one last time, a reassuring smile upon her lips, though her brown-green gaze was terribly sad. He sheathed the cold Ares in its home at his waist, lifted the golden Goblet from its place, brought it to his lips, and drank the blood. It was not until he was nearly done that he recognized its taste, smelled its scent heavily and with a pang of fresh grief at last, realized he drank Xavier Delacroix's cold, Vampire blood.

Chapter Twenty-Two

PHOENIX FYRE

The World was silent.

Nothing stirred in any corner of the World, which was no longer Dark, but brightening by the minute. And though it was night where the Goblet lay atop the snow, the sky was bright in a place now completely abandoned, its stone tunnels empty except for the Creature that walked through its hallways, searching as always, for the thing it would need.

For the power had shifted once again, and he knew, somewhere in his addled mind that the beings in the clouds were coming. All of them.

For war.

For things had not changed.

And as he sauntered toward the room toward the end of the hall, bent double to keep his head from scraping the ceiling, he was not surprised when the man, glowing with golden fyre appeared in the doorway, leaning against it, his strength not returned to him. Not yet, anyway.

But he was on his feet.

And as Darien stared at the Vampire who trembled, not used to the strange power that flowed through his weak veins, he let out a roar, unable to do anything more.

The Vampire's violet eyes found him in their sockets, and with a cry of what Darien guessed was fear, pulled a hand from his midsection, and pointed the palm toward Darien, a burst of brilliant fyre leaving his palm as he did.

Darien thought only of his brother as he went up in the scorching flame.

* * *

Victor Vonderheide stared at his trembling hand, the smoke that left it, and then at the massive pile of black ash in the narrow hallway, disbelief blanketing his mind.

He didn't understand what had happened—it made no sense, no sense at all.

One moment he had been staring upon the terrifying, soulless eyes of Eleanor bloody Black, and now—well, now he didn't know what had happened.

He was sure he had died, his spine cracked, but save the odd ache, the trembling of his limbs, he felt more or less fine.

He stepped forward, unsure what more to do, the woman's endless caves the maddening mess he had always remembered, but on instinct more than anything, he found the entrance, climbed the steps, and inhaled fresh, cold air.

He blinked in the light that greeted him as he did so, unsure why it was morning, for he had the strangest feeling it should have been night.

And there he felt it: something was off about the Earth, something so very wrong. But what it was, he could not know, could not entirely sense.

And where is Eleanor? Her Creatures? Where is Xavier and his smug face?

Unsure if he wanted to see either Creature after what Eleanor had put him through, he cracked his neck to release its stiffness, surprised when a surge of what felt like liquid heat slid through his veins.

Bewildered, he tried it again on the other side, nonplussed when it happened again.

He stared at his shaking hands closer now, able to see what looked like golden blood within his veins, past his skin so pale.

"What on Earth?" he whispered, as the sky erupted in fire, what sounded like millions of voices across the World crying out in fear.

* * *

Bel led the charge, darting through the sky as the others pressed on behind him, whoops of excitement and yells of focus leaving their throats.

He did not bother to stifle his smile, for he felt it as well: Excitement to move, and at last.

He just found it odd Syran had pulled them to such a remote place.

And he was sure it was far too soon. The others had not yet reached Shadowhall, had not prepared the necessary things to see their passage to Earth safely.

But something else had made it easy.

The sky had opened up willingly.

And as he flew, spreading his bright blue wings wide, he wondered what on Earth it could be.

* * *

Philistia Mastcourt breathed a sigh of relief as the white gates opened and Evian was already standing there, a look of anxiousness plastered across his face.

"Took you long enough," he chided, eyeing the Vampires in the arms of the strange Creatures and her own. "What's happened to them?"

"No idea," she said breathlessly, having used her magic to get them there. She was absolutely winded and desired nothing more than to eat and sleep, but by the look on his serious face, sleep was the last thing he would grant her. "Evian, please, that was quite a journey to make."

He waved a hand to a waiting Enchanter who brought forward a jar of orange liquid. "Drink," he said as the Enchanter handed her the jar.

She knew what it was, knew it a matter of them running out of time that he even offered it to her, but still she took it, drinking it down fast. When she was finished, she handed the jar back to the Enchanter who took it kindly, stepping back in line with the others that she just realized had stood there as Evian had done, impatient.

"What's going on?" she asked, wiping her lips, feeling her weakness and exhaustion leave her.

"The Phoenixes," Evian said, and she could finally see the fear in his eyes, "they have landed somehow Philistia. We didn't do our duty. We must expect them to be cross with us. We must expect war."

She stiffened, not expecting this news at all. "What? How do you know they landed?"

"To the south," he said, pointing in that direction.

She turned as did Amentias and Aciel, to eye the only part of the World that was not blanketed in night. Above many trees the sky was lit up as though morning, and even from the great distance she could make out the small, glowing figures that were zooming to the ground.

"Tremor preserve us," she whispered. She stared back at him, eyes wide. "What on Earth shall we do? We'll never make it to Shadowhall in time!"

"We do what we were taught to do," Evian said, a glint of mischief in his eye, "we serve those greater than us no matter the cost."

Chapter Twenty-Three

GOLDEN BLOOD

Christian Delacroix opened his eyes.

The ground beneath him was cold, the wind that pressed against his front was cold, and what his fingers brushed against was very cold.

He thought it strange, so much cold about him, when he remembered, with a pang of grief, the sight of Aleister pressing the sword into Xavier's back—

He sat up, turning his head to where they were, part of him surprised to still see them there, just where they were left, Xavier still crying, Eleanor still caught in her surprise.

The hand was on his face, bringing his gaze around, and he eyed Alexandria Stone, not understanding why she was still pale, why her eyes were red as she stared upon him.

"Why didn't it work?" she asked, and he looked around at the others who were rising from their own unconscious states, save the Enchanters and Elf. They had kneeled at their chosen Creature's side attempting to rouse them.

"I don't know," Christian said, eyeing the Goblet in the snow. It was very dull, the gold almost black now. Its contents were indeed drained, and he wondered what would happen. Wasn't he the rightful King? Wasn't he meant to drink it and end all of this? Weren't they to be human now?

"Maybe it takes a while to sink in?" Alexandria offered, but as he rose to his feet, helping her to her own, he had a feeling that wasn't the case.

He felt no different from before; he didn't know why he was still a Vampire at all. He should be human, shouldn't he? *We should all be human...*

"What on Earth happened?" Dragor's voice could be heard within the trees, and Christian eyed the dark bark, able to see the gruff Vampire, black sword in hand, blue eyes angry in the dark. "Shouldn't we be human?! You did drink from it, didn't you, Christian?"

"Of course, I did!" he called back, "it's why we all took a nap, wasn't it?!"

"Leave it to Dracula to ruin things further," Peroneous muttered some ways off from the Order. Christian had the sneaking suspicion the Enchanter was trying to run off before the Goblet's blood had passed his lips.

The Goblet's blood.

He tore his gaze from the bewildered Creatures before him and eyed the plain Goblet once again. No trace of blood lingered atop the snow and he nodded, mind spinning.

"I did drink it," he whispered.

The hand was on his shoulder, and he blinked upon her, her brown-green eyes filled with fear, her brow furrowed as though she saw something he could not.

He turned to her fully, placing two hands on her shoulders, willing her to come around. "Alexandria—Alexi, what is it?"

He waited, the fear in her eyes inspiring his own, but how distant her gaze was. It was as though she stared across valleys, seeing things she did not wish.

He blinked in the dark, the steady glow of white light illuminating her front, but it was not from her, he realized with a start, tearing his gaze from her to eye the Members of the Order. They had left their places in the snow to stand at his back, anticipation filling all their serious, tired gazes.

"Alexi—please," he whispered, turning back to her, never releasing his hold, "come back."

And with a gasp of cold air, she blinked rapidly, her brown-green gaze present as she stared at him.

Without a word, she grasped his arms as though he would vanish if she did not.

"It's the Phoenixes," she said, her fangs glistening in the night, "a-and Victor, Christian. I thought he was dead but he's...somehow he's alive—"

"Impossible," Aleister said, "we saw him die, didn't we?"

"I think we can rule out the 'impossible,' now, Aleister," Aurora Borealis said curtly.

Alexandria snarled and all Creatures stiffened. Her eyes were now red, her voice distorted from its usual pleasant air, "Listen to me! Victor Vonderheide is alive—and the Phoenixes—they have landed."

"But wouldn't Syran have told us?" Dragor asked, and all heads turned to the trees where the Phoenixes were last.

They were gone.

A colder fear entered Christian's cold heart, and he understood what had her so scared. "We failed," he said to the trees, Xavier's statue, "we are still Vampires—the Goblet didn't work. They'll kill us."

And before anyone else could utter a word, a large shadow swept over them. He looked up, his voice dying in his throat.

The bottom of the white Dragon and its gold talons shimmered against the stars, and as they all tensed, waiting for certain death or worse, the long white figure removed itself from the Dragon's back, his long white hair billowing in the wind the Dragon's large wings created.

Evert the Ancient Elder landed without a sound beside Xavier, his long staff in hand, his deep blue eyes penetrating and fear-filled as well. "What happened?" he asked, panic in his old voice. "You should all be human!"

Christian stepped from the group of Creatures, moving toward the Ancient Elder. He kept a hand on the handle of the Ares though it no longer burned. "We should. We're not. But we've just been told that the Phoenixes—all of them—have landed, and those Phoenixes that were with the Order of the Dragon are nowhere to be found. What does this mean?"

Evert's old face dropped, now appearing terribly cold. "They'll hunt what remains of the Dark Creatures down and end them all," he said seriously.

Christian heard a sword sway in someone's shaking grip. "And what of you? Come here to kill us were we not what we were meant to be?" It was Dragor.

Evert's blue eyes stared at this Vampire for quite some time, and Christian realized he could hear nothing else in the World, not the sound of woodland beasts nor the sound of the night: cries of humans, his prey, the rustle of a Dragon's wing, nothing.

"I'm not here to kill you, silly Vampire," Evert said at last, turning his cold gaze to all of them. "I'm here to save you. We can get to the bottom of this later, right now we must go into hiding—the Phoenixes are on the move, and will not cease in their desire for the blood of you strange, troublesome Creatures."

All watched as the large Dragon began to land, her wind pushing them all away, back toward the stone stand where the Goblet had sat. Her golden eyes gleamed as she stared at them knowingly.

Bowing her head into the snow and lowering her wings, Christian realized she was allowing them her back.

He wondered how all of them would fit onto the Creatures large back at all, when Evert waved the staff and they were all blanketed in a soothing golden light.

"Now, Creatures," Evert said, his voice regaining its commanding air, "let us go. There is clearly nothing for us here."

And as Dragor withdrew from the crowd, sheathing his sword and the others followed, Christian eyed the statue of Xavier and Eleanor that remained intact just beneath the Dragon's wing, and he realized the sky was no longer filled with the suffocating dread that had become so familiar to him these past months.

He could not find it in himself to feel relief, indeed, he could feel nothing but fear, a sickening fear that stuck tohis heart and throat, and he realized all he desired to do was scream.

He smiled, however, when Alexandria reached him, clasping her hand in his, and as she led him to the Dragon's back, he realized he was the last to ride it.

They all took up the length of the Dragon's back, and he thought there would be no room for him, but as he climbed the wing and settled himself on what remained of the long spine behind Alexandria, he realized his seat was quite comfortable; it was as if he sat nestled in-between the wing blades.

Christian eyed the tall Creature who still stood on the ground, who stared after them as the Dragon began lifting itself from the snow.

"Wait," he called. "Aren't you coming with us?"

"I will meet you all soon, Christian Delacroix," Evert said, unbothered. "Vetus here will assure you make it to Tremor in one piece."

He blinked, unsure he'd heard what he had. But he needn't wonder for long for the older Creatures in front of him had gasped as they'd heard the name. Peroneous looked near tears, his brown eyes water-filled as he turned to eye them in what looked his surprise and equal fear.

Wondering who this Tremor was, Christian was distracted by all thought when Alexandria's hands ran across his own around her waist. He knew it a reassuring motion he wouldn't have been granted but a few days ago.

But so much had changed, he thought as he eyed the World from the strong Creature's back. And how new it seemed, how clear. There was no dread in sight, no darkness to fill his empty lungs and suffocate his blood.

He then wondered if this was how it was for the other Creatures before Vampires and Lycans filled the World.

But all fled him as the Dragon sped fast over the land, the cold wind whipping at their hair and faces, and the Ares at his side let out a flare of comforting heat at last.

* * *

"It failed, brother!" Bel shouted to the angry Phoenix who had appeared through the trees the moment his feet had touched ground.

"Failed and here we stand! And don't you dare try to protect your damned project any longer!"

"Something interfered!" Syran shouted back, Caligo eyeing the blue eyes so confused, stricken with pain.

I told him it would not work, he thought darkly, *but he desired to see the abominations right their wrongs. And now we are here. Quarreling amongst ourselves when we should be ending them all!*

Bel lifted a tan hand through the air, silencing the voices of the many Phoenixes that filled the woods in front of the low cave. All watched as he stepped up to Syran, dark blue eyes cold, swirling with what Caligo knew was his strange power. "What interfered?" Bel asked, mockingly. "What could possibly interfere with your *great* desire, your great *rule*, brother?"

"I know not!" he shouted, gone all manner of peace within the Head Phoenix's blood. "But something has ruined it—something has—for its own gain—allowed the Vampires to continue to live—something—"

"Is listening," Caligo finished, sensing the Vampire Creature nearby. It smelled of Vampire, yes, but also, strangely, Phoenix. But he did not sense both Creatures hiding behind trees, after all, only one...

Syran and Bel eyed him in the light, confused.

"Can you not sense it?" he asked, stepping to a cluster of trees most near each other. He rounded the bark, eyeing the scared, pale Vampire that leaned up against it, shaking with perspiration. His long silver hair clung to his sweat-laden shoulders, his thick, black traveling cloak hanging from two fingers, sliding against the ground.

"How are you alive, Creature?" he whispered, sure the others could not hear.

"What?" the violet-eyed Vampire asked, confusion blanketing his gaze.

"What *are* you?" he repeated, impatient.

From beyond the trees, a voice called, "Caligo? What's gotten into you? What do you sense?"

"Hurry," he whispered, hearing the footsteps nearing him.

At last the strange Creature seemed to understand what was at stake, should his answer not suffice, and he said, "I...am a Vampire,

I think. There is…golden blood," he said, raising a free shaking hand into the air, "in my veins."

And Caligo could see the Vampire was telling the truth: through the skin the Vampire's blood traveled through the veins gold in color. He would have thought the Vampire only a strange man if he had not seen the fangs in the Creature's mouth.

"Caligo?" Bel asked, rounding the cluster of trees, now. And as the dark blue eyes happened upon the Vampire, he readied his staff threateningly but Caligo held out an arm.

"Relax, Bel," he said, "he's no normal Vampire."

"No normal—he's an abomination! He must be put down!" Bel retorted, indignant.

Ignoring him, Caligo focused on the Vampire. "Go on, Vampire; tell us—how did you come to hold your golden blood?"

He blinked in the light, clearly expecting to be reduced to ash, further confused when it did not happen. "I…fought with Eleanor Black. She killed me…I—I woke up just minutes ago…with this blood in my veins."

"And tell us, Vampire," Caligo said, heading Bel off, "what…is your desire regarding your nature?"

"What?" both Bel and the Vampire asked, flustered.

"What is your desire regarding your nature? Do you wish to be human or remain a Vampire?" he asked.

"Just one moment—!" Bel began.

"I wished to stay a Vampire," he said without further thought. "Always a Vampire. It is what Dracula made me, after all. To be anything else…I cannot."

Caligo could not suppress the smile. *Of course! Of course!* "We have found the reason Syran's will could not be completed," he told a terribly confused Bel, waving a hand to the trembling Vampire, "this Vampire…imbued with Phoenix fyre, took over the will of Syran. He wished to remain a Vampire—so all Vampires remain Vampires, even if they drink from the Goblet."

"I don't understand," Bel whispered, staff dropping in hand. "How did this happen?"

"When we went to gather the thing that granted Syran entrance to Earth in the first place, we found this Vampire," he said, "Syran's messenger right beside it. Syran gathered the messenger but his fyre seemed to spark its last remaining essence, and that is what I believed allowed this Vampire to live…with Phoenix fyre within his veins."

Bel's mouth opened and closed, his long brown hair waving slightly in a breeze. "But how on Earth can a thing like this happen? Syran! Syran! Come here!"

Caligo stepped aside as a despondent Syran moved to them, confusion in his blue eyes as he eyed them both, then eyed Victor, blue eyes widening.

"What's the meaning—?" he began when Bel opened his mouth.

"He's the reason your Goblet did not turn the Vampires human, brother."

Caligo smiled wide, stepping side, sure the strange Vampire would face Syran's wrath at last.

But much to his dismay, Syran merely stepped up to the Vampire with Bel's words, and touched a cold, blood-splattered cheek.

"Incredible," he whispered, even as Victor shrunk from the touch as though pained, "I never thought it possible—my will overshadowed by an abomination."

"He's not an abomination any longer, brother," Bel said seriously, his gaze too upon the Vampire curiously.

Caligo frowned. "Father, uncle—are you not upset this Vampire is the reason your will is not done?"

Syran eyed him, a hand still on Victor's cheek. "We have something here, Caligo," he said, anger gone from his voice, "if this abomination can take in our fyre…what is to say the others cannot do the same? Look, he does not even burn in the light. They may be able to keep their existence if only imbued with our fyre."

"But we don't even know if they can withstand the form! If they won't go after the humans, taking their blood!" Caligo retorted at once, furious. *This is not what we need!*

Syran eyed Victor, and by the settling of his shoulders, Caligo knew his father was calm, eager to see his will done, no matter the cost. "Tell me, Vampire," Syran began, "do you feel the desire for the humans' blood?"

Victor blinked, apparently dazed by his brilliance, but said, "I feel…I don't know what I feel."

"Blood," Bel said urgently, "do you feel a desire to take blood?"

"I...no," he said dimly, but Caligo felt as though the Vampire was not telling the truth. Yes, his eyes darted from Phoenix to Phoenix as though searching for the correct answer.

"Indeed," Syran said, clasping a strong hand on Victor's shoulder, sending his knees to buckle slightly, "we've found our way." And then to Bel, "Gather the others. We prepare not to kill the Vampires, but give them our fyre. Give them life anew."

As Bel moved to obey his brother's wishes and Syran led Victor to the others, Caligo stared after them, anger burning beneath his skin, quite sure Syran had allowed a Vampire to trick him into destroying their World for a second time.

About the Author

B esides being addicted to vampires, blood, and a good, steaming cup of tea, S.C. Parris attends University on Long Island, NY, and is the author of A Night of Frivolity, a horror short story, published by Burning Willow Press. She is the author of The Dark World series published by Permuted Press, and enjoys thinking up new dark historical fantasies to put to page next. She lives on Long Island, New York with her family and can be reached on the web at http://www.scparris.net/

PERMUTED PRESS
needs **you** to help

SPREAD INFECTION

FOLLOW US!

f | Facebook.com/PermutedPress
🐦 | Twitter.com/PermutedPress

REVIEW US!

Wherever you buy our book, they can be reviewed! We want to know what you like!

GET INFECTED!

Sign up for our mailing list at
PermutedPress.com

PERMUTED
PRESS

KING ARTHUR AND THE KNIGHTS OF THE ROUND TABLE HAVE BEEN REBORN TO SAVE THE WORLD FROM THE CLUTCHES OF MORGANA WHILE SHE PROPELS OUR MODERN WORLD INTO THE MIDDLE AGES.

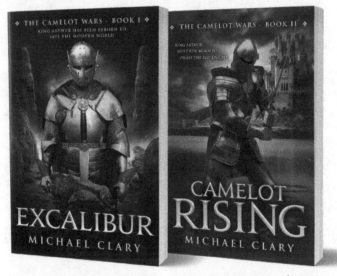

EAN 9781618685018 $15.99   EAN 9781682611562 $15.99

Morgana's first attack came in a red fog that wiped out all modern technology. The entire planet was pushed back into the middle ages. The world descended into chaos.

But hope is not yet lost— King Arthur, Merlin, and the Knights of the Round Table have been reborn.

PERMUTED PRESS

THE ULTIMATE PREPPER'S ADVENTURE.
THE JOURNEY BEGINS HERE!

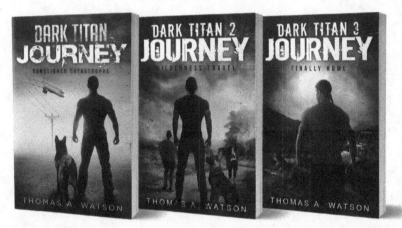

EAN 9781682611654 $9.99   **EAN** 9781618687371 $9.99   **EAN** 9781618687395 $9.99

The long-predicted Coronal Mass Ejection has finally hit the Earth, virtually destroying civilization. Nathan Owens has been prepping for a disaster like this for years, but now he's a thousand miles away from his family and his refuge. He'll have to employ all his hard-won survivalist skills to save his current community, before he begins his long journey through doomsday to get back home.

THE MORNINGSTAR STRAIN HAS BEEN LET LOOSE—IS THERE ANY WAY TO STOP IT?

An industrial accident unleashes some of the Morningstar Strain. The

EAN 9781618686497 $16.00

doctor who discovered the strain and her assistant will have to fight their way through Sprinters and Shamblers to save themselves, the vaccine, and the base. Then they discover that it wasn't an accident at all—somebody inside the facility did it on purpose. The war with the RSA and the infected is far from over.

This is the fourth book in Z.A. Recht's The Morningstar Strain series, written by Brad Munson.

PERMUTED
PRESS

GATHERED TOGETHER AT LAST, THREE TALES OF FANTASY CENTERING AROUND THE MYSTERIOUS CITY OF SHADOWS...ALSO KNOWN AS CHICAGO.

EAN 9781682612286 $9.99   **EAN** 9781618684639 $5.99   **EAN** 9781618684899 $5.99

From *The New York Times* and *USA Today* bestselling author Richard A. Knaak comes three tales from Chicago, the City of Shadows. Enter the world of the Grey–the creatures that live at the edge of our imagination and seek to be real. Follow the quest of a wizard seeking escape from the centuries-long haunting of a gargoyle. Behold the coming of the end of the world as the Dutchman arrives.

Enter the City of Shadows.

PERMUTED
PRESS